DEAD MEN DON'T EAT QUICHE

A MARTIN AND OWN MYSTERY

NINA CORDOBA

Art Director: Sierra Acy

Cover Art: Kostis Pavlou

CHAPTER ONE

Nick Owen

I flipped over on my left side for the dozenth time since I'd gotten into bed.

Sleeping still didn't come easy, although the reason for my insomnia had changed a few months ago. Johnny Chavez—the innocent defendant in the only murder case I ever lost—had won his appeal and that was a load off my conscience.

Truth be told, though, his face had already been replaced much of the time in my nightly visions with a prettier one. One with big, beautiful eyes the color of chocolate.

My cell phone rang. I turned over and stared at it for a few seconds wondering who could be calling at this hour. Even mom liked to limit her "emergencies" to between breakfast and midnight.

Had to be a wrong number.

I picked up the phone, checked the name on the screen, then blinked a few times to make sure I hadn't conjured it up with wishful thinking.

As soon as I confirmed I wasn't hallucinating, I tapped the screen to answer the call.

"Rika?" My voice came out higher pitched than I was comfortable with, maybe a little desperate. I wished I could have a Mulligan on answering.

"Nick?"

I sat up straight at the distressed sound in her voice. "What's wrong?" I said. "Are you okay?"

"Yes. It's my dad. He's disappeared."

"In Colombia?" I immediately regretted that I didn't know any more than any other dumbass American about Colombia—let's see, coffee...cocaine. Yep, that was it.

"No, he was here...in L.A." I'd never heard her sound so panicked, not even the night she nearly got blown up by the boss of our local crime ring. "He moved here a month ago. Now, his co-worker's been found dead and he's missing!"

Missing? "Missing" in this type of situation usually meant the missing person was the perpetrator...or dead. I suddenly felt like I had a brick wedged in my stomach.

"Are the police looking for him?"

"Yes..." The word came out as a sob. "But they're looking for him as a suspect! He wouldn't kill anyone, but no one's looking for him as a kidnapping victim."

While I tried to process what she was telling me, I heard her clear her throat. She took a deep breath and exhaled it slowly and I knew she was pulling herself together. The Rika I knew last summer was not a woman who cried easily. She made it through her bogus arrest, a shooting attempt with her as the target, and a bomb she had to disarm herself, all without shedding a tear, at least none that I saw.

But she cried when we said goodbye, and the memory of those tears clawed at my heart every single day. I told myself that if it was meant to be between us—if she still felt as strongly as I did once she was back home and wasn't depending on me to get her out of a murder rap—I'd hear from her.

A text. A call.

But I hadn't heard a peep from her since she drove out of my life. I figured she'd come to her senses and moved on with her life.

"I'm sorry." The sob was gone from her voice. "I don't know why I called you. It's just that you were the only person I..."

She seemed to have run out of words, and I didn't want her to hang up before I told her I was coming.

"I'll catch the first flight I can get," I said. "I'll let you know when I'm arriving."

Her sigh of relief whooshed through the phone. "Thanks, Nick... Thanks."

"No problem. See you soon." I hung up and grabbed my laptop to start searching for flights.

CHAPTER TWO

Rika Martín

I tried not to look into my rearview mirror as I gunned the accelerator, preparing to muscle my way into traffic on the I-10 freeway.

Forty-five minutes ago, I met Nick in the baggage claim area of LAX and everything was exactly as I imagined it.

I saw him first. He was wearing my favorite t-shirt—light blue and short-sleeved—that showed off his thick biceps as he pulled a suitcase off the conveyer belt. His buns of steel were covered by worn jeans he'd paired with cowboy boots.

As soon as he turned and my eyes met his, he strode over to me, sliding his arms around my waist, pressing me tightly to his body, his big hands scorching my back.

I curled my arms around his neck, resting my cheek against his chest, sucking in all the Nick pheromones I could fit into my needy olfactory glands. And those pheromones were still delicious, even if they weren't coated in the scent of Pillsbury Crescent Rolls as they often were when I stayed with him.

His body felt so good pressed against me, warm—like he'd brought some of the Texas heat with him—with hard manly muscles that gave a tiny bit under the pressure I applied. With Nick wrapped around me, I felt so cared for and safe. My eyes burned and I nearly cried with relief that he was here.

He tugged gently on a chunk of hair until I bent my head back and looked up at him. His eyes searched mine like he was doing an emotional scan of my brain, trying to determine how I was holding up.

And, in that perfect moment in Nick's arms, I was one hundred percent certain that everything would be okay.

Until a syrupy, twangy voice broke in, full of faux-enthusiasm mixed with pseudo-sympathy.

"You must be Rika!" It said.

When I leaned my head to the right to see around Nick, I found a tall, leggy blonde with hair that swooped up high above her forehead—thumbing its roots at the law of gravity—then cascaded down in layer after layer of pure sexy.

Exactly like his last two wives.

Someone please tell me Nick didn't get married again already!

Six months ago, after we'd discovered who the killer was and the charges against me had been dropped, Nick sent me away, citing his recent divorce and the fact that—even though he was only thirty-four—he'd already been married three times, as the reasons we shouldn't be together.

Like he wasn't relationship material.

And for the past six months, I couldn't bring myself to have a relationship with anyone else because all I could think of was Nick. Nick barefoot in his kitchen making me breakfast. Nick in court in his perfectly tailored suit, mesmerizing the jury with his deep voice and striking eyes. Nick, shirtless, in his jeans and cowboy hat, holding his extra-long hose.

But while I was obsessing about him, he hadn't called or texted once. Instead, he'd moseyed right along and found himself another...what?

Girlfriend?

Lover?

Wife?

How would I know? He'd introduced her by her first name with no further explanation.

Asshole.

I lost control of my eyeballs and they flicked to the rearview mirror. *Marla* sat in the back seat of my Honda Fit with little Gucci, Nick's Maltese—an unwanted residual from his last wife—in her lap.

Gucci was decked out in a pink and black zebra striped dress with a black tutu for a skirt. A pink bow adorned the ponytail on top of her head.

If there were ever a dog meant to wear clothes, Gucci was it, but what right did this Marla have to dress Nick's dog? I knew Marla did it because I was absolutely certain Nick would never be caught putting clothes on a dog.

My hot Latina blood—which I'd discovered was a thing when I caught Nick withholding evidence from me last summer—boiled up into my brain.

Marla. Who named their daughter "Marla"? I mean it just sounded like a bitchy name, didn't it? Truth be told, I'd never thought about it being a bitchy name before, but now...

I peeked at her again. She was wearing a slinky, blood red dress. Unless she was on her way to the Grammy Awards, it was cut way too low in the front and slit way too high on her left thigh. Plus, she was too tall. When we were standing near each other waiting for her three—*yes, three*—checked bags to come around the carousel, I felt like one of the seven dwarfs.

Grumpy. Definitely Grumpy.

The two Nick ex-wives I'd seen in Bolo were nearly as tall and every bit as blonde and sexy as Marla. I wished I'd at least worn heels so I could give my five-foot-five—okay, five-foot-four-and-a-half—inch frame a boost. I'd worn flip-flops, jeans, and what I thought was a flattering peasant top instead of my usual geeky t-shirts and hoodies, but now I felt like a schlub compared to sexy Marla.

Nick held onto the passenger door armrest, mashing his imaginary brake, apparently not a fan of my driving. I jerked the car to the right, purposely cutting off a red Lamborghini, no doubt being driven by another asshole who had three blonde exes under his belt.

Nick had been trying to control his reactions, but I heard an involuntary grunt escape his lips at what probably looked to him like a near-miss, since he'd spent the past few years in a town that only needed one stoplight, if that.

Ha! Serves him right.

When I called him night before last and he agreed to come, I felt such a sense of relief, I actually got a few hours of sleep. Nick Owen was coming to help me. We made a great team, and having him nearby made me feel safe and, by extension, my dad would be safe.

But this...

My eyes flicked to the mirror again, then sliced over to view Nick's ruggedly handsome profile, which only pissed me off more. No one should get to have a face that good, a freaking eight-pack of abs *and* be as smart as Nick was. And from the pictures I saw at his mom's house, he'd been hot his whole life.

Well, I guess "hot" wasn't the right word for his whole life. That would be creepy. Let's just say, he was a beautiful baby, a cute kid, and by high school he turned into this smoking hot chick-magnet sitting next to me.

No awkward phase with braces on his teeth or bad skin. Certainly, no extreme weight issues like the ones I'd had. And I was pretty sure he'd gotten to work his way through every gorgeous blonde in Texas.

Huh. I remembered that Texas Ranger-slash-super model "friend" who Nick called in on my case.

Make that, all the gorgeous blondes in Texas plus a few sultry brunettes mixed in as palette cleansers.

Asshole.

I jerked the steering wheel to the left unnecessarily. Marla's body flopped over to one side. Nick flung his hand out and braced on the side of my backrest to keep himself upright.

Stifling my satisfied smile as best I could, I said, "Sorry. It was a motorcycle. Came out of nowhere."

"I didn't see a motorcycle," Nick replied.

"I'm not surprised." I shrugged. "It must have been weaving through traffic at a hundred miles an hour. Thank goodness for my lightning quick reflexes."

"Yeah." Nick's voice was tinged with sarcasm. "Thank goodness." His face had turned completely toward me and I could see his narrowed eyes in my peripheral vision, assessing me.

Let him wonder why I was pissed. I didn't care.

"Do you want to fill me in on what happened?"

"Sure," I said. A lump formed in my throat, but I didn't want to cry in front of Marla. It was bad enough I cried the last time I saw Nick. I don't know what got into me. I hadn't cried since I was a little girl and my mom was murdered, except for a few months later when my dad wasn't allowed back into the country after his own mother's funeral.

But when it was time to leave Nick last summer, I blubbered like a silly teenage girl.

So embarrassing.

Pull yourself together, Paprika. My brain liked to annoy me with my real name when it thought I was acting stupid.

"My dad made a reputation for himself as head chef of one of the best restaurants in Bogota," I began. "He specializes in these fusion dishes, combining the flavors of other countries with Latin American ones. He's known for reinventing the quiche." Traffic ahead stopped suddenly and I came to a screeching halt six inches behind the car in front of us.

Marla's head flopped forward, then back again. My lips tried to turn up into an evil grin, but I squelched it before anyone could see.

"Shit!" Nick said. If he didn't stop with his passenger-seat driving, his big boot was going to put a hole in my floorboard.

I ignored him and kept talking. "The founders of Microtology —Steve and Valerie Kaporsky—happened to be in Bogota a few months ago. Steve fell in love with my dad's Triple Fusion Quiche when they ate at the restaurant where he worked. He offered him the head chef job here at the VIP Center and pulled strings to get him a quick green card."

"Back up a minute," Nick said. "What's Microtology, a company or...?"

I eased up a few inches, then turned my head to look at him. "You haven't heard of Microtology?"

He shook his head.

"The official name is the 'Temple of Microtology.' It's the latest Hollywood fad religion. From the research I've done, they seem to believe humans' negative behavior is being controlled by tiny microorganisms and parasites living in and on us. Their dogma is kind of convoluted and secretive."

Nick rolled his eyes. "Welcome to L.A.," he said.

"Hey, Bolo wasn't exactly the bastion of normalcy."

"You've got me there."

"Anyway, my dad's only been here a little over a month. Two nights ago, the head of security found his sous chef—Alberto Viera—dead and my dad was gone. He hasn't been seen since Sunday afternoon when he was working with Alberto. They were still there when the rest of the kitchen staff left at three—the restaurant only serves brunch on Sundays. The medical examiner places time of death at around ten-thirty that night."

"Are there any other suspects?" Nick asked.

"I don't know. The police haven't been very forthcoming with information. When they questioned me about my dad, though, it was clear he's a prime suspect."

"And why do you believe it wasn't him?"

Was he serious? I turned to look at him, then slammed on the brake when I saw the traffic stopping from the corner of my eye. Nick's head jerked forward and I was okay with that.

"Did you come all the way from Texas to side with the cops?" I yelled.

He lifted his hand and massaged his whiplashed neck. "I'm just wondering what you know about him, considering you've been in The States and he's been in Colombia for the past, what, fifteen or sixteen years?"

If I wasn't strapped in and driving in heavy traffic, I would have climbed onto Nick's lap and strangled him with his safety belt.

"Ya know," I said snottily. "There are millions of people in Colombia, and the vast majority are not dealing drugs or assassinating judges. They have teachers and doctors and lawyers, just like here."

"You're pretty keyed up," he replied. "Maybe I should drive."

"Hah! Like you could drive in L.A."

Nick sucked in a heavy breath. "Rika, I'm on your side, but I need to play devil's advocate and learn everything you know so I can help."

"All right." I took a deep, calming breath, but a Krispy Kreme donut sign still called to me from the side of the freeway.

A donut was exactly what I needed right now. However, in addition to the five pounds I gained while eating Nick and LeeAnne's meals in Bolo, I'd put on four more from pining over him since he'd sent me away.

"What's your dad's name?" Nick asked.

"Diego Martín. He started as a cook when he first came to the country. Later, he enrolled in culinary school and graduated right before my mom died. A few months later, he went to see his sick mom in Colombia and stayed for her funeral. When he tried to come home, immigration wouldn't let him back into the U.S. He worked his way up in restaurants and became known as a cutting-edge, creative chef in Bogota."

"Not exactly Scarface, in other words," Nick said.

I chuckled. Laughter was a surprise after how stressed I'd been. I was back to being glad Nick had come. "No. Besides, Scarface was a Marielito.

Nick raised his eyebrows.

"A Cuban."

Nick nodded thoughtfully. "Murder weapon?"

I pulled into the hotel driveway, then closed my eyes for several seconds. "Chef's knife."

Twisting in my seat, I looked directly into Nick's eyes, expecting them to be the bright Bondi blue color I remembered most when I thought of him, but found them gray-blue and contemplative.

"We'll figure it out," he said gently, and I realized he was searching my eyes for something. I wasn't sure what.

"We're here," I said, feeling weird about gazing into each other's eyes with Marla in the back seat.

"Good. I'll be back as soon as I check us in."

The word "us" jumped out at me and I clamped my teeth together. "Sure," I said. "No problem."

Nick

"Did you say two rooms sir?" the scrawny hotel clerk's eyes slid to Marla and stuck there. He was in his early twenties and looked like he was wearing his dad's hotel blazer. And he was clearly perplexed as to why I was springing for a separate room for the swimsuit model hanging onto my arm.

"Yep. That's what I said." I pulled out my credit card and laid it on the counter. His question was understandable, so I tried to keep the annoyance out of my voice as I fought the urge to shake Marla's hand off me.

Yeah, she was beautiful. But that didn't keep me from trying to ditch her and come to L.A. alone.

I still didn't understand how this kept happening to me. Just like with my last two exes—BreeAnne and Megan—I found Marla on the side of the road when I was on my way to help out my mom. Marla was clearly having car trouble, but I swear to God I had no desire to stop this time.

In fact, when I saw her long legs and voluminous blonde hair, I wanted to mash the accelerator and break the land speed record to get the hell away from her.

But then I realized she was crying and I've never been able to stand to see a woman cry. The memory of Rika's tears running down her beautiful face before she drove away from me last summer had been stuck in neutral in my mind. I knew it wasn't right to ask her to stay, but I didn't want to let go of one memory of her.

Regardless, female waterworks could always tear a hole in my chest, and that day on the way to mom's was no different.

Talk about a fatal flaw.

Next thing I knew, Marla—if that was her real name—was staying at my house, waiting for her car to get fixed. Then, her last paycheck from her previous job hadn't been auto-deposited into her account and her employers weren't returning her calls. Then, her new job in Corpus Christi fired her for not showing up for the first day of work even though she called and told them what happened.

Sounds suspicious, I know. But Rika claimed a lot of bad luck, and all of hers turned out to be legitimate. I didn't have the heart to fill Marla's tank with gas and tell her to hit the road when she said she had nowhere to go.

After several weeks, though, I started to wonder if she was

playing me. And still, I was willing to leave her alone in my house with all my belongings and fly to L.A. to help Rika.

Nothing in the world would stop me from going to Rika if she needed me. The idea of getting away from Marla was icing on the cake.

Unfortunately, she caught me putting my bag in the truck and was *thrilled* at the idea that *we* were going to Los Angeles. She had her bags packed in ten minutes.

"So, would you like one key or two keys to each room?" The clerk's wide blue eyes shifted back and forth between me and Marla.

What kind of stupid question was that? "Why would I get us two separate rooms if we were going to have keys to each other's doors?"

"Well...um..." His brows lowered as his face reddened. "A lot of men come on business trips with their, um, *assistants*," he glanced at Marla again, "but they ask for an extra room key in case they want to..." The pause was so long, I found myself leaning forward as if that would draw the rest of the sentence out of him. "...collaborate," he finished.

Oh. Got it. People used work trips as excuses to have affairs, but needed to book separate rooms for appearance sake.

I didn't have time for this shit. Rika was waiting in the car.

"I need to get going," I said to Marla.

"That's okay," she replied cheerfully. "Gucci and I will keep busy with a massage and room service."

At my expense, not that I cared as long as it kept her occupied and out of my hair for a few hours.

I turned back to the clerk. "Can you get someone to help her to her room and leave my bag in mine?"

"Certainly, sir."

"Just charge everything to the room," I told Marla, effectively giving her permission to go hog wild spending my money.

My friend Gabe was right. I needed professional help. My—

according to him—*pathological* need to take care of women now had me providing a free vacation at the Omni Hotel to a woman I wasn't even sleeping with.

The one woman I'd never regretted taking care of was Rika. When I'd seen her at the airport today, she'd been more beautiful than I remembered. I think she even put on the five or ten pounds I'd thought she needed to gain last summer, before I realized she was irresistible regardless.

That kiss we shared when I caught her in her superhero underthings was the hottest moment I'd ever had with a woman.

Any woman. Ever.

"Bye, Nicky," Marla was saying.

I hated being called "Nicky"' One of my exes called me "Nicky."

"Say 'bye-bye,' Gucci," Marla baby-talked to my Maltese.

Yeah. I have a Maltese. Don't ask.

"Come on, Gucci! Tell Nicky 'bye-bye'!" Marla watched Gucci as if she expected her to open her tiny mouth and start speaking English.

This is the dog who once spent thirty minutes barking at one of my old sneakers. I didn't see a second language in her future. And, by the way the other dogs looked at her when she barked, I wasn't even sure she was fluent in her first.

"See you later." I stepped back so Marla wouldn't try to insist I give Gucci a goodbye kiss. She picked up her paw and waved it at me.

I turned to face the exit before I let my eyes roll.

"Fuck," I muttered as I shook my head. *Fuck.*

CHAPTER THREE

Nick

"Where are we?" I asked when Rika pulled into the parking lot of a six-story building. The bottom floor was windowless and square. Each floor above it was a bit smaller than the one below, giving it a stair-step appearance. But the most striking thing about the building was its color—shocking, gleaming white like I'd never seen on a building before.

"The Microtology VIP Center," Rika said. "I want to try again to get a look at the crime scene."

We got out of the car and I followed her around back. My eyes caught on the tall fence blocking the main parking lot off from the back of the building where we were.

"Authorized personnel only. No trespassing," I read off the sign. "Are we gonna be breaking and entering, too?"

"The gate's open." She gestured toward it. "And we won't be *break*ing anything."

"All right, then." I shrugged. "Lead the way."

I'd seen this determined look on Rika's face in Bolo when she informed me that if she couldn't count on the shady sheriff to prove her innocence, she'd solve the case herself. She almost got herself killed, although her instincts were right on when it came to catching the accomplice and recognizing a clue that I didn't think would lead anywhere.

Regardless, whatever she needed to do now, I was in. If there was a chance in hell my dad was alive, I'd break into Fort Knox to find him. And, deep down, I wanted to be the guy who helped Rika get her father back.

Strange how you could still miss someone you hadn't seen since you were a kid. I couldn't visualize my dad anymore. I had to rely on pictures, and that bothered me.

Rika had been separated from her father for most of her life. She deserved more than a month of face time with him.

As we came around the dumpster behind the building, I saw an open back door, manned by a twenty-something male in a dark blue uniform and shiny badge.

Shit. A cop.

"Hey, J!" Rika called.

Hearing the casual, borderline affectionate way she addressed him made me take a closer look. He was about five-foot-ten, several inches shorter than I was, but still quite a bit taller than Rika.

His physique said Gold's Gym, but as we approached, I noticed his face looked like it was swiped from a member of a '90s boy band.

A strange sensation sliced through me. My jaw clenched and my hands fisted involuntarily. I hadn't felt this way since the night Rika came home from Barr's and informed me JimBob McGwire had mauled her in the parking lot.

I experienced an irrational urge to punch this cop in his poster-boy face.

"How are you holding up?" he asked Rika sympathetically.

As she reached him, he stepped forward and wrapped his arms around her in a hug that lasted over seven seconds.

Sympathy hug. What a lame move.

I flashed back to how great it had felt to have Rika in my arms when she greeted me at the airport. *I* certainly didn't squander my chance to hold her when I could. So, could I really blame this guy?

He finished off the hug with a kiss on her cheek.

Oh, yeah, I could blame him all right. Who the hell was this guy to her?

When he finally let go of her, Rika glanced at me. "Julian, this is Nick Owen. Nick this is Officer Julian Suriano."

As we reached out and gave each other the obligatory handshake, I watched him take stock of me. Sure, I was taller and probably better educated, but I wasn't certain I could compete with this warm, maybe Italian, maybe Latin vibe he was giving off.

Had they slept together? My gut clenched at the possibility.

I squeezed his hand harder than necessary in a ridiculous macho-man move I'd never even considered before. Then, I reminded myself I was here to help Rika find her dad, not run off her potential boyfriends like I *was* her dad. I released him and we both looked at Rika.

"Is there any way we can get in to see the crime scene?" she asked.

"Sorry," Boy Band replied. "CSI's back in there today. Not sure why."

Rika's shoulders dropped as she exhaled on a frustrated sigh. Boy Band shifted uncomfortably from one foot to the other.

Yep, he wanted her bad, and it was bothering him that he was so useless to her. I was enjoying his discomfort, although I did wish he had more information about the case.

"Can you get me copies of the crime scene photos?" Rika tried again.

"I'm not a homicide detective," he said. "I don't have access to the murder book." But when Rika's big chocolate eyes shone with disappointment, he added, "I'll try to get copies for you, if I can."

She smiled gratefully at him. I wanted to swipe that smile from her face and stick it in the front pocket of my jeans where Boy Band wouldn't dare go after it.

"Have you heard any talk?" Rika asked. "Were they able to lift fingerprints?"

"They think the killer did some cleanup afterward because the knife handle and some other items at the scene were wiped," he replied. "It's going to take a while for the lab to process the DNA they found in the kitchen and on the victim. Plus, the detectives are going to have a hell of a time getting it sorted because of the number of people who've been in and out of there on a regular basis."

Disappointment registered on Rika's face again for a split second before she willed it away. "Thanks for keeping me informed," she said. "If I need to talk to someone I can't track down on the internet, can you get me their phone number and address?"

"Sure," he replied, clearly dazzled by her pearly whites. But who could blame the guy? My heart seemed to trip over itself every time she aimed that smile at me. "Do you still have my email and cell number?"

"Yeah, I do. Thanks, J." She stepped forward.

Seriously? They had to hug again? The last hug was only three minutes ago!

I closed my eyes automatically. My teeth clenched as I entertained a fantasy that involved knocking Boy Band on his ass.

"Nick, are you all right?"

I opened my eyes to find the two of them had disengaged and were staring at me.

"I'm great," I said. "Let's go." I gave Boy Band a half-hearted chin lift and turned toward the car.

CHAPTER FOUR

Rika

I tried not to let my disappointment get the best of me as Nick and I climbed back in the car.

Focus. I needed to focus.

But my mind had been jumping back and forth between trying to determine the next logical step in finding my dad and fighting off the idea that I'd never see him again.

Just like my mom. She was abducted when I was eight and that was it. No more mom.

People were always talking about karma, but I didn't believe in it. I mean, what did I ever do to deserve having two parents taken away?

I started the car and headed to the exit.

"So, how do you know Ricky Martin?"

"Huh?" Had I zoned out on a conversation we were having about pop music? Not that I didn't have feelings about Ricky Martin. On one hand, as a Latina, I was proud of him for breaking through as an international artist. On the other, I was annoyed that he'd sold out and dropped the accent from the name Martín. On the third hand—a third hand was the super power I'd wished for since I was nine, so I could hold a Colombian beef *empanada*, a Mexican *empanada* with pineapple filling and a Hostess Ding Dong, all at once—

Wait, what was I thinking about? I'd gotten distracted by the carbs dancing in my head. Oh, yeah, on the third hand, I admired Ricky for coming out publicly as gay, an extra difficult thing for a Latin pop star to do.

But none of this had anything to do with our visit to the center. "What does Ricky Martin have to do with anything?" I asked Nick.

"You know, Boy Band, back there at the door."

Oh. I pictured Julian's face. He did look like he could have been a member of Menudo, the boy band my mom and aunts were crazy about when they were young.

"Julian and I were in a criminal justice class together at the community college before I moved to New York," I explained.

At the time, I'd been working as a receptionist and online skip tracer for a private investigation agency, trying to get my boss to take me seriously and let me work in the field. Then I moved to New York with my boyfriend Brandtt where I'd ended up as an E.coli tester in the lab at a meat packing plant—not as glamorous as it sounds.

When Brandtt broke up with me and I finally got back to L.A., I would have preferred working at a different agency, but the only P.I. firm job I could get was at the same place with the same sexist boss I had before I went to New York.

At least he was fine with me taking time off now, although he didn't offer me any help at all, since he knew I couldn't pay for it.

"Has he asked you out yet?"

I pulled into traffic and flicked my eyes at Nick. His voice was super-casual but his body seemed tense.

"Who? Julian?" What did Nick care about my love life? He's

the one who had me and threw me back. Well, he didn't have me as in *have* me-have me, but he could have had me. Instead he let me drive away.

Maybe he was asking about my love life so he could assuage his guilt over allowing me to fall for him. *Hard.*

I mean, if he wasn't going to seal the deal, the least he could have done last summer was avoid removing his shirt when I was in the vicinity. My recurring dreams about Twinkies, Ding Dongs and donuts were now interrupted by memories of Nick's hot Texas sweat riding his ab muscles like a roller coaster. And had he really needed to flex his biceps so tightly while lifting his extra-long hose?

Oh, yeah. We were talking about Julian asking me out. "I was already dating Brandtt when we met," I replied. "And I didn't see Julian again until my dad disappeared and I tried to get into the crime scene."

"Well..." Nick was looking out the passenger window, but, when I glanced at him, I saw a muscle jump in his jaw. "He will."

I rolled my eyes. Nick was being ridiculous. Julian was way too hot for me. Of course, I'd thought the same thing about Brandtt when we met. Weird how he got less and less good-looking, the longer I knew him.

"Where are we going now?" Nick asked.

"My Lita's house." I nosed my Honda through the stop-and-go traffic to the left lane.

"Your what?"

"My grandmother's. I've been staying there since I got back to L.A. I have some information we can go over there." I'd meant to bring my laptop with me, but had gotten so excited about the idea of seeing Nick again, I'd forgotten it.

I merged onto the 101 as Nick stared over his left shoulder, clearly not trusting my merging skills, and headed East. Lita had insisted I stay with her when I moved back from New York, citing my cruel abandonment of her in favor of that *careculo* Brandtt, as she called him. She wasn't letting me forget that I'd been away on the opposite coast for an entire year for nothing, as it turned out.

In hindsight, I realized my two-year relationship with Brandtt had been based on him liking the way I looked standing beside him in photo ops—he was only five-nine, but I was still quite a bit shorter than him, even in heels. He also liked the contrast between his blonde hair and blue eyes and my brown hair and dark brown eyes. It would have peeved him to have another blonde next to him, outshining his blondness.

As for me, after finally dropping half my body weight, I think I was so flattered to have a man as good-looking as Brandtt romancing me, I overlooked the clear signs we shouldn't be together. Like the fact that he hated both the Star Wars *and* Star Trek franchises as well as the Terminator movies.

Okay, maybe the later ones that James Cameron didn't direct, but how do you hate *Judgement Day*, with Linda Hamilton all buff, ready to kick ass and blow up Cyberdyne?

"So, I'll be meeting your grandmother?" Nick asked pulling me back into our conversation.

Ha! No way did I want him meeting my grandmother. "No, she's out of town with my aunts right now."

I'd lucked out on that one. Lita had this trip planned for a while. Ever since she won a five-night stay for four—in a vineyard bed and breakfast in wine country—at the church fundraiser.

According to Tía Margo, my grandmother bid twenty-five dollars for the prize in the silent auction, then hid the card so no one else could outbid her.

Lita defended her actions by pointing out that she'd been a devoted volunteer at the church for thirty years, and she'd never even been awarded the volunteer of the year plaque.

In other words, they owed her.

I'd turned down the offer to go, dying to have some time

alone in the house, so Lita had invited my two aunts and her best friend and neighbor, Mrs. Ruíz.

When my father disappeared, they were already packing for the trip. I decided to keep the information to myself. My dad was the only man in the world the women in my family thought highly of, and I couldn't bear to tell them he'd vanished, like his wife—their daughter and sister.

Not only would they be shocked and broken-hearted, but the house would become Grand Central Station, full of worried friends and relatives and friends of friends and friends of relatives. We were Latin, after all, and my grandmother had lived in this neighborhood for decades. Everybody knew her.

I needed space and quiet to figure things out, so I let them go on their trip without telling them, hoping I could find some answers by the time they came back. They left early this morning, none the wiser.

I stopped the car in front of my grandmother's stucco, Spanish Revival style house on a corner in a neighborhood the locals called "Ale," pronounced "Ah-leh." It was short for the word *Alemania* which means Germany in Spanish.

According to my grandmother, the houses were bought new by German families in the 1920's after some Ku Klux Klan members took over the local government in the mostly German city of Anaheim and started giving Catholic Germans a hard time there. A few years later when the Klan threat seemed thwarted, the German families moved back to Anaheim, but the name "Alemania" stuck, even though nearly everyone around here was Hispanic now. Mostly Mexicans, with enough El Salvadorians, Guatemalans, and Colombians to keep the soccer bets interesting.

As I unlocked the front door and Nick followed me in, I wondered if the house seemed claustrophobic to him. It wasn't tiny by L.A., regular people standards, but compared to his huge ranch-style in Texas, the rooms looked small and packed with furniture.

My grandmother's affinity for floral patterns and obsession with knickknacks didn't help any. More specifically, angels—cherubs, golden-haired angels, Gabriel blowing his horn, and one I was pretty sure was the Greek God Hermes, but I guess the wings on his feet were enough to qualify him as an angel in Lita's book. The miniatures and not-so-miniatures covered nearly every surface in the living room except for the spots that were cluttered with family photographs.

I'd been coming to, or living in, this house my whole life, so it never struck me before that large floral patterns and miniature angels didn't go together, aesthetically speaking, until I saw the room the way I thought Nick would view it.

To the left of the living room was the dining area, still in the same room. A shiny walnut six-person table with matching chairs took up nearly every bit of the dining space. The table could be expanded to fit two more people, which meant over a dozen people could eat at that table, based on how my grandmother and her Latino friends allotted space.

Plus, when you're Latin, virtually any excuse for a get-together will do, so my grandmother kept twenty folding chairs and two folding tables in the garage for outdoor parties. She had four bar stools at the counter separating the living-dining combo from the kitchen, when it was clearly meant for two stools.

I'd seen as many as forty people happily crammed into the kitchen-dining-living room with overflow on the front and back porches.

Anyway, that's why I couldn't tell my grandmother about my father going missing. Sympathy parties drew even more people than soccer finals and *quinceañeras,* since it would be wrong to stay away from a friend in her time of need. Genetically, I was one hundred percent Colombian, but the American in me couldn't think straight with all that commotion around.

At the back of the living room was a short hall that led to my room and the downstairs bathroom. I was originally upstairs, but when I was a freshman in high school, my grandmother noticed me huffing and puffing as I climbed up to my room and told me I could have the one downstairs.

I jumped at the chance—not literally or it would have registered on the Richter Scale—because the downstairs bedroom had been my mother's when she was growing up, and I'd always felt closer to her when I was in it.

Now, Nick followed me toward it, but my steps faltered as I reached the open doorway. My eyes paused on my Ms. Pacman comforter, flicked to the Hogwarts Express bookends on the shelf above it, then slid over to pause on my Wonder Woman desk lamp. God, I hoped he wouldn't look in the bathroom and see my *Doctor Who* Tardis shower curtain and matching toothbrush holder.

Embarrassment prickled over my skin. Nick was the polar opposite of geek.

"Um...I'm back in my childhood bedroom until I find an apartment," I said breezily. It wasn't a lie. I had been a child when I moved into this bedroom. However, I bought the lamp and bookends well after I qualified as an adult.

Nick already knew I was a geek, but that's different than exposing myself to him with the full-frontal geekiness of my room.

His gaze swept around, not missing a detail. His lips were pressed together, fighting off a grin.

Asshole.

I hadn't ever seen his childhood bedroom at his mom's house, but, assuming it was still intact, it was probably full of stupid football trophies. Not nearly as cool as my stuff. Depending on your definition of "cool," that is.

He strolled over to my bookshelves. "A helicopter?" he said as he picked it up from the top of the shelves.

"It's a mind-controlled helicopter," I replied. "I'm testing and reviewing it."

"Is this a job?"

"No. I review for an online company that sells geek stuff. I get to keep everything they send me for free."

"Like this?" Nick glared at the copter. "There's no such thing as a mind-controlled helicopter."

"There is," I said. "You're holding it. You put that headgear there," I pointed to the electrode cap, "on your head and fly it using brainwaves."

"And you've gotten this to work?"

"Yes, well..." I was pretty sure it worked, but I'd only had the chance to try it once before I'd found out my dad was missing. "I got it to lift off the ground and back down without crashing, but I couldn't get it to fly anywhere," I said. "I just need more time with it."

"Huh," Nick replied. "I think you're going to be glad you didn't pay money for it."

This bugged me, since Nick wasn't nearly as knowledgeable about technology as I was and had no business pre-judging something I was supposed to judge scientifically. However, he had flown all the way to L.A. to help me so I was in no position to be snooty with him. Not at the moment anyway.

I rolled out my desk chair and asked him to sit down in front of my twenty-four-inch HD computer screen. I already had my laptop plugged into it. When I was home, I often used the big screen for my skip tracing or online classes while I used the laptop screen to stay on top of social media.

Standing over Nick, I clicked open a file. "These are the Kaporskys—Steve and Valerie—the founders of Microtology," I explained. Steve's head was always the first thing that jumped out at me, since it was shaved completely. While on most men, this tended to emphasize the roundness of their heads, his looked almost square. Valerie wore a bob that had been bleached white. Not blonde. White. Like a piece of printer paper.

Both of them had dark brown eyes. Valerie's were warm, but Steve's fell somewhere between David Koresh and Charles Manson. Each time I saw his picture, I thought he was a man capable of anything, and I didn't want to imagine that he had possession of my father.

Nick stared at the screen. "Unusual-looking couple."

"Not for Microtologists," I replied. "They believe that shaving or bleaching hair is the best way to deter external parasites and other microorganisms. It's not required, but it is encouraged that they do one or the other to all the hair on their bodies."

I clicked to the next picture. "This is Alberto Viera, the victim." The photo was from when Alberto was still alive. He was gasp-worthy handsome with smoldering black eyes and dark hair, cut purposefully messy by some hairstylist who knew what he or she was doing.

I expected Nick to comment on this, but he didn't seem to notice the hotness of the victim. I guess when you were as gorgeous as Nick, hotness was just a fact of life.

"His hair is dark brown," Nick pointed out. "Does that mean he was only an employee, not a member?"

"I haven't been able to verify that either way yet." I appreciated the fact that Nick already had his thinking cap on. "This is Jason Kim," I said as I moved on to the next photo. "He's the one who found the body. He left the military after two tours and got a job in the VIP Center kitchen." Jason was Asian and, like Alberto, exceptionally good-looking, even sporting a white mohawk. I wondered if there was an appearance requirement for Microtologists and their employees. Maybe the best way to get new people into a cult is to have hot people hanging around the facility.

"Was he working in the kitchen that day?"

"He doesn't work in the kitchen anymore. After the Kaporskys got to know him and his history, they made him Head of Security for the VIP Center and he's worked his way into their inner circle. I've been trying to talk to him, but, no luck, so far."

My phone let out a hungry zombie sound and Nick jerked back before he caught himself and reacquired his cool. I stifled a laugh. I'd never gotten to be one of the cool people, so I kind of enjoyed it when they lost it, if only for a second.

"What the hell was that?" Nick asked.

"Incoming email," I replied.

"They offer that sound as an alert tone?"

"No, I jailbreak my phones so I can customize them however I want."

I'd noticed that Nick had gotten himself a phone like mine since I last saw him. He probably thought that made us even, but my phones would always do more than his.

I reached past Nick, clicking over to my inbox. It was an email from Julian, so I opened it right away.

I only got copies of the first three pictures, Julian had written. *I'll try to get you more later.*

I double-clicked the attachment. This time, I was the one who jerked backward.

The body looked worse than I'd expected. Once handsome Alberto Viera was crumpled on the floor with his legs bent underneath him as if he'd fallen to his knees first. One of his hands was on the large chef's knife protruding from his chest. He'd grabbed the blade instead of the handle and it appeared that his hand had bled along with the wound in his stomach. The front of his body was covered in blood and it pooled on the floor next to him. Lots of blood. More blood than I'd ever seen. His other arm was bent at a right angle as if he was waving.

I imagined him putting his hands up at the last minute to try to defend himself, then forgetting about his left hand completely as his right hand grasped at the knife in his gut. His eyes were open and vacant.

Nick and I studied the image in silence for several seconds before I clicked the next attachment—a tight shot of two quiches side-by-side, one slice missing from each of them. There didn't seem to be much to see there so I went on to the third—a delicate silver chain with a heart pendant which held a tiny colored stone.

He bent down to get a better look. "Well, there's something new," he said. "We didn't know there was a woman on the scene."

"Yeah, it looks like one of those you buy in twos and share with a best friend or someone you love," I replied. "Which means someone has the other heart. Teenage girls love that sort of thing." Oh, how I yearned for a friend I could give a BFF necklace to when I was a teenager.

"It looks like a cheap piece," Nick said. "Not exactly platinum."

I rolled my eyes inwardly, sure that Nick knew about expensive platinum jewelry from buying it for at least two of his wives.

And maybe Marla.

Suddenly, the front door rattled and I heard women's voices.

Very familiar women's voices.

"Oh, shit!" I whispered. "Why are they back?"

Nick looked at me with curious eyes, clearly ignorant of the catastrophe that had befallen us.

"Stay here," I whispered as I jumped off the bed and hurried to the living room.

My grandmother was standing next to the sofa, putting her keys back into her purse. Tía Margo was coming through the door. Tía Madi, the youngest of the three daughters my grandmother gave birth to, had already flopped down on the couch and pulled out her cell phone.

"Lita? What are you doing here?" I blurted in my grandmother's direction.

She let her purse strap slide down and rest on the crook of

her elbow. "*Madre de dios!*" she cried. "We've been sitting in traffic all day!"

Tía Madi looked up from her phone. "Wildfire," she said.

"They've closed off the road." Tía Margo added. "God's punishing mamá for stealing the vineyard vacation." Margo always goaded my grandmother, taking opposite positions to annoy her.

Tía Madi claimed her sister Margo suffered from MCD—Middle Child Disorder. When they were young, Margo pointed out the most ridiculous slights, like how Mariana—aka Mari, my mother, the oldest—and Madison, the youngest had been given multiple syllables in their names, while Margo only got two.

When I was younger, Margo and my grandmother were constantly at odds over me. My grandmother believed the best cure for my sadness over losing my parents—one to a killer and one to Homeland Security's post nine-eleven immigration policy—was fatty, carby meals followed by ice cream or *pan dulce* from the Mexican bakery a few blocks away.

Margo, on the other hand, thought I should be living with her and my cousins Sofia and Max, eating low-fat meals and exercising.

My grandmother won, which is why I went through junior high and high school with nicknames like "Hindenburg" and "Megaton."

Now, Lita was giving Margo the death stare. Her daughter was not allowed to call her a thief, regardless of how the vacation was obtained. Margo glared back at her, clearly in the mood to rumble.

It was never a great idea for the two of them to be stuck in a car for hours together.

Madi chuckled. I was never sure why she found their bickering so funny. I typically found it stressful, but maybe that was because so many of their arguments had been about me.

My grandmother looked at the ceiling and mumbled something in Spanish about God helping her with her ungrateful children.

Suddenly, both my aunts' gazes jerked up, focusing on the doorway between the living room and hall, and stuck there.

My own wildfire broke out in my stomach as I turned to look over my shoulder.

CHAPTER FIVE

Nick

I sat at Rika's desk for a couple of minutes, wondering what I should do. Would it be better to walk out and greet everyone? Or to let Rika bring them in here where I'd be staring into the computer, making it clear I was just working on the case?

The longer I sat here, the creepier it seemed that I hadn't made my presence known. Finally, I got up and walked to the living room.

A moment after I entered, Rika glanced back at me as if verifying what two of the other three women in the room were staring at.

The look on her face told me she was not the least bit happy to see me in here. But what was I supposed to do? Jump out her window like some horny high school kid?

One woman's back was to me, but I could see the faces of the other two. Both bore some resemblance to Rika, the most notable feature being their unusually big brown eyes. One had a fuller figure than Rika, her hair cut shorter, at shoulder length. The younger one, on the couch, had bright red lips and hair so black it might have been dyed that way. Since she was wearing a black t-shirt and black skinny jeans, she may have been going for a goth look, but she was too attractive to be scary-looking. In fact, she looked a lot like Morticia Addams in the old TV show re-runs.

Both women were way above average in the looks department, like Rika was. In fact, if the three of them were taller, they might be mistaken for a room full of models.

I realized while I'd been checking them out, their eyes were turned up, looking at me, shock apparent on their faces.

The other woman followed their gazes, then whipped around to see what they were staring at. When she saw me, her body tensed as if she were preparing for hand to hand combat.

As she examined me from the top of my head to my snake skin boots, I examined her right back.

She had the big eyes like the others, but darker, and was probably a looker in her day. Her hair was nearly as black as her younger daughter's except for the two streaks in front that had turned snow white. She was wearing a hot pink polyester pantsuit that looked both brand new and like it was designed in the 1970's.

Between that and the pink floral top she wore under it, she should have seemed approachable, but her nearly black eyes—along with the rest of her face—scowled at me with such intensity, I felt like I was getting a hex put on me right then and there.

Her lips parted and she glanced back and forth between Rika and me. "What is this?" she demanded. "What was this man doing in your room?"

Rika winced. "Lita..." she began, her voice higher pitched than usual, "this is Nick Owen. Nick, this is my grandmother Dolores Delacruz, and my aunts, Margo and Madison." She gestured to each in turn.

Wow, her aunts, huh? I would have believed her if she said those two were her sisters.

I offered her grandmother my hand to shake. "Nice to meet you, Mrs. Delacruz."

Her eyes darted down to my hand suspiciously, then back to my face again. "Why are you in my house?"

"Nick Owen?" Margo said. "Isn't he the lawyer from Texas?"

I nodded and started to smile at her, but she'd narrowed her eyes and was staring at me as suspiciously as her mother was.

Mrs. Delacruz drew herself up to her full five-foot-zero. "The man who took her and kept her at his house?"

Madison sighed and rolled her eyes. "The one who defended her for murder for free and saved her from a sniper."

Mrs. Delacruz ignored her and said, "You should be ashamed of yourself!" to me.

I turned to Rika. "What did you tell them about me?"

"I just told—" Rika began.

"Are you one of those child predators who molests little girls?" Mrs. Delacruz's glare was burning a hole in the space between my eyebrows.

"Mamá! She's been an adult for, like, six years now." Madison said. "Besides, he's hot. If he molested her, she probably enjoyed it."

Mrs. Delacruz turned toward the couch and yelled "*Cállate*, Madison!" at the same time her older daughter yelled, "Shut up, Madi!"

Rika's face darkened into what I assumed was a blush, judging by its flustered expression.

"What were you doing in Rika's room?" her grandmother asked again. "Did you hear we had gone and come over to take advantage of her again?"

That was it. I didn't know what Rika said to give them such a bad impression of me—and she must have said something—but I wasn't going to stand here and take this abuse.

"By taking advantage of her, are you referring to me posting bail for her, defending her in court, or giving her a place to stay when the sheriff confiscated her car and all her money?"

"No man does all that without expecting a return on his investment," she replied, narrowing her eyes even more.

"Lita," Rika broke in. "Nick is here for a legal conference. He stopped by to say 'hi' and I asked him to take a look at my computer. He...fixes things." Why was she lying? We both knew she was light years ahead of me, technologically speaking. "He's always fixing things for his wives and his mom and—" *Uh-oh*. She sounded like she was in full-on panic babbling. What the hell?

"*Wives?*" Margo's eyes bugged out like a cartoon character. "Is he a polygamist?"

I frowned, hard. "I'm not a polygamist." I couldn't believe I had to answer that ridiculous accusation.

"Lita, I need something from Eddie's," Rika said. "Are you cooking tonight? Is there anything we can pick up for you?"

"*Pues*, of course I'm cooking. How else would we eat?"

Rika grabbed her backpack-purse thing from the couch where she'd left it.

"You like Colombian food or Mexican?" her grandmother asked me.

"I guess I only know Mexican."

She blew out a snort and nodded as if I'd confirmed her low expectations of me.

"But I've always wanted to have Colombian," I added.

"Yeah, I'll bet you have," Madison said with a smirk. She glanced between me and Rika. When my eyes met hers, she wiggled her brows up and down a couple of times, just in case I hadn't caught her innuendo.

Her mother ignored her. "Paprika, see if Eddie has some *patacones*. I want to make *bandeja paisa*." She turned back to me. "*I'll* show you Colombian," she said in a tone of voice that sounded like a threat.

"Uh...great!" I replied.

~

Rika

Since it was winter—if you can call any time of year winter in L.A.—the sun had already set when I hustled Nick out of the house.

The last thing I needed was for him to spill the beans about my dad.

"What was that all about?" Nick asked as we turned onto the sidewalk.

"Well, my grandmother won this stay at a wine country bed and breakfast that was donated to the silent auction at church," I began. I was stalling. If I explained to him why I hadn't told my family about my dad, I'd have to tell him things I'd avoided talking about my entire life. "Since the trip was for four people—"

"No." He shook his head. "I mean, what the hell did you say to them about me?"

"Oh, that." I said. "Nothing. Well, nothing bad, anyway." I'd given my family the run down on the events in Bolo, but left out the part about how I'd only been broken up with Brandtt for a few days when I started having feelings for Nick.

A lot of them.

"You had to have told them something," Nick insisted. "They treated me like I was a cross between Bill Cosby and Roman Polanski. They hate me." He seemed really bothered.

I liked the idea that he wanted my family to think the best of him. I'd wanted his mom to like me, even though, under normal circumstances, I would have had no interest in ditsy Tammy Lynn whatsoever.

Or maybe Nick was so used to women swooning over him, he'd be shocked by any female rejection.

Yep. That was probably it. It had nothing to do with the fact that they were my family.

"They don't hate you," I said. "Not you personally, anyway."

He stopped in the middle of the sidewalk, next to Mrs.

Arguello's lemon tree. "Oh, they hated me," he insisted. "Did you tell them what happened that day in my bath—"

"No!" I yelled before he could say *when I kissed you in your underwear*, then I glanced over my shoulder at Lita's house and lowered my voice. "I didn't tell anyone about that. Besides, nothing happened."

Other than him rocking your world, you mean? my mind whispered.

Nick's lips parted and his expression said he wanted to argue the point. I couldn't discuss this with him, not now.

"They don't have a high opinion of men," I said. "They assumed you'd expect to be paid back in some way for everything you did for me."

"There has to be more to it. They were openly hostile. If you told them the truth—"

"Of course, I told them the truth! But from what I've learned, my grandfather screwed around on Lita, although she talks about him like he's a saint now that he's dead. My Tía Margo's husband was a... well, a *dick*." It wasn't a word I normally used, yet the only one that fit my ex-Uncle Kurt. My ex, Brandtt was a tool, but Kurt was a full-fledged dick.

Nick pushed out an indignant breath, clearly not wanting to be bunched together with the tools and dicks.

"Oh, I wouldn't recommend drinking anything my grandmother gives you unless it's water or in a sealed can or bottle when you get it."

"Why?"

"Her best friend Mrs. Ruíz—you'll probably meet her—is a Mexican *curandera*."

"A what?"

"A *curandera*, an herbalist. People come to her if they're sick or they think someone's given them the evil eye. I can't believe you don't know the term considering all the Mexicans there are in South Texas."

"I don't know any witch doctors down there."

"*Curandera*," I corrected him. "And you do know one. The lady who runs the bakery in Bolo. You buy tortillas for your breakfast tacos from her."

Nick frowned at me and shook his head. "Mrs. Hernandez? No way."

"Yes, way. She offered me a good luck potion one day when she came into Barr's."

"How would I not know this after all these years?"

"She's not going to offer it to *you*. Your people burned witches. Anyway, Mrs. Ruíz, Lita's friend, is convinced she has a truth serum, so watch out. My grandmother might try to use it on you."

"You believe in this stuff?"

"A lot of medicines come from plants," I said. "And she knows a lot about herbs. Maybe she's figured out how to make some herbal form of sodium pentothal."

At that exact moment, I saw a form in the shadows. In that same exact moment, Nick reached out, grabbed the form, wrenched its arm behind its back and pushed its face into the tree trunk.

I winced. "Hi, Eli," I said to the back of the form's head.

Was it awful that I was a *teensy* bit aroused by Nick's lightning fast display of machismo? Something fluttered low in my belly and I was breathing a little harder. I'd learned months ago that being around Nick turned me into a cavewoman, but I thought maybe the effects wore off when you crossed the Texas state line.

I was wrong.

"You know this guy?" He whipped Eli around to face me.

"Sure," I replied. "Nick, this is Eli Lippman, my stalker. Eli, this is Nick my...um...friend and sometimes attorney."

Nick released Eli, but as my words sank in, he narrowed his eyes, flicking them between us. "*Your stalker?*"

"Uh-huh," Eli said cheerfully. "It's been, like three and a half years now." He smiled affectionately at me like he was a husband talking about how long we'd been married.

Nick looked back and forth between us again as if trying to assess which one of us was the craziest.

"I lost her trail when she took off for Texas," Eli said with some annoyance. "I guess that's when you had her."

"I didn't *have* her," Nick replied. "She wasn't under lock and key. I just helped her out."

The two men stared at each other. I could sense the testosterone bursting through Nick's pores, forming a protective barrier around me, and found I enjoyed the feeling.

"Regardless," Eli turned to me, "did you get the candy?"

"Yeah," I replied. "It was great, but you know we don't really have an anniversary, don't you?"

Eli's jaw tightened. He jerked his chin toward Nick. "So, is this what you like now, Rika? This muscle bound, shit-for-brains—"

"Hold on a minute," Nick said. "I have seven years of post-secondary education under my belt and I was no slouch in any of them."

"Look, Eli," I said softly. "My dad is missing and we've got to go."

"Missing?" he replied. "I'll help you look for him. Whatever you want. Name it."

"Don't you think that would be crossing a line between stalker and stalkee?"

Eli nodded his head disappointedly. "See you later, Rika."

Nick watched him walk away before catching up to me. "I can't believe that 'crossing a line' line worked."

"I've learned Eli has some very strict ideas about his job," I said. "He's a very disciplined stalker."

"Humph," Nick grunted. "Have you taken out a restraining order?"

"On Eli?" I glanced back, but, as usual, Eli had melted into the shadows. "He's harmless."

If I were perfectly honest with myself, I guess I'd have to admit I was flattered by Eli's devotion. He'd started stalking me when I'd only lost half my excess weight. He was the only man who looked twice at me back then, certainly the only one to send me gifts and follow me around like I was a Kardashian and he was a paparazzo.

Nick grabbed me by the upper arm and whirled me to face him. "He's a stalker, Rika." He squeezed my arm tighter for emphasis. "One of these days, he's going to get it through his thick skull that you're not ever going to be together and then what?"

I shrugged. "He'll move onto someone else," I said. But just to annoy Nick, I added, "Besides, how do you know we won't end up together?"

His eyes had turned an intense midnight blue in the vague illumination of the street lights. "I know because you're a ten, and he's a two."

My breath caught in my chest. Nick's hot palm burned through my arm—in a good way—as his words wiggled into my brain.

Nick Owen—Nick *Freaking Gorgeous* Owen—had called me a ten.

A ten. *Me!*

And it wasn't like I'd been fishing for a compliment or he was trying to console me. He'd stated it like it was an obvious, known fact.

I tried to reconcile this ten version of me with the butterball Paprika I still carried around in my head most of the time.

A ten.

No. My chest deflated. He couldn't have meant he believed I was a ten. I'd seen two of his ex-wives and now Marla.

They were tens. He'd been exaggerating to make his point. He was a lawyer, after all.

Suddenly, I didn't want him staring at me anymore,

comparing me to the other women in his life, mentally reassessing the numbered category I belonged in.

"We need to get moving," I said. "Lita is going to need those *patacones*."

He fell into step beside me, silent for several minutes before he asked. "What's the real reason you haven't told your grandma and aunts about your dad's disappearance?"

Damn it. Here we go.

I sucked in a deep, slow breath. I looked ahead at the lights of Eddie's Easy Stop and Taqueria.

"I told you about my mom dying when I was eight."

"Yeah," he replied in a gentle tone.

"Um..." I'd learned over the years, there was no way to say this that didn't sound horrific, so I sucked in a deep breath and forced it out. "She was abducted in a parking lot and found a few days later."

I hadn't been able to put the word "dead" in. Found *dead* a few days later.

I heard the involuntary intake of breath. The sound I'd been trying to avoid hearing. The sound I'd heard many times before when my grandmother or aunts had to explain what happened. We didn't discuss it between us. We couldn't. But sometimes people would ask where Mariana was, if they were old friends of my grandmother's who'd moved away and come back to visit. Or where Mari was if they were my mom's old high school friends.

And they had to be told.

The truth was, I didn't want the way my mother died to be this huge thing in my life. Losing her was huge enough. Gargantuan. It was all I could deal with when I was eight years old and it was all I could handle now, after all these years.

I knew the way she died had shaken my family to the core. My grandmother and Tía Margo became even more suspicious of men than they were already.

It was harder to put a finger on how Madi had been affected, but I sometimes wondered if it was the reason she didn't date. And by didn't date, I mean, *at all.* I'd never known her to go on a date with a guy, and I'd seen no evidence she was gay. When anyone asked questions about her love life, she acted like they were being sexist, assuming her romantic relationships had to be the most important thing in her life because she was a woman.

Regardless, I refused to let the manner of my mother's death define me. I'd handled it by deciding when I was very young that bad stuff could happen to you anywhere, anytime. Even in a parking lot after your yoga class, apparently. It wasn't like my mother was staggering drunkenly to her car in the parking lot of a seedy bar.

There was no sense in constantly worrying about your safety.

I once read a news story about a plane crashing into a man who never flew because he was afraid. But he was sitting in his car on a road near the airport and poof! He was toast. This finished convincing me that, in the end, it's not what you're expecting that takes you out. If you're looking to the right, the bad shit will come from the left.

Anyway, I'd always crushed any image my mind tried to conjure of the crime into powder and let it float away. I'd still missed my parents desperately though, and tried to fill the giant hole they left with Colombian and Mexican comfort foods and sweets. Lots of sweets.

Nick leaned in closer. "I'm sorry," he said huskily.

I swallowed the tears that tried to rise up in my throat. "Not your fault," I replied as casually as I could. "And you lost your dad young, too."

"To an aneurism," he said, "not..." His voice drifted off. He couldn't say it either.

I didn't want Nick to pity me. There were a dozen emotions I wanted him to feel for me, but not pity. Never pity.

"Anyway, my dad is the only man in the world my Lita and aunts think highly of. If they find out he's disappeared after what happened to my mom, it will be drama city." I was trying to make my reasoning sound as practical as possible, even though the truth was, I didn't want to watch the looks on their faces as their hearts broke again. "I need to be able to think without the uproar," I finished.

"I guess that makes sense," Nick said, although he didn't sound quite convinced.

"They were supposed to be gone a few days. I thought maybe I could find him before they came back to town."

"And now?"

"I'd like to keep them from knowing as long as possible, if you don't mind."

"You mean if I don't mind playing the pervert who flew in to molest you while your family was out of town."

I shrugged and winced.

"Only for you, Paprika." He looked down at me, his eyes full of what I hoped was affection. Then, he put his arm around my shoulder, kissed the top of my head and propelled us toward the store. "Only for you."

CHAPTER SIX

Rika

When we walked back into the house, dinner preparations were in full swing. My grandmother had pots on the stove with oil or water or whatever in them—I seemed to have missed out on the cooking genes from both sides of my family—and my aunts were at cutting boards, chopping.

When I brought the bag of plantains to the kitchen, Tía Madi lifted her face, shifting a dirty look back and forth between me and Nick who was standing in the dining area. She hated being dragged into the kitchen and was clearly blaming us for it.

She'd planned to spend her evening drinking wine and eating dinner on a balcony overlooking a vineyard. Instead, my grandmother had decided they had to show ignorant Nick the wonders of Colombian cuisine.

I knitted my brow and poked out my bottom lip in my apologetic look. She instantly forgave me, smiling with a combination of fake-annoyance and affection.

My aunts loved me and had tried their best over the years to help my Lita make up for the fact that I'd lost my parents. Madi was still a teenager herself when my mom died, although she looked grown up to me at the time.

I set the bag in the kitchen and took Nick to my room, careful to leave the door ajar so my grandmother wouldn't think he was molesting me right under her nose.

His phone vibrated. He stared down at the screen for several seconds as if deciding whether to answer. He brought the phone to his ear. "Hello... yeah." As he listened, he took in a deliberately slow breath and exhaled it just as slowly. I heard chattering coming through the phone, but couldn't make out the words. "Yeah, fine," he said eventually. "I'll text it to you."

He hung up and tapped out a text. "Marla is coming by to drop Gucci off. She's going to some party tonight."

"A party? Does she have friends here?"

Nick shrugged like it was of no consequence to him and put his phone back in his pocket. He sat down at my computer to finish the article I'd been showing him before my family returned.

Weird. It didn't sound as if Marla asked him to go with her, and he didn't seem the least bit concerned that his woman—for lack of a more specific term—was attending some unknown event with unknown people.

"I was thinking," he said. "If we get stuck, we might have some luck with the chef who was working at the VIP Center before your dad took the job. I don't think he was a Microtology member, but he must have spent a lot of time around them. I know where he lives."

"Good idea," I said, grateful for the new lead. "How'd you find out about him?"

"I googled it after we stopped at the center," he said with an eyebrow flip, throwing my over-used phrase from last summer back at me.

"Google was so six months ago," I said in an uppity tone. "I'm using Bing now." Maybe that was a little overstated, but the last time we were together, I was the bumbling fish out of water. Now we were on my turf and Nick was not going to be superior to me in any way, except maybe brute strength if it was called for.

I thought of how much strength he'd had in his body when he'd pulled me against him and pressed his lips to mine.

Oh, jeez. How did I go from being determined not to let Nick get the best of me to daydreaming about his body in two seconds?

"Except when you try to make the word 'Bing' into a verb, you end up with 'binged' in the past tense," he pointed out. "Sounds like you're talking about binge drinking or binge eating."

"Yeah," I agreed. "I'm not sure they thought that through. There are other words with the same problem, though, like ting turns into tinged. But I decided to solve the Bing problem by spelling it with a double G, so the G doesn't seem like it should have a J sound. B-I-N-G-G-E-D. Bingged."

Nick chuckled, his gaze on me so warm, I wanted to test the temperature of his lips with mine. "You're one in a million, Paprika."

I didn't know how to respond to that, so I asked, "What's the chef's name?"

"Chef Ben Appétit." He pronounced the last word the French way.

"Are you kidding me?"

"I didn't name him," he replied. "And his birth name was Myron Roach."

I grimaced.

"I know," he said. "Terrible name for a chef. I don't blame him for changing it."

We spent some time showing each other articles we'd found online. One ex-Microtologist claimed the cult had a compound in the desert a few hours out of Los Angeles where they sent members who'd acted inappropriately, according to the church, and "re-educated" them. That was creepy.

The doorbell rang. I hurried to it, hoping to grab Gucci and slam the door in Marla's face before my grandmother knew what was happening. Nick was right behind me.

When I opened the door, Marla breezed in looking like she'd stepped off a page in a fashion magazine. She was wearing a second red dress—this one candy apple red—that went to the floor, the halter-style bodice v-ing almost to where I guessed her belly button would be. Although who knows where women that tall keep their belly buttons?

Nick does, my annoying brain reminded me.

The dress was saved from complete indecency by a chain mail thingy made from mock-Roman coins that formed a thick Y over the chest area, flowing down into a high, thick belt made of four more rows of coins. I frowned at the contraption, trying to figure out if it was sewn onto the dress or just a very large accessory Marla added after the fact.

Regardless, there was no question she looked fabulous. Since I didn't have the exceptional height needed to pull off this dress, nor the blonde hair-long legs combo that Nick seemed so fond of, I kind of hated her. I certainly couldn't compete with her for his romantic attention.

What had I decided in Bolo? Never give up the geek? Yeah, I was going back to my usual geeky self tomorrow now that I knew Nick already had a new blonde in his life.

"Here," Marla said as she thrust Gucci at Nick. Tonight, Gucci was wearing pink flannel pajamas covered in cupcakes. "She's already dressed for bed, since I'll be late."

Nick stared down at the tiny dog now lying on his forearm. By the time I left Bolo, he'd seemed to be getting used to the fact that his ex, Megan, had stuck him with her Maltese. However, I guessed the one thing worse to a macho guy like Nick than carrying around a toy-sized dog was carrying around a toy-sized dog that looked like it was dressed by a Hilton.

Lita came out of the kitchen, openly assessing Marla from head to toe. "Hello, I'm Dolores Delacruz, Rika's grandmother."

"Oh," Nick said, realizing he'd forgotten his manners. "Mrs. Delacruz, this is Marla Jones."

My grandmother took her hand briefly as she asked, "Would you like to stay for dinner?"

Marla glanced around the room, paling at the idea of spending her evening here instead of at whatever fancy gathering she'd managed to get invited to. "Thanks, but I can't. I'm going to a party with some friends."

"You have friends here?" Nick asked.

"I sure do," she replied gleefully. "New ones I met at the hotel spa today. They invited me to a party at a Hollywood producer's house!"

Nick shrugged. "Great. Have fun." He still acted as if he wasn't the least bit bothered about his woman running around to random parties with so much skin showing. He'd been a lot more bothered when I'd had to wear LeeAnne's hoochie clothes to work at the bar.

Uh-oh. Lita was wearing her curious face. "So, you came here with Nick from Texas?"

"Uh-huh," Marla said as she stepped back, anxious to be on her way.

"So, you are Nick's..." my grandmother prodded.

"Oh, we live together," Marla replied. "For a couple of months now. Nicky's awesome."

Lita nodded. Her narrowed eyes cut to Nick. "*Pues*, I guess every dog has his *date*."

"Don't you mean 'day'?" Marla asked helpfully.

"No."

Nick's gaze moved to me, but I averted my eyes. I'd just gotten confirmation that, four months after he'd told me he wasn't relationship material, Nick Owen had moved another woman in with him.

A lump rose in my throat, but I was absolutely not going to

cry in front of him again. I reminded myself I'd only called Nick here to help find my dad.

Marla reached the door. Nick stepped forward and opened it for her.

"See y'all later," she called. "And, Rika." Her gaze turned fake-sympathetic. "Good luck finding your daddy." She hustled out on her super-high heels.

Nick closed the door behind her as my heart sank into my stomach. At some point, the female chattering had stopped and the house had gone dead quiet—probably when the spectacular Marla walked in.

All eyes turned to me—my grandmother's, Tía Margo's, Tía Madi's, and Nick's which were apologetic.

"What did she mean by that?" Tía Margo asked.

Both my aunts closed in, finishing the semi-circle of people in front of me. "Um..." I began, "It's *Papi*..." My throat closed. I'd managed to box up my emotions—more or less—and focus on this as a case to solve. If I said the words aloud, I didn't know if I could hold it together in the face of my family's shock and grief.

Nick stepped next to me and placed a comforting arm around my shoulders. "That's why I'm here," he said. "Rika's dad disappeared a couple of days ago and we're trying to find him."

"*Madre de dios*," Lita grasped the crucifix she always wore around her neck.

"Oh, my God!" Tía Margo cried at the same time as Tía Madi whispered, "Disappeared...?"

I knew all of them had just been sent sixteen years back in time to when my mother had disappeared.

Tears filled their eyes simultaneously.

"No!" I heard myself scream in a tone of voice I'd never used on them before. "No! It's not like last time. Someone else was murdered, but if they'd wanted to kill Papi, they would have done it then. He's only been kidnapped and..."

Tears were streaming down their faces. Madi swiped at hers with the back of her hand and blinked fast, trying hard not to be as dramatic as her mother and sister. For some reason, her tears seemed worst of all, maybe because she was typically so blasé and sarcastic.

I couldn't handle this. "Nick. Explain things to them. I have a couple of leads to follow on my computer. Call me when it's time for supper." I pushed past them and fled to my room.

Sitting down at my computer, I widened my eyes and swallowed hard until the threat of tears passed. Then I bingged everything I could think of, that could possibly relate to the Temple of Microtology.

~

Nick

A part of me couldn't believe Rika had walked away and left me to fend for myself with her female relatives. However, I was the one who brought Marla into her life and she'd blurted out the one thing Rika was trying to keep quiet. Besides, it was clear she was almost in tears when she left the room, and I knew that wasn't typical for her.

I'd admired the mostly calm way she'd handled herself in Bolo, as well as her determination to solve her own case. But this was different. This involved the possibility that her one remaining parent was gone. Maybe forever, as much as we didn't want to say it.

Mrs. Delacruz motioned silently for me to sit in a bright floral arm chair. I sat, and Gucci squeezed herself between my thigh and the armrest. The three women sat down on the equally bright floral couch.

Mrs. Delacruz closed her eyes, then swiped at them with both hands. "Tell us," she said in a much quieter voice than I'd heard her use thus far.

I explained what little I knew about the murder, which drew

gasps from all three women. Then, I told them how Rika's father had gone missing at the same time and hadn't been heard from since.

"*Diego...*" Mrs. Delacruz whispered. She clung to her crucifix like a life preserver. "My poor Rika." Tears spilled down her cheeks as if a dam had broken behind her eyes.

Dismayed at her drastic change from badass to broken-hearted, I glanced at her daughters for help.

Margo, who'd been giving me the stink-eye since we met, was staring straight ahead, tears dripping off her chin, her hands shaking like I'd never seen hands shake before. Madi, previously flip and sarcastic, was blinking fast, staring at the floor.

Did I mention that I couldn't stand to see a woman cry? And now I had three of them weeping silently in front of me, which was three times as many women as I'd ever seen cry at once, except maybe at a funeral.

My mind whirred, searching for the right thing to say, desperate to make them feel better, but how was that possible? They'd been through this before and the outcome had been horrific.

God, there wasn't a word to describe the misery this family had endured.

Not knowing what else to do, I took off to the bathroom near Rika's bedroom where I found a box of tissues. When I got back, none of them had moved or spoken, which I was pretty sure wasn't normal for these particular women. I put the box in Margo's lap since she was in the middle, and I sat back down. But she didn't look at it or me. Just kept staring off into space, shaking.

I got up again, bent over and pulled three tissues from the box, stuffing one into Mrs. Delacruz's fist, another in Margo's, the last in Madison's. Madison began dabbing at her face. Margo still stared into space. Then she started to do this involuntary sniffing thing that jerked her entire body while she continued to shake in between.

Mrs. Delacruz rocked back and forth, her thumb and forefinger rubbed the crucifix as she murmured something in Spanish that included the names "Mariana" and "Diego."

Two of these women seemed to be going into some type of shock and the other was in no shape to help. I ran up the stairs and opened doors until I found a linen closet. Grabbing three blankets, I hustled back down. I wrapped one around Margo first, since all the color had drained from her face, and another around Mrs. Delacruz's shoulders. The last I hung around Madi, who murmured "Thank you."

I glanced at the hallway, wishing Rika would come back. But how could I expect her to handle this? Her father was the one missing.

This time, when I sat down, I reached out to Mrs. Delacruz, taking her hand. "Look, I don't know what Rika told you about what happened, but she had a sheriff who was trying to railroad her straight to prison for murder. She convinced me to try to solve the case instead of only concentrating on the trial. And we did."

All eyes were on me now, assessing, wanting to believe. "That's why she called me," I went on. "We make a good team."

Mrs. Delacruz peered at me with such intensity, I could feel it all the way to the back of my brain. "I can't lose my Paprika," she whispered. "I can't have her in danger."

I squeezed her hand. "I don't think there's anything we can do to stop her from looking for her dad," I replied. Mrs. Delacruz gave a slight nod of agreement, but rubbed her crucifix faster. "I can promise you something though," I continued. "Last summer, I put myself between Rika and a sniper who was determined to kill her, and I'd do it again. Without a second thought."

The looks on all three of their faces changed, but I couldn't tell if they were good changes or bad.

Madison leaned forward at an angle toward me and peered into my brain, just like her mother had done. "Do you *love* her?"

They all widened their eyes, waiting for a response.

I gasped in a tiny measure of air before my chest tightened and stopped me from breathing. My gaze averted itself from theirs and I felt like I no longer had control of my facial expression.

"Uh...I..." The truth was somewhere in my gut, trying to work its way out while I tried my best to force it back down. "We're friends." I replied. "Good friends. We went through a lot together. Getting shot at...a bomb... It's like, um, army buddies. You know, you're forever connected when you..." I felt like I was rambling and needed to stop.

I was not this guy. I was an attorney. A litigator. In other words, a person who was in control of his mouth and what came out of it.

My eyes caught on a short but round woman who was coming in the back door into the kitchen holding a large skillet.

This reminded me of what was going on before Marla showed up. I saw a chance to distract them. "Is dinner burning?" I asked.

Rika's grandmother shot off the couch and into the kitchen faster than I would have thought a woman her age could move. Gucci jumped to the floor and started barking. Madison scooped her up and held her to her chest like a kid with a Teddy bear.

"Delia! I thought you were in here!" Rika's grandma said to the woman. She removed a lid and stirred the contents of the pot.

"Mrs. Ruíz," Madison explained to me. "Our neighbor."

"How could you think I was here?" Mrs. Ruíz said defensively. "You called me at my house a few minutes ago and asked me to bring your big pan back."

"It's okay," Mrs. Delacruz whispered, realizing she'd been unreasonable. She patted Mrs. Ruíz on the back as if her neighbor was the one who needed consoling. "It's okay. Everything will be okay." She sounded as if she was trying to convince herself.

Margo kept staring off into space. By the look on Madison's face I had the feeling that, any minute, she was going to continue the interrogation about my feelings for Rika as a way of distracting her sister.

I didn't have any answers for her. Or, maybe I did, but I wasn't about to say them aloud.

"I'd better go check on Rika," I said. I shot up from the chair and got the hell out.

CHAPTER SEVEN

Rika

We sat down to eat—Nick, Tía Margo, Tía Madi, Lita, Mrs. Ruíz, and me. My grandmother insisted Nick sit directly across from her. My pulse quickened as I glanced at him to my left. I knew from past experience that this wasn't good, and Lita would spend a lot of time glaring at him while he was trying to eat.

I suspected this was an intimidation tactic she picked up on the mean streets of the village where she grew up in Colombia. When Tía Margo thought her husband Kurt was cheating on her, my grandmother lured him to the same spot Nick was sitting with the promise of Mexican *chilaquiles*—Mrs. Ruíz's recipe—and questioned him like the gestapo, staring menacingly at him until he broke down and admitted to seeing not one, but three other women.

I mean, he was a six-foot-two "corn fed white boy," as he used to say. He was a fireman who power lifted weights in his free time, but he crumbled like a stale cookie under my tiny grandmother's scrutiny. I peered harder at Nick and tried to send him a psychic message—which I didn't believe in—telling him he'd better keep his mouth shut about our half-naked make-out moment in his bathroom.

Lita had indeed gone all out and made *bandeja paisa* which she considered a dish, but was really about nine different things piled on one plate. Nick took a bite of meat and a bite of *arepa,* chewing them together in his mouth. “Mmm...this bread’s even better than a tortilla,” he said. The frown lines on my grandmother’s face grew softer, and she relaxed back in her chair. However, Mrs. Ruíz leaned forward, her eyes narrowed at Nick.

Uh-oh. I hoped she didn’t have her herbs on her.

Nick’s head turned and, although I couldn’t see from where I was, I was pretty sure he winked at Mrs. Ruíz when my grandmother wasn’t looking. Mrs. Ruíz batted her eyelashes shyly and gave him a conspiratorial smile.

Seriously? That’s all he had to do?

Hot people could get away with murder. I shoved my fork into my *carne molida*, forgetting, as usual, that people claimed I was in the hot category, now. I still couldn’t see it about ninety percent of the time. And I hated being naked near a mirror because I always seemed to end up staring at my thighs, wondering if they were normal-sized or still too fat.

I was certain growing up struggling with my weight made my current reality completely different than Nick’s reality, since he’d grown up secure in the knowledge that he was hot stuff.

Hm... My grandmother tended to run hot and cold with some people. A part of me hoped she’d give Nick a hard time again in the future to balance out the injustices toward people in the world who could never get out of trouble with a compliment and a wink.

The knob jiggled, then the front door opened.

“What the...?” Nick muttered before he went speechless.

LeeAnne strolled in and dropped her fake-Miu Miu handbag on the couch. “Oh, am I late for dinner?” she asked disappointedly.

"It's no problem," Lita said. "We just sat down."

Mrs. Ruíz had easiest access to the kitchen so she hopped up to get LeeAnne a plate.

Nick's lips were parted, a bewildered expression on his face. I followed his line of sight to LeeAnne in her gold lamé spaghetti strap top that turned to gold lamé peek-a-boo fringe from her ribs down. She'd paired it with antique wash jeans, giant hoop earrings and high wedges with a crisscross of shiny silver and gold leather right behind her toes. Her fingernails and toenails were painted deep red with gold and silver swirls.

Sure, it was a little over the top, but I figured it was a big step up from the bedazzled t-shirts with suggestive messages on them that she wore back in Bolo. Plus, there was hardly even any cleavage showing tonight.

"I got your text," LeeAnne said to Madi. "I'm sorry y'all's trip didn't work out." Then she noticed Nick. "Jesus Christ Superstar!" she shouted. "If it isn't No—"

Nick bent his head forward and eyed her like a bull ready to charge.

"Nicholas Bernard Owen," she corrected mid-word.

Tía Madi cracked up. Nick turned his narrowed eyes on her. "Sorry," she said. "It was just the Bernard thing. It's, um, unexpected."

I pressed my lips together, trying not to laugh. I'd had the exact same reaction when I heard Nick's middle name for the first time.

LeeAnne took her place in front of the plate Mrs. Ruíz had laid out next to my grandmother.

Since LeeAnne had been with me when the police came to the house and talked to me about my father, I couldn't hide it from her. I told her to keep quiet about it, though, and she did.

However, I hadn't told her Nick was coming, mainly because I wasn't convinced she could keep more than one secret at a time.

"What the hell are you doing here?" Nick asked loudly.

I turned to him, confused. "You didn't know she was in L.A.?"

"No," Nick said. "She closed down the bar and left town. When I tried to call to check on her, her cell phone was shut off."

"I needed a California number so I could seem legit in my business pursuits," LeeAnne said. "Besides, ReeAnne knows where I am. And Dwight, of course."

LeeAnne had thought she'd never be able to leave Bolo because of her brother Dwight. He was an adult, but he had Asperger's Syndrome, was a loner, and didn't always act in ways that endeared him to others.

However, Dwight met a young woman—Petra—at one of the support group parties he and LeeAnne attended. Petra had a sister with Asperger's and wasn't intimidated by Dwight's—sometimes startling—communication style. And it turned out that they had a lot in common. She owned an entire collection of Spider-Man comics to go with his Spider-Man collectibles. The two of them were now living together in the house LeeAnne and Dwight had shared.

"ReeAnne has been in Waco with her sick mom for the last couple of months," Nick replied. "And, when I called Dwight and asked how I could get a hold of you, he told me he wasn't 'authorized to divulge that information'."

LeeAnne rolled her eyes and laughed. "That sounds like Dwight. I check on him almost every day, but you know he's not one for small talk and gossip, so he didn't mention you asked about me." A devilish gleam sparkled in her eyes. "It's cute that you were so worried about me, though."

Nick sucked in an irritated breath.

When I'd first met Nick and LeeAnne in Bolo, I'd been jealous, thinking they were exes. Later, I'd realized their history was more of the sibling nature, annoying the hell out of each other, but being there for one another when the chips were down, ever since they were kids.

"So, why are you here?" Nick asked.

"Following my dreams," LeeAnne said. "I've been staying here with Rika and Lita, working at a boutique until I break in as a celebrity stylist."

"I can't imagine what celebrity would want you to style them," Nick replied, his eyes sweeping up and down her outfit and clearly not liking what he saw. "I can't even imagine what kind of boutique would hire you."

"Oh, you can't, can you?" LeeAnne wobbled her head as she spoke, but her hair didn't budge. The L.A. hairstylist who cut it flat-out refused to recreate the Dolly Parton—circa 1985—hair LeeAnne preferred. They compromised on a style that still gave LeeAnne's platinum blonde hair lots of layers and volume. Then, LeeAnne came back and curled, fluffed and teased it to achieve the most height and width possible.

Nick shook his head in response, confirming his stance regarding LeeAnne's fashion sense.

LeeAnne put her hands on her hips, confirming she was ready to rumble. "I'll have you know that I am employed at the favorite boutique of Ms. Mariah Carey and Ms. Britney Spears," she said haughtily.

Nick snorted. "I guess that explains it."

My Tía Margo had been watching the exchange with her "studying" face. "Did you two used to be together?" she asked, thinking she had them figured out.

"No!" LeeAnne and Nick yelled simultaneously.

Tía Margo's chin drew back and her brows popped up in an expression that said, *Did you really just yell at me on my turf?*

Nick closed his eyes and drew in a calming breath. "Sorry. Didn't mean to yell."

"I'm sorry, too, Margo," LeeAnne said as she took her place across from Mrs. Ruíz. "Nick and I have known each other since we were kids."

Tía Margo chuckled. "So, you turn into kids again whenever you're in the same room?"

Nick pretended he hadn't heard her and started stabbing at his food. LeeAnne gave a shrug that more or less confirmed Margo's analysis.

Moments like these reminded me Tía Margo was more than just my aunt. She was also a licensed therapist who specialized in the one area anyone who knew her personally would think she should absolutely not specialize in—marriage counseling.

I never understood how she did her job while believing that ninety-nine percent of the men in the world were assholes or worse, *and* while she was still pissed off at her ex-husband who she'd divorced years ago. Plus, like my Lita, Tía Margo had been extremely suspicious of men since my mother's death.

But she'd already opened her counseling practice before her marriage blew up and couldn't afford to change course at that point, especially since she had two kids she needed to support—Sofia and Max. Sofia was two years younger than I was and had recently moved into an apartment with a roommate. However, Max was away at college, which was crazy expensive, and his dad claimed to have no money to spare.

Personally, I couldn't imagine Tía Margo doing anything other than telling her female clients to set their spouses on fire, but not until after they'd bought a stun gun and zapped him a few hundred times.

I say this because it was the fantasy she shared one night at the dinner table when her kids weren't around. In reality, she'd screamed expletives at Uncle Kurt in two languages and divorced him.

Margo got a ton of referral clients from satisfied couples who'd used her when they were having problems, so I assumed she somehow put her personal issues aside at work.

I watched as she glanced curiously at LeeAnne, Nick, then

me. Even from several chairs away, I could see the vertical concentration line that always appeared between her eyebrows when she was trying to find the answer to a crossword puzzle... or a human one.

"Nick," she said while I held my breath. "Rika said you were trying to get out of criminal law. What are you doing now?"

That wasn't so bad. Just a normal dinner question.

Nick didn't look like he agreed. "I'm assessing my options," he replied.

"Yeah," LeeAnne jumped in. "Nick doesn't *have* to work like the rest of us," she tipped her head at him. "Oil wells."

The look on Tía Madi's face went sour. "A real environmentalist," she said sarcastically.

Nick huffed out an angry breath. I remembered how he didn't seem thrilled when he confessed to me the reason he could afford to spend money from his own pocket prepping for my trial.

"The mineral rights contracts were in place decades ago," he mumbled. "Before my dad died."

"But luckily his dad set up a will and he knew that Nick's mom wasn't exactly—"

"LeeAnne!" Nick said her name like he was her father and she was about to get grounded.

"You know I love Tammy Lynn," LeeAnne replied. "But she's no rocket scientist. She was the best Sunday School teacher I ever had, though." I tried to imagine Tammy Lynn having enough knowledge on any subject to be qualified to impart it to a bunch of children. "She used to tell us lots of pageant stories."

Puzzled looks passed around the table.

"Like, Christmas pageants?" Lita asked.

LeeAnne laughed. "No, like beauty pageants. Nick's mom was a pageant girl when she was young, won crowns and trophies and sashes..." She twisted her mouth to one side in a thinking pose. "What was my point again?"

"You were talking about Nick and his oil wells," Tía Madi said helpfully.

Nick gave her a sidelong glance that said, *Thanks for nothing.*

Madi lifted her head into a regal pose, fake-smiled at him, then gave him her version of a pageant girl wave.

"Oh, yeah, it's just that Tammy Lynn was never good at handling money. Nick's uncle helped him until he got older. Now he's diversified and..." She turned to Madi, "I guess he must feel guilty about the environmental thing because he gives a lot of money to clean energy non-profits."

Nick nearly choked on the food he'd been chewing. He took a large gulp of water then asked, "How the hell do you know all that?"

"Harlin was at the bar one night doing your taxes." She glanced around the table. "Harlin Deets is the only CPA in town," she explained. "He does everybody's taxes."

"He *did* everybody's taxes," Nick replied. Apparently, Nick wasn't thrilled with Harlin's policy of tax transparency for his clients.

"*Entonces*, how much money do you have?" Mrs. Ruíz asked.

Like my grandmother, Mrs. Ruíz had a habit of blurting out inappropriate questions—or at least questions that were inappropriate by American standards—without shame. I was never sure if the two of them did this because they were immigrants and the rules were different in their countries or because they were old ladies who didn't give a crap what anyone thought of them.

Sometimes I blurted too, but I blamed it on the fact that I'd grown up with my grandmother.

Nick stuffed some plantain into his mouth, making it clear he was no longer participating in the conversation.

LeeAnne's mischievous gaze travelled around the table before she mouthed, "I'll tell you later," to Mrs. Ruíz.

I was starting to feel bad about putting Nick through all this.

I'd gotten him to come all the way to L.A. to help me, then run off to my room and left him to deal with my freaked-out family, and now his life was fodder for the gossip mill, except the milling was happening right in front of his face.

I decided I'd better save him before they started asking about his ex-wives.

"Has anyone seen Gucci twirl?" I asked enthusiastically.

Gucci's head popped up from Tía Madi's lap. Her tiny black eyes scanned all the faces, trying to determine who'd said her name.

Nick claimed she was "dumb as a box of rocks," but she always seemed to recognize the opportunity for a treat.

I grabbed two small chunks of *carne molida* and stepped a few feet away from the table, which officially put me in the living room.

"Come on, Gucci!" I said.

Before Madi could move her to the floor, Gucci sailed off her lap and raced to me like the star of one of those Mighty Dog commercials.

One look at Gucci twirling around on her hind feet in pink cupcake pajamas and everyone forgot about Nick. They ooohed and ahhhed and laughed and clapped. Then they all wanted to hold treats over her head and make her dance.

"*Ay, qué* cute!" Mrs. Ruíz kept saying, using her favorite Spanglish phrase.

As soon as Nick's plate was empty, I said, "Nick and I have some more work to do to get ready for tomorrow." No one would dare argue now that they knew about my dad.

Nick stood and picked up his plate, but Lita and Mrs. Ruíz insisted he leave it and they'd take care of it.

Once he'd followed me to my room, he shut the door behind him and let out a huge sigh of relief.

I still felt terrible. "Look, Nick, I'm sorry about everything. I thought they'd be out of town. I never meant to have you come all the way over here just to be treated like a child molester and given the third degree. You totally don't deserve that and—"

Nick seized my upper arms near my shoulder. I glanced down at his fingers digging urgently into my skin, then lifted my gaze to his. His eyes were intense in a way that made my pulse pound in my ears.

"Stop apologizing," he said. "After everything you and your family went through with your mom, your dad is missing."

"But that's not really your problem and—"

His hands jerked, giving my body a little shake. "Don't you know by now I'd do anything for you?"

I stared up at him, not sure how to respond. His statement sounded like something a leading man in a romantic movie would say to the woman he loved, but we weren't even dating. He had someone else. Someone else who was totally his type and would probably be his fourth wife.

"Thanks, Nick," I said as I broke eye contact and glanced at my computer. "Ready to get back to work?"

"Sure," he replied. He looked from one of his hands to the other as if surprised at the strangle-hold he had on me.

His grip relaxed. Once released, I immediately decided freedom was over-rated. I didn't want to be free of Nick, and it was clear he cared about me in some way. He just didn't care about me the same way I cared about him.

I sat down and clicked through the Microtology website to Suzee Driver's bio as I tried to ignore the warm imprints Nick's fingers had made on my...on my...

My heart throbbed extra hard in my chest.

On your arms, Paprika. Just on your arms.

Sure. The imprints he made on my arms.

~

It was two o'clock in the morning when LeeAnne pulled her old TransAm into the VIP Center parking lot.

I'd noticed something when Nick and I stopped by. Well, on some level, I'd noticed before because when I saw the three identical cars, I remembered they were there the first time I'd gone to the center, right after the detectives spoke to me about the murder and my "fugitive" dad. The other reason they caught my attention was because I'd never seen this type of car or the logo displayed on the back of each one. They had an odd almost triangular shape, smaller in the front and wider in the back.

The cars were parked side by side in the VIP Center parking lot. I recalled my dad had once mentioned that the center kept a small fleet of cars for employees and special guests to use. When I texted Julian, he said there hadn't been any warrants issued to check Microtologists' cars, thus far. In fact, it was entirely possible the police didn't know these vehicles belonged to the center yet.

I didn't tell Nick because I was afraid he wouldn't be okay with me trying to get into these cars, especially if they were locked.

Also, I was afraid I'd get Nick into enough trouble to lose his license to practice law and, although he didn't seem to want to practice law at this point, he put in a lot of work to become an attorney. I didn't want to be responsible for taking that away from him.

However, I had to search these cars. If someone who worked at the center wanted to cover up a murder or transport a witness —namely my father—to another location, they might have used one of them to do it.

After Nick left, I talked to LeeAnne and she was ready to roll within a few minutes. She also informed me that she knew how to break into cars without anyone being the wiser. I didn't ask for more explanation because she'd already told me her parents had been ne'er-do-well types, not to mention her ex-husband, who'd turned out to be a major heroin dealer.

There was no sense in dredging up any bad memories unnecessarily. I was nervous enough about the crime I was about to commit. I didn't need LeeAnne riled up.

However, the music she was playing in her car on the way to the center gave me pause.

Normally, LeeAnne was partial to male country singers and female pop divas.

When we first got into the car, I was distracted by my plans, and my mind barely registered that fact that the upgraded stereo she'd plugged her phone into was playing Steppenwolf's *Born to be Wild* followed by Pat Benatar's *Hit Me with Your Best Shot.*

Aerosmith's *Janie's Got a Gun* did get my attention as did the next song *Mama Said Knock You Out* by LL Cool J. It was followed by *Dirty Deeds Done Dirt Cheap* by AC/DC.

By that point, LeeAnne had taken to singing or rapping along with every word of the songs. It felt to me like she was getting herself hopped up on beats so she'd be ready for eminent warfare.

When she and AC/DC's Bon Scott started singing about concrete shoes, cyanide, and TNT, I turned the stereo down.

"LeeAnne, you know we're not about to do a drive-by, don't you?"

"A drive-by?" LeeAnne gave me a quizzical look. "How would a drive-by shooting help find your dad?"

I wasn't sure whether to be relieved by her logical reasoning or disturbed that she'd only ruled the drive-by out because it wouldn't help in this specific circumstance, which meant she might be okay with it otherwise.

I gave my head a quick shake as I told myself I was letting my anxiety get the better of me. Previously, I'd only ridden in LeeAnne's car in the daytime. Maybe this was her normal nighttime playlist.

She braked at the next light. "Don't worry, though," she said. "I'm prepared for anything." She reached under the driver's seat and pulled out a huge handgun that looked like something Jesse James would have used in a train robbery.

Holy crap!

I automatically crossed myself, even though I hadn't attended a mass in years. "Oh, my God, LeeAnne! Put that away!" I lifted my hand as if it would shield me from an accidental discharge, even though she wasn't pointing it at me. "We're not going to shoot anybody!"

"This is for defensive purposes only," she replied as she stuffed the gun back under her seat. "If anybody comes after you, I can pick them off before they can say 'Boo!'"

When we were in Bolo, Nick told me LeeAnne could shoot the whiskers off a hamster. Or maybe it wasn't a hamster. A muskrat or a squirrel, perhaps?

Whatever. The point was, LeeAnne had been a great shot since she was a little girl.

I closed my eyes, planning to use visualization techniques to calm myself and imagine a positive outcome, but that was cut short when Iced-T began rapping "Fuck the police," over and over again.

I recalled that there was no love lost between LeeAnne and the sheriff back in Bolo who'd tried to send her brother Dwight to jail for a crime he didn't commit.

Jeez, I hadn't brought Nick with me tonight because I was afraid he'd be too cautious and law abiding to let me do what I needed to do. Now, I was questioning my sanity in bringing LeeAnne for the opposite reason.

"Where are the cars?" she asked, looking around.

I spotted them inside the closed gate. "Damn it!" I said. "They're inside the fence. The gate's the kind that needs a remote or a code."

"If you'd told me, I would have brought a bigger gun."

I was pretty sure that any gun bigger than the one she had with her would have to be a rifle or a shotgun. Of course, for all I knew, her grandfather might have had a machine gun in his collection. I'd only seen a small part of it when I'd visited LeeAnne's house in Bolo.

"Why would you need a bigger gun?" I asked.

"If I aimed it at the place where the gate locks together..." LeeAnne mused.

Another thought hit me. "Does my grandmother know about these guns?"

"No," she replied. "I keep this one with me all the time so it's only inside when I am, and the others are in a storage unit a few blocks from the house."

I found it a wee bit disturbing that the storage facility near our house probably held enough fire power to arm every gang member in L.A., but that was an issue for another day.

I looked up at the building and something caught my eye. "Shit! I didn't even think about security cameras," I said as I mentally kicked myself for such an obvious mistake. There were two cameras, together, on this side of the building. One faced the parking lot outside the fence. The other was pointed at the parking area inside the fence.

"No problem. I got that covered," LeeAnne said. She reached under her seat again and pulled out a can of black spray paint along with a black garbage bag with holes in it.

"Is Hermione's handbag under there?" I asked.

"Who?"

"Nothing." I shook my head. "LeeAnne, we didn't even stop at a store. How do you have spray paint?"

"I always keep it with me," she said. "Never know when it'll come in handy."

I opened my mouth to ask more questions, then realized this was probably one of those things I didn't want to know about LeeAnne.

I stared at the twelve-foot iron gate and figured I wouldn't be searching cars tonight after all.

"Damn it," I muttered again.

"Is that fence all that's stopping you?" LeeAnne asked. I've been climbing over barbed wire fences since I was knee-high to a cockroach. This one's got footholds all over the place and it doesn't even have barbed wire at the top."

I scanned the fence and gate, bottom to top. It was all iron, but the gate had crossbeams about three feet from the bottom and top with fancy curves decorating the portion in between.

I was starting to see the footholds she was talking about. "So, you think we can climb it?" I asked.

"I know I can. And you're strong and wiry. You can do it."

I'd begun exercising back when I decided to lose the weight. That was over four years ago, so I had quite a few workouts under my belt. But my goals were all about increasing my metabolism and burning calories. I had no idea if I'd developed any fence-climbing muscles.

LeeAnne pulled the garbage bag over her head, adjusting it until the holes matched up to her eyes and nose. She got out of the car and glanced around as she walked up to the gate. She squatted and slid the gun through the gap between the fence and the pavement, so it was waiting for her on the other side.

Tonight, she was wearing the most practical outfit I'd ever seen her in—a pair of stretch jeans, a black t-shirt, and Keds, which I didn't even know she owned until now.

She came around to my window. "Wait here just a minute," she said. She ran over to the spot where the fence met the building, scrambled up the fence and sprayed the lenses of both cameras.

I got out of the passenger side and walked over to the gate. It looked a lot taller now that I was standing at the bottom of it. I didn't want to climb that high, but I really didn't want to be the reason this operation failed, especially considering what was at stake.

Sucking in a lungful of courage, I grabbed the fence with my fingers, perched a foot on the lower crossbar and hoisted myself up.

Unlike LeeAnne, I did not climb the gate like I climbed one every day. And I immediately found muscles in my hands and arms that I'd never worked out in the gym.

I was only five feet off the ground when my nerves kicked in. If you'd asked me before if I had a fear of heights, I probably would have said no. However, normally, when I went up high, I was inside something—an elevator, a stairwell, an airplane—and not dependent upon my own strength and agility to keep me safe.

I imagined falling from the very top and wondered just how much it would hurt and which body parts I was most likely to break.

Twelve feet didn't sound that high, but the pavement in the lot looked more like concrete than asphalt, and concrete was hard. I hoped I didn't get my foot caught in the fence and fall upside down on my head.

"Come on, Rika! You can do it!" LeeAnne whisper-yelled from the other side. She was already on the ground.

I felt like a wuss. I mean, I was kind of a wuss, but I didn't enjoy feeling like one.

I shoved my fear into a box and locked it away, forcing my unwilling hands and feet to climb up again and again until I reached the iron bar running across the top. My hands in a death grip, I threw my leg over before I had a chance to back out.

But, as I straddled the bar, I experienced a moment of vertigo and my stomach lurched.

I swayed from side to side, then tried to reposition my hands for more stability, but my palms were sweating, making me feel even more apprehensive.

"Just get your left foot on that curlicue and bring your right foot over," LeeAnne instructed. "Like dismounting from a horse."

Why LeeAnne assumed I knew how to dismount a horse, I didn't know. But, at this point, it was just as dangerous to turn back as it was to keep going. I managed to get over, and the climb down was much faster than the climb up. I tried not to think about the fact that I'd have to climb the fence again in order to get out.

When I was safely on the ground, I turned and saw LeeAnne at the farthest car—the one closest to the building's back door—waiting for me, the driver's side door already open.

I jogged over to her. "How did you do that so fast?" I asked.

"It was unlocked," she replied. "I guess it's for the best. I've never had to break into one of these keyless cars before."

She looked kind of miffed that she didn't get a crack at it, though.

"I'll stand here and watch the back door of the building," she said. "After you get done with this car, I'll sit inside it and keep lookout while you search the others. It has the best view of the door and we're not sure if anyone's in the building at night."

Yeah, LeeAnne was a bit too at ease with our criminal activity for my comfort, but this was no time to quibble.

"Okay," I said. "Sounds like a plan." I sat down in the passenger's seat of the car and closed the door. Pulling my cell phone from my back pocket, I turned on the flashlight and shined it around the interior.

Whoever had been driving this one was a smoker. The car smelled like stale smoke and ashes with hint of something else I couldn't identify at first.

I checked the cup holders and found nothing. The console in the middle held a phone charger cable and a couple of gum wrappers. The wrappers sent a jolt of anxiety through me, since gum wrappers nearly sent me to prison in Bolo.

I shook it off and opened the glove compartment, which held a manual and some insurance information.

Finally, I stuck my hands under the seats, which turned out to be the storage area of choice. I pulled out a mostly full pack of Marlboro Cigarettes from the driver's side. Under the passenger's seat, I discovered a half a pack of Newports and a quarter of a cigarette that looked suspiciously homemade. I lifted it to my nose.

It was weed, and despite the fact that I wasn't an experienced pot user, if I'd had a lighter I might have smoked the rest of it just to calm my nerves.

Once I was sure I'd found all there was to find, I moved to the next car as LeeAnne took my place in the first.

The contents of this one were more interesting. Within a minute, I found a box of condoms and two pairs of women's underwear—one in white cotton, size small, one in lacy white satin, plus-sized.

It was starting to look like the Microtology employees had designated different cars for different purposes—smoking car, fornication car, and...?

I scanned the parking lot, then moved quietly to the final car. I could still see LeeAnne's silhouette in the first one I'd searched. It was both comforting and frightening to know she was there, keeping watch with her six-shooter.

Sliding into the front seat of the last car, I noticed a drastic difference from the other two. The first two cars looked and smelled like they hadn't been cleaned out in at least a week, if not longer. This car was pristine, the dashboard, steering wheel and leather seats gleaming in the light from my phone.

My shoulders deflated as I realized I was unlikely to find anything here. Either this car was kept clean, maybe for VIP Microtologists, or it had been thoroughly cleaned since its last use.

I checked the glove compartment, console, and under the

seats, but they, too, were clean as a whistle. I was shining my light on the back floorboard, thinking how this had been a colossal waste of time when I heard the slam of a metal door.

I threw myself onto my stomach, across the front seats, then lifted my head until I could see out the passenger side window. A man in a white western shirt, white jeans, and white boots came ambling along the sidewalk looking into his phone.

My phone buzzed and I glanced around for it. Damn it! It had fallen between the seat and the door. I reached down and managed to touch it, but it fell farther down, almost under the seat. Since it was at a slant, facing up, I could see the text from LeeAnne.

It's okay. Headed to truck.

I glanced back at a white pickup truck, parked behind the car I was in, facing the fence. Then I checked out the guy. Despite having a face that resembled Richard Branson, but clean-shaven and with snow white hair on top, he looked like a guy who would drive a pickup truck. I mean, he was wearing cowboy boots. I hadn't known a lot of men who wore cowboy boots, but I was pretty sure they were required to drive a pickup truck unless they traveled by horse.

He stopped walking as he typed into his phone, then smiled, probably having a text conversation with a friend.

Determined to finish the search, I hung my head below the seat and reached in from the front to get my cell. As the screen popped on, light hit the carpet, and something glimmered.

A necklace, perhaps?

I reached back and grabbed it, then focused my cell's flashlight on it.

"Papi!" I whispered. My heart jumped up into my throat and I couldn't swallow.

In my hand, was a ring on a chain. A ring I knew well. It was my mother's wedding ring that my dad had worn around his neck since she died.

Most people who met him never knew he'd vowed he would wear it for the rest of his life in memory of my mother, the only woman he'd ever love. They didn't know because he wore it inside his clothes, usually between a button-down shirt and the t-shirt he had on underneath.

My phone buzzed again, but I was so shocked by my find, I ignored it for a moment before picking it up and reading it.

Run! I'll cover you.

I looked up and saw the man come around the car to stand next to the driver's side, still immersed in his texting.

Holy shit!

It was too late to run. Plus, I didn't want LeeAnne firing shots and possibly killing or maiming someone. And I certainly didn't need to be arrested. The detectives would use it as an excuse to grill me about my father, wasting valuable investigation time.

Getting up on all fours, I crawled over the console to the back seat, glancing at the driver's side window to make sure the man's back was still pressed against it. Clearly, we were wrong about the pickup truck, but maybe he was just going to sit in the car and do whatever this car was designated for.

Let's see, I'd already been in the smoking car and the sex car, what was this one for?

Drinking?

He didn't have a bottle or can with him.

Shooting heroin?

Surely, he'd be in a bigger hurry to get a fix if he were a heroin addict.

Masturbation? He could watch porn on his phone and...

Eek! I didn't want anything to do with a strange man's private moments...or parts.

The trunk! Maybe I could hang out in there until he finished whatever he'd come here to do.

I hoped the seats came down so I could climb in there and hide. I really had no idea whether this guy was involved in my father's disappearance or was just a mild-mannered Microtology employee, but either way, I didn't want him to find me.

I grabbed the seatback with my fingers and pulled. When that didn't work, I ran my hands around the leather, yanking on anything I could until half the seat came down. I scrambled into the trunk.

I'd barely pulled the seatback into place when I heard the car door open, then shut a few seconds later. I lay down in the trunk, my knees to my chest, psyching myself up for what could be a long wait. I hoped this wasn't the Dungeons & Dragons car.

The motor started and the car began moving backward.

Was that the sound of the gate opening?

He was actually going somewhere! Panic shivered through me at the idea that I was in the trunk of a car with a strange man behind the wheel. I imagined the faces of my grandmother and aunts when LeeAnne had to explain to them that I was gone. Nausea filled my stomach and for a moment, I thought I might throw up. Then I realized if I didn't get out of this, I might never see Nick again and that made me really, really sad.

I shoved those thoughts into a dark corner of my brain and made myself think.

The driver would have to stop the car before turning onto the street because this was Los Angeles, California, not Bolo, Texas, and we had cars on the roads at all times of the night and day. I ran my hand along the front of the trunk until I found a release lever.

When we stopped, I would simply lift the lid of the trunk, jump out and run to LeeAnne's car.

The car began moving forward. I knelt on the bottom of the trunk for stability, but put my other foot flat on the floor so I'd be ready to jump out. The top half of my body was smushed down, my face even with the raised knee.

I closed my eyes, trying to estimate how many seconds it would take to reach the road.

Any moment now, he should slow to a stop.

Instead, the engine revved and the car swung to the right, causing me to topple onto my side and roll. Now I could hear car sounds all around us.

Holy shit! He didn't stop, which meant I was going with him to Zeus knew where!

CHAPTER EIGHT

Rika

My phone vibrated. When I reclaimed it from the floor of the trunk, LeeAnne's name was on the screen.

"Yeah?" I answered.

"It took me a sec to get over the gate," she said. "Are you on the other side of the building?"

That confused me. "The other side of the building?"

"Rika," she said like she was trying to mentally shake me. "Where did you run when you got out of the car?" She thought she could just drive around the VIP Center and pick me up.

"I didn't get out," I replied. "I'm in the trunk. He turned right."

"Holy shit!" I heard more cursing as the Trans Am's engine roared to life. "Can you get a license plate number for me so I'll know when I'm behind the right car? I just turned out of the drive and I'm looking at a mess o' taillights."

"I'll try," I replied. I popped the trunk latch, opened the trunk and bent forward to try to see the plate.

That's when the driver braked hard and three things happened—my phone flew from my hand, my body rolled and hit the back of the trunk, which was also the back of the car seats, and the trunk slammed down and clicked closed, not necessarily in that order.

The car immediately took off again. It was pitch black now as I felt around for my cell. The longer I couldn't find it, the more stressed I got until the stress reached down and released all the panic I'd shoved into that box in my gut. I moved around the trunk as fast as I could, feeling, feeling...

Got something! But too big to be my phone.

Just a jumper cable set.

I had to accept the thing I absolutely didn't want to accept—my phone must have fallen out of the trunk when I was trying to get a plate number.

I took stock of my situation. I was being driven to an unknown location by a strange man. If I tried to jump out while we were moving, I might surprise the driver behind us and get run over. I had no phone to call LeeAnne with, in fact, no way to call for help now or when I arrived at our destination. And I now knew opening the trunk was a bad idea. The floppy lid was too heavy for me to control. If the driver had accelerated instead of braking, I would have rolled out onto the street.

I wiped away the nervous sweat that had accumulated on my forehead as the car accelerated, then accelerated some more.

Going this fast could only mean one thing—we'd entered the freeway.

Damn it! Could I please catch one fucking break tonight?

I remembered my dad saying we made our own luck, but that was before my mother died. She certainly hadn't made that happen. For a split second, I imagined her being taken away in the trunk of a car and a wave of nausea rippled through me.

I sucked in a breath and whooshed it out. If I was going to get out of this mess, I needed to find a way to make my own luck.

As much as I didn't want to deal with cops right now, they might be my only hope...if I could signal for help.

I began feeling around, looking for the place where the side of the car curved into the back. My pinky touched a flap.

This had to be the fabric that often covered a light assembly. I slid my fingers along it and pulled. I heard the sound of Velcro separating and a stiff fabric square came off in my hand.

Behind that, I found the plastic taillight assembly I'd been looking for. Pulling and pushing every protrusion, I finally squeezed the right ones together and the taillight assembly popped out into my hand, lights attached. That left only the exterior light cover.

Bracing with my hands, I placed my foot on it, then bent my leg and kicked, leading with my heel, over and over again.

I felt it loosen and I lay down on my stomach to finish knocking out the cover with my fist. When I broke through, a stream of light shone in from the car behind me.

Yes! Something was finally going right for me!

As I stuck my arm through the hole I'd made, I hoped I didn't cause an accident. It had to be freaky to see a hand where a taillight should be. At this time of night, some of the people on the road were probably tipsy or wasted and would think they were hallucinating.

Oh, well, there was nothing I could do about that, so I began flapping my fingers around. I started with a classic bye-bye wave, then decided a side-to-side *Hey, I'm in here!* wave might work better. When it didn't, I moved on to a parade wave, a royal wave, and even a bendy one-finger wave when my wrist got tired.

"Please memorize the plate number," I pleaded with whomever was out there. "Please, please call the cops." I knew no one could hear me, but the words seemed more powerful when I said them aloud.

Though the car was speeding along pretty fast, time seemed to crawl as I tried to get someone's attention. I'd learned some sign language from a YouTube video, so out of desperation, I started signing the letters *H-E-L-P* in case there were any deaf drivers behind us.

Why I thought sign language would do for a deaf person what my waving hand sticking out of a taillight, flopping around like a fish wouldn't, I did not know. All I knew was that we were getting farther and farther away from where we started and if this guy caught me in his trunk, he might carve me up and barbecue me like those cannibals in *The Walking Dead*.

Then, the car braked suddenly and I rolled back at an angle. My wrist was caught in the hole I'd made and pain sliced through it, radiating up my arm. It was so bad, in fact, I was afraid I might pull back a nub.

Luckily, the car sped up again and my body rolled forward. I brought my hand in and examined my wrist as best I could by the road lights. It was red, but not broken. Not yet, anyway.

Threading it back through the hole more gingerly this time, I began waving again, ignoring the ache in my wrist.

A horn sounded.

And by "sounded," I mean it played the first eight notes of *The Yellow Rose of Texas*. I'd only met one person who had a custom horn like that.

I pulled in my hand and stuck my eye to the opening. All I could see were headlights beaming from the car behind.

Then I thought I heard someone shouting my name, so I pressed my ear to the hole.

"...worry, Rika. I'm going to shoot his tires out!" That was LeeAnne's voice.

Shit, a tire blowing at this rate of speed was extremely dangerous. And I didn't even know for sure the driver was a bad guy.

I mean, I was a trespasser and a snooper, but I couldn't let some man I didn't know get injured just because I snuck into his car. I made a split-second decision, put both my feet to the back of the seat and pushed. It gave way and I crawled into the cab of the car.

The driver was tapping his fingers on the steering wheel to the beat of the country-western music playing on the stereo. He clearly had no idea what was happening.

I looked out the back window in time to see LeeAnne change lanes and accelerate. She was trying to pull up next to us.

I needed to put a stop to this now before anyone got hurt.

"Sir?" I'd spoken too quietly. He didn't hear me over his music and the road noise.

I cleared my throat and took in a big breath. "Excuse me, sir."

The driver jerked, looked into his rearview mirror then turned his face to see me better. I got a look at a pair of very startled blue eyes framed in wrinkles.

He turned back to the road, but gave his head a quick hard shake. "Don't tell me I'm seeing things again."

Again? Uh-oh. I hoped his normal hallucinations didn't involve his neighbor's Pekinese telling him to kill short-ish Hispanic women. Actually, I didn't know that the Son of Sam's neighbor's dog was a Pekinese—*I should really bing that*—but that's how I'd always imagined it.

Regardless, I wasn't sure what to do. If the driver thought I was a hallucination and I told him I wasn't, wouldn't he just think his hallucinations were trying to trick him?

Having not experienced any hallucinations myself, I didn't know how they worked.

I could only see the side of his face now, but it looked to me like he was squeezing his eyes tight, then opening them again. After several rounds of this, he checked the rearview mirror.

Decelerating, he turned to look at me again, but this time, he stuck a finger out and poked me in the chin. I figured he might have been aiming for my chest because a chin is a really weird place to poke someone.

"What the fuck?" he exclaimed. "Who the fuck are you?"

I guess he believed I was real now. I tried to come up with a plausible explanation.

"I'm sorry," I said. "I'm...um...homeless and I was sleeping in here."

Okay, maybe that wasn't the most plausible explanation, but there were a lot of temporary and permanently homeless people in L.A., since the cost of housing was sky high.

"Where?" he asked. "In the trunk?"

"Sure," I said, as if it were the most normal thing in the world to take a nap in someone's trunk. "I'm sorry I surprised you. Could you just pull over and let me out?"

He eyed the shoulder ahead suspiciously. "Is this some sort of carjacking thing?" he asked. "If I pull over, is your boyfriend going to jump out of the bushes and shoot me?"

Although I was flattered that he assumed I had a boyfriend, this comment made me wonder about his intelligence. Assuming I had a boyfriend, how could I possibly predict the exact spot the driver would stop on the side of the freeway so said boyfriend could pop out and jump him?

Of course, considering my predicament, maybe I didn't have the right to question another person's intelligence.

I glance over at LeeAnne, whose front passenger window was now even with me in the back seat. She was holding her big gun in one hand while pulling the seatbelt with the other, mouthing the word "seatbelt," like she wanted me to put mine on.

She was driving with her elbows.

Shit! LeeAnne's going to get her drive-by after all, except I'm in the other car!

"Look, mister. My friend over here..." I stuck a thumb toward LeeAnne, "is worried about me and she's going to shoot out your tires any second, so if you could just pull over and let me—"

I stopped talking when, instead of pulling over, he pulled a gun from his boot. It was black and not as long as LeeAnne's Jesse James gun, but it still looked pretty lethal to me.

"I guess she thinks she's the only one with a gun?" he asked loudly. "Say hello to my little friend."

Okay, that was the worst Scarface impression I'd ever heard, mainly because it was done with an Indian accent, not a Cuban one.

His window started sliding down and he stuck the gun out, aiming toward LeeAnne's car.

"Nooooo!" I screamed. I flung myself at him and was crouched half-over the console, pulling his body toward me before I'd even made a conscious decision to jump him.

His gun went off, loud, reverberating in my ears. In my peripheral vision, I saw LeeAnne swerve, but her head was still on her body and I was grateful for that.

The driver pulled the gun in. He turned it, like he was going to use it on me.

For a split-second, I was looking straight into the barrel. Since that was the last place I wanted to look, I grabbed his wrist with both hands. The struggle caused the steering wheel to get jerked back and forth, the car swerving in and out of its lane. As we struggled over the gun, several more shots went off, blowing small holes in the ceiling over my head.

The streams of light from streetlamps shone in through the roof and reflected on the dash forming a near-perfect rectangle. I was reminded of those dot-to-dot geometry worksheets my teacher gave me in Kindergarten.

Shit! Was my life flashing before my eyes?

I glanced at the windshield and saw the brake lights of dozens of cars up ahead, but the driver was looking at me.

"Look!" I yelled as I pointed at the windshield. "Stop!"

He turned and mashed his brake. The tires squealed and I went tumbling into the front floorboard along with his gun.

The traffic must have started moving immediately because we began to accelerate just as two more shots rang out, except these sounded different.

The ride turned bumpy and we lurched to the right. The car

slowed. I pulled myself up just as we rolled to a stop on the shoulder.

"Fuck!" the driver was yelling. "Fuck that fucking bitch!"

I felt his gun underneath me, grabbed it and pointed it at him.

"I asked you nicely to pull over and let me out," I said. "When you didn't, legally, you were kidnapping me."

Okay, I didn't actually know if this would count as a kidnapping considering how I'd crawled into his trunk voluntarily, but it was all I could come up with. This was such a strange situation, there might not be any laws on the books to cover it. The driver didn't intend to kidnap me, and I didn't intend to carjack him.

The man scowled at me and I could see signs of too much sun on his leathery face. I guessed his age to be mid-fifties.

"Fuck you!" he said again. "Give me back my gun and drive off with the cunt who shot at me." He jerked his head to indicate LeeAnne who'd stopped a few car lengths in front of us and was now in the process of backing up.

He did not just say what I think he said!

I mean, normally, I wasn't bothered by profanity, but this guy just called my friend, a woman who'd risked her life for me, the c-word.

"Take it back!" I yelled. I could hear how childish it sounded, but I had adrenaline coursing through my veins like it had never coursed before. "You do *not* call my friend a..." I couldn't say it aloud. "That word!"

"I'm not taking it back," he said stubbornly. "And I don't think you even know how to use that gun."

Damn it! He was right! I wasn't sure if there was a safety or something I had to cock before pulling the trigger.

One reason I didn't know these things was because I was self-aware enough to realize that I never, ever wanted to shoot anyone.

Even if they call your best friend the c-word? my mind asked.

That was a tough one.

Just then, LeeAnne emerged from her car, gun in hand.

"Fine," I said. "My friend's coming and she has no trouble using a gun. In fact, she can shoot the whiskers off a hamster at a thousand yards." I was pretty sure I'd gotten the animal and the distance wrong, but I was under a lot of stress.

He looked horrified at the thought. "Who shoots hamsters?"

Since this was L.A., it was entirely possible there was a hamster rescue group he was a part of. Angelinos were a lot better at rescuing animals than people when it came down to it.

"It's an expression," I waved the gun around threateningly. "Apologize!"

"I'm not apologizing," he said. "You broke into this car and she shot out my tires!"

LeeAnne was at his open window. "Apologize for what?" she asked.

He looked at me challengingly, which pissed me off even more. "He called you the c-word!" I blurted.

LeeAnne's eyes narrowed on him as her face turned murderous. Her thumb slid up over the hammer of her gun. She lifted it and pointed it at the driver.

Damn! I really should get some help for this blurting problem.

"Um, LeeAnne?" I said uber-calmly, hoping my calmness would transfer to her.

She ignored me. "When I got divorced from my lying, cheating, abusive husband, I swore if a man ever called me that word again, I'd put a bullet right between his eyes."

Crap! I just wanted to put a scare into the guy. LeeAnne was looking at him like he'd be having his midnight snack with Osama Bin Laden.

I searched for a way to distract her, then remembered the wedding ring. "LeeAnne, I found something, but I dropped it somewhere in the car."

"Okay," she said. "I'll keep an eye on this guy for you in case he needs another hole blown in his nasty mouth."

I checked her face to see how serious she was. She threw me a wink and I relaxed.

Taking the driver's gun with me, I opened the back door and looked around, then pulled the seatbacks down to check the trunk. From this angle, with both seatbacks down, I could see the ring, still on its chain, along with my phone, wedged under a jumper cable set.

I grabbed them, stuck the phone in my pocket and held onto the necklace.

I got out, slammed the doors closed and walked around the car to LeeAnne. "Found it," I said. I thought I heard a siren. "We'd better get out of here."

The residents of L.A. were used to a lot of things, but surely another driver had called 9-1-1 on us by now.

LeeAnne and I ran to the car and jumped in. Her tires squealed as we tore away from the urban cowboy.

He yelled, "Fuck you, you c—"

I didn't hear the last word clearly, but I was pretty sure what it was.

LeeAnne glanced back, then burst out laughing. "Woo-hoo! Thelma and Louise, baby!" she said. Then she put up her hand for a high-five—my least favorite means of congratulations, since it took hand to eye coordination—but I couldn't leave her hanging. I slapped her hand and smiled at her.

LeeAnne was kind of crazy, but she was also really awesome. She and I didn't have a lot in common on paper, but I hadn't had a lot of friends in my life, so I appreciated her, crazy or not.

At the next light, she checked her own clothes than gave me a once over. I did the same and thought I didn't look so bad for having climbed a giant gate, being tossed around in a trunk and being involved in a shootout.

LeeAnne's gaze moved to my lap. "What've you got there?"

I looked down at my hand in my lap and stared at the ring. I hadn't had the chance to process this new development yet.

Any laughter that was waiting inside fizzled out, and my chest felt funny, but not funny ha-ha. Funny opposite of ha-ha.

"This was my mom's wedding ring. After she..." The words "was murdered" hung in my mind like a neon sign, but I found it nearly impossible to utter the phrase aloud on a regular day. On a day my father was missing, I certainly couldn't say it, even though LeeAnne knew the story.

"...died," I said. "After she died, my father put it on this chain around his neck and vowed he'd never take it off."

"So, he was in that car," LeeAnne said.

A horn sounded behind us, alerting LeeAnne that the light had turned green. She moved her foot to the accelerator and twisted her mouth into a thinking pose.

"What do you think that means?" she asked cautiously. I could tell she didn't want to be the one to list the possibilities aloud and freak me out any more than I was freaked already.

"I think they got him into the car and, when they were distracted, he took it off and stuck it next to the seat as a sign."

"Yeah..." LeeAnne said, keeping her eyes on the road. "That's one possibility."

I blew out a breath. "LeeAnne, I know it's not the only possibility, but it's the only one I can deal with right now."

She gave a quick nod. "I got it."

I knew she really did get it because both her parents had died young. Unfortunately, not saying the other stuff didn't keep me from thinking about it.

For a brief second, I saw my dad unconscious in the car, the chain falling off while white-haired, white-clothed men pulled him out.

I thought about telling the detectives, but, besides the breaking and entering charge we'd have to face, they'd just say I couldn't prove he was wearing the chain that night. He could have used that car at any time. None of this proved he was abducted to them. But to me...

I turned to my partner in crime. "Thanks, LeeAnne," I said. "It's hard to believe we've only known each other half a year. You've done so much for me."

She slowed and gave me a meaningful look. "Well, hun, you've done a lot for me, too. I'm in L.A., living the dream." She smiled broadly at me, but her eyes were kind of watery. I wasn't sure if she was imagining how I'd feel if my dad turned out not to be okay, or if she was choked up over our friendship, and I didn't want to ask.

~

We got home and tiptoed past my cousin Sofia, who'd come over and, as she often did, fallen asleep on the couch. This was actually a lucky break. Since Marla had texted Nick that she had more plans tomorrow, I'd told him to leave Gucci, and I'd have someone take care of her tomorrow while we were investigating. That someone I was referring to was Sofia.

LeeAnne went up to bed while I peeked into my room looking for Gucci. She'd helped herself to my bed and was lying on her side, her tiny head on my pillow.

I realized I couldn't go to sleep without taking a shower. All that gate climbing and rolling around in the trunk and nervous sweat had made me feel too grungy to sleep.

When I got out of the shower, my phone was playing an old country song—*All My Exes Live in Texas.*

It was Nick's ringtone.

Originally, when I was sobbing my way back to L.A., brokenhearted, I'd set it to James Blunt's *You're Beautiful* because it's about being in love with someone who's out of your league, or at least that's how I interpreted it.

Later, when I didn't hear anything from him, I'd gotten a wee bit tipsy on my Tía Madi's margaritas and, when she fell asleep on the couch, I'd convinced myself Nick had to be an asshole, considering his three ex-wives. I'd decided to change his ringtone out of spite after spending an inordinate amount of time looking for just the right song.

I looked at my Death Star wall clock. It was three in the morning. Why would Nick call me now?

As I reached for the phone, I decided his mom had concocted an emergency to make him fly home, and he was about to abandon me.

"Nick?" I said after I'd touched the screen.

"What the fuck, Rika?" was all he said in reply.

That didn't sound like Nick. I mean, it was his voice, but he usually had better phone manners.

I put the phone on speaker for a moment so I could check my texts. Could I have butt-texted him something *What the fuck?* worthy?

Nope.

I touched the speaker icon again and held the phone to my ear. "Did you call me at three o'clock in the morning just to cuss at me?"

Nick blew out a breath. Through the phone, it reminded me of an angry bull—one that had already been poked with pointed sticks in a bullfight, not that I'd ever seen one.

"LeeAnne told me what happened."

What? My best girlfriend called and ratted me out? Why would she do that?

Wait, maybe she didn't. Maybe he was talking about something else.

I decided playing dumb was the best way to go for now. "Told you?" I said.

"Damn it, Rika! You went to the VIP Center in the middle of the night—why would you have me come down here if you're not even going to let me take care of you?"

Did he just say, "take care of you"? I didn't like the sound of that one bit.

"You thought I brought you down here to take care of me?"

He didn't reply, but I could still hear his angry breathing.

Well, he wasn't the only one who was angry. Sure, I hadn't been at my best last summer in Bolo, but in my real life in Los Angeles, I was not the kind of woman who needed a man to take care of her. I'd been employed part or full-time since I started tutoring in high school. The only lapses in employment I'd had since then were when I quit my job to follow Brandtt to New York, where I snagged a new job within two weeks, and when I'd left New York and gotten stuck in Texas. As soon as I got back to L.A., I'd started working again.

Take care of me. Ha!

"I asked you here because we make a good team. We bounce ideas off each other, come up with plans. I don't need you to take care of me. I can take care of myself."

"It didn't sound like you took care of yourself very well tonight."

"I'm home, and I'm in perfect health," I said snottily.

That was a teeny weeny lie. I had some bruises and scratches from rolling around in the trunk and my wrist really hurt, but at least I didn't need medical attention.

"Shit," Nick muttered. "You and LeeAnne are gonna be the death of me."

"How are we going to be the death of you? You were asleep..." I thought of sexy Marla. "...or whatever, in your fancy hotel!"

"Exactly," he said. "I was supposed to be with you."

"I didn't need you. I already had a plan."

"Rika!" He said my name like a father would when his small child was about to run into the street.

Annoying.

"What, *Nick?*" I said in what I hoped was the same tone of voice.

"You can't go running around town, looking for evidence

without me. You're five-foot-two and weigh about as much as a scarecrow. If anything happened..."

I felt the steam boil up inside me and puff out my ears. I didn't know which of his stupid comments to address first, but after a couple of seconds of aggravated speechlessness, I decided to take them chronologically.

"First of all, I *can* go running around town looking for evidence if I so choose, since this is still a free country, last I heard. And I am not five-foot-two. I'm five-foot- four-and-a-half..."

Wait, did he say I looked like a scarecrow? Or that I weighed the same as a scarecrow? I ran to the bathroom and looked at my panty-clad body.

A part of me wanted to be thrilled that someone compared my weight to that of a scarecrow. They were stuffed with straw and straw didn't weigh much. On the other hand, scarecrows were not known for having attractive bodies, so it couldn't possibly be a compliment.

I decided to leave that alone because I did not want to get into a conversation about my body with Nick.

Nick breathed out long and slow in what sounded like a frustrated sigh. "Look, Rika, I came all the way up here from Bolo—"

"Is this some kind of guilt trip?" I asked hoping that saying it to him bitchily would relieve the guilty feeling that had unfolded in my chest. It didn't work.

"No," he replied. "Not a guilt trip. I'm just saying, I came here to help you, so don't go running around town, investigating without me."

That did seem reasonable.

"Fine," I replied. "I'm tired. I need to get some sleep.

"Okay." His voice was gentle now and I felt even guiltier.

"Nick, I do appreciate... I mean, I—"

"Glad to be here," he replied. "And LeeAnne just called me because she was worried about you. The guy had a gun."

I didn't know what to say to that. "Thanks" really wasn't adequate for a guy who saved you from a murder rap, then flew thousands of miles to help you find your father.

"See you tomorrow," he said. And he hung up.

~

Rika

The next morning, I picked Gucci up from my extra pillow where she'd been curled with one paw over her eyes, clearly not a morning person. Neither was my cousin Sofia, however, she was an extreme dog person. Not the *put a bib on them and feed them from a spoon* extreme, but she loved dogs and one of her two jobs was as a trainer at a dog-training facility.

This morning, she was lying on her side on the sofa, leaving just enough room for a tiny dog. I lay Gucci gently on the couch, hoping she wouldn't cause a fuss. She wiggled around a little, then wedged her tiny nose under Sofia's side to block the light from her eyes. She was super cute when she wasn't barking bitchily at me.

When I'd called Nick to tell him I was picking him up, he informed me he'd gotten a rental and would meet me. I found this highly annoying. I was pretty sure it was because he didn't like my driving. I wanted to tell him about my perfect driving record—with the exception of the time I landed his truck in a ditch in Bolo—but since he didn't come right out and say that was why he rented the car, I would have sounded like Dustin Hoffman in *Rain Man* just blurting it out.

It was also extremely annoying that he'd stayed at the Omni with Marla last night, no doubt feeding her chocolate covered strawberries and having wild sex.

I imagined Nick holding a strawberry, gazing at me with those Bondi blue eyes as I ran my tongue over the chocolate. After that, my brain kept flipping back and forth between the chocolate and the hotel sex, unsure which I was more envious of, and wondering whether the Omni room service staff dipped their strawberries in milk chocolate or dark.

Stop thinking about chocolate!

The situation I was in now was the perfect storm of stress that could plunge me back into the eating binges like when I was a kid. When they began, I'd been depressed over my mother's death and my father's inability to get back into the U.S. to be with me. As I'd grown heavier, my anxiety over school increased as the stares, jeers, and bullying got worse.

I reminded myself that stress was not an excuse for eating. That's what my Jilly Crane counselor would have told me. I signed up with Jilly Crane when I decided I needed to change my life and couldn't afford to do Jenny Craig. And, my counselor—they all went by Jilly—was instrumental in helping me lose the weight, even if I had never met her in person. Unfortunately, she hadn't replied to any of my Skype messages lately and I had no idea where she lived, so I was on my own.

Walking over to the front window, I opened the curtain a smidge and peeked out.

No cops. Interesting.

LeeAnne's car was easy to trace and was probably recorded on a security camera before she blacked out the lenses. The fact that the Microtologists hadn't called the police on us made me think there could be a major conspiracy going on. Icy fear shivered down my back as I wondered what that meant for my father.

No. I couldn't dwell on those thoughts or I'd be no good to him. I could not lose it, no matter how scary the possibilities seemed.

I went back to my room, grabbed my phone and left.

I parked in front of the VIP Center and called Nick on his cell. He said he was a block away.

A couple of minutes later, a huge black GMC Yukon turned into the parking lot. When it pulled up next to me, the window slid down to reveal Nick.

"Holy mother of Zeus!" I said. "Are you planning to carpool with the Lakers while you're in town?"

"I was lucky to get it," he replied. "Everything else they had in stock was designed for pygmies." He glanced at my Honda Fit as if it were just another example of a pygmy car. I was about to argue that my car was perfectly comfortable, until I thought about how Nick was several inches over six feet tall and did seem a little squished in my car yesterday.

Although it looked like an impossible task in the center's tiny spaces, he managed to park the Yukon between two other cars in one smooth arc.

When Nick stepped down from the truck, I couldn't stop my eyes from giving him a thrice-over. He was wearing his jeans and brown cowboy boots, like I'd seen him a few times in Texas. But what caught my eye was the worn brown bomber jacket which made his shoulders appear even wider than they had before. Underneath was a blue and brown vertical striped button-down shirt.

I thought I'd seen Nick at his hottest when we were in Texas, but bomber jacket Nick...

I felt light-headed and had to remind myself to breathe.

That's when I realized he was examining my attire, too, and I wished I'd put a little more thought into it this morning. But Lita had distracted me, falling back into stress-feeding mode—which was extremely dangerous with the stress-eating mode I was in—trying to serve me an eight-course breakfast, while I was trying to get out the door on time.

I glanced down at my choices. It was chilly this morning, so I'd thrown on a red, pull-over hoodie, jeans and sneakers.

The corners of Nick's mouth were turned up slightly. His eyes held an expression I wasn't quite sure how to interpret.

"Rock, paper, scissors, lizard, Spock," he read off my shirt.

"Yeah, it's—"

"I know," he said. "I've watched *The Big Bang Theory*."

I felt like such a geek, standing in front of cool, hot Nick. I needed to distract him from his examination of my clothing, which could lead to him noticing the extra pounds I'd gained since Bolo if he hadn't already. "Actually, the game was invented by Internet pioneer Sam Kass back in the 1990's," I blurted.

Great. Now I was dressed like a geek and babbling like c3po.

"Is that right?" The corners of Nick's lips rose another half-inch and his eyes warmed. He'd looked at me this way a few times last summer, and it always made me aware of the blood rushing through my veins. Mainly because that expression made me feel like he was appreciating me in a way no one else did.

Or maybe this was his *Rika is such a weirdo* face. What did I know about men, really?

"Yeah...not that it matters..." I gave my head a quick shake, to rid myself of the embarrassment. A breeze kicked up and blew a strand of hair across my face. His gaze didn't leave me and my insides started to shake and kept shaking until I blurted out, "Why are you staring at me?"

He chuckled. "I mostly saw you in LeeAnne's clothes when you were in Bolo. It's still new, seeing you dressed as yourself."

What did that mean? Nothing good, surely. I'd gotten this unisex hoodie from ThinkGeek.com not Victoria's Secret.

"You look...cute," he said.

Cute? Nick wasn't attracted to cute. Nick was into women who won pageants and got mistaken for models.

His eyes were still warm as he reached out and slid his index finger across my forehead then down the stray strand of hair, tucking it behind my ear. "You always looked great in red," he said.

My skin tingled along the imaginary line where he'd touched me. My knees went weak and for a split second, I thought I was going down.

Wait. Why was he flirting with me when he had a girlfriend or fiancé or wife—*please not a wife*—back at his hotel?

Asshole.

I couldn't believe I'd forgotten about Marla and almost kissed him—twice—last night. Feeling awkward, I lifted my hand and re-tucked the same hair he'd tucked a moment before.

His gaze caught on my wrist and his hand shot up lightning fast to grab my arm. I'd had other things on my mind this morning and hadn't noticed the ugly purple bruises from my wild ride in the trunk. But Nick definitely noticed. His body went rigid and his eyes darkened as he stared murderously at my wrist. I braced myself for another round like last night only in person this time.

He took several breaths and I got the feeling he was mentally counting to ten. His grip loosened and slid down until his thumb and fingertips captured the tips of my fingers. "I go with you," he said.

I shook my head. "What?"

"Until we find your dad, where ever you go—I don't care where it is—I go with you. Got it?" His eyes were like twin thunderstorms as they peered into mine, I realized they'd morphed from angry storms to concerned ones.

The only other man who'd ever looked this concerned about me was my father. I guess I'd thought that's how it would always be because, when I saw the emotion in Nick's eyes, my lungs stuttered with the shock of it.

"Sure," I whispered. A frog had taken up residence in my throat, so I cleared it and said, "Of course."

He released my fingers. "LeeAnne said you found your mom's ring?"

I nodded and pulled the ring out of the neck of my shirt. I

hadn't been able to bear leaving it alone on my nightstand. I never liked to think of my mom being alone, wherever she was, and the ring...

I shook it off. *Whatever.* Like a lot of my feelings, that one didn't make any sense.

LeeAnne must have filled Nick in pretty well. Or maybe he could see the emotion this ring evoked in my eyes because he didn't ask any more questions. Instead, he glanced up at the building. "So, what's the deal here?"

I stuffed the ring back into the neck of my hoodie. "We have an appointment with Suzee Driver. She's the VIP Center's manager and acts as the spokesperson for Microtology with the media."

"In other words, she'll be full of shit."

"She will be," I replied. "Unless she can't be."

Nick's brows drew together as he tried to decipher my cryptic message. But I wasn't in the mood to be forthcoming. The information I'd obtained was mine. Nick could be a bit macho-mannish at times, and I didn't want him taking the lead on this one. He could just wait for the rest of the story.

"Oh, and Suzee thinks we're cops," I added. "So, don't blow our cover."

Nick looked at me like broccoli had sprouted out the middle of my forehead. "You want me to impersonate an officer of the law? That's a crime."

"It's only a misdemeanor. Besides, as long as we're not flashing badges or wearing uniforms, we're in the clear. I introduced myself on the phone as Detective Martin. I didn't say anything about working for the LAPD. I'm a private detective."

"I thought you were a private receptionist."

I gave him a threatening look—although he didn't look very threatened—and took off for the front entrance. With several strides of his long legs, he caught up and pulled the glass door open for me, which was also annoying. I was in no mood to have to thank him for his chivalrous actions. Not while he was still with *Marla*.

After checking in at the desk on the first floor, a security guard escorted us to the fourth floor where he left us in a waiting area decorated in white. White floors, white faux leather chairs, and glass end tables with white legs. Every space we'd passed through had a large, white air purifier like this one did, and every surface was spotless.

"I heard they take cleanliness very seriously." I was afraid to sit and risk sullying the stark perfection of the waiting room.

"No kidding," Nick replied. He sat down, apparently not as concerned as I was.

A minute later a youngish African-American woman came out of a nearby office. Her face was sweet, her expression earnest, with eyes that were bright and glowing golden brown. Her dark hair fell in adorably messy ringlets to her shoulders. I'd grown up envying ringlets because my cousin Sofia had them while my hair was stubbornly straight.

I glanced at Nick, as he stood, to see if he was noticing Suzee's ringlets, but his face was unreadable.

"Hi, I'm Suzee Driver," she said with a welcoming smile.

"I'm Nick Owen," Nick said, like he was in charge of this operation. "This is my partner, Rika Martin."

Mar-teen! My mind insisted, then I remembered I'd been the one to change the pronunciation this time. I didn't want Suzee to hear *Martín* and ask if I was related to Diego, the chef.

"You're detectives?" She was examining our attire.

"Under cover," I said. "Homicide could use some help and we weren't on assignment right now."

Nick frowned at me. But if he just used his crafty lawyer brain, he'd realize I still hadn't claimed to be a police detective. I hadn't even lied. We were working undercover as detectives instead of our regular jobs and homicide definitely needed some help if my dad was their prime suspect.

"Come into my office and we'll talk," Suzee said in a tone that implied we were going to talk about our love lives and what kind of music we were into, instead of murder. I followed behind her, noting her chic white pantsuit with a top that wrapped at the front and was tied in a bow on the left side. She looked both professional and approachable.

When we stepped into her office, we were confronted with even more white. A white desk topped in blonde wood and more white pleather chairs—but with fancy curved armrests, this time—facing the desk.

My gaze darted back to the desk. On a plate, resting under a glass cover, were a pile of cookies coated in white powdered sugar.

Be still my heart.

I tried to peal my eyes away from them. I knew exactly how one of those cookies would feel on my tongue, the powdered sugar caressing my longing taste buds.

"Have a seat," Suzee said cheerfully as she sat in her white leather executive chair behind the desk. She uncovered the cookies and pushed the plate at us. "Help yourself. What can I do for you?"

I focused on her, although the cookies were still visible in the corner of my eye. "We have some more questions for you about Alberto Viera's murder," I said before Nick could take over. I'd used the word "more" because I knew she'd already talked to the cops, and I wanted it to sound like we were continuing where they left off.

"Sure," she said.

"Some new evidence has come to light. A video on his computer." I watched her face, trying to note any change in her expression. Nick's head jerked to look at me. He watched me with his eyes narrowed, probably not appreciating the surprise. Although I hadn't seen the evidence, Julian had heard about it and texted me early this morning.

She tilted her head slightly. "A video?"

"Yes. Of you and Alberto." Her brows lifted but I saw no sign of distress. "Of you and Alberto having sex," I added.

"Oh." She chuckled. "Does he still have that?"

"He *did*," I said, to remind her that Viera was dead.

Nick fake-cleared his throat, reminding me to tread lightly. "How long were you two involved?" he asked.

I had to admit Nick was good at choosing the right words. Almost any other phrasing could have made Suzee defensive.

"Well," her lips turned up into a half smile that seemed part-nostalgic, part-mischievous. "I wouldn't call it 'involved,' exactly. There were a few times I was here late, he was here late. Things happened."

Nick's gaze settled on me. He lifted his eyebrows and I knew he was asking where I wanted to take the interrogation, since this evidence was new to him.

"It looked like hidden camera footage," I said. "Was Alberto trying to blackmail you?"

"Oh, yeah." She swatted her hand through the air as if shooing a fly. "A while back. Threatened to show it to my husband."

"And what did you do?" Nick asked.

She tilted her head to one side casually as she shrugged one shoulder. "Nothing. I told him to go ahead."

Nick's brows lowered, his expression skeptical. "Nothing, huh?"

She shrugged again.

"Is it possible he did show it to him, and your husband was angry enough to kill him?"

Suzee laughed like Nick had made the silliest joke ever. "You don't know who my husband is, do you?"

We shook our heads.

"He's Darson Dare." The name rang a bell with me, but Nick was still staring at her questioningly, so she went on. "He's the radio shock jock from the *Truth or Dare Morning Show*. He's always talking about our marriage and women being bitches and whores. If he'd heard about me and Al, he would have told all of Southern California about it the next day on the radio. In fact, if he could have pulled some audio off it, his listeners would have heard me panting and telling Al what a big dick he had."

Nick and I exchanged *What the fuck?* glances.

"Dar is all about his art," Suzee explained. "That's what he calls what he does for a living—*art*." The eye roll that followed made it clear she didn't agree.

"Is your husband a Microtologist?" I asked, more out of curiosity about the couple than anything else.

"Sure. Steve and Valerie jump-started his career. They matched us up personally."

"Matched you up?" I hadn't heard about this aspect of the cult. "Like on a date?"

"Like, to be married. They said the two of us balanced each other. He's blunt and brash. I'm diplomatic and discreet."

She didn't seem that discreet to me.

"What about the Kaporskys?" Nick asked. "Weren't you worried about Alberto leaking the video to them or the press?"

"No, I knew Al's threats were empty. He wouldn't have done anything to piss Steve and Valerie off. They have all kinds of connections in this town. They would have taken him down, one way or another."

"As in killing him?"

"As in discrediting him. Getting him blacklisted from working in the best restaurants in L.A. You'd be surprised how many Hollywood elite are Microtologists. Even some of your bosses for that matter."

This confused me for a split second until I remembered she thought we were cops. Interesting, the way she sneaked that threat in about our bosses so casually. But, that's why the Kaporskys hired her, I supposed.

"Do you know of anyone else who might have had it in for Viera?" I asked. "Anyone angry with him?"

"As I told the other detectives, Al knew how to make a woman..." Her gaze wandered off to stare at something out the window only she could see. "...feel *muy especial*," she finished with a sexy lift of her eyebrows. "Like you were the only woman in the world. And he had the *chorizo grande* going on down below, if you get my drift. He knew how to work it, too. Enough to make me go bilingual."

I just stopped myself from rolling *my* eyes this time. While it was true that I'd only experienced one *chorizo*, I didn't understand the attraction of them being so big. It wasn't like there was some cavernous space to fill.

Then I remembered I was five-foot-four (and a half) and small-framed. Maybe some women did have galaxy-sized black holes and needed giant man parts to fill them.

I wondered if I could bing that before I realized it would probably just get me a lot of weird porn.

My mind flipped through a file of Nick's women—BreeAnne, Megan, Marla... Maybe that's why he needed them so tall. My eyes flicked down and caught on his crotch.

Hm...

"So..." Nick's voice interrupted my thoughts, "you think Alberto was having affairs with other women?"

"Are you kidding?" Suzee laughed. "If it had boobs and a booty, he hit it."

"And how did you feel about that?" He was speaking in his smooth, casual attorney voice—the one he used for witnesses in the courtroom when he was trying to lull them into coming clean. "It would be understandable if you were jealous."

Suzee snorted. "I knew the score with Al from the jump, but his wife probably didn't sign up for this. Have you spoken to her?"

"He was married?" I asked.

"Yep," Suzee replied. "Isn't everyone?"

"Nope," Nick said. Although, I noticed he didn't explain that he had been married *three* times, assuming he wasn't married to stupid Marla, yet. Wait, did that nope mean they weren't married? My lungs expanded like they were being filled by a helium tank. "What about Diego Martín?" Nick's question pulled me back to reality.

"Oh." Her face fell. "He wasn't interested. What a shame. I do like those hot Latin types."

This time, I had to shut my eyes so I could roll them without Suzee seeing.

"I was referring to his disappearance," Nick said.

"What about it?"

"Do you know anything about it?"

"No. The police seem to think he killed Al, but that's hard to imagine. Diego wasn't like that TV chef that goes around screaming at everyone. He always seemed calm and under control. Sometimes kind of sad, though."

A lump formed in my throat. My dad hadn't looked sad when my mother was alive. That came after she was murdered.

"And how was his relationship with Alberto?"

"Great, as far as I could tell. They became friends immediately, laughing all the time. They teased each other about being Mexican versus being Colombian, but it all seemed good-natured. I've been operating under the assumption that Diego was murdered, too. I figure they just haven't found his body yet."

A gasp escaped my lips when she said, "his body." My hand jerked out, grabbed a cookie from the plate and shoved the whole thing into my mouth.

Sweet mother of Betty Crocker...

The moment the sugar registered on my tongue, a pleasant wave of endorphins swooshed through my body. My eyes closed involuntarily.

I opened them to find Nick and Suzee staring at me, the same odd expression on both their faces. I swallowed and tried to focus on questioning Suzee again.

She'd seemed more candid than I'd expected. Maybe the Microtologists weren't involved in my father's disappearance. But would the Kaporskys or Jason Kim tell Suzee if they were?

Nick stood. "Thanks for your time."

I stood too, even though it bugged me that he'd made a unilateral decision to end the interview. Did he think he was in charge here?

Suzee came out from behind her desk and slid one of her business cards from an acrylic cardholder. She jotted something down on the back of it and handed it to Nick. "Call me anytime," she said, her brown eyes throwing heat into his blue ones.

I snatched the card from Nick's hand. "Thanks! We'll do that," I replied super-cheerfully.

We turned toward the door, but another question came to me. "One more thing..."

Suzee lifted her eyebrows, a helpful expression on her face.

"Were Alberto and his wife members of the cul—um...*church*?"

"No, he was just an employee at the center," she replied.

"All right, thanks."

As Nick followed me out, I glanced down at the card. Suzee had scrawled another phone number on the back—her personal one, no doubt.

When we got to the parking lot, I turned to Nick to say something, but got distracted by his expression. His lips were pressed together like he was trying to suppress a smile.

Holy mother of Zeus, his eyes were dreamy today! Extra-dreamy, in fact. Was it my imagination or were they even more beautiful in L.A. than they'd been in Texas?

"So, do you want to hold onto that?" he asked as a cocky smile spread across his face. His eyes flicked down to the card I was holding.

"Do *you*?" I asked him with a challenge in my voice that was only appropriate for a wife or girlfriend to use in this circumstance. "Considering there's a woman waiting for you at your hotel?" I added, as if I cared about Marla.

And one waiting here in front of you, my mind whispered. But no way was I saying that aloud.

"Rika, Marla and I—" Nick began.

"What did you think of Suzee?" I interrupted. I couldn't stand to hear any details about Nick and Marla. I was already on the edge of a meltdown with my dad missing, which was way more important than whatever stupid Nick was going to tell me about him and stupid Marla.

"I don't know," Nick said. "She seemed casual and forthcoming, but it's her job to spin information for the public. The best public relations people are the ones who make you feel like they're being totally candid."

"Yeah." I thought for a moment. "And she did try to redirect us onto Alberto's wife, who isn't affiliated with the cult or the center."

"Yep, I noticed that, too," Nick said. "I think we need to talk to her and Suzee's husband."

I was already on my phone, bingging away. "Darson Dare is going to be out in public this evening," I said. "Announcing for a charity roller derby event." I switched over to messaging and texted Julian about an address for Alberto's wife. I turned toward my car, walking while texting, but Nick put a hand on my back and propelled me in the direction of the Yukon.

"Hey, Rika?"

As I hit the send button, he cupped my jaw with one very warm hand and stared down at me. My gaze met his, then his eyes slid down to my lips.

My breathing shallowed as I waited for him to swoop down and kiss me.

He rubbed a thumb across my mouth. "There. That's better," he said.

I looked down at his thumb, which was now covered in white powder.

Damn it! I'd forgotten about the powdered sugar on the cookies. Why didn't Nick tell me the sugar was there so I could lick it off? I could really go for some powdered sugar now that I knew there was no kiss coming.

Squelching my sigh, I didn't bother to argue about who was driving. I let my shoulders sag as I headed for the Yukon.

CHAPTER NINE

Nick

I drove toward Mrs. Delacruz's house with a very quiet Rika. Her grandmother had called and left a bunch of messages telling us to come by for lunch.

Rika had listened to them on speaker phone. Her "Lita" seemed very concerned about Paprika eating enough during this stressful time. Diana Viera's office was in East L.A. anyway, so, after hearing the messages, I'd decided to stop at Mrs. Delacruz's on the way.

I figured that if the grandmother who raised her was so worried about her food intake, Rika probably had a history of forgetting to eat when under stress.

Truth be told, when I first met her, I'd thought she was a little too thin. I was relieved when I came to L.A. and found she hadn't dried up and blown away. Seeing her today, I was sure she'd put on a few pounds—just enough to look healthy and not quite so fragile—although she was still petite in every way.

My takeaway from all this was that she was a lot better off living with her grandmother than living with Brandtt, but I didn't think much of that idiot regardless. If I'd met Rika under different circumstances and made her mine, I wouldn't be stupid enough to break up with her.

When we stopped at a red light, I looked over at her. She hadn't said anything since we'd gotten into the truck except when she called her cousin about bringing her car home for her. Apparently, Sofia's car was in the shop and she worked near the VIP Center and could walk over, use a spare key Rika kept hidden on her car and bring it home. After that conversation, Rika stared out the passenger window silently.

I knew the second she realized I was watching her because she pulled her shoulders back and straightened her spine, a sure sign her determination had returned. Suzee hadn't been much help, and Rika knew that every day we didn't find her dad made it more likely we'd never find him, but she wouldn't be kept down for long.

Rika was brave. Maybe the bravest person I'd ever known and I respected the hell out of her for that. That and her geeky smarts.

"Well," she finally said. "It's not like we expected Suzee Driver to blurt out the name of the killer. She was a place to start."

"That's right." I pulled the Yukon onto her grandmother's street. "We'll get there. Wherever your dad is, we'll get there." I pulled up to the curb in front of the house.

"Yeah," she said. "We'll get—"

She stopped talking suddenly. I followed her line of sight to the car parked in the driveway behind her grandmother's. It was a refurbished muscle car—a red sixty-nine Camaro.

"That looks like..." she whispered.

"Like what?" I asked.

She didn't respond. She just kept staring.

"Rika?" I prompted. She couldn't seem to take her eyes off the car.

Unsure of what to do, I watched her lips move as though she was reading the license plate to herself. "That's Julian's car," she whispered.

Suddenly, both her hands were at the door handle as she struggled frantically with it. "Fuck!" she said when she couldn't get it open.

"Hold on." I slid out of the driver's side. On the way around the truck, the idea that she was this desperate to see Boy Band stabbed at my belly in what I decided to believe was a hunger pang.

When I opened her door, she was sitting still, her hands over her face, shaking like a leaf.

"Rika?" I was used to her being quirky. Liked it, actually. But this mood was downright squirrely—in a hurry one minute, not moving the next.

"I can't get my damn seat belt off," she said.

Her voice didn't sound right. I leaned over her, released the latch and pulled the belt away.

"What's going on?" I asked.

"That's Julian's car," she repeated.

"Yeah?" I reached out and pried her hands from her face.

"So, why is he here?" As I watched her face, her eyes filled with liquid. "In person?" She opened them wide, blinking fast, and the tears seemed to evaporate.

"I don't know." I touched my fingers to her cheek, then turned her face until she met my gaze. I was taken aback by the naked fear I saw in hers. "Rika, what are you thinking?"

Instead of answering, she closed her eyes and deep-breathed. Seconds later she opened them and said, "We have to go in. My grandmother may be there alone."

I took her hand and helped steady her as she got out of the truck. She released my hand right away and headed up the walkway. The door was open. Through the screen, we could see Julian talking to Mrs. Delacruz.

Someone sat on the couch behind them. I only had a view of the legs, but I was pretty sure it was Madison.

"Rika!" Julian said as we walked in.

Rika's gaze took in Julian, then her grandmother. She glanced briefly at Madison before speaking. "Hi, Julian," she said guardedly.

"Where have you been?" Mrs. Delacruz asked. "Julian is here to see you, and he brought these flowers!" She pointed at a bouquet of pink and purple flowers, which were already in a vase on the coffee table near Madison. Rika's grandmother was beaming at Julian, making it clear she approved of him as a potential suitor.

What happened to that hating all men thing? Or did she just want Julian to keep Rika away from me?

My stomach filled with gravel. Felt like someone was mixing concrete in there.

He brought her fucking flowers.

I had the urge to punch Boy Band in the gut...hard, so he could feel like I did right now. Or maybe I wanted to kick myself because I'd never bought her flowers. I mean, I'd had three wives —although I didn't think the first one should count against me— I should know women liked flowers.

Why didn't I bring some to greet her with at the airport? Then, whenever she looked at the vase, she'd be cheered by my gift instead of Boy Band's.

"It was Nick, right?" he said as he stuck out a hand towards me to shake. I shook it, but couldn't take my eyes off Rika who was staring at the flowers, as the color drained from her face.

She looked at Julian. "Why...?" She had a frog in her throat she didn't bother to clear. Was she so thrilled with the bouquet that she'd gotten all choked up about it? "What...?" she began again. Her eyes jumped back to the flowers and stuck there.

She didn't look thrilled. Not one bit.

Hm...

"Oh, I have some more info for you," Julian said. He looked as confused by her reaction as I was. "You'd asked me to keep you posted...?" He paused, but when she didn't respond, added, "With anything new I heard about the autopsy?"

"That's it?" She asked, her eyes still shifting between Julian and the flowers. "You have more information?"

"Yeah. About the autopsy," he repeated.

I watched as Rika's body relaxed and the color came back to her face. "What have you got?"

"The official report isn't out, but I heard the detectives talking." He shifted closer to her and said conspiratorially, "Looks like the cause of death will be stabbing, which isn't a surprise. But the victim wasn't stabbed only once. The estimate for now is four to five times."

"Four to five times," Rika said, excitement creeping into her voice. "A crime of passion."

Julian nodded.

"Are the detectives looking at some of the women he was seeing for the murder now? And maybe their boyfriends or husbands?"

"I think they would be if Diego Martín—I mean your dad—wasn't in the wind. But they tend to assume the person on the run is the murderer."

Rika looked peeved, but determined. "Is that it?"

"That's it for now," Julian said, clearly wishing he had more for her than an unofficial third-hand report and flowers.

We stood there awkwardly for a moment.

"Is anyone hungry?" Mrs. Delacruz asked.

"No, thanks," Julian said. "I need to get back to work." He stepped forward and wrapped his arms around Rika for a hug, which lasted even longer than the VIP Center hug.

"Thanks a lot for stopping by," I said loudly.

He released Rika and said goodbye to her grandmother who headed to the kitchen, then he shook my hand again.

As I shut the door behind him, Rika made a beeline for the

flowers and that "hunger" pang hit my stomach again. Was she going to take them right to her room?

"Looks like you've got some competition, there, cowboy," Madison said with a smirk. Her face had been focused on her phone as if she wasn't paying attention, but now her eyes teased up at me.

I opened my mouth before realizing I had no response to that statement. Not one I could say aloud, anyway.

But Rika didn't seem to be listening. When she got to the flowers, she pulled them from the vase, dripping wet, strode to the corner of the living room and dropped them into the small trash bin I hadn't even noticed until then.

Take that, Boy Band. I wished she had done it in front of him, so he would take his flowers and his lingering hugs somewhere else.

I felt like a weight had been lifted off me. She didn't want his stupid flowers.

"Not a fan of flowers?" I asked playfully.

"Flowers are for funerals," she replied, her face harder than I'd ever seen it. "My father isn't dead." She sat down on the couch.

Huh? I mulled over her words for several seconds until it all made sense.

Damn. She'd freaked out because she thought Julian had come in person to tell her something terrible had happened to her dad. And he brought flowers which reminded her of when her mom died.

I tried to imagine the overwhelming number of arrangements the family received when Rika's young mother was kidnapped and murdered. The case probably made the news, which means the Delacruz family may have been drowning in flowers from people they'd never even met.

"Rika..." Madison murmured as she reached out to comfort her niece.

"No," Rika said as she stood and moved out of her aunt's reach. "I'm fine." She turned to me. "Are you hungry?"

"Starved," I replied, deciding to respect her emotional privacy. Then I realized I hadn't heard one yap since I walked in. I asked Madison, "What happened to Gucci?"

She looked up from her phone again. "Sofia took her along to her jobs this afternoon."

I imagined the day Sofia was having toting my bitchy little Maltese around with her. "Wow, I didn't mean to put y'all to so much trouble," I said.

Madison waved off my concern. "It's no trouble to Sofia. She loves dogs."

"Come and eat before it gets cold!" Mrs. Delacruz commanded.

I sure hoped Rika could eat after the drama of the past few minutes. I planned to make myself eat, even though the concrete hadn't completely cleared from my gut.

Rika hurried to the kitchen and grabbed a piece of round *arepa* bread, like the kind we'd had at dinner last night, and stuffed half of it in her mouth all at once.

"*Ay, no!*" her grandmother said. "Put your food on a plate and sit down!"

Watching from the living room, I felt a hand on my arm and turned to find Madison standing next to me.

"Thanks, Nick," she said too quietly for anyone else to hear. "For everything."

Nick

We found the victim's wife Diana Viera in a low-rent strip-center space in east Los Angeles that served as her office. Her long medium-brown hair was pulled back in a no-nonsense ponytail. She wore a simple white button-down blouse and a dark slim skirt.

Boy Band had texted Rika Diana Viera's information, including the fact that she was an attorney, but not the fancy kind. There was no receptionist, only a small waiting area with four chairs. However, she could see us walking in through her open office door.

When Rika introduced us as Detectives Owen and Martin, Diana surprised us with a confession, of sorts.

"I'm sorry," she said. "I wasn't completely honest with the other detective when he came yesterday. It's been bothering me. I was going to call today. I just hadn't found the card he gave me, yet."

As I scanned her desk, I could see how understandable it was that she'd lost the card. There were papers everywhere. Papers in stacks. Papers in files in boxes on the floor. Papers completely filling the wooden boxes labeled "In" and "Out" she'd put on her desk in a futile attempt at organization.

On the credenza behind her were more papers, a pile of unopened mail, and a long, stainless steel letter opener.

She needed a legal assistant...bad.

"Well, no need to look for it now," Rika said eagerly. "We're here."

Even though I wasn't touching her, I could sense the tension in her body as she waited to pounce on Diana's lies. I hoped she could control herself until we got the whole story from her. I wouldn't have blamed her if she'd grabbed Diana and shook her until she told her where her dad was.

"Oh, come into my office and sit down," Diana said as she led us through the doorway and moved stacks of papers from the folding chairs she'd set up for clients.

Rika sat, but remained perched on the edge of the seat. When I sat down, I tried to make up for her tension by appearing as laid-back as possible.

"What else did you want to say?" I asked casually, as if it was no skin off my nose, one way or the other.

The tone of my voice must have reminded Rika to be cool. She adjusted herself on her seat, allowing her back to relax against the chair.

"I told the other detectives Alberto and I had been getting along fine," Diana said. "Which was not the whole truth."

Rika's lips parted, then she closed them again and looked at me.

Good call. Diana might hear the stress in Rika's voice and get suspicious.

"But I guess there was more to it?" I asked.

"Yeah. Alberto could be a great friend and an awesome boyfriend. But he wasn't such a great husband."

I nodded sympathetically. "That's the impression we've gotten."

"He was a player, big time," Diana continued. "He loved women. And when I say he loved women, I mean he *luhhhhved* women. Lots of them. All the time. I was pretty angry when I first found out." Her gaze drifted off, settling on the only office window, which had a view of the stucco wall next door. "I hadn't slept with him in over a year."

"Why were you still with him?" Rika asked.

I wanted to smile at her profile. She'd managed to get it together after the flower incident, like she did every time there was trouble. Even though she denied it, it was obvious now that, below the surface, she was worried her father was already dead and was half expecting to be notified of it at any moment.

But she pulled herself together and kept trying to solve the problem no matter how scary the solution might be. Her determination was one of the things I admired most about her. My chest swelled with something that felt like pride, not that I had anything to do with it. Neither her courage nor her smarts had anything to do with me.

"That's the part I didn't want to say because it makes me sound like a pretty rotten person, especially now that he's dead." Diana said. "Steve and Valerie know a lot of people in entertainment and publishing. They introduced Alberto to an editor at one of the Microtology events. His story before he came to the U.S. was pretty dramatic and they eventually offered him a book deal. He was supposed to get a big advance from a publisher soon. As soon as he signed the contract, in fact, which he was expecting any day now. If we stayed married until after he got it, it would be community property, so I acted like I'd given up on trying to make him be faithful."

Yep. That's a woman for you.

Or at least that's what the women I'd married cared about.

Money. Expensive clothes, handbags, cars... There seemed to be no end to their pricey "needs." It always amazed me what some women would do, what they'd put up with, to have more stuff.

I always felt like Rika was different, but I'd only known her when she was fighting a murder conviction and fighting for her life. Maybe, in my head, I'd made her what I wanted her to be.

Diana looked down at the pen she was holding. "The money wasn't for me," she said. "I've been trying to start up a real legal aid office to serve the east side. A lot of people around here don't have the money to hire attorneys to protect them from rotten landlords. Women can't afford to hire a divorce attorney to get rid of their abusive husbands. And their teenagers go to jail a lot more than white, middle class teens would for minor crimes because the public defenders are swamped and their parents don't have the money to swoop in and get them out of trouble. And, sometimes, there are language barriers."

I checked Rika and saw her shoulders had dropped. She was fidgeting, drawing circles on the pad of her index finger with her thumbnail in a move most people would probably not notice, but I did.

She was disappointed. She'd been hoping Diana's confession would be more of a breakthrough. I watched Rika take in a deep breath and realized she was literally "sucking it up." I also knew when she was ready to go. We both stood.

"Thanks for your time," she said. "And good luck with what you're trying to do." She walked out and I followed her.

After we left Diana's office, Rika was quiet again and I didn't have much to console her with, so we rode in silence until we got back to her grandmother's house, since we had some time before the roller derby started.

"She could still be the killer," I said as I turned off the engine. "She had a chance to think since the cops talked to her the first time. Maybe she decided it wasn't that believable that they were happy when everyone knew he was cheating on her, so she made up a story to explain her lie. She is an attorney..."

Rika didn't respond immediately, her chest rising and falling with more deliberate breathing. My eyes caught on her breasts before I reminded myself how inappropriate staring at them was, especially now.

"Don't you think she came across as devoted to her cause?" she eventually asked. "She seemed really passionate about helping the community."

"Passion can take you in a lot of different directions," I pointed out.

Rika shook her head and sighed. "She was just so believable."

"Yeah," I agreed. I'd felt the same way when Diana was talking. "But we were both fooled the last time."

Her gaze met mine. She instantly knew I was talking about last summer. "Good point," she said almost cheerfully. "Let's go do some background searches on her and her husband." She smiled at me. Not her real smile. It was a close-lipped half-smile, but still more than anyone should expect of her right now.

I wanted to take her in my arms and kiss her if only because I admired the hell out of her. How did she motivate herself to be so great after all the things she'd been through?

Typically, the impulse to touch her came because I found her beautiful and sexy in a way I'd never known a woman to be before. She didn't need high heels—although she looked great in them—or designer clothes.

The top she was wearing when she met me at the airport looked like it had been embroidered with the red and orange flowers in some Latin American village. The white background against her soft brown skin made her extra hard to resist.

When I realized it was one of those tops with the elastic neckline that could be pulled down to bare the shoulders, I nearly tugged it down and planted a kiss there. I remembered exactly what her shoulders looked like from that day I caught her in my master bath.

Well, not just her shoulders. I remembered every detail about her, from the scent of her hair to the shape of her belly button—another place I wanted to put my lips.

Anyway, the geek hoodie she was wearing today was even better. The fabric was thin and fit close to the body, skimming over her breasts, teasing me to distraction.

As much as I didn't like L.A., it was hard to imagine getting on a plane and leaving her after this was over. The last six months had been miserable without her.

When we walked into her grandmother's house, Mrs. Delacruz and Mrs. Ruíz were in the kitchen cooking again. Rika's Aunt Margo was pacing the hall behind the living room that led to Rika's room and the stairs, talking on her cell phone. Her Aunt Madison was on the sofa, playing a game on her phone.

On the floor was a young woman I didn't know. She looked like she might be close to Rika's age, but she didn't resemble the other women in the room. From what I could see, she had a Marylin Monroe bombshell body that was covered in brown skin and topped with ringlets that hung past her shoulders. Since she was lying on the floor, her ass was on display in her snug jeans. It was pleasantly rounded like Rika's. Bigger, but in nice proportion to the rest of her body.

I assumed she was a friend of the family. Or a friend of Rika's, maybe.

Then I realized why she was lying on the floor. Her phone was in front of her face as she snapped pictures of Gucci one-handed while she rewarded her with treats with the other. "Hide, Gucci, hide!" she said.

I watched as my dumb-as-a-doornail Maltese flopped onto the floor and covered her eyes with both paws.

"How the—?" I began.

"Nick, this is my cousin Sofia," Rika said. "Sofia..." She tossed a thumb in my direction. "Nick."

"Hi," Sofia said before she went back to taking pictures.

"How did you get her to do that?" I asked.

"I trained her," Sofia said as though I'd asked the stupidest question ever.

I shrugged. "She always acts like an airhead when I try to teach her to do anything."

Sofia stopped photographing long enough to flash me an angry look. I wasn't sure what I did to deserve that, but I noticed her eyes seemed to be an unusual color, sort of an olive green in this lighting. She was looking at Rika as if asking permission to speak freely.

Rika pressed her lips together, clearly struggling not to laugh. "Go ahead," she said. "He's a lawyer. He can take it."

"With dogs, it's almost always user error," Sofia said.

I tilted my head and ran my tongue over my teeth, trying to decide on a response.

"She means it's not Gucci, it's—" Rika began.

"I know what she means," I replied. "Anyway, thanks for the dog-sitting."

Sofia smiled up at me like she respected the fact that I could, indeed, "take it."

"It's no problem," she said. "Gucci's adorable. Aren't you Gucci?"

My dog jumped up on her hind legs, pawed at the air, then delivered what looked like a thank-you kiss to Sofia's nose like she was ready for her own TV show.

"Do you mind if I use her for my video blog?" Sofia asked. "I'm doing a series on training tiny breeds."

"Knock yourself out," I said.

"Dinner is ready!" Mrs. Delacruz called. "Sofia, Gucci's dinner is ready, too. I put it in the little pink bowl."

"Gucci's dinner?" I asked. "You didn't have your grandmother cook the dog dinner, did you?"

"Sure," Sofia answered like it was the most normal thing in the world. "Gucci didn't want it raw, but it's still paleo." She pulled the fur ball to her chest and got up off the floor. "She needs a healthy diet."

Damn, I'd never get her to eat her dry dog food again. But it wouldn't be cool to be rude to my free dog-sitter-slash-trainer.

Instead, I said, "Awesome!" as I headed to the table.

Rika sat down at the table, looking completely calm and composed, but I could see the worry in her eyes. For her sake, I hoped we could get a real lead at the roller derby tonight.

CHAPTER TEN

Rika

By the time we got to the old warehouse district, where the event was being held, the sky had been dark for a couple of hours.

I looked up at the crescent moon and wondered if my father could see it, too.

It was hard to imagine him as a prisoner. He'd always been larger than life to me. He was tallish and handsome, and, although he cooked for a living, he was no sissy. He grew up in one of the worst parts of Bogota and had hundreds of stories about fighting the thugs who were trying to steal from him on the way to school and dodging members of drug cartels trying to force him to work for them.

One thing I hadn't thought about until now was how his abductors got him out of the VIP Center without a messy struggle.

But Jason Kim could have cleaned up the signs of my dad's abduction in order to make it look like he murdered Alberto then took off.

My father had been away from The States for fifteen years.

Maybe the Microtologists simply tricked him into a vehicle by telling him the cops were on the way but the homicide detectives wanted him at the station to report what happened. If he thought of Jason or one of his people as a friend, he probably wouldn't have been suspicious.

Or they might have had a weapon. God, I didn't want to imagine my father staring down the barrel of a firearm.

"Rika," Nick said gently. "We're here."

I knew we were here. He didn't need to state the obvious. And I didn't like the tone he'd used with me.

I mean, normally I would have loved the tone because, when he spoke to me in that gentle voice, it felt intimate, like there was more between us than a foul weather friendship and a couple of murders.

However, at this moment, his tone felt patronizing. Like he was being gentle with me because of my circumstances. Like I could shatter into a million pieces at any second.

He probably felt sorry for me because he knew about my mother and now with my father missing...

"I know we're here." My voice came out sounding defensive and annoyed.

Nick raised his eyebrows and tilted his head, examining my features, no doubt trying to determine what had brought the attitude on.

I didn't want to be examined, not when I was this vulnerable. I pushed back at the fearful voice inside my brain that kept trying to convince me my father couldn't see the moon now and would never see it again.

When I inhaled, my lungs fought me and my breath stuttered in my chest.

No! H to the E double L, no! I was not having a meltdown, no matter how badly I needed comfort. No matter how much I wanted Nick's arms wrapped around me to keep all the bad away.

He knew there was something wrong. I could see it in his

eyes. I could also see that he cared, really cared, and his sympathetic expression was causing a wall of tears to well up inside my chest and overflow into my throat.

I was not going to break down in this stupid truck with Nick watching. I'd been having trouble hiding my disappointment after talking to Suzee and Diana. And I'd practically lost it when I saw Julian and his flowers. But that was it. I would not play the weepy damsel in distress.

No f-ing way!

"Rika," he said as he leaned in. I wanted him to lean in, but only if he was going to kiss me and mean it. Otherwise, he needed to keep it all business between us, or, at the minimum, stay three feet away from me at all times. I didn't want his sympathy. At least, not as long as he had Marla in his life.

Fear and grief and jealousy began gnawing at my stomach again. I was suddenly desperate for food. But we were in Nick's rental, which had no emergency snacks whatsoever in it. My car typically had butterscotch drops, M&Ms, or at least gum to keep me sane until I could make it to a donut shop or home to my cheat drawer.

Nick's concerned eyes warmed in a way that made my throat tighten. Why was he looking at me with such care when he'd brought a date to my dad's disappearance?

My hand jerked up and slapped him. Not a full-on *I want to knock your face off* slap. It was halfway between a pat and a slap. Just enough to knock that sympathetic expression off his annoyingly handsome face.

It worked. He pulled his head back and frowned at me. "What was that?" he asked.

"You looked like you were losing it," I said. "Didn't seem focused on the task at hand." I reached for the door handle.

"I thought the same thing about you," he replied. "But I didn't consider violence to be a viable cure for it."

Oh, boo-hoo! I'd seen his big macho self working out in his home gym and planting bushes for his mom. My scrawny hand couldn't do him damage, even if that's what I had been going for.

As we climbed out of the truck, we dropped the subject, thank Hera, because for a moment, I'd had the urge to invoke Marla's name and out myself as a jealous girlfriend wannabe.

I slammed the truck door, hoping I'd trapped all my crazy, mixed up thoughts in there. Finding my dad was top priority. I didn't need any distractions, which meant calling Nick to L.A. might have been a stupid idea, but there was no help for it now.

Nick and I had figured Darson Dare might be in a hurry before the roller derby and busy during it, so we decided to come near the end and try to catch him after it was over.

The other option was to talk to him at the radio station, except there would be a receptionist and security to get through. His home was out of the question because Suzee might be there and we wanted to talk to him alone. Tonight was our best bet.

After a lot of muttering complaints on Nick's part about L.A. parking, he'd found a space along the curb that was big enough for the Yukon only three blocks from the venue, which I thought was pretty good, but he labeled "insanity," the same thing he said every time we had to park.

I knew from my time in Bolo that he was used to businesses having huge parking lots, large enough for the entire town population to park their pickup trucks in at one time. I'd thought it was a crazy waste of space, but it wasn't like people were clamoring for condos with scrub brush views. Bolo had the space to waste.

Several times, I'd pointed out to Nick that my car was a lot more practical in Los Angeles than his rental, but he said he wasn't driving around L.A. or anywhere else in "that tin sardine can," which my Fit found quite offensive. She was one of the safest cars in her class with high owner satisfaction ratings and certainly not made from "tin."

The parking lot was pretty quiet, but as Nick opened the gray metal door, we heard a burst of cheering and applause from inside.

When we walked in, a teenage girl with an interesting combination of pigtails and face piercings seemed ruffled by our presence.

"I'm supposed to charge you for tickets, except it's almost over," she said. "I guess..." she shrugged. "Just go ahead."

On both sides of the entrance were makeshift concession stands with drinks on one side and snacks on the other. The snack offerings included cupcakes and cookies baked by the team members.

Half of me was dubious of the hygienic baking practices of anyone who came to an old warehouse to get dirty and bloodied on purpose. The other half—okay, three-quarters of me—wanted a freaking cupcake.

As we passed the table, I leaned toward them and took a deep breath. *Mmmm...* I could smell the fudgy chocolate icing on the cupcake I'd locked eyes with the moment we'd walked in.

Nick was giving me a strange look.

Oh, jeez. I'd actually paused by the table, closed my eyes, and sucked in a huge whiff of frosted cake. So embarrassing.

"Do you want a cupcake?" Nick asked. "I've got some cash..." He lifted his chin to indicate the cash only sign as if he thought that was the reason I wasn't buying myself a cupcake.

"No thanks," I said. I inhaled the fudgy air once more and walked quickly away from the table.

The track was flat on the floor, not like the raised kind I'd seen in movies. From my research, I knew that this version was not quite as dangerous as the raised, slanted track because you couldn't get up to top speed. Still, as we made it to trackside, there was all kinds of evidence of the night's violence, from dirty uniforms to torn fishnet stockings, and one player had a swollen nose and blood all over "her" shirt.

Everyone had gone all out for the cause with official team

uniforms—one team's pink and black, the other's orange and white.

"I love their skirts," I said, wishing I had the nerve to dress in short skirts and fishnet stockings. I mean, I'd managed to wear the clothes LeeAnne lent me in Bolo while I worked at her bar, but whatever audacity I'd gained there left me as soon as I drove away from Texas.

No, that wasn't true. It had left when Nick gave me his lawyer version of an "It's not you, it's me," speech. I deflated like a balloon and any self-esteem I'd gained from the way he looked at me evaporated.

He was a good guy to take me in and help me out of my predicament, but hadn't wanted me to stay.

He was staring at the skaters as they blocked and hip checked the jammer. His eyes narrowed.

"They're taller than I expected," Nick said.

"Really?" I replied as I scanned the building for Darson Dare.

"Yeah," he said. "They all seem tall for women."

I paused in front of the rink. "You might want to look a little closer." I located the announcer's table at one end of the track and started down the center aisle between the bleachers, since it appeared we had to get to the front and walk by the track to make it to Dare.

Nick followed, still watching the players. "What do you mean?" he finally asked.

"I mean they're not women. This is an annual charity event. Members of the Gay Firefighter's Association compete with the gay cops. The money goes to a children's hospital."

Nick scanned the track again, then his gaze went to the crowded benches full of players who were sidelined for the moment. His eyes moved around like he was counting.

"You have enough gay firemen and cops here to pull off an event like this?"

"This is L.A.," I replied. "We have enough gay everything here for pretty much any activity you can think of."

Nick chuckled and looked at me with that warm appreciative look in his eyes and my anger at him from a few minutes before melted away.

He had the best smile I'd ever seen, and that includes movie stars and Osmonds. I smiled back at him, but felt my face heating. I turned away and started walking.

~

Nick

I couldn't help but wonder why any man—gay or straight—would agree to dress up in wigs and fishnets and take part in this craziness. Couldn't people give to the cause without requiring these guys to humiliate themselves?

Except they didn't look humiliated. They looked like they were having a great time. While they waited to be put back in the game, team members posed so people on the bleachers could snap photos.

Both team benches were set up on the same side of the rink, near the crowd, one at one end of the track and one near the other.

Clearly the first team, in neon orange and white V-neck jerseys were from the fire department. Most were wearing white miniskirts or short-shorts and orange or black fishnets.

As we walked by the Slaughter Hoes—which I thought might be a play on "water hose," but wasn't sure—someone from the bench called out, "Hey, Tex, nice boots!"

I stopped automatically. I'd been raised not to ignore a person who was talking to me and to always say "thank you" to a compliment.

A player in an eighties-style layered wig and an awful lot of makeup for someone with such a big Adam's apple, was waving. I checked over my right and left shoulders.

"Is he talking to me?" I asked Rika.

She chuckled. "Nick, these events attract a lot of gay men, and you're kind of a stand-out, gay or straight."

I glanced around at the crowd of people sitting on the bleachers and realized there were a lot more men than women here and many of the men were holding hands with each other.

I turned back to the track in time to see my admirer—Nate Balls of Fire, according to his jersey—tap Frisco Inferno and Firen DuHole on the shoulders. They smiled my way and fell in line behind Nate, who was coming toward me.

Now, I wasn't normally a homophobe and had no problem with men wanting to be with other men. However, I didn't know how to handle being catcalled or propositioned by one.

I turned and walked toward the far end of the track where the announcer and scorekeepers seemed to be.

"I'm not sure I've ever seen you look nervous before," Rika said tauntingly. "I assumed you never looked nervous. One would think that if you could look nervous, you'd look that way, say, when you're defending an innocent person who's on trial for murder?"

She was referring to her troubles in Bolo. Since the firemen seemed to have given up and gone back to their bench, I paused to watch the game. We couldn't talk to Dare before it was over, anyway.

"I know how to handle myself in a courtroom," I replied. "I just don't know what to do when a man comes on to me."

"Why don't you do whatever you do when a woman comes onto you and you don't want to marry her?" Rika smirked at me and I wanted to kiss the smirk off her face, even if she was making fun of me.

Sometimes I wished I hadn't told her I'd been married three times. It would have been nice to put all that behind me like it never happened and start fresh with her. But, if I hadn't spilled the beans, LeeAnne or my mom would have.

"When it's a woman," I replied. "I give her a wink and say, 'I'll see *you* later,' then keep on walking."

"So," Rika shrugged. "Do the same thing with the men."

"I'm not going to go around winking and flirting with men," I said. Then, for kicks, I added, "For all I know, that's how they all ended up here." I dipped my head in the direction of one team, then the other.

Rika laughed, which was the only reason I was continuing this conversation. When she was serious, Rika was a ten. When she laughed, a thirty. Too bad I only got to spend time with her during some of the most stressful weeks of her life. I'd like to see her laugh a lot more.

"Yeah," she agreed. "They were all perfectly straight until some tall Texan winked at them and then, poof!" She waved her hand in a magical gesture. "They turned gay." She laughed again, her brown eyes doing a little salsa dance just for me.

Whenever I replayed the events of last summer, which I did often, I was pretty sure of the moment she got under my skin. It almost happened the first night I saw her, when Danny was gloating about her arrest and she put him in his place. But I was still able to drive away.

However, the next day when I picked her up from the station, she zapped the hell out of me. She was funny and confident in a completely different way than I was used to. Maybe because she was confident in her intelligence and didn't seem aware of how knock-out gorgeous she was.

My previous live-in situations had been with either women who had lots of confidence in their exteriors, but not so much in their intellect, or women who were full of all-around confidence, but didn't have the brains to back it up. Or, maybe they didn't bother to keep themselves educated about the world because they didn't have to.

Unfortunately, my mother was one of these women. Not my sister DeeAnne, though. She'd always been the exception in my life, but she'd moved to Seattle, as far as she could get away from Mom, and I couldn't blame her for it.

It was a good move for her until her divorce last year. Now I got the feeling she was hurting. Of course, being around mom at Christmas didn't help any. Those two were oil and water. Mom wouldn't stop making comments about Dee needing another man, and Dee couldn't stop trying to make Mom listen to reason on a variety of topics.

My sister was a smart cookie like Rika. I always thought they'd get along well if they had the chance to meet. And the idea of the two of them becoming friends always caused a pleasant twinge in my chest.

I shifted on my feet so my left elbow was touching Rika's upper arm. It was a junior high move, but we were searching for her missing father. I'd feel creepy putting the grownup moves on her under these circumstances.

Not that I had any business putting the moves on her, period. The same things were true now that were true when I met her, except for the fact that she was no longer my client. But I was still about ten years older, not exactly ancient by most people's standards, but I felt like I was carrying around an entire airliner full of baggage.

However, away from Bolo, here in L.A., a relationship between Rika and me felt a little more plausible. Maybe because I'd put so many miles between myself and my old life.

"And Attila the Huney takes over for Rumpled Foreskin as jammer for the Queerstone Cops..." The announcer's voice broke into my thoughts and I remembered why we were here.

Did he just say, "Rumpled Foreskin"?

I was now stuck with an image I didn't want rattling around in my head involving another guy's junk. I glanced down and realized I could see into Rika's shirt from this angle. I tilted my head a bit to get a better view...for therapeutic purposes of course.

She turned toward me suddenly and I averted my eyes.

A horn sounded. "Come on," I said as if all I'd been doing was waiting to talk to the announcer. "Game's over."

CHAPTER ELEVEN

Rika

Nick and I stepped up onto the platform where Darson Dare was standing, stretching his arms in the air while talking to a young Asian woman holding a clip board.

Darson was good-looking in a Hollywood way, with a spray tan and perfectly fake-tousled white hair. His style was a cross between a used car salesman and an over-the-hill actor turned Vegas performer, even though he was probably still in his thirties.

"You have the sweetest ass I've seen in a long time," Darson said as we walked up behind him. The young woman's face reddened. She was working hard not to appear horrified at the inappropriateness of his comment. "You're leaving with me," he stated as if it had been decided.

Ick! I shuddered. Darson Dare got grosser with every word that came out of his mouth.

She tucked her hair behind her ear nervously. "Sorry. I have to get home," she said. "Early meeting tomorrow."

"I'll make it worth any sleep you lose," Darson replied, a slimy grin on his face. "Don't you want to get a little from the Voice of L.A.? You could be my own personal geisha."

What? He did not ask an Asian-American professional woman to become his personal geisha!

My eyes shifted to the woman, who seemed to be fighting a losing battle with her facial expressions. She probably worked for the non-profit that was putting on the event and didn't want to piss off the talent they might need again next year. But I could see she wanted to tell Darson Dare he was gross and the geisha girl comment was so out-of-line, he should be reported to the FCC. Although, I doubted the FCC concerned themselves with things that were said by on-air personalities when they were off air.

"I need to be sharp for the meeting," she replied. "We do event recaps right away before we forget about issues we need to fix for next year." She took a baby step to her right as if she was planning an escape from a predator but didn't want to make sudden movements that would incite his chase instinct.

Darson took a step to his left to block her, then reached out and took her free hand in his. Her gaze shifted nervously from one hand to the other.

Nick stepped up behind him, placed a hand on one of his shoulders and said, "Darson Dare?" His head jerked around and the young woman took the opportunity to reclaim her hands and move away, which I figured was why Nick had done the shoulder thing.

Darson turned around to face us, his icicle blue eyes trying to stab holes in Nick, but failing. Nick was not the least bit fazed by the likes of Dare.

I pressed my lips together to keep from smiling. In this close proximity, it was impossible not to notice how much taller and better-looking Nick was than him.

"No autographs," Darson said to Nick, then he noticed me and his lips turned up into a seductive smile. "Except you," he said in his velvety radio voice. "I'll autograph anything you want me to, Babe."

Nick's entire body tightened as if ready for action and the air between the two men turned thick with tension. Nick shifted closer to me in what felt like a protective move. But I wasn't going to be flustered by this egocentric idiot.

I jumped in before Nick had a chance to chastise him and possibly piss him off.

"I'm Detective Martin." I pronounced my name without the accent in case he was aware of my father. "This is Detective Owen."

"Yeah?" Darson's eyes skimmed leisurely down my body, which felt like I imagined a worm would feel slithering down my spine. I decided then and there that if he touched me—anywhere—I was going to kick him in the balls on behalf of womankind.

"Yeah," Nick replied in a no-nonsense voice. When I glanced up at him, I caught the muscle ticking in his jaw. I felt his arm move against mine and saw his hand close into a fist.

I got the feeling that if Darson touched me, I might not have the opportunity to kick him in the crotch before Nick punched him in the face.

"We have some questions about the murder," Nick finished.

"What murder?" Darson asked.

"Alberto Viera," I replied.

Darson stared at us blankly.

"The sous chef at the Microtology VIP Center."

"Oh," Darson said. "That wetback cook."

I gasped inwardly at the slur, feeling insulted on behalf of Mexicans, even if I wasn't one myself. This guy was as offensive in person as he was on the radio. I'd assumed it was an act.

"Why would you want to talk to me about him?" Darson asked.

This is where things got dicey. It wasn't exactly our place to clue Darson Dare in that his wife had fooled around with Alberto, but we did need to know if Darson had a motive for murder.

"We're talking to everyone who has a connection to the

Microtology Center," Nick said. "We understand you're a member of the Temple of Microtology and your wife's office is in the center."

"Yeah, I joined because they told me they had connections and could help me transition to TV," Darson said. "Same reason I married my bitch of a wife."

Wow. What a catch. However, I'd heard his voice on the radio at various times over the past few years—when I couldn't avoid it—and he was always saying something obnoxious.

Nick gave me a *what the hell* look.

That was understandable. Nick didn't ever talk about women that way, not even his exes. I could tell he felt like he should defend Suzee, despite barely knowing her.

I figured I'd better jump in. "Were you at the center much?" I asked.

"No, I'm only there when I have to make an appearance to keep Steve and Valerie happy. They know a lot of people in this town. Hollywood types, people with money to finance pilots and films..." He shrugged. "They're connected."

"How well did you know Alberto?" Nick asked.

"I saw him around," Darson replied. "I don't think we ever had a conversation. He wasn't in a position to help me, so there wasn't any reason for me to talk to him."

What an asshole. The only way he could be a worse person is if he were the killer.

"What about your wife?" I asked. "Did she ever mention Alberto?"

"Maybe," he replied. "But I mostly tune her out. For all I know, she might have been screwing him. She's a whore." He said the last sentence matter-of-factly to Nick as if he expected him to commiserate about women and their whorish behavior.

"Unlike you?" I glanced behind Darson at the place where the young woman had been standing.

Darson laughed. "Touché," he said. "How about you and I

meet for a drink, and I'll fill you in on everything I know about the people who work at the center."

I opened my mouth to accept the invitation. Sure, he was a creepy, racist, misogynistic man-slut, but he might have information that could be of help to me.

Nick beat me to the punch. "That won't be necessary," he said.

"I wasn't inviting you," Darson clarified. "I like my threesomes to be girl-boy-girl."

Nick tensed again and figured we'd better wrap this up before he decided he needed to teach Darson some manners.

Pulling my phone from my pocket, I asked, "Could you take a look at this?" I thrust the photo of the heart necklace from the crime scene in front of Darson's face. "Have you ever seen this before?"

He grasped my hand as if to steady the phone in front of him, but it felt like a move. I made a mental note to wash that hand as soon as I got near a sink. There was no telling where it had been.

"No," Darson answered after staring into the phone for several seconds. "But I'm usually looking a little lower than that." He illustrated his point by focusing all his attention on my chest.

A low growl came from next to me. I shifted my gaze to Nick, trying to send him a *be cool* message. At the same time, he sent me an *I'm going to shove this guy's head up his ass* look.

"This pendant didn't ever belong to your wife?" I asked, wiggling the phone to get Darson's attention back on it.

He checked the screen again. "That's not pricy enough for my wife," he said. "If it doesn't have a giant diamond on it, she won't put it on her over-rated body."

Well, okay, then. The one good thing I could say about Darson Dare was that he wasn't sugar coating his relationship to divert suspicion.

"Did you kill Alberto?" Nick asked.

Way to be subtle, Nick.

Darson chuckled. I searched his eyes as he responded, "No, I didn't kill him. And if I murder somebody, it'll be Suzee."

"Fair enough," Nick replied.

Fair enough? I threw Nick a disgusted glance.

He smiled at me, which I knew was code for laughing at me. "Let's get going, Detective Martin."

My lips parted to say "Mar-*teeeeen*," then I remembered, again, that I was under cover. Being around Nick totally addled my brain.

As we left the stage area, I noticed the crowd had only partially disbursed. Most of the attendees were either still in their seats or lined up near the track. The players were all doing their own thing—some performing skating tricks off track as others passed a hat along the railing to collect more donations from the audience. Others were engaged in an extended version of the game, but without refs, so the moves were getting wilder.

As we walked by, one of the firefighters on the track threw an arm out as Rumpled Foreskin was racing by him at top speed.

Rumpled went flying over the railing toward us.

I froze, just like I'd done whenever a ball came at me in P.E. class.

Nick started forward, then stepped back a couple of feet, thrusting out his arms in what was probably a reflex action from all those football games in high school.

In the second or two Rumpled was in the air, the building went silent. Every pair of eyes were riveted to his flying body.

He let out a horrified, "Shiiiit!" making it clear to anyone who didn't know him that he did not possess the power of flight. Nick made one last adjustment to the right...

And caught him.

To say it was an impressive catch would be an understatement. Rumpled Foreskin was medium height for a man with a slight craft-beer belly. I would have expected the laws of physics to require that Nick fall back on his ass after a catch like that.

Instead, he caught Rumpled, running back several steps until he found his balance.

Once steady, though, Nick seemed sort of shocked, like he didn't know what he was supposed to do with the man in his arms. In fact, the look on his face was the same expression crooks on TV have the moment after they've been shot in the stomach, before they fall to the ground.

"Why don't you carry me to your car, hot stuff," Rumpled said as he batted his false eyelashes at Nick.

"I don't have a car," Nick replied.

"Is that a Texas accent?" Rumpled asked with obvious delight. "Hey, ladies!" he called to the other players. "I've got myself a real, live cowboy!" Then he kissed—yes, *kissed*—Nick on the right cheek.

Nick jerked his head to the left. As the crowd erupted in laughter and cheers, he half-dropped, half set Rumpled on his feet, turned and walked toward the exit.

And I could swear, before he left the building, I saw the beginning of a blush appear on Nick Owen's cheeks.

When we walked into my grandmother's house, it smelled strongly of cumin, one of my all-time favorite aromas since it was used in my favorite Colombian and Mexican foods.

I glanced around, noting that the living-dining-kitchen area was so full, it looked like everyone in the neighborhood had piled in. There were people on the sofa. People around the dining table. People in the kitchen. The kitchen door was open and there were people in the backyard.

My cousin Sofia was camped out on the corner of the couch. The caramel ringlets I so envied hung over her face as she scrolled through her phone.

"Hey, So." I poked her arm with my finger. We used to have

poking contests when we were kids. We took turns poking each other in more and more ticklish spots. The one who laughed first lost. As we got older, the game morphed into a greeting.

Sofia looked up, just realizing I was there. She was a lot better at blocking out the noise of Lita's gatherings than I was. Her olive-colored eyes searched my brown ones sympathetically, as if checking to see if I was still mentally sound. Once she was satisfied, her gaze shifted to Nick.

Sofia smiled as her eyes shifted back to me. The mischievous look on her face sang, *Nick and Rika sittin' in a tree, K-I-S-S-I-N-G.*

I whacked her on the arm. Nick gave me a *that was uncalled for* look, but he was a man and had no clue about the secret conversations women had between the lines.

"Where's Gucci?" Nick asked. He liked to pretend he didn't have any use for the little ball of fluff, but he took good care of her. He glanced around the floor as if concerned she might have been trampled by the crowd. I was sure he never would have chosen Gucci as a pet if he'd done the choosing, but I'd caught her lounging on his lap while he scratched her behind the ear with his little finger a couple of times at his house when he was watching TV.

"She was getting stressed by all these people," Sofia said. "I have her resting in a little crate in Rika's room."

"And she's not raising a stink?" Nick asked.

"Huh?" Sophia said. "Oh, you mean all that barking? It's fine. I took her with me to the puppy class I taught this morning and worked with her some more after."

"You stopped her from barking?" Nick asked.

Sofia looked up at us in a way I'd seen many times before. She wanted to roll her eyes at us but was restraining herself because she didn't know Nick well. "Do you hear her barking?"

There were a lot of people in the house, but Gucci's high-pitched yapping could cut through the roar of a jet engine. If we couldn't hear her, she wasn't barking.

"Hold on," Nick said. "Are you telling me you trained her to do something else?" He'd told me it had taken a year for her to learn her name.

"Technically, I taught her *not* to do something," Sophia corrected. Her expression grew more serious. "Any word on your dad?"

I shook my head and was about to move on, but she touched my arm to stop me.

After tapping her phone a couple of times, she held it up to me. On the screen was an adorable picture of a dog snuggling with a baby goat.

Since Sofia was the artistic type, she always felt the best way to cheer someone up was with a visual. Since she was an extreme dog lover and I had a penchant for tiny goats, she saved pictures of dogs and goats together and pulled one up whenever she thought I needed my mood lifted. Those were the moments I appreciated her the most, whether her effort helped me feel better or not. It was her way of letting me know she cared.

Sofia and I had a strange relationship. Or, at least, I thought it was strange. In a way, we'd been close since we were little and had spent lots of time together. But I often found her staring off into space with an unhappy expression on her face. Worse, sometimes I caught her staring at me with a strange mix of emotions visible in her eyes. Emotions I couldn't sort out, but one of them looked a lot like resentment.

I never doubted that she loved me, but sometimes I had to ask her why she was upset with me. She always acted like she didn't know what I was talking about and insisted we were fine.

I glanced toward the kitchen, wondering if I could sneak into my room without speaking to my grandmother. Most of the eyes in the living room were focused on some major action in the soccer game on TV.

Mr. Garza, one of our Mexican neighbors from down the street, was camped out on a stool at the bar facing the kitchen so he could gaze longingly at my grandmother. His devotion to her was completely unrequited. In fact, she acted as though his attention peeved her, but he was determined to change her mind.

The story I heard from my aunts was that about twenty years ago, one year after my grandfather died, Mr. Garza came to my grandmother's house with flowers and an extravagant ten-piece Mariachi band to help him appropriately relay his passion for her.

When she turned him away, much to the shock of my grandmother's friends who regarded him as the catch of the neighborhood, he started mowing her lawn. She retaliated by hiring a landscaping crew to mow for her instead of waiting for my father or Tía Margo's husband to come.

Mr. Garza began checking her yard every day and the moment the grass was long enough for mowing, he would mow it, before the landscape crew got to it.

But Lita was not one to be thwarted so easily. She ordered her grass taken out completely and even dug up her precious flower bed and replaced everything with a cactus garden. Two Sundays later, Mr. Garza snuck over while she was in church and planted a "Red-headed Irishman"—scientific name *mammillaria spinosissima,* I looked it up—in the middle of her garden.

This is the part I remember even though I was probably only about four years old. Growing from the top of the large rounded cactus was a perfect crown of gorgeous pink flowers. It was the most magical-looking thing I'd ever seen.

My grandmother dug it up and gave it to Mrs. Ruíz.

Over the years, every time he saw a chance, Mr. Garza would make a new play and every time my grandmother shot him down. Yet, he seemed completely undaunted, determined that she secretly loved him and would be his one day.

He was her Eli, in a way, and I didn't understand why she had to be so testy with him. Her brutal rejection of Mr. Garza also seemed to ward off any other suitors, which I think was her intention.

After the repeated infidelities by my grandfather and Tía Margo's husband and the death of my mother, men were the enemy to the women in my family with the exception of my father and one of the priests at Lita's church (but not the other two who made the volunteer of the year decisions).

And, now, maybe Nick.

I gestured to him and he followed me to my room. My phone vibrated in my jeans pocket. My home screen showed an email from Julian had come in. I sat down in my desk chair and typed my password into the computer to pull it up on the bigger screen.

"I love Julian!" I shouted when I saw that he'd managed to get me some more photos.

Nick let out an odd snort behind me. I turned around and saw a look in his eye that said he didn't share my jubilation.

Asshole. Sure, he didn't seem to like Julian, but this was about my dad.

When I pulled up the pictures, there were several more of the body from different angles, which I didn't think helped any. I clicked open the next image. It was another photo of the quiches, but a wider shot than I'd seen before.

"Two glasses," Nick said, referring to the two wine glasses on the counter on opposite sides of the quiches.

"They look like there's only water in them." I enlarged the picture to try to get a closer look. "Or vodka."

"Would a chef put vodka in wine glasses?" Nick asked.

That was a good question. After many years in the restaurant industry, my father automatically used the appropriate glassware for the beverage he was serving, especially alcoholic beverages. But I didn't know if this would be true of Alberto. I didn't even know if Alberto was the one who filled the glasses.

Another photo was a closeup of a large chef's knife, presumably the one that had been sticking out of Alberto. Dried blood was visible on the blade.

Sofia appeared in my doorway. "Rika, some people just pulled up in front of the house."

"People?"

"Not from the neighborhood. It's a regular car, but they look like cops."

Sofia was good at identifying people and things at a glance. If she said they were cops, they were almost definitely cops.

I stood and rushed past her, through the living room, with Nick at my heels. When I looked out the peephole, I saw a dark-haired man and a blonde woman, both dressed in slacks and blazers.

They weren't just cops. They were the homicide detectives that called me in for questioning after the murder.

As I opened the door and stepped out onto the porch, I felt Nick at my back.

"Ms. *Martín*. I don't know if you remember us, but I'm Detective Winchell," the man said.

What kind of moron would I have to be not to remember them? They questioned me at the station before it became clear that they were treating my dad as a suspect and I ended the interview.

"And I'm Detective Hertz," the woman added, except she was staring at Nick, not me. And she was smiling.

A feeling I told myself was righteous anger—even though it felt a whole lot like jealousy—reared up inside me.

Was it too much to ask that she keep her head in the game for a murder investigation?

On the other hand, since my father was a suspect, maybe a distraction was called for, but I didn't want it to be Nick.

Detective Winchell's gaze shifted expectantly to Nick. "This is my friend Nick Owen," I felt obliged to explain. "Have you found my father?"

Detective Hertz looked at me like she didn't for a second believe that I was ignorant of my father's whereabouts. "No," she replied. "We haven't."

"Do you mind if we have a look around inside?" Detective Winchell asked.

I opened my mouth to speak, but Nick butted in. "Do you have a warrant?"

That was exactly what I was about to ask. I frowned at Nick and his buttinsky attitude. Then I remembered he flew all the way here at the drop of a hat to help me find my dad. I should quit getting annoyed with him and be grateful.

"What are you, a lawyer?" Detective Winchell asked sarcastically.

"Yeah, in fact, I am." Nick gave the detective a piercing alpha male stare which evoked some very inappropriate tingling in a very inappropriate place on my body.

I guess I had no business mentally berating Detective Hertz when I couldn't control my own reaction to hot Nick. Especially when he went all macho man.

Until I spent time with Nick, I had no idea that type of behavior would stir anything in me. I'd never gotten excited over men in uniform or men in western films or any of the typical hyper-masculine male stereotypes. But Nick...

Nick was different for reasons I didn't understand.

"So, you've lawyered up?" Detective Winchell asked. "Or is he for your father?"

"Nick Owen is a friend of the family who flew in to help when he learned my father was *abducted*." I overemphasized the word to make my point.

Detective Hertz didn't seem interested in my point. "According to the homeowner records, this isn't your house," she pointed out.

"It's my grandmother's house."

"Well, then, we'd like to speak to your grandmother."

Shit.

I left Nick at the door to stare them down while I hurried to the kitchen.

"Lita," I said, taking her by the elbow. She immediately recognized the seriousness in my voice and walked with me.

"Is it Diego?" she whispered. I could see the fear in her eyes.

"No," I replied quickly. "But I don't want the police to find him before I do. We need the detectives at the door to keep suspecting we're hiding him here."

She gave a single knowing nod then moved through the doorway.

After the introductions, Lita planted a hand on one hip and asked, "What is this about?"

"We're still looking for Diego Martín," Detective Winchell said. "I believe he married one of your daughters?"

"He was married to my daughter many years ago before she was abducted and murdered," my grandmother replied. "Your department never caught the man who killed her." She focused an accusing stare on them.

Detective Winchell looked momentarily chagrined, but not Detective Hertz. "We'd like to solve *this* case," she said. "Can we come in and look around?"

"Diego doesn't live here. He has his own apartment."

"We know, but we'd still like to look around here," Detective Hertz replied, clearly uninterested in a case that took place before she was even on the force.

My grandmother's chin raised defiantly. "Do you have a warrant?"

"No."

"Then quit wasting your time here and find out who killed that poor man and took Diego."

She turned her gaze toward Nick and me, flicked her head in the direction of the house and walked inside. We followed without another word to the detectives.

CHAPTER TWELVE

Nick

Rika was disappointed when we started out the next morning. She'd hoped to see Jason Kim, but everywhere she called, she was told he'd taken days off to go to a family member's funeral out of town.

The timing was suspicious, but we had others to interview who we hoped would be more forthcoming. We headed to the address we had for Chef Ben.

I drove, since I was a bit dubious about Rika's skills behind the wheel. She'd put one of my trucks in the ditch the first time she drove it in Bolo. And when she picked us up at the airport, she was driving like a crazy person, blaming non-existent motorcycles for her wild lane changes.

I wasn't sure if she was a bad driver in general or she was just a bad driver under stress, but I wasn't taking any chances.

Chef Ben Appétit lived in a swanky four-story apartment building in West Hollywood that had been painted cream and orange in what I guessed was a nod to art deco style. After spending what felt like an eternity looking for a place to park, I found a spot around the corner

We rode the elevator to the top floor and knocked. The door opened and a chubby, round-faced man wearing over-sized nerd glasses opened the door. His blonde hair had been shaped into a swirl on top that made me think of Jimmy Neutron.

And, did his glasses have lenses?

No. They didn't.

Weird.

Didn't know what to make of his outfit either. He was wearing a pair of bright yellow shorts and a thin cotton, navy-colored shirt, unbuttoned halfway down to expose a chest the color of bread dough. The shirt had wide panels of a miniature white floral pattern running down the right and left sides. He'd added a belt—my ex, Megan, would have called the color "fuchsia"—and some lime sandals.

I had no idea if the guy was completely colorblind or this look was cutting-edge L.A. fashion. If it was, you could count me the hell out.

"Yes?" He smiled at me while batting his eyelashes. I hoped he had something in his eye. "How can I be of service to you?" He kept staring at me even though the most beautiful woman I'd ever seen was standing right next to me.

I found it unsettling to be the object of flirtation from men two days in a row. Maybe I needed to change my aftershave.

"I'm Rika Martin and this is Nick Owen," Rika said. "We're private investigators looking into the death of Alberto Viera."

The man's smile faded. "Oh."

"Are you Chef Ben Appétit?"

I was glad she said it because I was afraid I wouldn't be able to get that silly name to come out of my mouth when he was standing right in front of me.

"Yes, but I don't know what I can tell you. I don't work at the VIP Center anymore."

Rika leaned in and said in a near whisper, "We thought you might have the inside scoop on some of the personalities there."

That was definitely the way to go. He smiled and cocked an eyebrow. “Girl, did you come to the right place,” he said, but he was looking at me again when he said, “Come,” and made a come-hither gesture with his fingers.

I reminded myself I was doing this for Rika and followed.

As we walked in, I was surprised by the look of his living room. I expected it to be decorated like Chef Ben was, but it was about as opposite from his clothing style as could be. The place was almost as relaxing as mine in dusky greens and grays with a mix of modern and ethnic art on the wall that I wouldn’t have known could be mixed so well together—not that I knew much about decorating. However, having three wives had forced me to learn the difference between peach, coral, pink and terra cotta, all words I avoided mentioning when around other men.

“This is a nice place,” Rika said. “Did you decorate it yourself?” After seeing her Ms. Pacman bedspread and what I thought might be Harry Potter wands hanging on the wall of her room, I was pretty sure Rika knew even less about decorating than I did. But it wasn’t a bad idea to compliment someone to put them at ease before questioning them.

“No,” Chef Ben’s eyes teared up instantly. “I let my boyfriend Rolf do it. My ex-boyfriend now.”

Did I say I hated to see a woman cry? I now realized I hated to see a man cry even more. With a woman, I could put a comforting arm around her or pull her in for a hug. With a man, I didn’t know the protocol. Where I came from, men didn’t go around crying, except for a few quiet tears at the funeral of a close family member. Certainly not in front of strangers.

Rika reached out and put her hand on his arm, saving me from having to decide what to do. “I’m sorry,” she said. “My boyfriend of two years broke up with me a few months ago. Well, actually, his doorman did. I came home and wasn’t allowed up to the apartment. My stuff was in the lobby.”

Chef Ben's eyes widened. He gasped, clearly incensed on her behalf.

Nice job, Rika!

I was pretty sure she hadn't been terribly upset over losing that dumbass Brandtt, but her comment was a great rapport-builder. Chef Ben patted her hand and motioned for us to sit down. She sat next to him on his couch. I took the arm chair opposite them.

"He must have been an idiot to dump a hottie like you," Chef Ben said. "Men are assholes."

Rika snorted. "And what was Rolf thinking? Aren't you the personal chef to the stars?"

Chef Ben nodded vehemently. "Yes, and I just received the contract this morning for my cookbooks based on the Microtology approved diet. I'm supposed to get a six-figure advance and Steve and Valerie are going to make them a required purchase for all Microtologists! I didn't text it to Rolf, though. I want him to hear about it when the publisher releases the information to the media."

"I wouldn't be surprised if he came crawling back to you," Rika said. "You're an awesome catch!"

Chef Ben wasn't crying anymore. In fact, a wide smile broke out on his face. "I think you're my new best friend."

I'd been mulling over the book deal. "Isn't it odd that the Kaporskys would be so supportive of a book that isn't written by an actual Microtologist?" I asked.

"Not really. I've known them for years now and their number one goal is to mainstream Microtology. They want to convince people it's a normal religion."

"And what's more normal than a cookbook?" Rika pointed out.

"Exactly!" Chef Ben replied.

"Just out of curiosity, why aren't you a Microtologist?" I asked.

"Well, for one thing, I'm not messing with this." He pointed both index fingers at his hair. "It's my trademark. I'm a natural blonde, you know. It's how I get the guys. Like a male peacock and his feathers."

I was pretty sure that the men Chef Ben had *gotten* either liked him for himself or were hoping for a gourmet breakfast in the morning.

Wait, this was L.A.

Make that brunch.

"I assume you're acquainted with Jason Kim and Suzee Driver?" Rika asked.

"Oh, sure. I used to see them every day. Now, Suzee, *she's* got some great wigs."

Rika blinked at him in surprised. "The one with the ringlets was a wig?"

Chef Ben nodded enthusiastically.

"Oh, my God! I wonder where she got it. I've always wanted ringlets!"

I couldn't imagine why someone as gorgeous as Rika would want to change anything about herself.

"Don't bother asking her," Ben replied. "She's really stingy with her beauty routine. Once I asked her what she'd done to get her skin so fresh and glowy and she told me she just washes her face. I mean, one Friday, she had a break out, then the next Monday, her skin was perfect and it's been perfect ever since... Just washed it, my ass!"

I decided I'd better get this conversation back on track. "Did you know the victim?" I asked.

"Al?" He nodded. "Sure. He was my sous chef when I worked at the center."

"Is there anyone you can think of who would want to hurt him?"

"That's a tough one..." Ben curled his upper lip and furrowed his brow as if giving the matter serious thought.

"Because he was such a likeable guy?" I asked.

He chortled. "No, because he had a habit of pissing people off. He and Jason used to argue about all kinds of stupid things—like Al leaving the back door open after going out to smoke his medicinal marijuana. And there were all those women he screwed. But he always called it 'making love.' Like you could be in love with half a dozen people at one time."

"Do you know who else?" I asked. "Besides Suzee Driver?"

"Well, off the top of my head, the restaurant hostesses..."

"Plural?" Rika asked.

"*So* plural!" He leaned in like he was about to tell a secret. Rika raised her eyebrows and leaned in too. "There was a lot of turnover in that position. It was usually filled by a young female Microtologist who was assigned there, then, after Steve and Valerie assessed her skill set, she'd get moved to another job. Al thought he was the welcome wagon, if you know what I mean."

"Wow," Rika said. "Anybody else?"

"Let's see, you know about Suzee. Then there was Valerie..."

"Valerie *Kaporsky*?" I asked as Rika and I exchanged *Holy shit!* glances.

"Yeah, and Jemima Harte, the actress. She's at the center a lot. The Kaporskys are trying to make her the face of Microtology from what I've seen."

"Do you think any of these women believed they were exclusive?" I asked. "Could someone have gotten jealous enough to attack him with a knife?"

"I'm not sure. I don't think Valerie would ever leave Steve, so it would be stupid for her to get that jealous. Although, I guess logic doesn't always rule in matters of the heart." He tilted his head to the side, but the swirl on top was not the least bit affected by gravity. It kept its structure, like a hat. "No, the more I think about it, the less I can believe Valerie was in love with Al. She and Steve spend most of their time together. Like, right now, they're at their weekly appointment at the Clarification Center and they always do it together. And Valerie's main priority is how her public actions represent Microtology. I don't think she'd lose control enough to murder someone. The one who seemed most infatuated with him was Jemima." Ben sighed dramatically. "All those beautiful leading men and she wanted to sleep with a sous chef."

Rika pulled her phone from her pocket. "Can you tell me if you ever saw any of them wearing this necklace? It was found near the body."

Chef Ben stared at her phone screen for several seconds. "It looks pretty cheap. Maybe it belonged to one of the hostesses, but I can't remember seeing it before."

Rika's blink lasted a split-second longer than a blink usually did. I could tell she was disappointed and frustrated but trying hard not to show it. "Well, thanks." She stood and I followed suit. "Can we contact you again if anything else comes up?"

"Of course," Chef Ben said. "I'm glad to help." He hugged Rika goodbye like they'd known each other for years. He stuck a hand out toward me, and I was glad to get by with a shake, at least until he gave it an extra squeeze. He winked at me. I took my hand back and opened the door. There had been plenty of gay men around at the University of Texas when I attended. None of them had ever come on to me. Here, I was getting hit on regularly.

Maybe I need to rethink my wardrobe. I checked what I was wearing.

Dark blue button-down shirt, jeans, boots and a leather jacket. Just normal clothes.

"Oh, one more thing," Rika said. I was already outside, but she'd lingered in the doorway. "Did the Kaporskys fire you to make room for the new chef?"

Chef Ben seemed momentarily taken aback by the question, but apparently decided not to be insulted by it, probably because it came from his new best friend. "No," he said. "I wanted out of that job. The restaurant grind isn't for me. I have bigger plans."

"Okay, thanks for putting up with all our questions," Rika said. "And good luck with your plans. I can't wait until I see you on the Food Network!"

Chef Ben beamed at her. "I can't wait for you to see me there either! Call me anytime!"

I'd noticed it was the second time Rika had done that "One more thing" thing. It was a smart tactic. Waiting until the other person's guard was down, then slipping in an important question.

In Bolo, I didn't get the chance to witness her interrogation skills, but I had to admit I was pretty damn impressed. And I enjoyed investigating with her so much, sometimes I almost forgot what was on the line.

She had to be good at compartmentalizing because you'd never know from her demeanor today that she'd been fighting off tears yesterday, afraid her father was dead.

Damn, I hoped we found him alive because now I knew that seeing Rika fall apart would break my heart in a way it had never been broken before.

"Well... we have some more women's names," Rika said as if trying to keep her hopes up. "Maybe we can find out who the heart necklace belonged to."

"So, I'm guessing you want to go to the Clarification Center now?"

She smiled. "I like it when we're on the same wavelength," she said.

"So do I." And I did.

Maybe I liked it a little too much for our own good.

Rika

Lucky for me, the Clarification Center was in an upscale strip mall only a few blocks from Chef Ben's apartment. I'd insisted Nick drive us straight there, even though I didn't have a clear plan of how we would get in to see the Kaporskys. I was just hoping the center took walk-ins.

My Internet search told me the Clarification Center was a kind of health spa where members went for treatments that supposedly kept them free of microorganisms and parasites.

When we walked into the gleaming white waiting room, the receptionist was on the phone. She mouthed the words, "I'll be right with you," and gestured to some white chairs.

As we sat down, I couldn't keep my eyes off her, specifically her hair, because I couldn't figure out how she'd gotten it to perform a virtual magic trick. It was pure white, the front poking out, forming a visor over her forehead. Then it doubled back to join the rest of her hair in a high ponytail that defied gravity by curving up and forward, the tip hovering over her head. The sides were layered and fell to right below her ears.

Bizarre as it looked, I was sure I'd seen this style somewhere before.

Hm... I typed "Jetsons" into Bing on my phone and there it was.

I looked at Nick. His eyes were narrowed, a quizzical tilt to his head as he studied the receptionist. I elbowed him to get his attention and showed him my screen. He peered down at it, then up at the receptionist, then back down at the screen again. He closed his eyes and shook his head.

He saw it too. She was sporting the Judy Jetson, a style I would have said was impossible to achieve if you weren't a cartoon.

He did a search on his own phone, found a picture and showed it to me. It was Jimmy Neutron. "Chef Ben," he whispered.

After that, each time we looked at the receptionist, we cracked up, then quickly looked down at our phones so she wouldn't know we were laughing at her.

It was nice having Nick around. We were totally on the same

wavelength when it came to sense of humor and, if ever I needed someone who could make me laugh, it was now.

Unfortunately, that thought reminded me of why I needed to laugh so badly. My stomach churned as the possibility that my father could have been murdered days ago, his body dumped on the side of a road like the one I found in Bolo, pushed its way into my head again. But I blew it up, scattering it into tiny unrecognizable thought fragments. The sick feeling remained, though.

I lifted my eyes to Nick's again. He winked at me and I instantly felt better.

At the same time, I wasn't comfortable with the power Nick held over my emotions. Once I'd pulled myself together after my mom's death and my dad's departure around nine years old, I prided myself on being in control of my emotional responses.

The awful things people said and did to me at school penetrated, but I didn't let my schoolmates see how their taunts affected me. I think if I hadn't made myself so stoic, the bullying would have happened all day every day instead of now and then. When bullies get no reaction, they tend to move on.

My Jilly Crane counselor had pointed out that I'd kept a tight rein on my emotions by keeping my mouth full of carbs so the feelings couldn't pop out.

Mmm... I could almost taste those pre-packaged mini-doughnuts Eddie always kept stocked at the corner store. For a while, I even entertained the notion of becoming Mrs. Eddie Robles, Junior, who was a year ahead of me in school. He wasn't much to look at, but someday he would inherit a store full of Hostess and Little Debbie's and Double Stuf Oreos, my version of Prozac.

"Yes, I've cancelled today's appointment, Ms. Peters..." The receptionist's voice pulled me back to reality. My gaze trailed down her chest, noting the white V-neck salon smock with black snaps down the front. "Sure, just call when you figure out your schedule."

She hung up the phone and looked toward the corner of the

room where a bald woman waited. I'd been so mesmerized by the receptionist's hair and my own thoughts, I hadn't even noticed a bald woman? I needed to get my head on straight. A private investigator should be keenly aware of her surroundings.

"Ms. Clayton, I'll take you back now," the receptionist said. She turned to us. "Someone will be right with you."

As I nodded back at her, my body tightened. This could be my chance. I scanned my memory banks, trying to recall whether Ms. Peters could be a recognizable female celebrity.

The only Peters I could think of was Bernadette Peters, who I remembered mainly from her role in *The Jerk*, which I considered a comedy classic. I'd never pass for her, but Peters was a pretty common last name. Besides, Bernadette Peters had been doing mostly Broadway for years, from what I'd heard. She probably lived in New York.

Another young woman appeared at the reception desk in the same type of smock. She had long, white hair, arranged in a fish-tail braid over one shoulder. Her nametag read "Coral."

"Have you been helped?" she asked.

"No," I replied as Nick and I stood. "Not yet."

"Do you have an appointment?"

"Yes."

I could feel Nick's eyes on me, and I hoped he played along. If I got away with this charade, I was going to kiss him goodbye like he was my husband and tell him to pick me up later.

I cleared my throat. "The name is Peters."

Coral checked the computer screen. "That's strange," she said. "Someone put you down as cancelled."

"No, I never cancelled. They probably just ticked the wrong box."

She nodded. "Yeah, that happens sometimes." She clicked on the mouse, then looked up and smiled. "So, I guess the two of you are ready for your couple's clarification massage lesson?"

I felt my eyes go wide before I got control of my face. I looked at Nick. His brows had climbed halfway up his forehead.

But no way was I passing up the chance to get in to see the Kaporskys. "Yep!" I announced cheerfully. "We're ready." I grabbed Nick's hand, lacing my fingers through his in case he was planning an escape.

Coral gestured for us to follow her and we trailed her into the back.

"Great wig," she said as we walked down the hallway. "I don't think any of mine are that shiny. Regardless, I have to wear a white one here—part of the dress code."

I nodded, hoping she wouldn't ask to try my "wig" on. "Wow, this place is bigger than I thought. Are all these rooms for clarification massage?"

"No, just these four." She gestured to the first four rooms. "The next two are for follicle control."

"Pardon?" Nick said.

"Follicle control. You know, shaving, waxing, etcetera. I can check the appointment calendar if you're wanting to get in today."

Nick's mouth opened, but I was afraid of what he'd say.

"He wants me to shave him his first time," I said, giving her a meaningful look.

She paused at a doorway and scanned Nick from head to crotch. "Just make sure you don't miss a spot." She threw a naughty half-smile my way.

His eyes narrowed at us, but she didn't seem to notice, since she was back to checking out his hot body. A burn erupted in my stomach and I wanted to poke her leering eyes with my fingers, *Three Stooges* style.

"So," I said more loudly than necessary to get her attention off Nick's privates. "Is this our room?"

"Yes, go on in and change into those robes." She pointed to two white robes hanging from a hook on the wall. The words *HIS* and *HERS* were printed on signs above them. "Take off everything except your underwear. Unless your underwear isn't white, then take them off, too. Helen will be with you in a moment."

We walked in and she shut the door behind us.

"What the hell?" Nick said as soon as she was gone.

"I had to get back here," I replied. "The Kaporskys are in the building somewhere!"

He looked at the door, then back at me. "How do you plan to get us out of this massage thing?"

"Just hurry and change into the robe so we look legit, then we'll try to sneak down the hall and look around."

"Fuck," Nick said as he grabbed the hem of his t-shirt and pulled.

That's when everything went into slow-motion. I felt my eyes bug out as he revealed inch after inch of tanned skin. I'd thought I remembered how mega-hot he was when I saw him shirtless in Texas, but I could swear he'd gotten mega-hotter.

And I'd heard of muscles rippling, but never thought about what that meant.

Now, I knew.

As he pulled his shirt over his head, Nick's muscles definitely rippled—like fans doing the wave at a sporting event—but from bottom to top instead of left to right. Okay, it was nothing like a sporting event, except for the fact that a person could easily sit around watching it happen for hours. And, by "a person," I mean me.

He turned to toss his shirt onto a chair, his back muscles flexing with his movements.

Mmmm.... Me and every other woman in the world who still has her eyesight.

He pulled the robe on and started unbuttoning his jeans. Our eyes met and something changed in his as if a new thought had entered his head and pushed out his annoyance. "Well?" He flipped his eyebrows and tipped his head toward my robe, still hanging on its hook.

Oh. I was supposed to change, too.

"Turn around," I demanded.

He lowered his chin and looked at me like I was being a silly girl. "I've seen you in your underthings..." The corners of his mouth turned up and I got the feeling he was both seeing me now in front of him *and* seeing me nearly naked last summer on his mental split-screen. "The superhero ones," he added.

Jeez, how could I ever forget that embarrassing encounter? Well, it had been embarrassing at first, then super-hot for a minute, then embarrassing again.

Regardless, being away from him had thrust me, full-force, back into my Oreo Double Stuf habit. I didn't want him to see me like this.

I glared at him. He exhaled loudly as he turned his back to me.

With *The Flash*-like speed, I tore off my t-shirt and bra, yanked the robe on and tied it. I pulled my jeans off from underneath. Luckily, my bikinis were made of white cotton today, so I could leave them on.

"Ready?" Nick asked. I turned around and noted that his robe covered him down to his calves while mine only went to mid-thigh.

Whatever. I didn't have time to lecture anyone here about their sexist spa-wear choices.

"Let's go," Nick said as he opened the door. We nearly collided with a woman who was standing in the hall, her fist in mid-air as if preparing to knock.

CHAPTER THIRTEEN

Rika

She was an older lady with pale, wrinkled skin, piercing blue eyes, and the requisite white hair, although it might have turned that color on its own.

"Oh!" she said when Nick opened the door. "Well, it looks like you're both ready."

"Uh-huh?" I squeaked. I rushed over and grabbed my pile of clothes from the floor where I'd abandoned them and laid them on top of Nick's on a white plastic chair in the corner.

"I'm Helen," the woman said. She came in and stood near the massage table. "Which of you is the masseuse for today's lesson?"

Nick's lips parted, but I was faster. "Me!" I raised my hand quickly. No way did I want him to have to sink his hands into my flabby flesh.

Although I was still below my original Jilly Crane goal weight by one pound, I needed to lose more like nine to feel comfortable with a man putting his hands on my body.

"All right, then..." she lifted the top of the sheet from the table and gestured for me to take it. "I'll turn away. After he takes his robe off and lies face down on the table, you can cover him to the waist with this."

"I... uh..." I stuttered as I took the sheet from her.

She turned her back to us.

Nick smacked me with another annoyed look, then turned, dropped his robe and lay face down on the table. My eyes boinged out of their sockets, my lids unable to blink.

Nick's ass was completely bare!

And I had never seen such a perfect ass in real life. It was neither tiny, nor huge. But it was rounded and muscled like a pro athlete's. My mouth went dry, my tongue somehow cutting off my air supply even though I'd been breathing through my nose.

My hands tightened on the sheet I was holding, as I imagined squeezing his gorgeous butt, one cheek in each hand, as he flexed in my palms.

Mmmmmm...

"Rika?" Nick's voice floated in through my lust fog.

"Hm?" My eyes were still on his ass. Then, for some inane reason, I blurted, "You're not wearing any underwear!"

Damn it! My gaze darted to Helen as I wondered if it seemed suspicious to her that a wife didn't know what her husband had or hadn't been wearing under his jeans.

"Remember, hon?" he said casually. "This trip was pretty sudden. I forgot to pack 'em."

I attempted to avert my gaze from his ass, but it seemed to be stuck there with superglue. I had to use every ounce of will power to peel them off Nick's delicious backside.

My gaze met his and I realized he'd been watching my expressions. But he didn't seem annoyed anymore. In fact, he was trying to suppress a grin and not quite succeeding.

His eyes had turned that beautiful Bondi Blue color they always did in florescent lighting and, at the moment, they held a mischievous gleam. My heart did a little somersault before I jerked into action, covering him from the waist down. As I imagined what I must have looked like, ogling his backside, my face heated with embarrassment.

"Ready," I said.

Helen turned around. "Where did you guys come in from?" she asked.

"Texas." I was glad Nick answered because my tongue was stuck to the roof of my mouth. "I have a job interview. We're trying to move here." He rested his face in the cradle.

"Great," she said. "I love it here. Plenty of Microtology friends. We'll start with the head and torso, today. If we have time, we'll proceed to lower body."

A thrill wiggled through me and I felt like a teenager, both excited and terrified at the same time. Did lower body include his ass? What about his boy parts? Would I be expected to put my hands on hot Nick's boy parts?

My girl parts got all giggly and wiggly at the thought.

Damn it! It was happening again, just like in Bolo. When I got too excited over Nick, I started making silly body part rhymes in my head.

Helen seemed to be waiting for me, so I moved up by Nick's head to stand next to her.

"Is he getting his head shaved today?" she asked.

"Yes, later, today," I lied.

"Good, we don't have to worry about how the clarifiers will affect his hair, then."

Nick's back muscles tensed. I was glad I couldn't see his face. I had a feeling he wasn't smiling anymore. His hair was noticeably longer than the buzz cut he sported when I met him. I wanted to believe he'd let himself go—from all the pining he was doing over me—but his body was still lean and muscular like he hadn't missed a work-out. Besides, the slightly longer hair looked just as good on him as the short style, maybe better.

Helen lifted a bottle from a table nearby. You can pick some of this up at the front desk along with the antibacterial supplements, if you don't already have those."

"Great, thanks," I said.

"First, you should wake up any microbes by putting both hands on his head and raking your fingers through his scalp."

I didn't know about the microbes, but I definitely liked the idea of running my fingers through Nick's hair. As my nails skimmed over his scalp, his hairs slipped across my fingers. The rest of him was so hard, I hadn't expected the hairs to be so soft. The urge to lean down and rub my cheek against them was almost irresistible.

My fingers slid to the top of his head, then down again, changing the angle each time to give him a thorough massage.

"How is that, Nick?" Helen asked.

"Great," he replied. I hoped he meant it. Even though we were here under false pretenses, I wanted him to think I was good at this.

"Now the clarifying oil," Helen said.

She lifted the bottle and I cupped my hands. As a small amount of warm oil drizzled into my palm, I had the feeling Nick was not going to like having this in his hair, but there wasn't much I could do about it now.

At Helen's instructions, I continued working on his head, massaging the oil into his scalp. When I heard no complaint from him, I was grateful. Maybe he didn't care about me the way I cared about him, but he was a good friend to endure this Micro-tology craziness to help me out.

His hand brushed my leg. I jumped, but managed to swallow the yelp that tried to escape my mouth. There was no reason to yelp. It was surely an accidental touch. My legs had been chilled from the air conditioning and his hand was shockingly warm, that was all.

But as I went back to work on his head, his scorching fingertips trailed lightly up the back of my calf.

That was no accident.

A hot shiver wiggled up my leg. Was he punishing me for getting him into this situation? Or taking the opportunity to do something he already wanted to do?

I remembered the times last summer when I thought we might kiss, but we didn't. And the time when we did kiss—boy did we kiss—but he put a stop to anything more. Then, as soon as the case was solved and I was free to go, he sent me away.

Well, he didn't send me away, exactly, but he didn't ask me to stay.

My grandmother's favorite saying about how men were the simplest of God's creatures came to mind. He was probably only toying with the diversion in front of him like a cat toying with a shoelace.

His fingers skimmed down to my ankle, then up again. When they tickled at the back of my knee, I jumped and let out a choked giggle. "Nick!" I cried.

Helen chuckled. "It's fine," she said. "We encourage our couples to enjoy this time together. Even use it as foreplay if they like."

Foreplay? With Nick?

Holy mother of Zeus!

"Now, slide your fingers down his neck," Helen instructed.

I tried not to let my hands shake as I slid my fingers over the nape of his neck. He moaned, or maybe it was more of a growl. The vibration made my fingertips tingle. Suddenly, my breath felt heavy in my chest.

Heat seeped from his body into mine, running up my arms and into my shoulders. But when it reached my abdomen, I remembered Nick had a woman waiting for him at his hotel. The heat turned from sexy warmth to angry fire.

I mean, what kind of asshole engages in clarification foreplay while sleeping with some blonde bimbo?

No, I didn't know for sure she was a bimbo, but it made me

feel better to think of her that way. And I did more or less force Nick into this appointment.

Regardless, I had the urge to smack him hard on his bare ass. But it was covered with the sheet and Helen was watching. Instead, I decided to try to give him Jimmy Neutron hair like Chef Ben had.

As I worked his neck with one hand, I used the other to push all his hair up and swirl it around on top of his head. I was afraid Helen would comment, but she simply smiled at me conspiratorially.

He didn't have enough hair to do a full Jimmy Neutron or even a Chef Ben. When I finished, it was more like a Woody Woodpecker.

"And now, the shoulders," Helen instructed. "His are thick for your small hands, but, remember, the purpose is clarification, not actual massage, so you're free to apply the oil however you like, as long as you're thorough.

I remembered the other times I'd touched Nick's shoulders. When he'd carried me from the truck the night I'd hurt my ankle trying to avoid being shot. When he'd kissed me in the bathroom half-naked. When he'd thrown me over his shoulder to escape a bomb. That one was a little fuzzy, since I'd lost a lot of blood by then.

Folding my hands over his shoulders, I massaged as best I could while enjoying the slight give of his muscles under my thumbs. At Helen's prompting, I continued down his back, until I reached the sheet covering his ass.

"All right, Nick if you could turn over now," she said. She held the sheet for him, averting her eyes as I semi-averted mine, grabbing another quick peek at his naked butt before looking away, so he wouldn't catch me.

"As you probably know, we have a different product for daily face cleansing, so start below his chin." After I'd followed Helen's instructions about clarifying Nick's neck and arms, she said, "Good! Now let's move to the chest area."

I stalled by adding more oil to my hands, nervous about handling Nick's perfect pecs. I turned back toward him and my eyes darted around, unsure where they should look.

When I pressed my palms to his chest, his gaze caught mine and held it. His eyes had changed to a dusky blue-gray like they did when he was angry, only he didn't look angry. He looked...

Intense.

His pecs felt hot under my hands, like burners on a stove. Something in my lower abdomen started to melt. Because Nick had looked at me like this once before. Right before he kissed me.

"You can move your hands now," Helen said.

Damn it. How long had I been standing here staring into Nick's eyes?

My face flushed hot again. I lowered my eyes and accelerated my actions, resisting the urge to linger on Nick's eight-pack. I didn't slow until I got down near his belly button and noticed the swell under the sheet.

What did it mean that Nick had gotten a stiffy while I rubbed oil on his chest?

If you didn't want him to have wood, you shouldn't have given him the Woody Woodpecker up-do. At that thought, a nervous giggle tried to escape my throat, but I forced it down into my lungs and held my breath until it surrendered.

Really, though, any man could probably get turned on while getting his body lubed up by a woman. I shouldn't assume it was personal.

"Well," Helen looked at a clock that hung on the wall near the door. "You have a few extra minutes, so I'll let you go ahead with the lower portion of his body while I leave the room." She raised her eyebrows at me knowingly. "Just continue down from where you are. Be thorough."

She winked and walked out of the room, shutting the door

behind her. I stared at the thick bulge under the sheet then back at my well-oiled hands.

Holy MOLY mother of Zeus! What did Helen think she was doing, leaving me here with naked, hard, oily Nick?

"Rika."

That was Nick's voice, but I couldn't look into his face. I also couldn't keep staring at the pup tent created by his erection.

"Rika!"

I looked into his eyes, unable to unwiden mine. "Hm?"

"Hand me my robe. This is our chance to get out of here."

"Oh," I said as I glanced around for his robe. My eyes flicked back to his pelvis. "Are you sure you can—" I stopped myself before I made a blatant reference to his aroused state.

I grabbed the robe from a chair and handed it to him.

Nick

As I willed the blood back to my brain, I opened the door and allowed Rika to step in front of me. We both leaned our heads out of the room to make sure the hall was clear. Hoping Helen had taken this opportunity to spend some quality time in the bathroom, I followed Rika past the other rooms, most with their doors closed, although some were open and empty. When we reached the end of the hallway, we had to turn right or left.

Rika paused and lifted her eyes to mine.

Damn. How many times had I wanted to dive headfirst into those chocolate pools? But now they looked up at me with more anxiety and concern than they'd ever held when it was her ass on the line.

Honestly, I thought it was stupid to be here. The Kaporskys were probably in one of those rooms off the hall. And, even if we found them, what were we going to get out of them?

I could only hope, if we found them, they'd slip up. Maybe

they'd be extra relaxed from their massages and confess to murder and kidnapping.

Yeah. Right.

Rika slipped her hand in mine. Maybe it was because we were pretending to be married, but it didn't matter. Any time I got to touch her was a good time.

I squeezed her hand reassuringly and was reminded of how small her frame was. If we got into trouble with all this sleuthing, would I be able to protect her? I mean, she was smart, but some situations took brute strength to get out of and a brute she was not.

I adjusted my hand so I could lace my fingers through hers. No good reason for it. Just a primal urge that made me want to feel as connected to her as possible.

Without a word to each other, we turned left. Our minds weren't always in sync, but I liked it when they were. Made me feel like maybe...

I shook the thought from my head and focused on looking casual.

Nothing to see here. Just a perfectly normal cult couple coming to their favorite hangout to do normal cult stuff.

We passed more closed doors and ended up in a large room with four different whirlpool baths. The smell of citronella seemed to be emanating from the one closest to us. That one was empty except for the water, but the other three held a smattering of bald and white-haired people.

My eyes caught on a bald woman who was speaking to one of the white-smocked employees. "Will it be done in the next half-hour?" she asked. She seemed to be referring to a red wig on a Styrofoam head the employee was holding.

"Oh, yes," the employee said. "It's a dry clean process. It only has to stay in the cube for fifteen minutes and it will be ready to go."

"Wonderful!" the bald woman replied.

Rika leaned into my side. "None of these people are the Kaporskys," she said.

We turned around and nearly ran into another young woman in a white coat—this one was billiard-ball bald—holding a tray. "Would you two like some cleansing juice?" she asked. Rika lifted her hand.

"No!" I said too loudly. If there was one thing I'd learned about cults, it was *never* drink the Kool-Aid.

Previously, I'd seen Rika grab food with lightning fast speed and practically swallow it whole after acting like she wasn't particularly hungry. I didn't want her to perform a similar disappearing act with the Microtology juice.

But a crinkle now marred cult girl's forehead. Was she suspicious?

"No, thank you," I said in a calmer tone as Rika's hand dropped to her side. "We've been put on a very restrictive anti-parasite diet." I turned to Rika. "Did you forget, hon?"

She made an *aren't I silly* face and shrugged. "Sorry," she said to the girl. "I keep forgetting. Have you seen Steve and Valerie? We were supposed to meet them after our treatments for a late lunch at some special restaurant they like."

I glanced at Rika, my chest swelling as I took in her matter-of-fact demeanor. I couldn't have been prouder of my fake wife if she were my real wife. No one would guess by the expression on her face or the tone in her voice that she was lying out her cute little ass.

"They're in a steam room." Cult girl glanced back over her shoulder. "Number three, I think."

We thanked her and headed back down the hall.

"What's with you?" Rika whisper-yelled. "You are not the boss of what I put in my body!"

Why was she so touchy all of a sudden? "You were about to take that drink she was offering," I replied. "It's cult science 101. You never drink the Kool-Aid. Haven't you heard of Jonestown?"

Rika rolled her eyes up at me. "You're starting to sound like LeeAnne with her bar science."

Like LeeAnne? "That was below the belt."

"I wasn't going to drink it," Rika said. "But it would have been nice to have something to do with my hands. I thought carrying a drink around would make us seem more legit."

We quit talking as we approached door three. We both took in deep breaths. I wished we had more of a plan, but I knew we'd have to play this by ear and see how forthcoming the Kaporskys were.

I opened the door and was walking in behind Rika, but nearly collided with her back as she came to a dead stop. At first, all I saw was more white—white walls, white floors, and white built-in seating that had the look of one long sofa running along all four walls. Then I saw what Rika had seen.

Steve and Valerie Kaporsky were there, lounging comfortably, their feet on white footstools, their eyes closed. Their towels were underneath them and both were naked as the day they were born. They were also smooth as the day they were born, each apparently having had every follicle of hair removed from their bodies, except for the white hair on Valerie's head.

My eyes caught on her breasts, which wouldn't have been bad for implants, except for the disturbing fact that her nipples pointed in and up, making them appear cross-eyed. The couple looked to be in their forties. Steve's belly had the beginning of a middle-aged pooch.

I nudged Rika forward so I could close the door behind us. It made a clicking sound when it shut and they opened their eyes and looked at us.

"Oh my God! Are you Steve and Valerie Kaporsky?" Rika asked in a high-pitched voice I'd never heard her use before. I couldn't help but wince, since the tone reminded me of my last two wives.

Both the Kaporskys smiled indulgently at her like they were

the royal family and she was one of their star struck subjects. "We are," Valerie replied.

"Is it all right that we're in here?" Rika asked. "We're new and we didn't know—"

"It's fine." Steve waved off her misgivings. "Sit down. We're always glad to meet new members."

The Kaporskys were sitting on the long part of the couch, near the corner where it made an L. We followed his gesture and sat on the shorter side.

I noticed Rika's gaze flitting to Steve's crotch. It darted away, then returned and held for several seconds.

My jaw clenched at the idea of her staring at another man's junk. Sure, Steve was bigger than average, but I had him beat by at least a few centimeters.

I tapped her as discreetly as I could with my elbow to get her horn-dog eyes to look somewhere else.

Anywhere else.

CHAPTER FOURTEEN

Rika

I felt Nick's elbow dig into my ribs and realized my eyes were still stuck on Steve's penis. There was something very wrong with it. Maybe he suffered from a birth defect. I wondered if it was still functional. If Steve's penis didn't work, maybe that's why Valerie needed to go to other men, like Alberto, for sex.

"Go ahead and get comfortable," Steve said. "Feel free to take your robes off."

Nick looked at me as if he was fine with it if I was.

Eek!

I stared back at him. *No fucking way*, I tried to communicate with my eyes.

The only thing more embarrassing than private nudity with Nick right now would be public nudity with Nick, the Kaporskys and whoever else wandered into the room.

"No, thanks. We're doing Hot Sauna," I said to Steve. "It's sort of like hot yoga."

Valerie sat up straighter, clearly interested. "But the sauna is already hot."

"Yes, but with *Hot* Sauna..." I ad-libbed, "...it's easier for impurities to leave your body because they have the terry cloth to absorb into. I read an article about it in an online science journal."

"Really?" Valerie said. "You'll have to send me a link to that. It sounds like something we could use."

"Sure," I replied. "The only thing you have to make sure of is that you're wearing sanitized, absorbent material, preferably white so it can be bleached."

The Kaporskys both nodded as if that made sense to them. Up until now, I'd assumed they were con artists, but maybe they were actually true believers.

I glanced at Nick and saw that he was working hard to keep a straight face.

"Oh, wow." I pressed my hand to my chest as if I'd suddenly recalled upsetting news. "I heard about the sous chef at the VIP Center. I'm so sorry for your loss. Were you close to him?"

I thought I saw genuine sadness cloud Valerie's gaze. "Well, he was an employee of the center, not a member of the church..." Her eyes drifted off like she was seeing a scene replayed on the white wall behind us. "But he was a charming man. He'd worked for us for over two years and, well...it was a shock." Her voice shook on the last few words.

Steve put his hand over hers comfortingly. I wondered if he knew his wife had slept with the man in question. "Alberto Viera will be missed," he said somberly.

Nick leaned in. "I guess that missing chef must be the killer, huh?"

"Diego?" Steve said. "Absolutely not. He's one of the finest chefs I've ever known."

"And a wonderful person," Valerie added. "Everyone loves and respects him. He's on the verge of becoming a member."

"Of Microtology?" I cried before I could get hold of myself. I adjusted my tone. "That's great!" But I noticed Steve had been giving his wife a silencing stare since her last comment.

She pressed her lips together.

"Diego is not the killer," Steve said as if that was that.

I gave what I hoped was a *no big deal* shrug. "Then, where is he?"

"I'm sure he just needs some time to himself after what happened to Al," Steve replied. "They'd become good friends."

"Most people are killed by someone close to them," Nick said. "Family, friends..."

"Well..." Valerie rolled her eyes. "I wouldn't put it past his wife to have a contract out on him."

"Val, maybe you need some clarification juice," Steve said half-jokingly.

I remembered that a central tenant of Microtology was about not speaking negatively of others. If you did, it meant you were "infested" with a microbe or parasite that had taken control of your personality. So far, though, I hadn't found Microtologists to be any less likely than a non-Microtologist when it came to bad-mouthing.

"I still keep wondering about that chef," I said.

"Surely, he would have turned up by now if he were innocent and alive," Nick added.

"Oh, Diego's fine," Valerie insisted. "He's getting his head on straight, that's all." She glanced at Steve.

Steve closed his eyes as if he was finished talking and wanted some quiet time. Valerie leaned back against the wall.

I felt like we'd gotten all we could out of them, which wasn't much. "We'd better get going," I said. "My husband," I tilted my head toward Nick, "has a defoliation appointment to get to."

Nick and I stood and headed for the door.

"Don't forget to send me that link," Valerie called. "My email is on the website."

"No problem," I said as I headed out the door.

"I'm not sure how productive that was," I murmured to Nick as we walked to the massage room to get our clothes.

He scowled at me. "Maybe that's because you couldn't take your eyes off Steve's package."

"I know!" I replied. "What do you think was wrong with it?"

He narrowed his eyes and shook his head as if I wasn't making any sense. "Wrong with what?"

"His penis. It didn't look right."

"It was a regular uncircumcised penis."

"Oh." Heat crept up my neck. It was times like this I was glad for all that pigment in my skin. I'd hate for Nick to know I was blushing.

He stopped in the middle of the hall. "You've never seen an uncircumcised penis?" He said it like he was having trouble believing it.

"No," I replied irritably. "Why would I?"

"You mean none of your boyfriends...?"

In the silence that hung between us, I recalled that Nick was ignorant of two major facts of my life. One, that I could have been a stand-in for Patrick from SpongeBob SquarePants during my teenage years. And, two, that I had only seen one penis, the one belonging to my previous boyfriend of two years, Brandtt, who I'd started dating at twenty-two.

Nick was still staring at me as if waiting for an explanation.

Great. I did *not* want Nick to know how inexperienced I was. When I thought about it, I realized he'd had more wives than I'd had lovers.

That was depressing.

"I haven't seen a lot of penises," I said. "I didn't go out a lot when I was young. My grandmother was old-fashioned and protective."

Maybe that wasn't the only reason I hadn't had a lot of boyfriends, but my grandmother was old-fashioned in a lot of ways and very protective. I was certain that, even if I had been asked out, she would have kept me from dating as long as possible, especially after what happened to my mother.

Oh, my God! For the first time, it occurred to me that my grandmother might have kept me fat for that purpose, thinking no one would kidnap, rape and murder me if I wasn't fuckable.

Hm... I tried to decide how I felt about that.

Nick stared at me for an extra moment as if he needed time to digest the information that I was twenty-four and practically a nun.

"Anyway," he finally said. "I thought the run-in with the Kaporskys was pretty productive."

"How?"

"They didn't flinch, even a little, when we brought up your dad and even more importantly..." He paused like he was delivering one of his jury arguments. "They talked about him in the present tense, both of them, repeatedly."

I scrolled back through my memory of the last fifteen minutes. "They did sound sure he was fine. Like they knew where he was, even."

Nick nodded slowly, lifting his brows at me.

"They have him."

"Yeah, Paprika... I think they do."

Nick

I glanced in the rearview mirror and saw the silver Nissan, two cars behind us. The same car that had been right behind us a couple of blocks from the Clarification Center, and one lane over, one car back a few minutes ago.

"We may have picked up a tail," I said. I opened my mouth again to warn Rika not to turn around, but saw it was unnecessary. She had flipped her visor mirror down, then checked the outside mirror on the passenger side.

I couldn't help but smile. She was pretty damn awesome.

"The silver one, two cars back?"

"Yeah." I checked the rearview again. "How'd you figure it out so fast?" There were four lanes full of cars going in our direction.

"Car body language," she replied. "Instead of being in line with the car in front of it, it's off to the left so the driver can keep us in view."

Traffic had come to a full stop. I turned and smiled at her.

"What?" she said.

"You're still pretty smart for a hot chick."

She chuckled and the genuine smile she aimed at me lodged in my chest and ignited a warmth that spread gradually through my body. Not just the hot attraction I'd felt for a lot of women, her included. It was a different feeling. The one that scares the shit out of a guy who's been married three times and has sworn off serious relationships with women.

Thank God she hadn't asked about what I was up to when she was massaging me at the Clarification Center. I don't know what got into me. I was lying there, trying not to get a hard-on from the idea that Rika's hands were sliding over my scalp—yeah, my scalp. Who knew that was an erogenous zone?—and I couldn't stop staring at her legs. Maybe because they were the only parts of her I could see with my face in the massage table cradle. Normally I was either staring into her big chocolate-colored eyes or checking out her ass when she wasn't looking.

But on the massage table, I was suddenly fascinated by her legs, which looked completely naked from my vantage point. And when she started massaging my head, I was overcome by the urge to touch her.

Before I knew what I was doing, my fingers were sliding up her smooth calf. Then she squealed, and I got this weird sense of satisfaction because I'd found a ticklish spot behind her knee.

Previously, I'd found ticklish spots on a woman annoying, the laughter getting in the way of the mood. But the idea of lying in bed with Rika, hearing her squeal and giggle sounded kind of nice.

My mind rewound to what she'd said about not seeing a lot of penises.

It was hard to imagine a girl as gorgeous as she was being so inexperienced with men.

And she'd had such an uncomfortable look on her face when she told me, like there was more to the story she was holding back. Some moments with her, it felt like we'd known each other forever. Others, she seemed to have this huge load of stuff she was carrying around that she wouldn't share with me, and that bothered me.

I mentally slapped my brain around a few times. I was here on serious business. The most serious business there was—so serious, people seemed to be following us because of it.

I wondered if Steve and Valerie sent someone after us. That would be pretty quick, though. We'd only spoken to them a few minutes ago. But maybe Suzee mentioned us to them or to the —supposedly grieving—Jason Kim. Or, the Microtologists might have tracked down LeeAnne's car from her midnight shenanigans with Rika, then found out who lived at the address.

I turned right, then right again into a residential neighborhood. After pulling up to the curb, I checked the GPS for alternate routes. Then, I watched my rearview mirror for our suspected tail.

"I think you lost them," Rika said.

"If that's all it took, they're not very good at this." I hoped they caught up to me when she wasn't with me. If there was only the driver in the car like there was now, I could confront him. If he had a passenger with him, I could at least get a plate number.

She was staring at the pavement in front of us, but I knew she was deep in thought. Sometimes I wished I could climb in her head and poke around. I had a feeling there were thousands of interesting thoughts in there I wasn't privy to.

Then it hit me that I'd never wanted to get into a woman's

mind before I met Rika. Into their pants, yes. All the time. But into their heads...

I skimmed through all the women I'd known and still couldn't recall caring much what they were thinking, other than wondering if they were going to let me into said pants in the near future.

Damn. This felt like an epiphany, but an unwelcome one, to be sure. Was I some superficial, emotionally distant jerk?

I'd thought I was a pretty good guy who'd made some mistakes in my choices where women were concerned. But what if it wasn't the women? What if it was me?

Then, I remembered how worried I was about what was going through DeeAnne's head after my dad died, but she was my little sister and I wasn't sure that counted.

If I was an asshole, Rika would figure it out sooner or later. She was smart and observant. Hell, maybe she'd realized it since I'd come to town.

"Am I a bad guy?"

Fuck. I'd said that aloud.

Rika's head turned slowly. She stared at me like she didn't think she'd heard right.

"Did I blank out and miss a conversation you were trying to have with me?" she asked. "Because otherwise, that was way out of left field."

Wow. She didn't answer the question. Maybe she did think I was a jerk.

I shook my head. "No. I was thinking and ended up thinking aloud."

"About being a bad person?"

"Yeah." I waved my hand dismissively, hoping she'd let it go.

"Nick, we knew each other for a few minutes before you took me in and put your life on the line for me," she replied. "And, now, I called you and you found the first available flight, drove all the way to Houston and flew here, just like that." She snapped her fingers. "I'll fight anyone who says you're a bad person even if it's you."

"Well, if you call me out, I get to choose the mode of fighting."

"And what would you choose?"

"Naked wrestling," I said. That was an easy one.

She burst out laughing. "Naked wrestling? That's not even a thing." She looked into my eyes and I had that drowning sensation again. Problem was, I didn't want to save myself. "Is it?"

"Sure, it is," I replied. "Bing it." I was certain if you typed "naked wrestling" into a search engine you'd find some naked people wrestling even though I'd never searched that particular phrase.

Rika shrugged. "It wouldn't be a fair fight. You're a lot bigger than I am, so all you'd have to do is get on top once and you'd win."

The image that sparked in my mind made it hard to suck in a full breath. "I'm pretty sure we'd both be winners in that scenario," I replied. "No matter who was on top."

I watched her swallow hard before her eyes snapped back to the street. "We'd better um...get...go," she stammered.

I chuckled at her profile, but she wouldn't make eye contact. Still, I couldn't keep the smile from taking over my face.

I'd gotten Paprika Anise all hot and bothered...and boy did I like it.

CHAPTER FIFTEEN

Rika

The next morning, I was in the shower rinsing the conditioner out of my hair, thinking about what we were going to do today. We didn't have a lot of likely suspects left to talk to.

As casual as the Kaporskys were, they had to be involved in this somehow, but it was hard to imagine either one of them as a crazed sous chef stabber. And there was something worldly and sophisticated about Valerie, whether she was photographed at a gala or sitting naked in a sauna. I couldn't imagine her wearing the cheap necklace.

Jemima Harte was at the top of our list to speak to today. She was young and possibly in love with Alberto. If she found out he had other women...

Or maybe she didn't even know he was married...

Plus, she was young and apparently wore her heart on her sleeve, so it was easier to imagine her being sentimental enough to wear a cheap heart necklace.

By all accounts, Alberto was quite the player. Maybe he gave her the trinket to make her believe she was more than just another conquest. Maybe she found out otherwise and went to the VIP Center restaurant to confront him, and threw it at him.

Nick and I had spent last night in my grandmother's living room on our lap tops, trying to track down Jemima's address. While Nick was trying to do it the hard way, by comparing drone photos of her house and the surrounding area with some Google Earth maps, I got on Twitter and tracked down a link to a site where her fans had posted her address.

After about fifteen minutes, I surprised Nick with it. Then, I taunted him with comments about working "smarter."

But Nick hadn't seemed bothered that I beat him at all. Instead, he gave me that warm look he always gave me at times like this. An affectionate expression that said he liked how my mind worked in a way no man had ever seemed to appreciate before.

Thinking about it this morning made me feel all melty inside, the same way it did last night. That was until my Tía Madi, who had been sitting sideways on the sofa, as usual, poked me with her toe and said to Nick, "Should I leave you two alone?"

So embarrassing!

And it would have been worse if she'd known about the ache I felt in my chest when he left. I flipped and flopped in bed, trying not to let myself think the worst about my father. But each time I forced my brain from that topic, I saw Nick "wrestling" stupid Marla in a king-sized hotel bed.

Ick!

Needless to say, I was tired and stressed this morning which meant I kept thinking about those little gingerbread pigs the Mexican bakery dropped off fresh at Eddie's every morning.

I got out of the shower, pulled on my underthings and Ravenclaw t-shirt—blue with silver letters—and was about to blow dry my hair when I heard pounding on the front door.

Nick was early! A thrill shimmied down my back as I pulled my jeans on and told myself not to be so excited. His coming early only meant he had a good work ethic, especially considering there was no pay involved in this job. It certainly didn't mean he couldn't wait to see me again.

I realized my grandmother had gone to the grocery store and I was the only one home.

I turned and ran to the living room so fast, the momentum slammed my body into the front door.

Great. Now Nick knew I was running like a maniac to get to him, which I definitely did not want him to know.

I took a second to catch my breath and re-arrange my facial expression before I opened the door.

When I did, Detectives Winchell and Hertz were standing on the front porch looking so smug, my heart did a flip and landed somewhere in my lower abdomen.

Had they arrested my father? But if they did, why would they come here in person and tell me?

"Hi there, Rika, I'm Detective—" I cut Winchell off. "I remember who you are." As far as I was concerned, L.A. homicide was the enemy as long as they were trying to railroad my father into jail. "I prefer Ms. Martín," I said in an uppity tone.

Normally, I didn't prefer "Ms. Martín" to "Rika," but if I had to call them by their titles and surnames, then they could show me the same respect.

"Alright, *Ms.* Martín," Detective Hertz said, her weird green eyes happy dancing. "We have this warrant..." She whipped it out of the pocket of her cheap navy slacks "...to search the premises."

"A search warrant?" I repeated. "Based on what evidence?"

"Doesn't matter," Detective Winchell focused his beady black eyes on me. "What matters is, the judge believed it was enough to warrant a warrant." He chuckled, clearly impressed with his little play on words.

That was when I realized there were three more police cars in front of the house and several uniformed cops were milling around in the yard, chatting with each other.

There was no way I could keep them out if they had a warrant. My grandmother was going to be super pissed about them handling her belongings, but I had more important things to worry about.

Letting my shoulders drop, I tried to look as resigned as possible to the search. "Whatever." I shrugged like a grounded teenager.

The detectives seemed to buy it. They turned, walked over to the uniforms and started issuing orders. I sprinted to my room, locked the door, then grabbed my laptop external battery and cord and threw them into my backpack. If they took my computer as evidence, they'd know Julian had been helping me and he could lose his job. Besides, I'd had my gear taken away last summer by the cops and damn if I was going to let that happen again.

Where was my phone?

I remembered I had it with me when I went to borrow some hand lotion from the upstairs bathroom.

Damn it!

I unlocked my bedroom door and peeked out. No one seemed to have entered the house yet. Still holding onto my backpack, I raced to the stairs. Unfortunately, I tried to take them two at a time and tripped, falling on my right knee.

Ouch!

I knew from previous experience that my legs weren't long enough to take the stairs two at a time, but some nutty part of my brain was convinced I would grow into it one day.

I'd barely made it into the upstairs bathroom and found my phone before I heard Detective Hertz's voice downstairs.

Tiptoeing across the wood floor to the pink floral area rug in my grandmother's bedroom, I locked the door behind me.

I ran to Lita's window and opened it. The window looked out over the side yard and since we were on a corner, I could escape without the cops seeing me.

Hmm... I examined the palm tree outside my grandmother's window. It wasn't ideal for climbing, not that I'd had a lot of experience climbing trees. There were no limbs to hold onto, only the nubby remains of old fronds that had long since fallen off.

Footsteps thumped up the stairs and I heard officers talking to each other in the hall.

Pulling the backpack straps over my shoulders, I climbed out the window and sat on the ledge.

The tree was close enough so I could touch it with my fingertips, but not so close that I could just wrap my arms around it and climb down.

I needed to jump, while wearing my backpack and throw my arms around the trunk. If I missed, I could land on the cement walkway that ran around the perimeter of the house.

A fall from the second story wouldn't kill me, but it would hurt like hell. I might even break something important, like an arm or an ankle, or worse, my laptop.

Someone jiggled the doorknob. "This one's locked," a deep voice said. "We're going to have to..." The voice faded as if the officer had turned and walked away. But I knew I didn't have long.

I looked down at the walkway again, imagining myself sprawled on it with blood oozing from my head. My Jilly Crane counselor had always told me to visualize myself succeeding, and I had lost an awful lot of pounds taking her advice.

I imagined myself flying gracefully like Hedwig the owl, catching the trunk effortlessly in my wings...or, um, arms. Bracing the soles of my sneakers on the outside of the wall, I prepared to fly.

The sound of a fist pounding on my grandmother's door startled me a split second before I'd committed to the jump.

I half jumped, half jerked, off the window sill. I stretched my arms toward the trunk, but caught it several inches farther down than I'd planned. Then gravity caused me to slide down a bit before my feet found some woody frond fragments to perch on.

This left me with bark burn I could feel on my face, inner thighs and torso.

I managed to climb down the rest of the way without doing any more damage to myself, except for some scratches on the inside of my arms.

Sneaking to the corner of the house, I peeked into the front yard. Two of the cops were still standing out there, gesturing with fake basketball throws like they were discussing a Lakers game.

Damn. My car was parked in the driveway a few yards from them.

Detective Winchell strode out to the front yard. "Did you see Rika Martín?" he asked the officers.

"Who?" the uniforms said in unison.

"The woman who came to the door." They stared at him blankly. "Hispanic...young? About five-three?"

Five-four-and-a-half! I wanted to scream at him, but didn't for obvious reasons.

The uniforms were still looking at him like they had no clue what he was talking about.

"Attractive..." Winchell tried again. "Slender..."

I closed my eyes and inhaled the word, savoring the sound of it.

Slennnderrrrr...

He was totally forgiven for getting my height wrong, but not for calling my dad a murderer, of course.

"Fuck!" Winchell said. "Did you two even graduate from the academy? Do you think this is a fucking field trip?"

The two officers looked at each other, then mumbled "no, sir" in unison.

"How about you pull your heads out of your asses, shut your traps, and observe what's going on around you.?"

"Got it," one of the cops replied. "Shut traps...observe around us."

"This..." Detective Winchell pointed at my Honda, "...is her car. Make sure she doesn't drive off in it without talking to me first."

Crap! That meant I was on foot, at least until I could get someone to pick me up. I headed down the street that ran along the side of the house.

As I rounded the corner onto another street that ran parallel to my grandmother's, I touched the screen until Nick's name popped up. I pressed "call."

That's when the low sound of a car motor caused me to look over my shoulder, expecting to find either a car I didn't recognize or a cop car. What I saw was a silver Nissan.

Correction. *The* silver Nissan.

The driver was wearing a hat and sunglasses so I couldn't ID him but it was definitely the same car that was following me and Nick yesterday.

Once the driver realized I'd noticed him, he sped up, passed me, then squealed to a stop right in front of me. The driver and front passenger doors flew open.

Holy mother of—

I turned and ran as my brain tried to come up with a benign reason two men who were following me would suddenly jump out of their car.

Nope. Abduction was the only thing that made sense.

My mother had been abducted.

My father, I was certain, had been abducted.

But this was one family tradition I would *not* be carrying on—not if I could help it, anyway.

There was some yelling of instructions and confusion behind me. After passing several houses, I looked back.

The tires of the Nissan were screeching as the driver made a three-point turn.

The other man—also in a ball cap and sunglasses—was out of the car and headed in my direction on foot.

I wouldn't be able to outrun him for long, so I needed to

outsmart him. I mentally searched my internal map of this block. There was one house up ahead that had fallen into disrepair years ago and stayed that way while the now dead owner's relatives fought over what to do with his assets, since owning real estate outright in L.A. was like owning a pot of gold.

Meanwhile, a broken latch caused the gate to hang open limply. Through that opening, anyone passing could see missing boards along the back fence.

I shoulder-checked again. The car was turned around. The guy on foot had gained some ground on me, but he was glancing back at the Nissan like he wanted to ride.

I took this opportunity to duck into the side of a house, two lots before my target. I skirted around the homes, staying close to the walls where there was shade much of the way from decades old trees.

I looked back once more. The Nissan was coming to a stop, the runner huffing his way to the passenger door to get back in.

While they were distracting each other—I hoped—I dashed out from my hiding place and raced to the abandoned house without looking back. I ran into the back yard, then pulled the gate closed so it wouldn't be so obvious where I'd gone. When I got to the back fence, I found two boards near each other missing with one rickety board in between still attached.

I pushed it, but it didn't budge. I grasped the next available boards to the right and left and leaned back as far as I could. Flexing until my sole was flat, I bent my knee and smashed my foot into the picket's mid-point.

The board exploded as my foot crashed through. I lifted my other foot over the cross support to the other side. I was now in the yard that backed up to the abandoned house. Luckily, the owners of this one hadn't bothered to finish off the part of their fencing where the gate would go. I hurried across the yard and emerged on a new street.

By the time I made the next corner, some of the initial adrenaline burst was fading and I was losing steam. I allowed myself to walk while I pressed my fingers into the stitch in my side.

Seconds later, I heard a motor, purring slowly along as if searching for someone and knew the Nissan had chosen the right path. I willed my feet to move faster, but I didn't have the energy left to keep outrunning a car indefinitely. Breathing in through my nose, out through my mouth like I was on a treadmill, I rounded the corner thinking how much heavier my backpack had gotten since I left home.

I looked ahead, trying to come up with another plan...

And saw that I was running toward seven—no make that eight—*cholos*.

CHAPTER SIXTEEN

Rika

So...

One of the reasons people in my neighborhood had stuck with the name *Alemania* or "*Ale*" for the twelve or so blocks around Lita's house was because they didn't want to be associated with some nearby areas that were crime infested. From what my grandmother had said, the gangs had tried to recruit in our neighborhood many years ago, but my grandparents and other residence stood up to them, adopting a zero tolerance for suspicious activities.

Lita always said she didn't escape the dreaded Colombian drug cartels to come to the U.S. and be tormented by a bunch of punk kids. Instead of acting fearful of gang retaliation, they formed a hard-core neighborhood watch.

I even heard stories about my grandmother rushing out of the house and throwing whatever she held in her hands at pimps and dealers when they were stupid enough to try to move onto our block. Since she spent a lot of time in the kitchen, the things she happened to have in her hands were cookware.

Those run-ins had become neighborhood lore over the years.

I could only assume the parts about her hitting said ne'er do wells—one in the back of the head with a frying pan, and one right between the eyes with Mrs. Ruíz's stone *molcajete*—were exaggerated. My grandmother was brave and tough and strong, but the combination of strength and aim it would take to do what the stories said she did just didn't seem possible, scientifically speaking.

Regardless, the *Ale* resident's hard line on criminals had worked. The gangs had never gotten a foothold in our neighborhood and stayed away from our blocks. As kids, we were taught to avoid the areas controlled by gangs or we'd be punished like we were in the gang.

My Tía Madi liked to claim that most of the kids weren't as afraid of their own parents as they were of my grandmother, and that some parents even used her as the boogeyman, as in, "If you don't stay out of trouble, Mrs. Delacruz is going to get you!"

So, anyway, I didn't know gang members and they didn't know me. And as I saw the curious and predatory expressions on the eight *cholos*' faces, I questioned whether I'd be better off getting abducted by the men in the Nissan.

I slowed from a full run to a jog as I measured my options. The gangsters would likely take my backpack and all its contents. That would be inconvenient, but not the worst-case scenario, since I'd been using the cloud to automatically back up my files. I still used the external drive out of habit but any data I had should be recoverable even if they took it.

Mere seconds stood between me and a decision one way or the other as my brain continued its risk calculations. Statistically, a person is supposed to be in much greater danger of being murdered if they get into the car with a criminal, and I had no idea what the Nissan goons would do to me. But with no one else out on the street to witness this, what would the *cholos* do to me?

I heard the Nissan's motor again and knew it would be

rounding the corner at any moment. A half-baked idea sparked in my mind, but could it possibly work?

Mentally crossing my fingers, I picked up the pace, running full tilt at the banger who appeared to be the head *cholo*. His head was shaved. He had a moustache and an oddly menacing strip of facial hair growing vertically, directly under the middle of his bottom lip, so long that the hair from his chin swayed with the breeze. As I got closer, I could see names tattooed gothic-style in black ink on his arms and on one side of his neck. On the other side was a portrait of Jesus.

"Hey, *mami*, what's your hurry?" he asked as he reached out toward me. I felt his boys closing in around me as my steps slowed. I stopped dead in front of him, grabbing his biceps with both hands as my body collided with his. He fell back a step then steadied himself.

I looked up at him with all the intensity I could muster. "They're coming!" I shouted into his face as I pointed in the direction I came from. "Silver Nissan!"

He narrowed his eyes at me, clearly suspicious of my game. In the split second I had to think, I decided switching to Spanish might be a good idea since these guys probably had mothers and grandmothers who made their most serious warnings in Spanish.

"*Ellos vienen aquí!*" I cried as I pointed behind me again.

It worked. The head gang-banger let go of me and started barking out orders in Spanglish. His minions began pulling various weapons—mostly guns—from their jacket pockets or the backs of their jeans. Some had a gun for each hand. They dispersed suddenly, jumping into the drivers' seats of several cars and re-parking them sideways to block off the road.

Then they got out and squatted down, using the cars as cover while they waited.

Holy mother of Zeus! I hoped whoever was in the silver Nissan were very bad people. These gangbangers had the firepower of a small army.

Once it was clear they had forgotten about me, I ran. And when I say I ran, I mean all-out, full-tilt running like my life depended on it, which it might because those *cholos* were going to be looking for me when they realized they were not defending themselves against a rival gang.

When the gunfire erupted, though, I couldn't help but look back.

The driver of the Nissan put the pedal to the metal when the first shot went off, but the car was hit with several pinging rounds before it passed out of sight.

The gang-bangers looked at each other questioningly. I heard their raised voices calling out "Qué pasó?" and "What the fuck, bro?" and the very relevant, "Who the fuck were we shooting at?"

I'd hoped I'd have more time for a getaway before the fact that they shot up a car for no known reason dawned on them. Unfortunately, just because you're a *cholo*, doesn't mean you're an idiot.

I ducked behind a parked car, pretty sure they'd be looking for me at any second. I lay flat on my stomach, watching from underneath the car to see what they would do next.

They met up in the middle of the road to pow wow, and one of them pointed in my general direction, but another one pointed in the direction the Nissan had gone.

I couldn't hear what they were saying—maybe arguing about whether to come after me or go after the Nissan—but I didn't want to wait around to find out. I checked the yard nearest me for cover, then rolled over, jumped up and ran until I was behind a thick palm. None of the bangers noticed me, so I ran a few more yards and crouched on the other side of some shrubs.

Just as I was trying to peek through them, I heard a motor right next to me. Then somehow the various parts of my brain got confused and started working against each other. My feet turned away from the car to run while my head turned toward the street to see if the men in the Silver Nissan were coming after me. Instead, I saw LeeAnne idling near me in her old Trans Am.

At that point, the parts of my brain tried to sync up and turn my legs back around. But instead of turning back and heading for LeeAnne's car, I somehow ended up crashing through the shrubs and falling face down on the lawn.

Obviously, your weight wasn't the only reason for your P.E. issues, some snarky part of my brain pointed out.

I did *not* have time to recap my disastrous childhood and asked that part of my brain to please join the other parts in helping me get away from this damn bush.

"*Mira*!" I heard someone yell, followed by a bunch of other yelling in two languages. Since "*mira*" meant "look," I figured someone had seen me.

"Oh, my lord! Rika, come on!" LeeAnne cried from the driver's side window. Her car was facing the gang members so she had a clear view of them, including a guy with the word "*muerte*" tattooed in a gothic font on his forehead. I hoped LeeAnne didn't know the meaning of that Spanish word or she might take off without me.

I managed to pull my feet from the other side of the shrub, but my backpack was still tangled. I couldn't reach the branches that were holding me captive, so I thrashed around like a wild animal until I got loose. Then I raced to LeeAnne's car as a couple of the *cholos* came at us on foot while the others ran to their cars.

I made it around to the passenger's side, grabbed the handle, flung the door open and threw myself in.

As I shrugged out of my backpack, I became aware of my body for the first time since I'd left the house. Every muscle seemed to be pained or strained in some way.

"How did you find me?" I asked.

"Nick said you butt-dialed him and it sounded like you were in trouble. When I saw the cops at the house, I figured you were on foot."

LeeAnne's eyes scanned me top to bottom. "Did those guys do that to you?"

I glanced down at the dirt and blood, plus one sprig of leaves hanging from the bottom of my hair. "No, not exactly—" I began. But when I looked up, LeeAnne's eye were big as saucers.

"Jesus Christ Superstar!" she whispered in a shocked tone, quieter than I'd ever heard her use before.

My eyes followed hers to the head *cholo* who was walking toward us with his right arm extended, a gun in his hand, turned sideways, gangsta style. "Seat belt, Rika," LeeAnne said. I guess I didn't move fast enough because she snapped, "Seat belt! Seat belt! Seat belt!" and took her foot off the brake.

I grabbed the belt and snapped it into place. When I looked up, the *cholo* was still coming at us with the gun aimed right at the windshield. I expected LeeAnne to try to turn the car around, but instead she aimed it directly at the gang leader.

"Shit, LeeAnne!" I cried.

Her eyes didn't leave her target. "He wants to play chicken?" I could tell the question was rhetorical because she said it in a voice Clint Eastwood would use to ask you to make his day. "Oh... I can play chicken." She mashed the accelerator.

"But—" was the only word I managed to get out. In fact, it was the only word stuttering through my brain—*but, but, but, but, but...*

We were suddenly racing straight at him, and he didn't look like he was going to give in. I mean, he'd probably done a lot of bad things, but he hadn't done anything to us, and I couldn't imagine how we'd explain running over him to the police who were only a few blocks away.

"Lee—" I began, but it was too late. We were going to hit him head on. Then, one shot pierced the air as he flung himself out of the way. Since he'd shot while on the move, we didn't even take a hit.

"Yeah, I thought so!" LeeAnne said as she gave him the finger just to rub it in. He couldn't have seen it, but some of his boys certainly did as their cars screeched past us, squealing tires as they turned around to give chase.

I nearly said something about not pissing them off more, then realized it didn't matter. I'd already duped them into an altercation that had nothing to do with them and they were out to get me.

LeeAnne, appearing completely calm and in control, rounded the corner fast enough to throw me against the door of the car. "Sorry, hon," she said as she checked the rearview.

I realized we were headed toward the 405. "Not the freeway!" I said. "It's nearly a.m. rush hour." Actually, most of the hours of the day in Los Angeles were like rush hour in other places, but rush hour in L.A. meant you could easily be stuck in one spot on the freeway for long enough to be murdered several times over.

LeeAnne's phone sounded. "Check and see if it's Nick," she said.

I'd totally forgotten about starting to call Nick until LeeAnne reminded me, but, in my defense, I did have a lot going on.

I checked the phone. It was Nick, so I touched the screen. "Hello?"

"Where are you?' he asked. "I'm at your grandmother's house and there are cops everywhere."

One of the bangers came up behind us in a classic low-rider Chevy, clearly threatening to hit us. LeeAnne punched the break.

A strangled "EEEEEEEK!" came out of my mouth as we were hit hard from the back.

I heard metal crunching and tires squealing. When I turned to see what had happened, the front of the car behind us was smashed, the fender bent in against a front tire. The car behind it appeared to have hit it from behind.

"Another one bites the dust!" LeeAnne said gleefully. "Guess they weren't counting on my custom steel bumper." She smiled victoriously.

"Who are you?" I asked, suddenly wondering if LeeAnne's down-home charm was a cover for her real occupation as a female James Bond.

LeeAnne cackled. "Those punk kids aren't gonna get the best of us!"

"Rika! Damn it, Rika!" I looked down and realized Nick was in my lap. Well, Nick wasn't, but his voice was. I snatched the phone up and put it to my ear.

"Nick?"

"What the fuck is going on?"

"We're being chased by gangbangers."

"Wha—" he began, then as my words sank in, he said, "Where are you?"

"A few blocks away."

"Well come back this way," he said. "They won't mess with you with all these cops here."

"Yeah, but..." I noticed LeeAnne's body language and checked over my shoulder. Two of the other gangster cars had come around the corner. "I ran off when the cops came because I didn't want them to get my computer. Even if they don't have a warrant for LeeAnne's car, seeing us racing through the streets with gang members on our tail might count as probable cause."

"Send me your GPS link," he said.

I clicked into an app that let Nick see our progress on a map. "Done!"

"Okay, watch for the Yukon. When you see me coming at you, swerve as far left as possible. Meet me at that used car place outside your neighborhood."

"LeeAnne, Nick says—" I began.

"We don't need his help," LeeAnne cried. "We're doing just fine." She bent over the phone, yelled, "Girl Power!" into it, and mashed the accelerator again.

"Fuck!" Nick said. "I'm on my way."

Two shots rang out. We didn't get hit, but I could see the

gunman in the passenger side of the car. "He's about to shoot again!" I said.

LeeAnne was already on it, yanking the steering wheel to the right and to the left to make it harder for them to aim. My body rolled to the door, then back towards her.

"LeeAnne," I said firmly. "When we see Nick coming, you're supposed to swerve left as hard as you can."

She turned the wheel drastically again as I braced myself on the door. Multiple shots rang out.

"LeeAnne!"

"Yeah, yeah, fine," she said.

Seconds later, tires screeched and Nick was rounding the corner and coming right at us. LeeAnne stopped swerving and headed straight for the Yukon.

I hoped she was onboard with the plan because I didn't think she or Nick would accept being the "chicken" if they were playing for real.

"Left, LeeAnne!" I raised my left hand and pointed, just in case she didn't know her right from her left.

"I heard you," she said. "I know what I'm doing."

The vehicles were nearing each other and gangsters were still on our tail. I envisioned the horrific multi-vehicle accident we were going to die in.

Right when we were about to collide, my eyes slammed shut, LeeAnne swerved to the left and, apparently, Nick plowed straight through.

I turned and opened my eyes in time to see the Yukon hit one car in the front left fender, forcing the vehicle to the right, where another was traveling next to it. Tires squealed and there were some scraping and crunching sounds.

The gangster's cars were all jacked up. The one he'd hit directly had a bent wheel. Nick backed up enough to disentangle himself from the wreck. Then he put the truck in Drive and passed them.

However, the cholo in the low-rider car to the far right started backing up, apparently not out of commission. Nick put the Yukon in reverse and squealed backwards, forcing the car onto the curb and over a large shrub. The motor kept revving, but the car no longer had all its wheels on the ground and was stuck in the bushes.

At that point, Nick waved us on, following behind us. LeeAnne drove to the edge of the neighborhood, avoiding my grandmother's street, which we presumed was still full of cops.

She pulled into the used car lot Nick had mentioned and parked. "Hell, yeah!" she cried. "That's what happens when you mess with LeeAnne Barr!"

"Hell, no!" I heard Nick's voice coming from my phone as he pulled up next to us. "LeeAnne Barr, I will tan your hide if I ever catch you driving like that again!"

LeeAnne rolled her eyes.

"Don't roll your eyes at me!"

She leaned up and looked past me at Nick in his Yukon. "You can't see me roll my eyes from there!"

"Yet, I know you did it," he replied.

LeeAnne hunched over and screeched into my lap, "Nicholas Bernard Owen, you are not my daddy!"

Nick jerked the phone away from his head as if her voice had just punctured his eardrum. His face looked murderous.

"Maybe we should lock the car doors for now," LeeAnne said. "Until he's cooled down."

And, despite the cops and the *cholos* and the guns, I burst out laughing.

CHAPTER SEVENTEEN

Rika

As we wound our way up the road to Jemima Harte's house, my excitement level rose with every foot of elevation.

It was all falling into place in my mind. Jemima Harte—young and dramatic—found out the older man she loved was married or sleeping with other women, but without any actual sleeping going on.

From what I'd read, she'd just turned twenty, but she'd been a TV star for years and had recently broken into feature films. She probably didn't remember a time when she couldn't have everything she wanted. Hurt and angry, she rushed over to the VIP Center looking for Alberto. When she found him, she saw the food and the two wine glasses and realized he'd been romancing someone else that very night.

She picked up the knife Alberto had been using and rushed him, taking him by surprise, stabbing him repeatedly in her flash of rage. She tore the necklace off and threw it at him. Or maybe it broke during the struggle.

But that didn't explain what happened to my father.

Nick paused the Yukon in front of a house. I craned my neck to see the address. "This is it," I said. "Go ahead and park."

"Where?" Nick asked. "There are already two cars parked behind each other in the driveway."

I shrugged. "The drive's long enough for one more vehicle," I pointed out. "Even this monster."

"It's rude to block other cars in," he replied. "Normally, I'd park on the street, but there's no shoulder to speak of. Someone could come around the curve and plow right into it. I can't believe a movie actress can't afford a wider drive."

"It's a trade-off to get the view. There isn't unlimited space on the side of a hill like there is in the flatlands of Bolo."

Nick puffed out a disgusted sound. "I don't know how people live like this." He pulled into the driveway and parked behind a white convertible.

We got out and followed the narrow concrete path around to the front door, which turned out to be double doors—one plum colored, the other fuchsia.

As we stood in front of them looking for a doorbell or knocker, I said, "Well these doors certainly make a statement."

"Yeah," Nick agreed. "They say, 'I'm bat-shit crazy'."

He bent forward to examine the two iron decorations hanging on the doors. On the door to our left, a right hand seemed to be protruding toward us from the inside. The hand was palm down. In its fingers was a ball that was flat on the side that met a piece of iron attached to the door. The other door had the same thing, except it was a left hand instead of a right.

Nick lifted the first hand and let it fall. It emitted a metallic clang. Now that he knew for certain what it was, he put more effort into it, and it went "bang, bang, bang."

"That's so cool!" I said. It was the type of thing that would fit perfectly in a Harry Potter movie, or *Game of Thrones*, or *Doctor Who*.

Hm... Had I seen it on *Doctor Who*?

I became aware of Nick's eyes on me. His head was tilted slightly to the left as he watched me from under his lids. His lips were curved in a vague smile.

Was he laughing at me?

No, his eyes had that look again, the admiring one that warmed me from head to toe, even though I had no business being warmed by Nick.

Both doors opened. A tall, older white-haired man stood before us, dressed in a traditional butler tux, except it was bright white instead of black.

"How may I help you?" he asked in a posh British accent.

Nick and I exchanged looks that said, *What the hell? Who keeps a butler dressed in a tux nowadays?*

I turned back to the butler. "We're here to see Ms. Harte," I said.

"And whom may I say is calling on her?"

"Detectives Owen and Martin," Nick said. I noticed he liked to give himself top billing, plus I was pretty sure he was enjoying the chance to mispronounce my name when my hands were tied, metaphorically, and I couldn't correct him.

"We're here about the murder of Alberto Viera," I added.

"Oh, dear," the man said. "Please come in and wait in the foyer." He stepped back to let us in, then waved his hand at some furniture, to use the term loosely.

It was an acrylic two-seater bench. Half of it was the height of a normal bench seat, the other half was nearly a foot taller.

As the butler walked away, I hustled over to the taller side and sat on it, so, for once, I could be taller than Nick. The down side was that it left my feet dangling, making me feel like a small child.

Nick's lips quirked up. He stepped over, sat on the shorter side, and turned his face toward me. I wasn't taller. We were eye-to-eye.

So annoying.

As he looked into my narrowed eyes, his mouth spread into a full-on teasing smile, his eyes twinkling sapphire blue at me.

So beautiful.

Our faces were so close, mere inches apart. He was all I could see. I could smell his pleasantly light aftershave. I was suddenly dying to run my hands up his freshly shaven cheeks.

As I stared back at him, his eyes darkened to cobalt. His smile faded. His gaze dropped to my mouth. His tongue darted out to wet his lips.

My breathing grew shallow. I could feel him willing me to come closer. Suddenly, my lips seemed to have strings attached to them. They were puppet lips and Nick was the puppet master. My mind fought against the pull, even as my face moved slowly closer to his. Centimeter by centimeter...

"Sir, miss," the butler said. I jerked away from Nick and straightened up. "Ms. Harte will see you now."

Wondering what the hell was wrong with me—considering the seriousness of the situation—I tried to slow my heartbeat as Nick and I stood and followed the butler to another set of double doors, which he opened for us.

"Detectives Owen and Martin, miss."

I glanced around the room looking for Jemima, but didn't see her. Her modern-weird decorating style was continued into the living room, most of the furniture so oddly shaped it was hard to tell what purpose it was meant to serve.

Forty or fifty feet from us, between the living and dining areas, sat a clear fiberglass piano. The strings and other guts were done in bright neon colors. It would be super cool in an elementary school music class, but I wasn't sure about an adult living room. Then, I recalled all the Harry Potter and Doctor Who stuff in my bedroom and decided maybe I wasn't the person to judge home decor.

Regardless of the furniture, the room was breathtaking because of where it sat. It had glass walls on three sides and hung off the edge of the hill, offering a sweeping view of Los Angeles below.

"Come in," a light, high-pitched voice said. I scanned the huge area again and found Jemima half-lying on a bright orange chaise lounge, the only comfortable-looking furniture in the room.

Typically, things appear larger as you get nearer. However, the closer we got, the skinnier the actress seemed. In fact, if she hadn't been wearing a long white dress, my eyes might have missed her entirely.

A jealous burn rushed through me so fast, I wondered if it was turning my face green. How did she stay so thin?

Probably had a personal chef. I was always convinced keeping my weight down would be easier if I had a personal chef who would prepare and serve low-calorie meals, removing eating decisions from me entirely.

I guess I did have a personal chef, in a way, but my grandmother always seemed convinced the more she fed me, the happier I would be, even when my body puffed up like Jabba the Hutt.

Jemima didn't get up off the lounge or even sit up—likely too weak from lack of food—so Nick and I walked over to where she was lounging.

"Hi, I'm Nick Owen. This is my partner, Rika Martin."

Jemima lifted a hand and we took turns shaking it, very carefully. I felt like I was holding a tiny bird.

"Nice to meet you." She ran the fingers of one hand down her long white hair, which was pulled around onto one shoulder. "I'm sorry. You've caught me at my low-energy time of the day. Steve says my bioflavonoids are off. You know, residual damage from the circadian parasites I consumed on that last press tour. I'm hoping a few more sessions at the Clarification Center will clear me up."

Circadian parasites? Holy mother of Zeus, she was stupid! It sounded like Steve and Valerie were pulling random terms out of their asses and presenting them as fact.

I mean, sure, Jemima was only twenty and had spent her childhood as an actress. But weren't child stars required to have tutors? Didn't she have wi-fi and Bing? Or at least Google?

A familiar feeling oozed into me. The feeling of superiority, like I used to get when I was a teenager and watched America's Next Top Model, treating myself to an Oreo every time one of those boney girls said something stupid.

Some people play drinking games. I played eating games. I justified it by reminding myself that my game didn't have me mowing down pedestrians in my car...unless they were between me and my next box of Double Stufs, that is.

Nick slid his gaze toward me, with a *Did you just hear what I heard?* expression on his face. However, as I opened my mouth, he placed a hand between my shoulder blades, which I knew was a warning. He was aware that I was prone, on occasion, to blurting out rude things at stupid people. In fact, the very first time Nick laid eyes on me, I was letting Deputy Dan know how stupid he and his boss were, even though he had me in handcuffs.

"Well, thanks for taking the time to see us," I said. Nick's hand dropped away. I missed it immediately. I wondered if I could fake an *I'm about to blurt* face so he'd put it back where it was.

"Oh, I'm always glad to help people now. I wasn't so much before my earwigs were cleared, but that was the microbes talking." Had Steve and Valerie fed her that old-wives tale about earwigs burrowing into your brain? She only needed to do a quick search on the Internet and she'd know better, assuming she could read.

She gestured at the weird furniture nearby and said, "Please, sit."

I made a quick assessment and sat on a mushroom-shaped thing. I felt a little like the blue caterpillar in *Alice in Wonderland,* but it was reasonably comfortable. The only piece left in this furniture grouping was a chair shaped like Cousin Thing from the *Addams Family*—a hand with a wrist as the base, the palm forming an awkwardly angled seat. Oh, and it was bright red.

Nick stared at it for several seconds then said, "I'll stand if you don't mind." He placed a hand on his lower back. "Sciatica," he added, but I was sure he thought he was too cool to sit in such a ridiculous chair.

"Oh." Jemima glanced at the chair. "I guess that might not be very comfortable," she said as if she'd just this second realized it. She sat up and turned sideways on the lounger, her perfectly pedicured feet—visible in her fancy flip-flops—coming to rest on the floor. "Would this be better?" She patted the spot next to her.

I would have thought I couldn't be any more jealous of her than I already was, but when Nick flashed his gorgeous smile at her and sat down beside her, I was sure I'd suddenly developed a very specific super-power. One that would enable me to snap her scrawny body like a pretzel stick.

"Thanks." Nick's voice was soft and tinged with affection. Sure, he might be playing her to get more information, but the tone was the same one he used with me when he told me I was pretty smart for a hot chick.

Jemima beamed up at him. Sitting together, they made the most beautiful couple I'd ever seen.

I wanted to pull her angel-white hair out, one strand at a time.

We'll see how Nick looks at you when you're bald, you skinny little skank.

Wow. This was the side of me I didn't like, and it only happened when I watched Nick interact with other women.

My dad's face appeared in my mind, as it had over and over in the past few days, and I felt guilty for my petty thoughts. I pressed my lips closed and let Nick work his hot lawyer magic on her.

"I'm sorry about Alberto," he said. "I heard you knew him. Were you close?"

Tears filled Jemima's eyes and I felt even worse about my

pettiness. The mention of the victim's name brought her grief to the surface. I could feel her tears in my throat. If anyone understood how awful it was to lose someone close to you, I did.

Jemima sucked in a big breath and straightened. "I forgot my manners. Are you thirsty? I don't have alcohol, but I have several teas and juices...and sparkling water. Oh, and nuts and berries if you're hungry."

Was she stalling for time now that she knew for sure why we were here?

"No, thanks. I'm good," Nick said.

"We just ate," I said. After the cops, the car, and the *cholos,* we were all hungry, so Nick, LeeAnne and I stopped and ate before she went to work.

"Jemima?" Nick said in a gentle but firm voice. Her gaze met his. "Were you and Alberto just hooking up or would you say you were serious?"

She'd begun shaking her head during the "hooking up" part of the question. Her lips parted and I was sure she was about to say she and Alberto were in love or something of the sort. But then her eyebrows pressed down and her lips flattened as if she was reliving a particularly bad memory—one that had made her very angry.

"I don't just 'hook up'," she finally said.

"Were things good between you and Alberto before he died?" Nick asked.

I watched her carefully as her expression changed, her body language relaxed down to her fingers and toes. It was like seeing her morph into a different person.

"They were great." She projected her voice more than she had since we'd come in. "He said he was leaving his wife as soon as he could square it with Valerie and Steve. He even told me he'd become a Microtologist for me."

Nick flicked his eyes at me. He knew she was lying too, I could tell, but he hadn't figured out what I had. Jemima had used her acting skills to become someone else right in front of our eyes. I'd been backstage and on set with Brandtt before. I'd seen how some actors could just decide to be someone else and change into that person almost instantly.

Jemima would not be breaking down and confessing to murder. Not today, anyway.

"Did you know about the other women?" I asked.

Her eyes were icy and cool as she said. "There were other women before me, but not once Alberto and I started seeing each other. We were in love."

"Do you know of anyone else who would want to hurt Alberto?" Nick asked.

"Huh," Jemima snorted. "Have you talked to his wife? It sounded to me like they hated each other's guts."

"What about the missing chef?" Nick asked. "Do you think he did it?"

"Diego?" She sounded surprised at the notion. "I'm sure he didn't do it."

Nick and I exchanged a glance. I forced myself to breathe normally. "How do you know he didn't do it?" I asked.

"Steve and Valerie told me. They said he needed some time before he went back to the kitchen where his friend was killed. I assume he's out at the ranch."

"The ranch?" Nick repeated.

"Yeah, that's the nickname for the Purification and Remediation Retreat in the desert."

"Have you been to this retreat?"

"Sure. Just a couple of months ago when my parents visited. Steve and Valerie took us all. They have a huge, gorgeous house there, not far from the private golf course. Steve took my dad out to play on it. My parents have even become Microtologists now." She wobbled her head side to side. "Well, they aren't bleaching or shaving their heads because they live in a small town in England and people would think they'd gone mad."

She twirled her finger next to her head in the universal sign for "crazy."

So that explained the unusual accent, which was mostly West Coast American, but with occasional touches of Brit.

"We need to talk to Diego Martín," I said. Do you have an address for the ranch?"

"Sure." She shrugged. "It's on the pamphlet right over there on my desk. You can take it if you want."

I hopped off my toadstool, went to the bright yellow desk she'd indicated and grabbed the pamphlet. It was the ticket to my father, I could feel it. I wanted to close my eyes, hold it to my chest, and click my heels together like Dorothy from the *Wizard of Oz*.

Nick stood too. "Thanks a lot for your time," he said. "We know how valuable it is."

She looked up at him from under her lashes. "Come back any time, Detective Owen." She smiled a smile that was simultaneously sweet and seductive.

"Call me Nick," he said.

My eyes shifted to him to give him a murderous look, but he was gazing at Jemima.

"Thanks, a lot, *Nick*..." She smiled up at him gratefully. "...for everything you're doing to find Alberto's killer."

She stood, lifted herself on tiptoes and gave him a kiss on the cheek. My hot Latina blood—which was apparently still a thing —boiled up from my stomach and overflowed so fast into my limbs that my hands started itching.

Itching to smash into her sneaky pixie face, that is. It was times like this I needed some girlfriends to hold me back and stop me from cutting a bitch.

LeeAnne was the only person I'd consider a girlfriend and she'd probably encourage me to go for it. I'd never cut a bitch before. I'd have to do some online research, buy the right kind of knife, and maybe practice on some cantaloupes.

Nick headed for the door and I followed, then remembered a very important thing I'd forgotten to do.

"Oh, Ms. Harte...?" As Nick opened one of the double doors, I turned and walked back to where she was sitting. Hopefully, I'd find my dad at the ranch, but the murder still needed to be solved if I didn't want him to go to jail.

She smiled at me, the picture of openness and innocence. "Yes?"

Innocent, my ass! Pulling my phone out of my pocket, I tapped and swiped until I got to the picture of the heart necklace Julian had sent me. "Is this yours? Someone lost it at the VIP Center."

I watched her expression as she looked at the screen. I thought I saw a sign of recognition, then it was gone. "No, not mine," she said.

"Have you seen anyone wearing it around the center? One of the restaurant hostesses maybe?"

"No, sorry. I haven't seen it on any hostesses either."

I felt like she was being evasive. "Have you seen anyone wearing this necklace...ever?"

She clasped her hands together in front of her, pushed her shoulders back and looked steadily into my eyes. "I've never seen that necklace before in my life."

My teeth clenched. She knew something and not telling me might mean my father could go to jail for murder. He could be in danger right at this very moment. A part of me I'd never met before swirled up from my gut, took control of my brain, and my finger swiped right on my phone screen.

Jemima made a strangled sound. Her hand jerked up, first to her chest, then to cover her mouth as she dashed from the room.

The butler appeared at the living room doors where Nick was standing. "You may want to see to Ms. Harte," Nick said to him. "She seems to be a little under the weather."

The butler hurried through the living room to the side door Jemima had gone through.

I walked past Nick, who followed behind me.

"You showed her Alberto's body?" Nick asked.

"Yep," I replied.

We stepped outside the front door and he shut it behind us. "Was that necessary?"

I couldn't miss the judgement on his face. "Yes, it was necessary!" I yelled. "She knows who that necklace belongs to and she's not telling us."

"You don't know that. And the poor kid is thin as a rail. She can't afford to barf up any more meals."

Hearing Nick stand up for Jemima and point out her thin-as-a-railness was the last straw. "So, you think she deserves your special Nick Owen love and kisses because she's blonde and thin?" I spat.

"*What?*"

I double-timed it toward the Yukon but with his stupid long legs he caught up and walked beside me.

"I said, 'Those gorgeous, *THIN*, model-actress types always need the special Owen sauce to make them all better!'" That wasn't exactly what I'd said, but I was beyond caring. Between Jemima not telling me everything she knew and Nick acting so concerned about her, I was losing my battle with control.

"Rika, what are you talking about?" he yelled back. "*You're* a gorgeous, thin, actress type."

I immediately noticed he left out "model." Because I was too short and chunky, no doubt. Wait, had he just called me "thin"?

Now my mind was all jumbled from feeling angry and jealous and flattered all at the same time. "I'm not an actress type," I said.

"You've certainly been doing a lot of acting since I got to L.A., *detective*." He reached the car door before me and opened it.

Annoying.

"Whatever." I hauled myself up into the Yukon and looked away until the door slammed next to me.

CHAPTER EIGHTEEN

Rika

I didn't speak to Nick once on the ride home. I just stared out the window at the setting sun. When he asked if we should pick up food for me to eat, I shook my head. There were always plenty of leftovers and snacks at Lita's house. And I was in the mood to eat alone.

I was in the mood to eat a lot, alone.

Despite the feeling we'd gotten yesterday from the Kaporskys that my father was still alive, I couldn't stop negative thoughts from popping into my head constantly.

Diego Martín was not a man who would allow himself to be held indefinitely. Knowing my father, he might let them think he was resigned to whatever they had planned for him, but he'd be watching for vulnerabilities. Then, the first viable chance he got, he would try to escape, and what would his abductors do to him when he did? I felt like they must be armed or they couldn't have held onto him this long. How far were they willing to go to keep him quiet?

Then there was Jemima. She recognized the heart necklace. I

knew she did. What I didn't know was who she was protecting by not admitting to it.

Herself? One of the hostesses she befriended at the VIP center? Valerie? Suzee? Some other Microtologist?

And stupid Nick had made me feel ashamed for showing her Alberto's body. I hated seeing him look at me like I'd kicked a puppy. I hated even more that he'd felt something for Jemima, even if it was only sympathy.

Girls who looked like her had been my worst tormentors in high school even though it was the boys who did the things that were obviously mean, like throwing food at my head.

The skinny blonde girls could torture me just by existing. And by murmuring things to each other as I walked by that I couldn't always make out. But I didn't miss the way they were covering their mouths as they spoke, their eyes shifting to me, then darting away again. They always acted so sweet and innocent with teachers, but I heard them snickering behind my back all the time.

When Nick pulled up in front of my grandmother's house, I popped the door open, planning to wave goodbye and run inside. I felt tears of frustration and fear accumulating behind my eyes and my throat was tight.

I wanted my dad back. And, if I couldn't have that tonight, I wanted to sit in my room and cry and eat the contents of the pantry. The best thing Nick could do for me was drive away and leave me alone.

The sky was dark now, but the streetlights were probably enough to give me away if the tears started flowing. Losing my mom was already too much to bear and, though I pretended as best I could, that pain never really went away.

"Pain" wasn't even the right word for it. It was more like I had this huge vacant place in my soul where my mom used to be and the edges left from where she was torn out still ached most of the time.

I jumped out, hoping Nick would understand I didn't want company.

But he wouldn't let me escape that easily. He got out of the truck and followed me to the door. When we were standing on the porch, he took me by the arms like he was about to shake me. Except, when I looked into his eyes, they were full of concern and maybe something else I couldn't deal with at the moment.

"Get some sleep," he said. "We'll find your dad. If the person who killed Viera wanted your father dead, he would have been found there in the kitchen alongside Viera."

My eyes welled up at the thought of my father lying dead in the Microtologist restaurant. Nick's brows drew together like he was in pain, and he pulled me against him. "I'm sorry," he said. "I shouldn't have said it that way."

I couldn't resist the comfort of his body. My hands skimmed around his waist until my arms encircled him. My nose, which was smushed against his chest, took in the scent I could never forget. I wanted to crawl up inside his shirt, chest to chest, where all the bad people in the world would disappear and we would be safe and warm together.

Maybe that was a lot to expect from a shirt, but I'd always felt better when some part of Nick was touching me, even inadvertently. I considered myself a feminist, but at this moment, all I wanted was to bawl my eyes out in Nick's big strong arms.

No.

I couldn't break down now. My Papi needed me.

Suck it up, Paprika!

"Paprika?" Nick said at the same moment my inner voice was calling me by my full name. Could he hear my thoughts?

And why did his voice sound so gentle? I'd successfully blinked back the first wave of tears, but his tone nearly undid me.

"Remember when you were in Bolo?" He continued. "You fought your own murder charge. You stood up to the cops. You escaped a shooting attempt. Hell, you disarmed a bomb."

I chuckled at this, pulling back until I was looking into his eyes. "I wouldn't call what I did 'disarming'."

"Hey, it got the job done. And you never lost your cool...or your determination."

I thought I'd lost my cool a whole bunch of times when I was in Bolo, but Nick's affectionate, admiring expression made me wish I could view myself through his eyes. I remembered feeling that way a lot last summer, too.

"You'll get through this," he said. As I nodded and released him, he spread his arms out wide as if displaying himself. "And you've got your loyal sidekick at your beck and call."

I laughed out loud this time. It was hard to imagine someone as tall, handsome, and smart as Nick being anyone's sidekick, although, he had always shown respect for my mind, and we did make a pretty good team. We seemed to take turns being the sidekick, in deference to each other's strengths and weaknesses.

It was nice. Even though I hadn't known him that long, he was one of the best friends I'd ever had. Him and LeeAnne. My chest squeezed as I thought about how two people I didn't know a year ago had both put their lives on the line for me.

I swallowed hard. "Thanks, Nick... I mean, for everything."

"I told you when you left Bolo to call me if you ever needed anything," he said. "I'm glad you finally called."

A light breeze blew a strand of hair into my face. He captured it between two fingers and followed it down, his fingertips skimming my brow, my temple, and my cheekbone before he tucked it behind my ear. My chest felt hot and the sensation spread up my neck and down into my belly.

"I hope you'll always call," he said. "Missed you at the dinner table. We had some interesting conversations."

My eyes escaped his, fixating on the front of his shirt while his words sank in. Had he truly missed me? Did he regret not asking me to stay?

But, then why hadn't he called or texted? We weren't even

Facebook friends. And how was he able to move on with Marla while I was still one hundred percent stuck on him?

He kissed the top of my head. "See you tomorrow." He turned and walked toward the Yukon. "Get some sleep," he repeated. "We have a big day."

We did. We were planning to go out to the Microtologist compound in the desert.

I let myself into the house, missing Nick even before I heard him drive off. I was glad no one was home, though. I vaguely recalled my grandmother mentioning she was in charge of an event at the church tonight. Knowing Lita, she'd dragged my aunts, LeeAnne, and possibly my cousin Sofia, along with her to help.

Gucci was lying on one end of the sofa. She opened one eye. She was a girl who needed about twenty hours a day of beauty sleep and was not happy when you interrupted one of her dozen naps, unless it was to give her a treat. Since, I wasn't holding a treat, she closed the eye and went back to sleep.

At least I had some time alone to decompress before dealing with their questions about my progress in finding my dad.

But the house didn't feel right. Didn't smell right. I thought about the search warrant and glanced around to assess the damage.

I'd called my grandmother because I was afraid walking in on a bunch of cops—mostly men—rifling through her things would give her a heart attack. Or, more likely, land her in jail once she beaned a police officer with a cast iron skillet. Then, I'd called Mrs. Ruíz to make sure she was there for moral support and to try to keep my grandmother away from anything she could use as a weapon.

The two of them must have had at least a couple of hours here because the living, dining and kitchen had been straightened up. Some of the angel figurines were turned backwards or sitting in the wrong place, but I was sure Lita would resettle them when she got back.

My room was a disaster. Because I didn't have a ton of space, I kept a lot of my things in under bed storage boxes. The police had pulled them out and dumped them all over the floor of my room.

My mattress was slanted haphazardly on its box springs. Nausea filled my stomach as I picked up my original Nintendo game console. Someone had pried it open and left it on my dresser with its guts hanging out, like it had been drawn and quartered.

I couldn't deal with the mess right now. I turned my back to it, sat down at my computer, and bingged the address on the brochure Jemima had given us, eventually finding some aerial photographs. There were several buildings on the property, all of them bright white. I could see the golf course Jemima mentioned. After more time on the internet, I learned the private golf course was built by previous owners of the property before the Temple of Microtology bought it.

I clicked back to the image of the golf course and noted its very green appearance. Whether the Kaporskys cared about helping their fellow man was arguable, but they certainly weren't worried about water conservation in the middle of the California desert. The fairways were green and the greens were even greener.

When I ran out of research ideas, I went into the kitchen to look for a comfort snack. I'd learned several years ago from my Jilly Crane counselor that stress was a food trigger for me and I shouldn't let myself use carbs as mood enhancers. But I'd fallen halfway off that wagon staying with Nick. Now with my dad missing, I just didn't have it in me to resist.

The stainless-steel refrigerator my aunts had gotten my Lita for Mother's Day yielded a cache of leftover beef *empanadas*, which I liked, but I was craving something sweet. Turning to the pantry, I found a package of Double Stuf Oreos and ripped it open. Pulling out the first cookie, I twisted it apart and began chewing one side as I looked forward to scraping the creamy white filling off the other with my front teeth.

I stepped back to the fridge to get some milk. Something changed in the room and it took me a second to understand what it was.

The light that normally reflected in the stainless steel from the back porch was partly obscured. Icy fingers gripped my stomach as I whirled around. My eyes scanned the window over the sink, then moved to the back door, then the window on the other side of the door.

I startled, gasped, then coughed as chunks of cookie flew from my mouth. I dropped the rest of the package, but was barely aware of my cherished Double Stufs crashing to the floor.

This was because I couldn't take my eyes off the face at the window. The creature staring back at me was horrifying, its nose bent at a strange angle, its eyes freakishly wide, its mouth open, spitting saliva onto the glass. And it was making the most bizarre sound—somewhere between a screech and a howl.

I froze, unsure if I needed a silver bullet to shoot into its werewolf heart or a spike to jam through its zombie eye. And it seemed to be struggling like it was caught in a trap. Its cry grew louder and its shoulder smashed the window so hard, I thought it would break through.

I flipped around and reached into the drawer where my late grandfather's barbecue utensils were kept. The giant meat fork caught my eye and I grabbed for it as I spun back around to check on the monster.

"It's all right, Rika!" I heard a familiar voice say. Another face appeared next to the werewolf-zombie. It was Eli's face. "I've got him!"

Just then, the front door burst open. LeeAnne had her key in the door, but Nick muscled past her. "Rika, we have a problem.

That silver car from—" He stopped dead in his tracks as he saw the creature against the window. "What the fuck?"

"I'm not sure," I said. I walked to the back door and tried to go out first, but Nick grabbed me by the arm and forced me behind him—*annoying*— then strode out with me at his heels and LeeAnne at mine.

When we came around the corner of the house, we found the perpetrator still smashed against the glass, one arm painfully hiked up behind his back by Eli as Eli's other hand pressed the back of his head into the window.

My imagination might have gotten a wee bit away from me because now I realized the sound wasn't really a screech or a howl. The window guy was moaning from the pain.

But the weirdest thing about the picture was that the stranger was several inches taller than Eli, broader-chested, and had noticeably thicker arms—actually, his body type was the same as the passenger in the Nissan that had been following me—but Eli had him completely under control.

"Jesus Christ Superstar!" LeeAnne cried. "You're strong for such a little guy."

Eli ignored her and glanced at the neighboring houses. "Do you want to question him out here or inside?"

"Inside," I said. I didn't want the whole neighborhood to get involved in whatever this was. And they would get involved, believe me.

"Come on," Eli ordered. He turned the monster around and, now that it wasn't pressed against the glass, its features were fairly normal for a man, his bulbous nose being the most prominent one. His head was shaved bald and he was wearing a full-length trench coat.

I turned to look at Nick and noticed his eyes were narrowed, but he seemed to be focused on Eli more than the perpetrator.

Weird.

Eli hustled his captive to the door and we followed. By the

time the stranger was sitting in a chair in my grandmother's kitchen, his coat had fallen open revealing white jeans and a white t-shirt underneath.

"Clearly you work for the Microtologists," Nick said. "What's your name?"

"Sherome."

"Sherome what?"

"Just Sherome," he replied.

Nick looked at me impatiently as if the guy was speaking a foreign language and I was the translator.

I shrugged. "This is L.A. His name might just be Sherome."

"She's right," LeeAnne agreed. "Like Cher or Madonna."

Nick shook his head as if to shake off the stupidity of my home town—like he could talk, being from Bolo—and said, "Alright, then, *Sherome,* who, specifically, are you taking your orders from?"

"Marshall," Sherome gave up immediately. So much for commitment to the cause. I was kind of hoping we'd get to rough him up a little.

"Marshall who?"

"Marshall Mahaffey."

"And who does Marshall take his orders from?" I asked.

"He's high up. I guess it would have to be Steve, Valerie, or Jason...or maybe Suzee."

"Well, that narrows it down," Nick said sarcastically. "What did they tell you to do?"

"Just to keep an eye on you two, I swear."

"And why did you stay with Rika when I left?"

"Well, no offense, but she's a lot better looking than you are."

Nick's body went rigid as his eyes changed color right in front of me. Weird how they could turn both darker and icier at the same time. A shiver wiggled down my back. I hoped he never looked at me that way.

He tilted his head menacingly, grasped the front of Sherome's t-shirt and used it to pull him up out of the chair. "Yeah, she's beautiful, alright," Nick agreed. My heart did a little skip and a jump at hearing Nick call me beautiful. "And what were you planning to do about that?" His eyes shot killer laser beams into Sherome's. "Besides the peeping Tom stuff you were already doing, I mean."

"No-no... *No!*" Sherome stuttered. "I wasn't going to... I didn't mean to..." Nick released him. He fell back into the chair and caught his breath. "I was supposed to try to see what she was up to on the computer and whether she had a security system."

Nick put his hands on his hips and focused his glare onto him again. Sherome cringed as if he thought a smack down could be coming at any moment. "They want to plant a couple of bugs."

"Listening devices?"

"Yeah."

"For what purpose?"

"I don't know. They don't tell me why. They just tell me what to do and I do it."

Hmm... Just following orders. I wondered if that cancelled out the stuff about me being better-looking than Nick.

I looked at Nick. No one was better looking than he was. But he *had* said I was beautiful. Warm glowy tingles spread over my skin. They felt awesome until the tingles converged and morphed into a hot craving between my thighs.

Not now! Jeez, you'd think my girl parts would understand that I was in the middle of a crisis and should not be distracted by Nick, no matter how embarrassingly aroused I was by his macho man act.

Sherome looked from Nick to me. "Look, you guys, I'm just an actor, and Marshall said there was a producer who's a Microtologist doing a spy thriller. Said this would be good research for the role."

Nick closed his eyes and shook his head. "A fucking actor," he murmured as if to himself. He opened his eyes and pointed at

Sherome. “Empty your pockets.” Sherome’s eyes shifted from Nick to me to LeeAnne. “Now!” Nick added.

Sherome jumped up and pulled a baggie from one of his pants pocket and threw it on the dining table.

“All of them,” Nick said.

Reluctantly, Sherome reached into one of his trench coat pockets and pulled out another plastic bag, laying it next to the first. Nick began patting him down, while I examined the contents of the baggies.

The first contained several penny-sized listening devices. If the evidence hadn’t been right in front of my eyes, I wouldn’t have believed someone wanted to listen in on me. I hadn’t lived the most exciting existence, with the exception of my weeks in Bolo.

Finished with his search, Nick put his fingers to Sherome’s chest and pushed. Sherome fell back into the chair.

I picked up the second bag. The items in this one were also small and round, but they were different. I opened the bag and took one out to examine it. It was thicker than the others.

“Oh, my God!” I cried as realization dawned on me. “These are cameras.”

All eyes were suddenly on the tiny camera in my hand. All except for Sherome’s. His eyes were flitting around the room like he was trying to plan his escape.

LeeAnne lifted one of the cameras from my palm and held it at eye level. “Holy hell! You were going to watch us, you sicko!” She took three steps forward and kicked Sherome in the shin hard.

“Ow! Fuck! *Fuck!* he cried as he covered the injured spot with his hand. But he was lucky. If he’d still been standing I was certain LeeAnne would have aimed higher.

I thought Nick couldn’t look any angrier than he already did, but I was wrong. I was standing a couple of feet away from him and I could still feel the angry heat rolling off his body.

“You were installing cameras to watch my...?” He paused and

looked at me and I got the feeling his mouth had gotten stuck on what to call me. "...friends?" He finished.

"No! I wouldn't have been watching!" Sherome insisted. "I was just supposed to follow you. And if Marshall texted me tomorrow, I was supposed to plant the surveillance stuff when you left. That's it."

"'That's it'?" LeeAnne cried. "You were *just* gonna plant bugs and cameras in a house where three women live?" She kicked his other shin and he let out a yowl. "Fucking asshole!"

I considered the fact that my grandmother and LeeAnne and I lived here, but my aunts and cousin Sofia often ended up crashing here for the night, especially if they didn't have work first thing in the morning. It was disgusting to think that some man in a room somewhere could be watching us all as we changed clothes, showered, or ate entire packages of Oreos in one sitting.

Okay, the last one was just me, but what a woman binge eats in the privacy of her home is her own business.

I dropped the cameras on the table and rubbed the creepy crawly feeling from my arms.

"Can I go now?" Sherome asked.

"Sure, after I call the police." Nick pulled out his phone. I opened my mouth to argue, but one look at the gleam in his eye told me we were on the same page.

"No, please. No cops. I was in jail once for a DUI and I don't want to go back there."

Nick pulled a trim wallet out of his back pocket and handed Sherome a business card. "That's my cell," Nick said, pointing to his number on the card. "If you get any more orders, you'll fill me in. Unless you want me to turn you into the cops as a sex offender."

"Uh...uh what?"

"You were peeking in the window at a woman. That's how the

perverts start before they move on to other stuff, like collecting panties and exposing themselves in parks."

"No! There's no other stuff! I would have closed my eyes if she got undressed, I swear."

"Just keep me informed and you'll be fine," Nick replied.

"Sure. No problem." Sherome held up Nick's card. "I'll keep in touch. Thanks." He scurried out the front door.

Nick glanced around. "Where's the other creep?"

"Huh?" I hadn't seen another one.

"Eli."

Oh, Eli. "He never came inside," I said. "Stalker code or something. He's probably gone." Eli seemed to enjoy appearing and disappearing on his own schedule. "Thanks, Nick. We'll be fine now."

Gucci suddenly jumped up from the corner of the couch and started barking. Nick pinched the bridge of his nose and shook his head slowly. "You're the worst watch dog I've ever known," he said.

Gucci tilted her head as if to say, "You don't need to have dog skills, when you're this cute, Bernard." I was convinced she called him by his middle name. She barked three more times, which I interpreted as, "Now, serve me!"

"Well," Nick said. " I'm going to take this..." He picked Gucci up from the sofa. "...out for a walk. Then I'm sleeping on the couch tonight."

"We'll be fine," I said. "You should go back to *Marla*." I tried to keep the childish tone out of my voice when I said stupid Marla's name, but didn't quite succeed.

"Yeah, and I'm here with her now, anyway," LeeAnne added.

"As comforting as that may be," Nick said sarcastically, "I'm sleeping here."

"But my grandmother—"

"I'll talk to her. I'll tell her I'm tired and don't want to endanger the public by driving across town. She'll be fine with it."

His confidence that he could charm my formidable grandmother into agreeing with whatever he said was annoying. Especially since it seemed to be true.

LeeAnne stuck one hand on her hip like she was about to start something with Nick. But the truth was, I didn't want him going back to Marla tonight.

"Whatever," I said with a dismissive wave. "I'm going to bed."

"Me too," LeeAnne said, apparently deciding to let it go this time. "I'm beat. Goodnight y'all." She clomped up the stairs in her platform heels.

I lingered for an extra moment, my body not quite willing to leave Nick's presence.

"Goodnight, Paprika." His voice oozed over me like warm caramel. He shifted toward me almost imperceptibly and, for a moment, I thought he was going to touch me. I really, *really* wanted him to touch me. But he turned and took Gucci out front.

"Goodnight, Nicholas Bernard," I murmured too quietly for him to hear. I smiled to myself at the sight of him towering over little Gucci while she squatted in my grandmother's cactus garden. Then I turned and went to bed.

CHAPTER NINETEEN

Nick

After Rika's grandmother came in and I explained my presence to her satisfaction, she went to bed. I stayed up doing Internet searches. I was glad I'd bought a phone like Rika's. It was ten times faster than the one I'd been using.

But for the first time since I came to L.A., I wasn't searching the topic of Microtology or the people involved in it. I was checking into Eli Lippman.

I hadn't liked the idea that Rika had a stalker, but he really had come across as a harmless trust fund type who had nothing better to do than follow beautiful women around. Since he didn't appear to be an immediate threat and we had Rika's dad to find, I'd let it go. Truth be told, I'd practically forgotten he existed in the hours since I first saw him. He was a little guy, not much taller than Rika. Just didn't make that much of an impression.

Until tonight.

How had he managed to disable a guy nearly a foot taller and twice as wide as he was?

I was certain now that I needed to know more about him. Problem was, there were quite a few Eli Lippmans on the Internet. There were Eli Lippmann doctors, Eli Lippman lawyers, Eli Lippmans who were in show business related jobs. Eli Lippmans kept popping up all over the country and, if Eli was short for something else, like Elliot or Elija, or if he went by his middle name, there were even more of them.

Maybe I was going about this the wrong way. Where would a guy like him get the skills and confidence to immobilize an oversized peeper so easily?

I touched the search field and began looking for any site that might have military records and that's the last thing I remembered.

~

I was dreaming that King Kong had his hand around my throat and I couldn't swallow. Women's voices were speaking in quiet, rapid-fire Spanish.

I couldn't understand why they were speaking so quietly. Why weren't they yelling, "Help, this man's being strangled by a gorilla"? Or whatever the Spanish equivalent was.

I breathed in a familiar scent. My stomach growled and woke me up. I opened my eyes and found Gucci's furry body lying crosswise on my throat. King Kong was nowhere in sight.

All at once, I remembered where I was and sat up. Gucci rolled down my chest into my lap and curled up, her paw covering her tiny eyes as if she wasn't ready to face the stressful day of eating and sleeping ahead of her.

She reminded me of my last ex-wife, who was Gucci's owner until she dumped the pooch on me and ran off to France. I liked dogs, but not in a million years would I have picked this prissy ball of fluff. Whenever I walked—or as she preferred, carried—her around, I felt like I was wearing a shirt that said, "I'm here and I'm queer." But maybe that was for the best, if I took my track record with women into account.

"Oh, we woke you up," Mrs. Delacruz said apologetically. Then she rattled some angry Spanish off to Mrs. Ruíz, who was in the kitchen holding a spatula.

"I didn't wake him!" Mrs. Ruíz said emphatically. "It was you and your noisy plates. Why did we need the plates already? The *juevos* and *papas* aren't even finished yet!"

I sucked in a lungful of bacon-scented air. "It's fine, ladies," I said. "Gucci needs to go out anyway." At this, Gucci cracked one eye open and looked up at me with a *Say what?* expression.

She acted clueless most of the time, then she'd suddenly give the impression she could understand exactly what I said. Made me wonder if she was playing the dumb blonde because she thought it made her cuter. I'd known too many women like that and I didn't find them so cute anymore.

I took her out and, when we walked back in, Rika was coming into the living room. My breath caught in my chest when I saw her.

Her lids were half closed like she'd just awakened. Her hair was the tousled bedroom kind. But, best of all, was her attire.

She was wearing a T-shirt with the words *Hogwarts O.G.* across her breasts. It hung as far as her hips and that was it, except for a pair of white bikini underwear.

I swallowed hard as I fought the urge to back her into the bedroom and use one of her wands to make her clothes disappear. My dick throbbed so hard at the sight of her, my entire body jerked.

As I tried to get my nether regions under control, she stopped in the middle of the room to rub her eyes. "Coffee," she murmured to herself.

"Morning, Paprika," I said.

Her body jerked, her eyes opening wide. "Oh, my God!" She glanced down at herself. She twisted her shoulders as if she was going to turn and run, then changed her mind. Instead she pulled the bottom of her t-shirt down as far as it would go, and backed out of the room.

Damn. For a second there I thought I was going to get a peek at her bodacious backside.

"Was that Rika?" Mrs. Delacruz asked as she stepped from the kitchen. She looked toward Rika's room.

"Yeah, I think she forgot something." I grinned inwardly, knowing the thing she'd forgotten was that I'd spent the night here.

Well, that and her pants.

Mrs. Ruíz came up behind Rika's grandmother. "We're making tacos with bacon, eggs and potatoes," she said. "I made the flour tortillas myself. You like tacos, don't you?"

"Love 'em!" I said.

Mrs. Delacruz frowned at me.

I smiled at her. "I've never eaten better than since I met you two ladies."

She pressed her lips together as if trying to control a smile. "Well, we are the best cooks in Alemania," she said.

I heard a clomping noise and looked up to see LeeAnne coming down the stairs in platform high-heeled stripper shoes.

Since before she was even a teenager, I'd been worried her choice of attire was going to attract the wrong element into her life. I'd tried to clue her in since she was twelve and I was thirteen, but LeeAnne never listened to anybody about anything.

She'd ended up married to an abusive asshole and, since her divorce, she seemed to go out of her way to keep any man she dated at arm's length.

It was a shame. As annoying as LeeAnne could be sometimes, she was still one of the most good-hearted people I'd ever known.

Rika came in again, wearing pants, unfortunately. She avoided eye contact, which bothered me until I realized she was probably just embarrassed.

"Breakfast will be ready in ten minutes," Mrs. Delacruz said. She and Mrs. Ruíz had gone back to cooking.

"LeeAnne, Nick," Rika whispered. When we looked at her, she jerked her head toward her bedroom and we followed.

"We need to get to the compound today," Rika said. "So, I asked LeeAnne to help us."

I looked at LeeAnne, then back at Rika, "Help us what?" LeeAnne was the last person I'd want to take with me on a covert mission.

"We're going to have to look like Microtologists to have a chance of getting in there. LeeAnne is going to style us."

"No way is LeeAnne Barr 'styling' me," I said. "Whatever that means."

"Nick, she can take care of this kind of thing a lot faster than we can. She'll get the clothes and accessories while we make our plan."

I shook my head. Being clothed and accessorized by LeeAnne was the stuff of my nightmares, or, at least, it would be after this, I was certain.

"Text me when you've got things together," Rika said to LeeAnne, completely ignoring my head shaking.

"Great. I just need both of y'all to text me your sizes."

Damn it. If I kept arguing the point, I'd be a selfish asshole, since this was about rescuing Rika's dad. I bit my tongue, but I couldn't rework my expression.

"Don't worry." LeeAnne patted me on the bicep. "I won't tell anyone what sizes y'all wear."

"Why would we be worried about that?" I asked, a tad insulted.

LeeAnne smiled mischievously and walked to the kitchen. "I've got some important stuff I've got to do," she said. "Could I get my taco to go?"

"Of course, *mija*," Mrs. Ruíz said. "I'll make you one just like you like it, with extra bacon."

I rolled my eyes and Rika caught me.

"Is this going to be a problem for you?" she asked.

Hell, yes, it was a problem for me. I wasn't proud of it. I knew I'd been petty to keep this childish feud going for so long. But it was a habit that was hard to break. "No," I said. "There's no problem. We're going to find your dad if we have to do it in Catholic school girl skirts," which was a distinct possibility considering what a big Brittney Spears fan LeeAnne was.

Rika chuckled. "I wouldn't mind seeing you in a Catholic school girl uniform."

"Back atcha," I replied.

~

Rika

I decided we'd meet LeeAnne outside the boutique so as not to have to explain ourselves to my grandmother and aunts.

They loved my father and were thrilled when he came back to L.A. after all those years. However, when push came to shove, "Paprika's" safety would be top priority. Even my Tía Madi, who tried to pretend she was too cool to worry, had watched me like a hawk when I was in her care. I was the only piece of my mom they had left and they'd tried their best to guard me from any danger.

While I appreciated their concern, I didn't have time to deal with the drama. My father was probably being held in the desert by a bunch of cult members, and I had no idea what they were capable of.

I hoped he was being held by them. The other possibility was unthinkable. I'd been through that horror with one parent already.

An all-too familiar sensation tried to swell up in my chest, but I sucked in a huge breath, pushing the accompanying emotion as far down into my guts as possible.

I'd known emotions came from your brain since I was a little girl. What I never understood was why I felt them so hard in my stomach, which would ache until I filled it with doughy sweets or chocolate.

When Nick and I pulled up in front of the boutique, I texted LeeAnne. Five minutes later, she came out with four shopping bags and set them next to the boutique's cargo van that was parked directly in front of the shop. As Nick and I got out and walked up to it, she went back in, then came out with another bag and a black plastic case.

"How long is all this going to take?" I asked, anxious to get to my father. If he wasn't at the Microtology compound in the desert, I didn't know what I'd do.

"Oh, don't worry," LeeAnne said. "I can do this on the way while y'all take turns driving." She handed me the keys and gestured for Nick to get into the back.

Nick and I exchanged glances that said neither of us was comfortable with LeeAnne being in charge of this operation, but she did have the costumes and the van.

I shrugged. "Okay," I said as I opened the driver's side door. On the way to the compound, I tried to focus on driving and listening to LeeAnne and Nick behind me because I did not want to dwell on my fear of not finding my father or, worse, finding him... I couldn't even allow myself to think the last word in that sentence.

LeeAnne spent the next twenty minutes organizing her stuff while Nick clicked around on his phone. Was he texting Marla? I wondered what he could possibly talk to her about. Or his ex-wives for that matter. The two I'd met in Bolo seemed ditzy and shallow.

Come to think of it, I'd only seen each of them for a few minutes and hadn't exchanged words with either. Maybe I wanted them to be ditzy and shallow.

Whatever.

I wondered if Nick and Marla had any stupid pet names for each other. It was hard to imagine Nick calling a woman snookum or pookie wookie or love muffin, or letting one call him a silly name. Even the classics like "honey" and "sweetheart" were hard to imagine coming from Nick. When we were a fake couple at the Clarification Center, he'd called me "hon," so I figured, in real life, he'd probably go for a simple monosyllabic choice, like "babe."

I liked the warm tone in his voice whenever he called me Paprika even though I'd never been thrilled with my full name. I tried to imagine him calling me "babe" in that same tone. *Paprika...babe... could you hand me that—*

"What the hell?" Nick said, jarring me out of my thoughts.

I checked the rearview mirror, but there wasn't enough light in the back of the van for me to get a clear view.

"What's your problem?" LeeAnne asked.

"This is a mullet. I look like a blonde Billy Ray Cyrus, circa 1991."

LeeAnne laughed. "I was thinking you looked more like a blonde David Spade in *Joe Dirt*."

I burst out laughing. I wished I could see Nick's expression.

"You didn't have something more in the Billy Idol family?" he asked.

LeeAnne snorted. "Like you could pull off Billy Idol."

The curiosity was killing me, but I couldn't look back while driving the van. It didn't handle like my Honda and I didn't want us to fall off the road on the way to rescue my dad.

"Besides," LeeAnne added, "nobody says 'circa' in real life."

"I'm not wearing this thing," Nick replied.

"It's either that or I shave you bald."

"No!" I yelled, much too dramatically. But Nick looked so handsome with hair. "It's just that..." *Think Paprika.* "Um...you've done so much already, flying here to help me and all. I'll feel terrible if you sacrifice your hair, too."

Nick let out an angry grunt I was sure was meant for LeeAnne. "What are you doing now?" he yelled.

"Just hold still."

"Hell, no, LeeAnne. I'm not wearing makeup!"

"Billy Idol wore makeup." Now, I was sure LeeAnne was just poking the bear for her own amusement. Microtologists were not required to wear makeup.

Nick escaped LeeAnne's clutches and slid into the seat next to me. "When you find a good place to pull over, I can take over the driving."

I glanced at him and giggled at the shape of the wig. Then I did a double take.

Damn it! Even with a white mullet and a scowl on his face, he was still hot. How was that possible?

Jeez. Nick could walk into a bar wearing a blonde mullet wig and still pick up whoever he chose, I was sure of it.

Annoying.

CHAPTER TWENTY

Nick

By the time we reached the sign announcing the Microtology Purification and Remediation Retreat, LeeAnne was decked out in a white denim skirt, a tight white tank top and white cowgirl boots, which I thought was pushing it since we didn't want to attract too much attention.

I didn't want her here at all, but she did save us a lot of time on clothes and wig shopping.

I suspected she had a good laugh at my expense when she bought me the mullet wig.

Rika was in the front passenger seat in white jeans and a clingy white t-shirt. The white wig—long and straight—with heavy bangs—looked surprisingly cute on her.

LeeAnne had purposely bought low cut tops for her and Rika, believing that men were horny idiots who could be distracted from almost anything by cleavage. As my eyes gravitated to Rika's breasts for the umpteenth time, I had to admit LeeAnne was right.

Not aloud, of course.

After a minute on the paved drive, a guard station came into view. My stress level climbed steadily the closer we got. There was a good chance we wouldn't be allowed in, and, because we were in the Mojave Desert, Plan B would suck. It was winter, so daytime temperatures weren't bad, but if we had to hike in from another direction carrying our own water, this mission would take a lot longer than expected and we could be facing some very cold temperatures if we were still out there when the sun went down.

I pulled up to the guard station and idled next to it. A tall Aryan-looking man stepped out to greet us. I touched the button to roll the window down.

"Hi," I said. "Steve sent us to check out the electrical."

"There's something wrong with the electrical?" he asked. "My AC is working in here fine."

I turned to Rika and took the clipboard she was offering. It had been her idea to bring one. She said she'd seen on some news magazine show that most people will allow a person into their homes if he or she is carrying a clipboard.

"My understanding is that it's localized," I said. I lifted the top sheet on the clipboard. Each page was a blueprint of a different building with all the electrical wiring included. Rika had tracked down information about the original owner of the property this morning. He'd found them in a file on his computer and emailed them to us.

The second the guard saw the blueprints he said, "Well, if Steve wants you to check it out, I guess you'd better." He hit a button and the mechanical arm that had been blocking our way lifted.

I glanced at Rika and saw her eyebrows lift in surprise before she hid the expression.

"Be pure," the guard said.

"Yeah, be pure," I replied. I'd read that was a commonly used farewell for Microtologists, but we hadn't encountered it with the L.A. group. Maybe out here, since they were all Microtologists, they didn't feel pressured to act normal—or at least as normal as anyone else in L.A.

We found a parking spot near two large buildings. These weren't our first search choices because we thought it was more likely Rika's dad was being held in a particular building in the back. It appeared to have tiny rooms that could have easily been made into cells.

However, I didn't want to park farther into the compound because I'd noticed how easy it would be to block off the alleys between the buildings with vehicles if someone sounded the alarm. Then the cult would have four captives instead of one, assuming her dad was here.

Damn, I hoped he was here. I didn't want to see the look on Rika's face if this mission turned up zilch.

Rika and I got out and met at the back of the van. We opened the doors. I reached in and got the drill case, handing it to Rika. I picked up the large toolbox we'd gotten from Mrs. Delacruz's garage that had belonged to Rika's grandfather.

LeeAnne hopped out. "Let's go," she said.

"Where do you think you're going?" I asked.

"Same place you're going," she replied with typical LeeAnne attitude.

"We're trying to be inconspicuous."

"I can be inconspicuous."

"Not in that outfit you can't. I'm no local, but I'm willing to bet that Dolly Parton hair and cowgirl boots aren't the norm in Southern California."

"You mean I went to all this trouble and you're cutting me out of the action?"

"Nick," Rika intervened. "She was super helpful with JimBob last summer."

That was not the thing to remind me of now. "If by 'helpful' you mean she let you put your life on the line and go outside alone in the middle of the night with JimBob McGwire!"

Rika pressed her lips together and stared at me.

Shit. I couldn't resist those eyes, even when they looked at me like I was being an ass.

"It's your operation," I replied.

LeeAnne picked up a tiny roll of electrical tape and hopped out of the van.

"Don't strain yourself," I said sarcastically.

She smirked at me. "I work smarter, not harder."

I slammed the van doors shut and the three of us walked through the alley toward our target building. As we neared the door, a lanky guy with a white man-bun stood outside, vaping. I didn't know if he was some sort of guard since he was dressed all in white like every other Microtologist.

"Let me handle this," LeeAnne whispered as she pushed past me. "Hey, hon!" she called in her unmistakable Southern accent.

I mean, sure, I probably had a bit of an accent too, but there were varying levels of Texas accent and LeeAnne was at about a nine out of ten.

"Are we allowed to do that?" she pointed to Man-bun's vape pen. "The vaping I mean."

The man nodded. "As long as you only use the Microtology brand of juice," he replied. "It's got microbe-killing properties."

"Seriously?" LeeAnne said as if it was the most fascinating conversation she'd ever had. "Can I smell it?"

I thought this was an odd request until I noticed that as the guy nodded and held out the vape pen, she took a step forward and thrust her breasts out in a move no man could ignore.

She waved the vape pen under her nose, closed her eyes and let out an "Mmmm..." sound that seemed too intimate for outdoors.

It worked, though. Vape guy's eyes were glued to her chest. His tongue came out and wet his lips like he wanted a taste. I cringed inwardly, since, for some reason, I'd thought of LeeAnne as a sister for most of our lives.

"We'd better get to work," Rika said.

I could only imagine the stress she was under, wondering if she was about to be reunited with her father or hit a giant roadblock.

"See ya later?" LeeAnne said to the thin man as if she was going to be around later and they might hang out.... Later," he stammered.

Shit. We were just putty in their hands.

"Sure, yeah

I reached for the door handle and man-bun didn't try to stop me. When I opened the door, we walked into a blindingly white room. The only person around was a ruddy-faced, heavy-set young woman.

"You're up, Stud Muffin," LeeAnne whispered as the door closed behind us.

I threw her a *hush up* look and approached the desk with her and Rika right behind me.

"Hi," the young woman said. "Can I help you?"

I looked at her name tag. "Rochelle, is it?" I asked. "That's a pretty name."

"Yeah?" She shrugged. "I've never been crazy about it."

Her attitude toward me seemed pretty indifferent. I felt like I'd already struck out with her. But this was for Rika so I tried again. "Well..." I began as if I was about to reveal a secret. "Maybe it wasn't the name, exactly." I peered into her eyes meaningfully.

I was surprised when she shrugged again and looked at me like I was boring her. That had never, ever happened to me before with a woman I was trying to get to know.

LeeAnne stepped forward. "We're here from L.A.," she said. "We usually work at the VIP Center. Do you ever get to come into town?" She sat her mini-skirt clad ass on the corner of Rochelle's desk, which seemed like the last thing you should do in front of a person who already seemed over you.

Except, when I checked Rochelle's expression, she didn't look disinterested at all. Her eyes were riveted to LeeAnne's body, just like the vape guy outside.

"She smiled shyly. "Not yet," she replied. "But I'll be in L.A. for the quarterly member gala next month."

"Great!" LeeAnne said. "Maybe we'll see each other there!" She reached into her back pocket and pulled out what looked like a business card and handed it to Rochelle.

"Cool!" Rochelle said.

"We'd better get busy," I cut in. "The electrical won't inspect itself."

"Yeah, okay," LeeAnne said reluctantly.

Rochelle glared at me. Her scowl was the universal one for cock-blockers everywhere. Only maybe lesbians didn't call it "cock-blocking."

I gestured down at the clipboard. "Looks like we need to take this hall to get there." I pointed at said hallway.

Rochelle glanced at my clipboard.

"Okay," LeeAnne said, but she took another longing look at Rochelle. "I'll see you later?"

Rochelle brightened again. "I hope so," she replied. "Be pure."

"Be pure," LeeAnne repeated, but managed to make it sound alluring.

Rika took off down the hall with me and LeeAnne behind her.

"Wow, you're going to be the belle of the ball at the next Microtology shin dig," I said sarcastically.

"Always am!" LeeAnne replied.

"What was with the card?"

She pulled another one from her pocket and handed it to me. "That's a fake number," she said. "It's how I get overly persistent men to leave me alone."

I looked down at the card. "LeeAnne Timberlake?" I read.

"You never know," she said. "I may be his next wife."

I snorted, then checked over my shoulder to make sure no one was following us.

"I hope they don't think they have a secure operation here," Rika scoffed.

"Yeah," I replied. "All a person has to do is put a wig on and not be deterred by the fact that there's a guard station.

"They must have my dad locked up," she said. "Otherwise he would have escaped this place by now."

I didn't point out the other possibility. That the Microtologists could have killed him and dumped his body in the desert, never to be found.

As we walked down the hall, we looked through the small windows in each door. Most of them seemed to be used as storage rooms for extra furniture, cleaning supplies, dry goods and lots of boxes full of who knew what.

When we got to the end of the hall, there was a solid, locked door, but it had a set of keys hanging on a hook right next to it.

I took the keys and started trying them in the door.

"Why would someone lock a door, then leave the key right next to it?" LeeAnne asked.

"Because they're trying to keep someone in, not out," Rika replied.

That was exactly what I was thinking. I glanced at her to see if she looked okay. Her face was unusually blank, her body taut, her breathing shallow and rapid. She was using every ounce of her will power to keep from banging on the door and screaming for her dad. I could feel it.

I went back to what I was doing, but could still see her clenched hands. As I tested one key after another, I wondered if we'd be celebrating the return of Diego Martín tonight or...

I couldn't think about the "or" yet or what it would do to Rika. I had to focus, one step at a time.

The key I was holding slid into the lock and turned. I opened the door to find a wide hallway with six other doors running down the left side. These doors each had a small window like the others we'd seen. But they also had good-sized slots. The kind you could slide a food tray through.

"Oh, my God," Rika and LeeAnne cried together. Rika dropped her drill case and ran to the first door and peered in. I put the tool box down and was right behind her. The tiny room held a cot with a mattress and blanket, a sink, and a toilet, all white.

"It's a cell," she whispered.

"And it looks like someone has been living here." I was basing this on the fact that the blanket was rumpled and a pair of white slippers sat at odd angles just under the bed.

"Those look like women's slippers," Rika said. "They're definitely too small for my dad."

By now, LeeAnne was standing behind us on her tiptoes, craning her neck to see. Rika and I moved on to the next cell.

This one was neat as a pin, bed made, no shoes.

In the third room was a haphazardly made bed and some slippers, but we couldn't get a good look at those because they were so far under the cot.

The fourth room was perfect, but empty, without so much as a blanket. The mattress looked brand new. In fact, it was still wrapped in plastic. The smell of bleach wafted from under the door.

My heart plunged to my stomach. The new mattress and bleach odor made me think of a murder scene clean up. I glanced at Rika, hoping we weren't on the same wave-length this time.

As a criminal defense attorney, I'd seen photos of murder scenes the perpetrators had tried to clean up. Rika wasn't an attorney. But the color drained from her face as she stared into the cell and she was blinking hard.

Damn it!

We moved on to the fifth cell. It was tidy and made up. No slippers.

I tried to figure out what we'd do next if the sixth cell was empty. Rika was due for a major meltdown. She tried to be flip and stoic, but as I'd gotten to know her, I'd learned to recognize the signs that she wasn't as okay as she pretended to be.

Her eyelids blinked rapidly. Her thumbnails were fidgeting with the pads of her fingertips. She went still as a tomb as she stared toward the last door, but didn't approach it.

"It's okay," I said. I slid my hand across her back in what I hoped was a comforting move. Then I stepped past her and looked into the sixth cell window. "Looks like this one's been occupied recently. There's a shirt—"

Rika was by my side instantly. I moved back so she could get a better view. "Oh, my God," she said. "That's my father's shirt."

CHAPTER TWENTY-ONE

Rika

"He's here!" I cried as both hope and fear expanded inside me. What if I'd gotten here a day or an hour or a minute too late?

"We've got to check the other buildings" Nick said.

"Yeah, maybe they take them outside or to a gym for exercise," LeeAnne chimed in.

Bless you LeeAnne. That was a much better thought than the ones that had been going through my head.

We left the cell area and took the back hall to the other side of the building, then proceeded down the hall we hadn't checked yet. The rooms appeared to be used for storage like the rest of the building. We could see inside every one of them and didn't find any humans.

Instead of going by reception again, we doubled back to an exit door we'd seen.

"LeeAnne," Nick handed her the van keys, "Go back to the van until you hear from me. Let us know if the guards get suspicious."

LeeAnne nodded, her eyes wider than usual. I'd expected her to argue because she always argued with Nick. Then I remembered she was one of the best-hearted people I knew and would never want to jeopardize my dad's life.

"I'll tell the receptionist we found an electrical problem and I need to get some more tools," she said. "Maybe that will keep her from wondering what's taking so long."

I grabbed her arm. "Thanks, LeeAnne," I said.

"It's all good, Rika." She said it cheerfully, but I saw the worry in her eyes. "He's here. You're gonna find him." She smiled at me, then turned and walked toward reception.

Nick pushed the door open. Sunlight streamed in as I realized it led back outside.

When we stepped out, I nearly collided with a short chubby white guy who looked about eighteen, even with his head shaved.

He nodded at us. "Be pure," he said with a smile.

"Be pure," we replied.

He turned to move on, but I put my hand on his arm. "Hey," I said. "Have you seen a man with my coloring around here? We seem to have lost him."

"Oh, yeah," he replied. "The Mexican guy?"

I opened my mouth to correct him, but Nick gave me a look that said we didn't have time for a cultural awareness lecture.

"Uh-huh," I said as I gave Nick a look that said I didn't need his silent lectures about my near-lectures.

"You'd better hurry if you want to catch him. He's on his way to his purification ceremony at the temple." He pointed to a building I could barely make out at the top of a tall hill behind a shorter hill.

"Do you know when he'll be back?" Nick asked.

"He won't be. Once they go up there, I never see them again."

Nick and I exchanged wide-eyed glances.

"Where do they go?" Nick asked.

The guy shrugged again. "Not sure. That information is need-to-know only, and I'm stationed here at the P. and R. permanently, so I don't need to know." With another "Be pure," he turned and walked inside.

Nick and I peered back at the bit of building we could see in the distance. There was a dirt road leading to it. Without a word, we both turned and jogged toward the front of the compound where we'd left the van.

When we got there, LeeAnne was standing next to it while one of the guards pulled a tire off the rim. She hurried over to us.

"What's going on?" Nick asked.

"They were gonna make me take the van to some garage at the back of the property," LeeAnne said. "They said Steve and Valerie don't like maintenance vans sitting in the front parking lot. I told them 'okay,' then punctured a tire with my hunting knife when they weren't looking."

"Your hunting knife?" I repeated.

She lifted her skirt to reveal a thigh sheath with a knife handle protruding from it.

"You didn't realize that could cause a problem if we needed to make a quick getaway?" Nick whispered angrily.

"I didn't have time to think," she replied. "I just acted."

"Damn it," Nick said. "We're going to have to run to the building at the top of the hill and get Rika's dad, assuming he's really there. Text me when the tire's back on."

"Sure thing," LeeAnne replied.

Nick and I turned and ran in the direction of the Purification Temple, knowing we'd need to pace ourselves to make it all the way. Actually, *I* needed to pace myself. Nick could get there faster without me.

I was just about to tell him to go on ahead when we passed the stables. I'd seen them on the blueprint but assumed they were empty.

They weren't. Several horses could be seen in their stalls inside through the open stable doors. One horse was saddled and tied in the shade, but I didn't see any sign of a rider.

"Look, Nick!" I pointed at the stables. "You can take us on that horse!"

He didn't look happy with my suggestion. "You think just because I'm from Texas, I know how to ride a horse?"

For a moment, I considered whether my expectations of him because he was from Texas were like being racist, or maybe "statist." But then I decided that anyone who looked as natural in cowboy boots and a hat, as he did when we were in Bolo, had to know how to ride. "Is this like the gun thing?" I asked, referring to our run-in with the Satan worshippers in Bolo.

Nick huffed out a loud breath, scanned the area, then strode over to the horse. He grasped the handle thingy on the saddle, stuck his left foot in the stirrup and mounted like he did it every freaking day of his life. I ran up behind him, trying to decide how to get on.

"Don't stand behind her," he said as if it should be obvious. "We don't know this horse. She could be a kicker." He jerked his head. "Come on."

I walked around to try to get on, but he said, "Left side," in a tone that implied I was an idiot for going right. "You always mount from the left." When I came around, he reached an arm out and pulled me up behind him.

He made a clicking sound and jiggled the reins and the horse started walking. When he pulled the reins to one side, the horse turned and we were headed up the hill. I grabbed the back edge of the saddle seat.

"This *is* like the gun thing," I said accusingly. "Why would you pretend you couldn't ride at a time like this?"

"I haven't been on a horse since I was ten," he replied.

He'd told me he was ten when his dad died. I wondered if that had something to do with why he stopped riding.

He shook the reins and tapped his heels again. The horse broke into a trot.

Nick seemed completely in control of the animal. I was still irritated, but wasn't sure if it was because he could ride a horse with the skill of Zorro or because he'd acted like I was stupid for not knowing which side of the horse to mount on.

Or maybe it was because I was scared to death about what these Microtologists had done to my dad at the Purification Temple and just wanted to focus on absolutely anything else.

I pulled my phone out of my pocket and searched, "Why mount on left side of horse?"

"Ha!" I said a moment later. "Mounting from the left was a tradition that began because most men were right handed and wore their swords on the left. There's no good reason for it now. I knew horses weren't smart enough to tell left from right."

Thrusting my phone out in front of him I jiggled it tauntingly. The horse chose that moment to step in a pothole, giving me an extra jostle. The phone slipped out of my hand.

As I cried out, Nick used his lightning fast reflexes to catch the phone just before it would have hit the horse's neck and slid away. He glanced back cockily as he handed it to me. "Put it away," he said.

I rolled my eyes behind his back and tried to stick my phone in the only place I had easy access to at the moment—my bra. But since I didn't have voluminous breasts and therefore didn't have a voluminous bra, it didn't fit. I had no choice but to hang on to it until we dismounted and I could stick it in my back pocket.

Nick looked down at my hand, then he reached back and pulled my left arm around him. He did the same with my right, crushing my chest against his back.

He pried the phone from my hand, and just as I opened my mouth to protest, he pressed my palms against his hard abs. Not only could I no longer remember what I was protesting, but the comforting warmth of his body allowed me to take the first full breath I'd taken since we found the cells. Maybe the best thing about Nick was that he made me feel safe. My insides turned soft and gooey at the thought.

Nick tapped the horse with his heels and made a clicking noise. The horse took off at a gallop. I caught sight of the dirt road rolling underneath us and the goo in my stomach turned to nausea. I'd never realized horses' backs were so high off the ground.

Closing my eyes, I tightened my hold on Nick.

For a moment, squeezed against his strong body, I felt like nothing bad could happen as long as we stayed just like this—my front against his back. Actually, his front against my back would probably feel pretty good too.

And my front against his front...

I let out a dreamy sigh, causing Nick to turn and check on me again. The corners of his mouth turned up a little and he winked at me, which I interpreted to mean, "We got this."

I smiled up at him in hopeful thanks, then pressed my cheek against his back.

Once we made it up to the temple, he reined the horse in next to a utility shed about twenty yards from the building. He tied the reins to the doorknob, and we jogged toward the main building.

The place was surreal, sitting on top of a hill in the middle of the desert, bright and modern and pure white. Instead of a doorway at ground level, there were exterior staircases on the right and left, curving to the second floor like a set of parentheses. Each staircase had a wall on the outside of it, the height of a banister.

I glanced around the white-graveled parking lot and counted four golf carts. Did that mean there were four people here, including my dad? Those weren't bad odds—me, my dad and Nick against three other people.

I probably shouldn't count myself, especially if the three turned out to be men. Nick could handle himself, though, and my dad grew up fighting his way out of trouble. Either of them could probably knock a guy out and take on a second. That's what I hoped, anyway.

However, if each cart had brought two people and they tried to stop us from taking my father away, we were in trouble.

I hurried to the left staircase. But Nick used his long legs to get ahead of me. When he reached the first step, he paused and took my hand, probably so I wouldn't freak out and go running up the stairs into trouble.

His assumption that I couldn't handle myself in this situation was insulting. But I guess I had no real proof I could thwart a gang of Microtologists.

The McGuire triplet in Bolo was tall, but he was just one drunken idiot. I doubted that I could flirt my dad's way out of this mess. I did have some knowledge of self-defense, but it was mostly from watching YouTube videos.

As we approached the top of the stairs, Nick squeezed my hand reassuringly. That's when tears burned behind my eyes. I wasn't sure if they were tears of gratitude that he was here with me, or tears of fear because I had no idea what shape my dad would be in when we found him.

What if he'd already been *disappeared* by the Microtologists?

Nick released my hand. "Stay here until I get a read on what's happening," he instructed.

I didn't reply. It was nice that he wanted to protect me, but I had to see my father and I wasn't willing to wait a moment longer to lay eyes on him, so I followed directly behind Nick.

At the top, we found ourselves in an open-air hallway or "breezeway," as we called it in one of my schools when I was a kid. In fact, the building was a rectangle made up of four breezeways. The floors and the Roman pillars holding the roof up were made of white marble. Instead of being at the door of a typical building, we were looking outdoors again. This place hadn't been built on top of a hill. It had been built *into* the top of the hill, kind of like an amphitheater.

A canal-shaped pool ran down the middle of the structure

from the far end, where several people stood, and ended right below us. Leading down to it was a flight of stairs.

In other words, it was designed so you walked up just to walk back down again.

Nick grabbed me by the arm and pulled me behind a pillar. "Peek around and see if you can spot your dad," he said.

I poked my head out just enough to see the people across the way. A heavy-set man with pinkish-white skin stood at the end of the pool, dressed in a shiny white robe. On his shaved head, he wore a white, pyramid-shaped hat.

His voice rang out as he spouted some mumbo jumbo about what an important step purification was in their "church."

On one side of him stood a man dressed in white linen pants and a tunic. His hair was shaved into a snowy white Mohawk. Although he had a lot more pigment in his skin than the man who was speaking, he didn't look like my father.

I narrowed my eyes and focused hard on his features. "It's Jason Kim!" I whispered. "I saw his picture on the website."

Nick leaned forward with me and looked. "Which one?"

"Mohawk. So much for that family funeral he was supposed to be at."

Next to Jason was another man—tall and muscular—who was too young and light-skinned to be my father. He wore white jeans and a white t-shirt tucked in. His size and demeanor screamed "henchman" to me. An icy shiver shot down my back.

My eyes shifted to the final man, who wasn't my dad either. His hair was stark white against his expresso-colored skin.

Skin the same color as mine.

"Oh, my God!"

"Sh!" Nick yanked me back behind the pillar. "What's wrong?"

"My dad's hair is white!"

"Yeah?" Nick's tone said he didn't get it.

How could I explain about my dad's little quirk? "He's really picky about his hair," I began. "He has a special hairstylist he uses and, sometimes he re-cuts parts of it himself if he's not happy. He uses different hair products depending on the weather that day."

Nick's brows drew together as if he couldn't possibly relate to that degree of fussiness over one's hair.

"He would never bleach it white," I said, finally getting to my point.

"Do you think they've gotten to him?" Nick asked. When I gave him a questioning look, he added, "Brainwashed him?"

"No!" I whisper-shouted. Then I flashed back to the time I spent a few years ago researching mind control. A person didn't have to be stupid or naive like Jemima to be brainwashed. Almost anyone could be if the washers knew what they were doing. The books I'd read by cult defectors had made that very clear.

After watching my face for a moment, Nick said, "He may not go with us willingly. We might need a Plan B."

"No," I repeated. "My dad will choose me over them, brainwashed or not." I'd never encountered my dad in a brainwashed state. I certainly hoped he'd pick me.

"There's another staircase." Nick pointed at the lower level. I could see the bottom steps a few yards from where my dad was standing.

The priest—or whatever he was—began descending into the pool. Were they going to do a protestant-style baptism on my father?

"Let's go!" I took off to the right. Nick followed me around the corner, along the breezeway until we found the stairs. As we descended, two things struck me: The strong smell of chlorine bleach and the very green grass outside.

Nick's eyes followed mine to the outdoor area. "This is where the golf course ends," he gestured to a couple of stray golf carts near the grass, which, because of the slope of the hill, were only three feet below us on this side of the building. "Now that I know the lay of the land, I'm going to get the horse and bring her around the building. When we get your dad, you two can ride away on it."

"We don't know how to ride," I replied, panicked by his suggestion.

Nick grasped my arms just below the shoulders. "Did you see how I made him go?"

"Yeah," I replied. "But—"

"Just get on him and make him go to the main road. I'll catch up with you in the van." He handed me my phone and I stuck it in my back pocket.

"Nick." I shook my head. "I can't—"

He cut me off. "I've seen you in action. You can do anything you set your mind to Paprika Anise." Leaning down, he pressed his lips to my forehead.

An emotion I didn't have time to deal with swelled up inside me. I blinked back tears. "But how will you get away?" I realized at that moment I'd be every bit as brokenhearted if I lost Nick permanently as I would if I lost my dad.

"Oh, I'll get away," he said. "Don't do anything to draw attention to yourself until I get back with the horse." He jumped off the breezeway onto the grass and jogged off.

I found another pillar to hide behind so I could watch what was happening. The priest mumbled on, using the word "purification" a dozen more times. My eyes began to burn and I thought about the high concentration of chlorine in the pool. Was being dunked in that much bleach dangerous?

And why were Jason and his sidekick here? Would they jump into the pool and drown my father while he was getting purified?

The priest gestured to my dad and he grabbed the hem of his shirt and pulled it over his head, handing it to Jason who quickly handed it off to the henchman.

I was relieved to see no signs of abuse on my father. No bruises or cuts visible from where I was standing.

After a few more words from the priest, my father walked to

the edge of the pool. I couldn't let him get in there, especially with two dangerous men looking on.

I stepped out from behind the pillar. "Papi!" I shrieked before I'd consciously decided what to do.

His head jerked up. "Rika?" Then he was running toward me. I glanced out the other side of the breezeway.

No Nick. I'd jumped the gun.

As my father reached me, I saw Jason and the giant hurrying in our direction. My dad's hands reached out to me, but instead of the hug I was expecting, he grabbed my upper arms, much like Nick had earlier.

"*Están locos*," he whispered. "And they think I'm with them. I've been going along like I believe all their crazy shit." He turned and saw Jason coming at us, his eyes on me. "*Corre*, Rika!" my father said. "Run!"

A part of me wanted to run because my father was telling me to so fervently. But I didn't go to all this trouble tracking him down just to leave him here.

"Hey!" Jason called out as he approached. "This is off limits! Who are you?"

A second before he reached me, my dad's hands left me. He spun around and I heard the dull smack as his fist connected with Jason's cheek.

Jason staggered backwards several feet, caught himself on a pillar, then immediately stalked forward, except now my father was his target instead of me. As he drew close, he turned to one side and threw a badass kick at my father's mid-section. My dad sucked in his abs and curved his spine, avoiding the kick by millimeters.

The fight was on, but I caught movement in my peripheral vision. The henchman, who was the biggest of all the men present, was stomping toward me. What kind of sense did that make? I was half his size.

His mouth was closed, but his eyes were saying, *Fee-fi-fo-fum, I smell the blood of a Colom-bi-an.*

Eeeek!

I could only think of one defensive measure that had any possibility of working.

Pretending to be afraid, I covered my face with my hands so my thumbs would be up high without tipping him off. I watched the floor. When I saw his white cowboy boots, I looked up as I jabbed my thumbs straight into his eyeballs.

"Shit!" he screamed in a surprisingly high-pitched voice. As he rubbed his sore eyes, I checked and found my dad and Jason throwing punches at each other.

Jason was a security professional, but my dad had been fighting his way out of trouble since grade school. He had some moves.

I turned back to my attacker in time to see that he was squinting his blinky red eyes at me murderously, coming at me again.

Before I had a chance to move, I felt my feet leave the floor. I was levitating, my body swinging around in mid-air.

Have I finally gotten my superpower?

Once my feet were on the ground again, I realized Nick had been responsible for my flying. He'd swung me behind him and was now between me and the henchman.

The henchman was a freak of nature, taller and thicker than Nick. When his hands balled into fists, veins popped out all over his arms.

In a flash, Nick's elbow rocked back and his fist struck the underside of the henchman's chin. The guy went down like a sequoia, crashing onto the marble.

Nick and I turned to see Jason, who now had a black eye and a cut on his face, punch my dad in the stomach. The momentum jerked him back into a pillar. I heard his head crack against the marble and he went down.

"Papi!" I cried as I rushed over to check his pulse. It was still strong, but he was unconscious.

I looked up in time to see Nick land a jab to Jason's nose. Blood rushed out, but Jason didn't seem to notice as he threw a left into Nick's gut. This time, Nick was the one who didn't seem to notice as his fist caught Jason's gut, sending him flying into the pool.

Without a moment's hesitation, Nick came over and grabbed my dad under his arms, dragging him toward the golf course. I snatched up his feet to make the job easier.

"Change of plans," Nick said, tilting his head at a cart. We deposited my dad into the passenger side. "LeeAnne texted me that the tire's about done. I'll be on the horse. Follow me. I want to get there first to take out any resistance."

Take out any *resistance*? I felt like I'd stumbled into a *Star Wars* movie.

Nick untied the horse from the other golf cart and mounted him effortlessly. I got in the driver's seat of the golf cart and turned it on. I'd never driven a golf cart before, but how hard could it be?

I mashed the accelerator as the hill sloped downward. My dad slumped forward and right, his arm dragging on the green.

"Shit!" I slowed and curled my arm around his neck. Then I hauled him to me, pulling until his head lolled on my shoulder, his left arm hanging inside my right arm as I drove.

As I sped up again, I noticed Nick glancing back repeatedly, but he wasn't looking at me. He was looking behind me. I checked over my shoulder and saw a very wet Jason Kim getting into the other golf cart.

"Gun it!" Nick yelled.

I stomped the pedal down as far as it would go. My cart accelerated to the unimpressive speed of about fifteen miles per hour.

Glancing back, I saw Jason "chasing" me at the same speed. It occurred to me that a guy in his shape would probably have a better chance of catching me on foot if my dad hadn't tired him out with all the punching. I pressed my arm against my father's chest, relieved to feel his heart still beating.

Then, I had a weird out-of-body experience in which I imagined what this scene looked like from a distance—Nick on a horse, racing across a golf course, being chased by me and my unconscious dad in a golf cart, while I was being chased by another golf cart. I nearly chuckled, wishing my dad were conscious because I knew he'd find this hilarious.

Maybe this wasn't an appropriate time for hilarity, but I'd found my father and he was still warm and breathing. I was so glad to have him back with me. If I could just get him away from—

Pop. Ping.

The two sounds got my attention. I'd heard that ping sound before, in Barr's parking lot, in Bolo, when I was getting...

Pop. Ping.

...shot at.

I turned and saw Jason's hand above his steering wheel. It was holding a handgun that was pointed right at me...or my dad. And I was pretty sure those shots were pinging on the metal poles that held the canopy on the cart. Way too close for comfort.

"Stop!" he yelled. "And I won't hurt you."

Maybe he was just shooting at me to scare me into cooperating. But maybe he wasn't.

I swerved to the right, then to the left as quickly as the cart would maneuver, but I realized there were two problems with this. One involved mathematics: If two carts are going the same speed, one swerving and one going in a straight line...

Jason would catch up to me.

Second, while I was swerving, he fired off two more rounds and they both hit the cart.

A gust of wind blew into my cart, head on, creating some resistance, slowing my progress as it tugged at my wig.

Then I had a ridiculous idea! I checked back to make sure I was directly in front of Jason who looked like he'd stopped shooting to rub some sand out of his eyes.

Looking ahead at the sand trap it had likely come from, I reached up and pulled the pins from my scalp and tossed them away. I held onto the wig with my fingertips until I saw the sand stir again, then I let go. A strong breeze blew into me, swiping the wig from my head. A second later, Jason let out a strange sound. I turned to see my wig devouring his face like a deranged albino rabbit.

I couldn't believe that stunt worked, but this was my chance to make an escape. We'd been following the route of the course which sloped gradually down the hill in front of me, but that was making us an easy target.

Hoping I wasn't about to kill us both, I jerked my wheel to the right. The cart went over a steep embankment, bouncing down the rocky slope. It suddenly felt like we were going too fast and I tried to slow down, but we were at the mercy of gravity and rough terrain now. I kept one hand on the steering wheel and used the other to hold my father's upper arm tightly against my body.

When the front tires banged into a large rock and the back of the cart lifted higher than the front, a wave of nausea hit me and my eyes shut involuntarily. This was like riding a jackhammer.

Then the cart came to a standstill and I opened my eyes to find us sitting on the grass at the fifteenth hole.

Another shot rang out.

Nick!

I looked up to see him, still on the horse, charging Jason's cart at full speed. Jason was pointing the gun straight at him.

"No!" I screamed.

Jason got off another shot before Nick dived off the horse onto him. I couldn't tell who was winning the wrestling match that ensued, but I was relieved to see the gun fly off the course and wedge in some rocks.

Seconds later, Nick stood on the course above me. "I can see the van," he called. "Get moving! I'll catch up!"

When I turned, LeeAnne was waving at us from the bottom of the hill, looking over her shoulder as if expecting trouble. I mashed the accelerator again and headed down the course as fast as I could.

CHAPTER TWENTRY-TWO

Rika

As I neared the van, LeeAnne opened the double doors. Nick had managed to get back on the horse and catch up to me, but this time he stayed directly behind me until we were down the hill.

I was pretty sure he was using himself as a human shield in case there was more shooting from Jason or his henchman. Instead of making me feel better, I was just as stressed, imagining another shot ringing out and Nick slumping over the horse.

"Where are the guards?" Nick asked LeeAnne as he dismounted. I checked over my shoulder. No Jason or henchman.

"They got an emergency call and took off up the dirt road," she replied.

I looked at Nick as I got out of the cart. "By now they've probably gotten another one telling them to come back here." I started tugging on my dad's arms.

"Let me do that," Nick muscled me out of the way. He put his forearms under my dad's shirtless shoulders and pulled him right out. I grabbed his feet again and we laid him in the van.

"Jesus Christ Superstar!" LeeAnne cried as she ran her index finger down my father's abs. "Who's the hottie?"

The question threw me for a minute before I remembered she hadn't met my dad. She'd been out of town with one of her new boutique friends when he got to L.A. Then, they'd both had new jobs and their schedules weren't in sync, so whenever my dad was at Lita's, LeeAnne was gone and vice versa.

I slapped her hand away. "This is my dad!" I replied. "*Not* a hottie!"

"He may be your dad, honey, but he's definitely a hottie."

I applied an elbow to her belly, forcing her back so she'd stop feeling up my father. "I need to check his pulse," I said, even though he was clearly still alive. I just wanted to think I was helping him somehow.

"I'll do it!" LeeAnne said. But instead of putting her fingertips to his neck or wrist, she laid her entire palm over his left pectoral muscles.

I smacked her arm, hard.

"Ow!"

"If you touch him again, I'm filing molestation charges."

"Shit," I heard Nick say.

LeeAnne and I turned to see the guards from the gate pull up behind us, both of them casting wary glances Nick's way. I wished someone would look at me like that, but nobody considers you much of a threat when you're my size unless you're Jet Li.

Damn I wish I were Jet Li right now.

"Look," the bleached blonde one said. "You three are free to go, but you can't take him." He gestured to my dad.

"I'm not leaving without my father," I said as forcefully as I could.

"Yeah, he's going with us," LeeAnne confirmed.

Their eyes cut to us momentarily, then they focused their attention back on Nick, the obvious threat. LeeAnne and I stepped forward anyway, flanking Nick as he faced them down.

He kept his gaze steady and his voice calm as he said, "I know you have a job to do, but I'm sure you didn't sign up for kidnapping and holding a man against his will."

"According to my intel, he came here willingly," the bald one said. "And you're the kidnappers. We're just going to get him out of the van and—"

I pointed at my dad. "He's my father," I yelled. Then, I pointed at baldy. "And *you* aren't taking him anywhere!" On the word "you," I jabbed my finger so furiously, it poked him in the chest.

He grabbed me by the wrist in what was probably an instinctive reaction. But I didn't like his hand on my wrist, so I lifted my foot and slammed my heel down on his instep.

"Fuck!" he cried. When he bent double to nurse his injured foot, I smashed my knee into his forehead.

He staggered backward a couple of steps, holding his head.

Then things moved really fast. My actions seemed to snap LeeAnne into bar-brawl mode. She kneed Blondie in the groin. She must have done a stellar job because he fell to his knees holding his package and groaning.

But the bald one didn't go down so easily. He recovered, took three steps, grabbed me by the arm and yanked me toward him.

I'd been unaware of what Nick was doing while I attacked a man twice my size, but, now, his fist came whistling by my face and smashed Baldy right between the eyes. He fell back on his ass as blood spurted out his nose.

Now Nick was the one pointing. "You don't touch her," he said menacingly. "*Ever.*"

My body flushed hot. The girly parts between my thighs quivered.

Jeez! Tell me I'm not turned on by a guy punching another guy out for me. That was so high-school cheerleader. Or how I imagined them to be since they never gave me the time of day when I was in school. But, no question, my body was totally aroused, completely ignoring the disgust my brain was experiencing at my cave woman response.

Baldy touched his face then stared at the blood on his hand. "Oh, my God! I'm supposed to start work on a pilot in two weeks!"

"A what?" Nick asked.

"A pilot, you know, for a TV show? I'm an actor."

Nick did a quick headshake and looked at me. "Another actor?"

But the blonde guard was on his feet again. He pointed at me. "That bitch touched him first!" he said in a surprisingly whiny voice for a grown man. "Then this bitch—" He pointed at LeeAnne, but stopped talking as Nick stalked toward him.

Nick seized the front of his shirt and glared into his eyes. "Call them bitches again," he said.

The guard pressed his lips together, his eyes so wide he resembled a cartoon version of himself.

Nick released him and turned to us. "Let's get going before you ladies have to take down Jason and his goon, too."

The guards were silent, giving us nothing but dirty looks. Nick chuckled as he got into the driver's seat. I didn't see what was funny about fighting off crazy cult members. I climbed in and sat on the floor next to my dad and LeeAnne took the passenger seat.

Once we were out of the compound and on the highway, Nick shook out his right hand and checked his knuckles. They were bloody. I hoped most of the blood belonged to other people.

"It's been a long time since I've seen you deliver the Nick Owen right jab," LeeAnne said with a chuckle.

"Yeah, I forgot about your secret weapons." He glanced down at her knees. Then they both cracked up. LeeAnne held her fist up. "Time to bump it out, homey," she said. Her lips turned up in a full-on smile. Nick smiled back and lifted his fist, then winced when she hit it with gusto.

My heart warmed. It was nice to see them like they probably

were when they were kids instead of the way they'd been since I met them—snarking at each other in person and defending each other when the other one wasn't around to hear.

LeeAnne twisted in her seat, focusing on my dad. "Did they drug him?"

"No, he got in a fight with Jason Kim, the security director," I replied. "Ended up hitting his head on a marble pillar." This was the first chance I had to examine him. He had a cut on his cheek and another over his eye, but they didn't look too bad. There were probably bruises, but I couldn't see them in the dark van. No blood was coming from the back of his head, but I knew that wasn't necessarily a good sign.

"LeeAnne," Nick said as he handed her his phone. "Can you search for the nearest hospital and put the address in the GPS?"

I stared down at my father's face as I considered what Nick had said. "No," I said firmly. "We're not taking him to a hospital."

"What?" Nick glanced back at me like I'd lost my mind.

LeeAnne put a hand on Nick's arm to keep him quiet. "Rika, honey, we've got to take him to a hospital." She spoke to me like I was in shock and not thinking straight.

"No," I replied. "Once he's in a hospital, he's basically in the cops' hands. They can put a guard by his door. I may not be allowed to see him or speak to him. If he comes to, they may arrest him."

"Rika!" Nick said as if trying to jar me back to reality.

"Nick!" I replied sharply. "We both know what happens when the cops are convinced they have their killer."'

"And with the arrest warrant out on him, you're harboring a fugitive," he pointed out.

Like I cared about that sort of thing when my dad's whole future was in jeopardy.

"Look," I said. "He might look like just another Colombian criminal to you..."

Nick slowed the van and twisted his body to look at me. His

expression revealed anger and maybe hurt at what I'd said to him.

My words had been careless. Nick had never, ever denigrated my dad or Colombians. He'd simply expressed concern about how a jury in Bolo would react to my lineage.

I squeezed my eyes shut and shook off the guilty feelings. I didn't have time to deal with Nick and whatever emotions we evoked in each other. I had to take care of my dad.

"My father's reputation is everything to him," I said. "Not only as a chef, but as a person. He wouldn't want his picture on the nightly news as the defendant in a murder case. We have to find out who killed Alberto."

"Rika," Nick tried again, his voice calm and concerned.

But I interrupted. "Do you remember last summer when I thought LeeAnne could have been involved in the murder, and you told me she absolutely wasn't?"

"Aw, did you stick up for me, Nicholas?" LeeAnne asked, a mischievous gleam in her eye.

Nick ignored her as he glanced from the road to me. "Yeah," he said quietly.

"Well, now I'm telling you that my father was not involved in this murder and I don't want him to spend one day in jail for a crime he didn't commit. We're taking him to Mrs. Ruíz."

"The witch doctor?" Nick cried.

"*Curandera!*" I corrected. "She's an excellent herbalist and a certified nurse practitioner."

"Does the licensing board know she's doing all this other mumbo jumbo on her patients?"

"I don't know, Nick," I said angrily. "Do you want to call them right now and tell them?"

If I had a phaser, he'd have been zapped already. I'd only have it set on "stun," but surely it would sting a little. "I've seen Mrs. Ruíz set broken legs that healed perfectly. Everyone in the neighborhood uses her. Plus, she *knows people*."

"What does that mean?" Nick asked.

"Just head for my neighborhood and you'll find out."

Nick

I pulled the van into the well-lit parking lot. The sign above the door said, "24 Hour Emergency Care." I assumed it was one of those private urgent care facilities, since there didn't seem to be a hospital attached.

Rika was holding her phone to her ear as she talked to Mrs. Ruíz.

As I started to pull into a parking space, she lifted the receiver away from her mouth. "No, not here. She's meeting us around back." Rika flung her arm out in front of me, pointing to the alley behind the building.

I cruised around back, stopping near a door in the alley. An older model Ford Taurus was sitting nearby.

Its lights flashed twice.

"That's her," Rika said.

As Mrs. Ruíz emerged from her car, I cut off the van's engine.

"Can you help me get him inside?" Rika asked.

"I'll help!" LeeAnne said, her voice too enthusiastic for the circumstance. Rika cut her eyes toward LeeAnne, as if suspicious of her intentions.

"What are we doing back here?" I asked, but Rika was already out of the van. I got out and walked to the back.

The back door to the building opened. A young Latino in a white lab coat peeked out. He motioned for us to come on, but Mrs. Ruíz grabbed the door. "Go help," she said to the young man. Then she whisper-shouted, "This is my cousin's son Roberto."

Roberto came up and offered his hand for a shake. "Most people call me Rob," he said.

"Nick," I replied as I shook his hand.

"Rika," Rob said as he turned to her. He gathered her in his arms as if it was the most natural thing in the world.

My body tensed, ready to intervene and pull them apart if he held on too long.

"I've heard what's been going on. I'm sorry you had to go through this." His voice resonated with feeling. Had I sounded that sympathetic when she called me? I mean, I'd felt it, but had I truly expressed it?

He pulled his head back, looked into Rika's eyes and said, "Are you okay?"

"I'm fine," she said, appearing perfectly comfortable in Rob's arms.

A nerve twinged in the back of my neck. I knew who he was to Mrs. Ruíz, but what was his relationship with Rika? I reached up and rubbed the feeling away.

"You're so brave," he said, pulling her tight against him again. "If there's anything you need—"

"I'm fine," Rika said into his shoulder. "I've got Papi back."

Rob released her and moved to get her father. He took his feet while I grabbed Diego under the shoulders. We carried him to a gurney that was waiting inside the door.

"We tried to wake him up on the way over," LeeAnne said loudly.

"Shhh!" Roberto said. "The doctor's asleep in the room next door.

"Shouldn't you go wake him up?" I asked.

"No!" Rika, Mrs. Ruíz, and Rob whispered simultaneously.

"This is, um..." Rob looked around the group, "...on the down low."

I frowned at him then Rika. "Down so low he's not going to see a doctor?"

"*Pues*, why do you think I'm here?" Mrs. Ruíz asked, obviously insulted. She followed the gurney as Rob pushed it to the opposite side of the building from where the entrance and doctor's room were.

"Rika!" I took her by both shoulders and shook her a little. Up until now I'd thought she was one of the smartest people I knew. Now...well, I wasn't sure. Maybe she was in shock. She didn't seem to be thinking straight. "Are you really going to trust your unconscious dad to her?"

She grabbed my hands, peeled them off her shoulders and thrust them away, her eyes sharp and angry. In fact, I'd never seen her look so angry. "Do you *really* think you care more about my unconscious father than I do?"

My lips parted, but I didn't know how to answer the question. Of course she had to care more about him than I did. I'd never even exchanged words with him. But she wasn't thinking straight right now. "Rika—"

"If she were a white male in a lab coat, you'd believe whatever she, I mean he, said. But since she's a Hispanic woman she's not qualified to treat him?"

Whoa. What the hell brought that on? Now I was the one who was angry. "No. Because she's not a real doctor, she's not qualified to treat him."

Rika looked at me like I was the crazy one. "She has a vast knowledge of Mexican, Chinese and Ayurvedic herbal medicine, *and* she has a doctorate in nursing. Healing is her life, and much of the time she's done it for free, not because she expected it to make her a millionaire."

"How was I supposed to know all that? Until a few minutes ago, you made it sound like she was mixing up potions in her caldron!"

"I never said she had a cauldron!"

I realized the cauldron might have come from my own imagination.

"Whatever," Rika said. "If Mrs. Ruíz believes he needs to go to the hospital, I'll take him, but I hope he doesn't because once the cops get him, he'll be railroaded to prison." Her eyes filled before she batted the liquid away with some quick blinking. "I'm scared to death, but I'm trying to think big picture and do what's best for him!"

I got it. She was even braver than I thought. She could have taken her father to a hospital. That would have been the easy thing to do. Then the doctors and cops could take over. It would be out of her hands, but she'd know her dad was alive. Instead, she was keeping her wits about her, recognizing he wouldn't want to spend his life in prison for a murder he didn't commit.

"Okay. I get it," I said. "But I'd appreciate it if you wouldn't make me out to be a misogynistic bigot when you haven't given me all the information."

She put a hand on one hip—never a good sign from a woman—and said, "Maybe you should just have some faith in me by now." Her eyes bore into mine. "Sometimes I know what I'm doing."

Most of the time she knew what she was doing. *Shit*. I looked back in the direction her father had been taken.

"Rika." I cupped her jaws in my hands and looked deep into her eyes. "I have more faith in you than you'll ever know. I was afraid you were in shock, with everything that happened."

I watched liquid form in her eyes again before she blinked it away. Stepping forward, she pressed her body to mine, wrapping her arms tightly around my waist. Her cheek was against my chest and I couldn't stop my hand from caressing her hair. Or my lips from touching the top of her head and lingering there.

We were both quiet for a moment. She relaxed into me and I pressed my cheek against her head. "I'm on your side, Paprika," I murmured. "Always." And as capable as she was, in that moment I wanted to cover her with an invisibility cloak—yeah, I'd finally watched Harry Potter so I could feel closer to her—and hide her away from this scary, sad, dangerous world.

She didn't try to move away, so I just kept holding her as the minutes ticked by, until our breaths matched one another's and I started to feel like we were one organism.

I liked that feeling more than I'd ever liked anything in my life.

Her head jerked at the sound of footsteps. We both turned toward Mrs. Ruíz, who was hurrying down the hall to us. "The MRI is finished," she said. "And, Rika, your father is awake.

Rika's eyes widened before she broke out in a run toward the MRI room. I strode behind her, hoping her father could give us the information we needed to solve the murder.

"Papi!" she cried when we reached the doorway.

Her father was sitting in a wheelchair. He threw his arms wide and she bent to give him a hug. He pulled her so tight, she fell into his lap. He held her close. "My Paprika," he said. "You look so beautiful! You've lost so much weight!"

Hmm...what weight?

Rika pulled back and looked at him. "Papi, I lost the weight a few years ago."

Confusion clouded his features. "Years?"

"Rika," Mrs. Ruíz called as she motioned Rika to where she and I were standing.

Rika extracted herself and walked over. "He has some memory loss," Mrs. Ruíz said. "He doesn't even remember why he's in L.A."

The remainder of the happy expression from moments ago slid from Rika's face. "He doesn't remember the murder?" she whispered.

"No, *mija*. He doesn't."

I noticed Rika's hands moving. She was running her thumbnails over each fingernail. Her eyes flicked left, then right, as if she was literally looking for a solution to this new problem.

"Is the memory loss permanent?" I asked.

Mrs. Ruíz shook her head. "Probably not. Not all of it, at least.

It's hard to say what he'll eventually remember, but he's awake and he recognized Rika and me and even Roberto."

Rika's gaze met mine. "Do you know what a prosecutor is going to do with my father's 'convenient' memory loss in court?"

I nodded. "But we can keep investigating. We found him. We can find the killer." I didn't want Rika chasing killers, but I couldn't shake the memory of the look on her face when she heard about the amnesia. For one rare moment, she'd looked defeated.

"I don't know who else to talk to," she said, dismay obvious in her voice. "I thought if I just found him..." She glanced at her father, who had his hands on the arms of the wheelchair and was trying to stand.

"Roberto," Rika cried.

Roberto, who'd been watching our exchange from beside Diego's chair, realized what was happening and spoke to Diego in Spanish.

Diego replied in a sharp tone of voice.

Rika shut her eyes. When she opened them again, her determination had returned. "Mrs. Ruíz," she whispered, "do you have anything safe to give him to keep him sedated?" She glanced at her father again. "I know him. He's going to insist he's fine and want to go back to work, if he remembers where he works. If he doesn't, he may try to hop a plane to Colombia to go back to his old job. He doesn't *not* go to work."

"I have something I can give him," Mrs. Ruíz answered. "And I'll stay with him at my cousin's house so the police don't find him." She dropped her voice to a whisper again. "But if we tell him the truth—"

"He's not going to want to be in hiding," Rika said. "He'll think it's cowardly. He'd probably want to go speak to the police or to Alberto's wife—when he remembers she exists. He was Alberto's boss. He'll think it's the right thing to do to pay his respects. Then she may report him to the cops."

Rika had been gesturing with her hands as she often did when she spoke. Mrs. Ruíz took one and patted it.

"Don't worry, *mija*. We'll take care of him. You do what you have to do to prove him innocent...after you get some sleep."

"Yeah, okay." Rika's eyes shifted back to her father. She took a deep breath. "Okay."

CHAPTER TWENTY-THREE

Rika

By the time Nick was walking me to my door, all the adrenaline had left my system and I couldn't decide if I was more hungry or tired.

After using the key to unlock the deadbolt, I turned and looked up at Nick, trying to compose a sentence to thank him for helping me find my father.

Someone had forgotten to leave the porch light on—probably LeeAnne, since I'd sent her home while we were getting my dad situated with Mrs. Ruíz—so the porch was dark. Nick's eyes were dark and colorless in the shadows, yet, somehow, they were as compelling as when they were Bondi Blue.

"You were amazing today," he said. "Brave and kinda badass." His fingers encircled my arms above my elbows. As his thumbs skimmed over my not-so-impressive biceps, he chuckled. "You beat up guys that had about a hundred pounds on you."

I smiled at his exaggeration, since he'd done most of the beating up. Then his last words sunk in and I didn't like the thought of him mentally estimating my weight.

But he was smiling at me with such admiration in his eyes so I fought off the urge to ask him how much he thought I weighed. I always got the feeling he saw something different when he looked at me than I saw when I looked in the mirror. A part of me was desperate to view his image of me.

Come to think of it, though, one big reason I wanted the image was so I'd know how many pounds I needed to lose to be Nick's perfect woman and that wasn't exactly a healthy mental attitude.

I visualized an action-figure sized Wonder Woman pushing the unhealthy thoughts out through my ears. I still hadn't given Nick the thanks he deserved.

"Nick," I whispered because my throat was closing from the gratitude that was overwhelming me. "Thanks for—"

That's all I got out before he bent down and captured my mouth with his. His lips were gentle, at first. A light touch, like an answer to my whispered words moments before.

Then for a split-second, I thought it was over. But our mouths barely lost touch, before he came back in for more.

My lips parted like it was the only thing they could possibly do with Nick on them. His tongue wasted no time, pressing into me, sweeping across mine.

There was a sound from deep in his throat. I felt the vibration as I heard it and answered it with a high-pitched moan.

He dragged me against him and my arms slid up over his shoulders, curling around his neck. One of his hands cradled the back of my head, his fingers holding me firmly as if escape was not an option.

As if I'd want to escape.

He retreated for a split second, then came in harder, his tongue thrusting into me, his free hand sliding down my back until it was pressing my hips into his.

I could feel him growing and hardening against my abdomen, and my heart pounded in my ears. I pushed my tongue into him, but he only allowed it for a second before reclaiming control of the kiss, again, thrusting even farther inside me.

Heat shot through my body and I thought my knees might give way. But they didn't have a chance because his hands were suddenly cupping my rear end, pulling upward until I was on my tiptoes and his hardness dug into my pelvis.

The sensation unleashed something wild I never knew I had inside me. I didn't just want to have sex with Nick anymore. I wanted to devour him. I wanted him to devour me. I didn't want to stop until we were so consumed by each other we couldn't find our way out of us.

I captured his bottom lip, scraping my teeth across it. He growled, kissing me so savagely, I wasn't sure I'd survive it.

I lost my balance, hitting the door with my back, but he followed. His lips touched my neck and I experienced a full-body shiver. His thigh moved between mine and hit the spot—a spot that hadn't been hit by a man in quite a while. The pressure sent a jolt of pleasure through me all the way to my toes. But when he pushed his thigh in harder, I got dizzy and my head dropped back, hitting the door a moment after Nick's boot did.

The result was a lot like a knocking sound.

Shit! If we kept this up we were going to wake up my grandmother. I imagined Lita coming to the door, chasing Nick away, then questioning me about why I was practically having sex with a man who already had a woman.

Lita had been cheated on too many times to have sympathy for women who knowingly seduced a man that was already taken. And I certainly wasn't okay with being the other woman.

It took all the strength I had, mentally and physically, to pull away. He held on until he saw the look in my eyes and let go.

Dizzy, I wobbled back and landed against the door.

He put his hands on his hips, looked down at the cement under his feet, and took in several deep breaths. When his gaze met mine again, his brows were pressed down in a sort of angry-confused expression.

Really? Did he think every woman he was momentarily attracted to was supposed to sleep with him regardless of any other women in his life?

No wonder he'd been divorced three times.

His lips parted as if he was going to speak, but either he didn't know what to say or he was holding back angry words, I wasn't sure which. However, I did know that I didn't want to have a fight on my grandmother's porch about Marla. Besides, I still needed Nick to help me prove my dad's innocence.

"I'll see you tomorrow," I said in a business-like tone. Or as business-like as a person can sound when she was just seconds away from a fully-clothed orgasm. I pulled my shoulders back and cleared my throat. "Lita said to remind you she's making breakfast."

Nick's lips parted again. Hands still on his hips, he closed his eyes for several long seconds as he took in a huge breath.

"Goodnight," I said.

"Night," he replied with a chin lift, but he didn't walk away. He watched me, blank-faced, as I escaped into the house.

Nick

As the door closed in my face, I had no idea what had happened.

Well, I knew what had happened. I just didn't know why it happened. Or more precisely, why it didn't.

I braced my hand on the doorframe as I waited for my body to return to normal. Although, I wasn't sure it had felt normal since the last time I made out with Rika in Bolo.

Every damned night since then, my mind had drifted to the image of her, standing in my master bath in nothing but her

Batgirl bra and panties. I'd seen a lot of women in skimpy clothing—revealing dresses, bikini bathing suits, lacy lingerie...

But there was something about Rika that pulled at all different parts of me at the same time. Sometimes when she looked up at me with those big brown eyes, I thought she might pull me apart completely.

I used to have a type. I liked 'em tall and blonde with big boobs—real or otherwise. But since Rika left Bolo, I'd been doing double takes whenever a petite brunette passed by. Then my brain would remind my body that it couldn't be her and a twinge of disappointment would echo through me from my head to my feet.

I'd managed to keep myself from calling or texting her for six months because I didn't think I was right for her. She was smart and beautiful and she could do better than a guy who'd been married and divorced multiple times. Shouldn't she be with someone who wasn't a decade older with a century's worth of baggage to show for it?

But, being here in the dark with her at four o'clock in the morning seemed so right. I always missed her most when I woke in the middle of the night, even though the two of us had never shared a bed.

It felt like I should be able to open my eyes and see her sleeping on my other pillow. Then I'd be able to go back to sleep instead of tossing and turning, thinking of her all night.

However, if she were next to me, I'd want to reach out and pull her closer. Maybe press my crotch against that sweet little ass of hers. Then I'd probably be kept awake by the wood her sweet little ass provoked, so maybe my sleep was screwed either way.

But it would be so much nicer to be awake with her in my arms than not.

It wasn't all about me, though. It had to be about what Rika needed, too. And, although the attraction was clearly there between us, some part of her must have realized I wasn't it for her or she wouldn't have cut me off with no explanation.

As I walked back to my Yukon, I checked my phone.

Good. Nothing from Marla.

Hopefully, she'd already found herself the sugar daddy she was clearly looking for.

She had to have known her days were numbered with me. I'd quit making any meals and stocked the kitchen with only lunch meat, bread and peanut butter.

I'd even suggested if she was staying in Bolo, she apply for the job opening at Dill's Dollar Store, which I knew she wouldn't take in a million years.

I was hoping she'd be gone when I got back from L.A., but maybe her coming along was the best thing that could have happened. There were a lot of wealthy men in this city.

My eyes paused on Rika's name in my text contacts. I clicked on it and typed, *Goodnight, Paprika*. Then I caught myself and hit the backspace key until I deleted every letter.

Now at the door of the Yukon, I reached into my pocket for the key fob and hit the unlock button.

"Hey!" I heard a male voice say.

In the truck window, I caught the reflection of movement behind me and slowly turned around.

CHAPTER TWENTY-FOUR

Rika

Once I was in the house, I headed straight to the kitchen for a snack. Checking the refrigerator, I was disappointed not to find any beef empanadas. Then I spied a familiar foil shape and my stomach growled with glee.

Mrs. Ruíz had left some tamales! I fumbled with the foil and tore off a corn husk, not bothering to warm it up. As I bit into a *tamal*, I realized it was one of the special bean ones.

All the Mexicans I knew who made tamales, including Mrs. Ruíz, fixed the beef and pork varieties, but only she made the ones with pinto bean filling.

My stomach cried out in delight.

Or maybe that wasn't my stomach because it sounded exactly like the word "hey" spoken in a man's voice. And it sounded like it came from outside.

Nick?

I jogged to the front window and pulled the curtains aside. The Yukon was parked across the street with the driver's side toward the house. Nick was standing with his back to the door, facing two equally large men in black trench coats.

This was disturbing because black trench coats weren't typical L.A. street wear. But even more disturbing was what I saw below the coats—the bottoms of white pants and white sneakers.

Unlocking the window as quietly as possible, I slid it open. Now I could hear voices more clearly.

"Where's Diego Martín?" One of them said. "We know you're one of the people who kidnapped him."

"He's getting treatment for a head injury," Nick replied.

"He needs to come back with us. We can give him treatment."

"It's not the type of problem that can be fixed with a Clorox bath." Nick's voice was sarcastic and it worried me that he didn't seem concerned about these guys. We didn't know what they were capable of.

"We can't go back empty handed. Either you tell us where the chef is, or we're taking you to our boss."

"You can try," Nick said.

Oh, shit! As hot as I'd found Nick's macho man actions in the past, daring bad guys to do bad guy things to him was scary as hell. In the second that followed, all kinds of options rushed through my head.

I moved to the front door, but stopped myself before opening it. Even if they didn't have weapons, I wouldn't be much help. I'd gotten lucky at the compound, but this time the bad guys were clued in on what was going on.

In a split second, my mind scanned through my options.

Damn it! I'd insisted LeeAnne store her Jesse James gun with the others after our wild night. My grandmother was not okay with guns in the house, and I didn't want her to be angry enough with LeeAnne to ask her to leave.

I was awesome with my Luke Skywalker lightsaber. Unfortunately, it only worked at Comic-con, where the other geek would concede defeat when I swiped it across his or her mid-section.

We had kitchen knives, but I'd have to get close to use one and those guys had longer arms than I did. They could hold me away from them with a palm to my forehead while I flailed around, like a scene from a cartoon.

There was only one other option I could think of. Poor Nick would still have to use his sore fists, but, if it worked, he wouldn't be taken away or injured.

I hoped.

I ran to my room and got my mind-controlled helicopter, then raced up the stairs and into the second-floor bathroom. The window was already open. From this angle, I could see that one of the men really was holding a gun.

Holy shit shit shit! What if I sent the helicopter out and it startled him into shooting Nick? But by Nick's stance, I could see he wasn't backing down from them and could be shot at point-blank range at any moment.

I had to have faith in the partnership we'd formed back in Bolo. I remembered how in-sync we were, driving the trucks out of that parking lot under sniper fire like two pros on *Dancing with the Stars,* if *Dancing with the Stars* were sponsored by Ford, that is.

Nick would see the helicopter coming and prepare to take evasive actions.

I hoped.

I set the helicopter on the window sill, pulled on the head gear and did what I did best—used my brain.

The copter lifted from the sill shakily, veering off to the left, then over-correcting to the right.

Damn, this was hard. And I hadn't considered the fact that I could hit Nick in the face with it. What if I marred those beautiful features forever?

Maybe this was a bad idea.

"I'm not going with you," Nick said in his smooth lawyer voice. "Are you sure you want to pull that trigger?"

"Yeah, I kind of do," one of the men answered as he lifted his gun higher.

Noooo! I thought. At my lack of concentration, the helicopter dropped like a stone, nearly hitting the sidewalk before I refocused my thoughts and managed to make it hover there. Using all my mental energy, I adjusted its course, lining it up with my target.

It was hard to be sure in the dark, but I thought Nick's head lifted slightly, his eyes flicking to the helicopter before settling back on the goon again. Or maybe it was my wishful thinking.

But I didn't have time to rethink my plan. Not now that there was a gun involved.

I focused my mind one hundred percent on the goon with the gun. As the helicopter whirred across the street, it rose too high. I over-corrected again, nearly crashing, but, just in the nick of time, it lifted, flying almost effortlessly toward the group. I focused with all my might on the spot I wanted the helicopter to reach.

Bam! It hit the gunman on the right side of his head, bounced off and hit the other goon on the left side.

Holy mother of Zeus! A double bammy!

At the first bounce, when the gunmen's head jerked right, Nick pushed the goon's gun hand upward and punched him in the face. He crumpled to the ground.

Meanwhile, the other guy had hit the pavement face-down, his hands over the back of his head as if he thought bombs were dropping. Nick took the gun from the crumpled goon, and stood over the cowering one, his boot resting on the back of his neck.

Adrenaline pumping through me, I raced downstairs and into the garage looking for some rope. I didn't find any, but I did find duct tape. I grabbed it and ran out front.

The guy who'd had the gun was moaning.

"If you'll tape this one's wrists together." Nick glanced at the man under his boot. "I'll have a talk with the one who wanted to shoot me."

"Sure," I said. I'd never gotten to duct tape someone's wrists together, but it was on my bucket list.

Nick kept his foot where it was until I got the guy's wrists together behind him and began wrapping them, then he directed his attention to the other one. "Sit up," he commanded.

The man pushed up from the pavement. He was the white-blonde security guard from the compound, the one who'd called me a bitch! His lips were bloody.

"You made me bite my tongue!" he cried. "I could bleed to death!"

I had the urge to bing whether someone could die from biting their tongue, but I didn't have my phone on me.

"You held a gun on me," Nick said.

"A prop gun," Blondie replied. "We're just actors, dude!"

"That's not an excuse for holding a gun on someone!" Nick shouted in a voice louder than I'd ever heard him use before. "This isn't a fucking TV show! Holy shit, what's wrong with this town?"

"Nick, we need to find out—" I began.

He nodded but waved me quiet, clearly in no mood to relinquish control of the situation.

I decided that was fine with me as long as he could get them to talk.

"Answer my question and you'll be free to go," Nick said.

I was relieved he wasn't insisting on calling the police. Until we solved the murder case, the less interaction we had with them, the better.

"Okay," Blondie said. "Whatever. I didn't sign up for all this."

"Who gave the order for you to come here?"

"Jason Kim," he gave up immediately. These Microtologist were definitely not CIA material. We hadn't even waved a branding iron in front of him and he was singing like a canary.

"Did the order come down from Steve and Valerie Kaporsky?" Nick asked.

"I don't know. I mean, I assumed it did, but he didn't say."

"Fuck," Nick said.

The word made me glance back at my grandmother's

bedroom window. She generally didn't allow men to curse in front of her, even though she'd been known to use expletives from three different countries.

I was glad to see the house was still dark and the curtains were in place. These idiots should have been glad, too. If she knew they'd pulled a gun in front of her house, she'd be beating them with her frying pan by now.

When I turned back, Nick was looking at me. "You wanna help me rough them up some more? See what else they know?"

"Sure, I do," I replied, even though I could tell by his expression he wasn't serious. "They only need one eye a piece," I added. "Oh, and LeeAnne left a pair of her spike heels in the living room. Gouging out an eyeball with a high-heeled shoe might be cool." I smiled an evil smile, or, at least, that's what I was going for.

The guy I'd duct taped chimed in. "No, really, you guys. Nothing comes directly from Steve and Valerie. Nothing like this, anyway. We only know what Jason tells us to do."

A new thought entered my head.

"Is Jason married?" I asked.

Blondie looked surprised then answered, "Yeah, he's married to Loraine."

Nick's eyes met mine and I knew we were on the same wavelength again. "Did she know Alberto?" he asked.

"Sure, she used to work as a sous chef with him at the VIP Center."

"When?" I asked.

His eyes rolled upward as his thumb counted off on his fingers, "I think she left four or five months ago. I'm not sure when she was hired because it was before my time there."

"Any problems in Jason's marriage?" Nick asked.

Blondie managed to shrug, even though his hands were still secured behind him. "I don't know anything about his personal life. It's not like we're buddies or anything, not that he's a guy you want to be buddies with."

"And you don't know Loraine personally?"

They both shook their heads, but Blondie added, "I said 'hi' to her a few times in passing."

"What does she look like?" I asked.

"Caucasian. Not bad looking, even with her head shaved."

Nick looked at me. "You done with these guys?"

"Yeah," I said, suddenly anxious to see them go. "I'm done."

"Get out of here," Nick said. "If you bother us again, I'll beat the shit out of you, then call the cops. They've got cults in jail too, except there they call 'em gangs."

Scaredy guy's eyes got wide. He struggled to get up from the pavement. His partner grabbed him by the arm and yanked him up, leading him to the passenger side.

They were gone in a matter of seconds.

Nick watched the car drive away. "These Microtologists have the worst henchmen I've ever seen."

"Have you seen a lot of henchmen?" I asked. "They say most criminals aren't that smart. Besides, I don't think the Microtologists were expecting to need henchmen. The murder still reads like a crime of passion. It looks to me like they just grabbed some of their actor members to follow us around, hoping they could act like criminals."

Nick nodded. "Steve and Valerie are no brainiacs as far as I can tell. I'm not sure how they've managed to get as far as they have."

"They just latched onto some of the dumber actors like your girlfriend Jemima." I smirked at him.

"Not my girlfriend," he replied. "I like women with more gray matter between their ears."

"Really? Because the women you—"

He grabbed my chin with his index finger and thumb and I stopped talking.

"Lately," he added. Then he stared into my eyes as if he wanted to make sure I caught his meaning.

My heart did a little flip and my lips parted before I realized I had no response to that.

Time to change the subject. "I can't believe we didn't find out about Jason Kim's wife sooner," I said. "If she and Alberto had an affair, both she and her husband are suspects."

Nick closed his eyes and massaged the bridge of his nose with his thumb and forefinger. His knuckles were a mess. A big glob of guilt settled in my stomach.

His eyes popped open. "If she did it, that would explain the extra chef's knife at the crime scene. And maybe Jason's covering for her."

"Or Jason could have done it out of jealousy and he's covering his own ass," I said. "But that wouldn't explain the knife...unless he took it on purpose to frame her for the murder, then had second thoughts afterwards."

"Or Steve and Valerie insisted he cover for her afterwards."

I leaned back against the Yukon. "Damn it," I said. I was so freaking tired and we'd just added new suspects to our list.

"Hey," Nick said gently. He slid his hand behind my neck, his thumb caressing my cheek. "How long's it been since you've gotten a full night's sleep?"

I thought about it for a moment. Since the murder, I'd been busy and worried. I'd probably averaged about four hours a night. "It's been a while," I said.

"We know your dad's safe now. Why don't you try to sleep in? Get eight hours and maybe after we've slept on it..."

"Yeah," I agreed. "I do feel pretty impaired." I turned toward the house and saw my helicopter in the middle of the street. I walked over and picked it up. "But not too impaired to drive this..." I wiggled it tauntingly, "...with my brain!"

Nick chuckled and came close again, lifting the copter from my hand. "You could have put my eye out," he said.

"Not unless I was aiming for your eye," I countered. Yes, it had seemed dicey at the time, but no way was I admitting that now.

He reached up and smoothed the hair back from my face. The contact sent a wiggle of warmth down my back. "Yep, that brain of yours is a deadly weapon all right," he said. Then he bent and kissed me on the forehead.

My insides went squishy when his lips touched my skin. But another sensation burned low in my belly. It made me want to grab him and pull him against me and kiss him on the lips again.

"Goodnight, Paprika." He released me and my next breath came out weighty, like the sigh of disappointment it was.

Nick touches had way too much effect on me. I was wrong in thinking having him around made me safe. There was nothing safe about Nick Owen.

I snatched the helicopter from his hand, and went home.

~

Rika

The Yukon's tires squealed as Nick turned into the VIP Center parking lot.

Julian had texted me forty-five minutes ago, telling me he'd been sent over to remove the crime scene tape. The restaurant kitchen could be cleaned and in use as early as tomorrow.

We hadn't gotten the full eight hours of sleep we'd planned, since we went to bed after four in the morning and the texting started a few minutes after ten, but six hours was better than four.

I was determined to get into the kitchen and have a look around no matter how many detectives and crime scene investigators had been through it already.

Julian was standing at the back door of the VIP Center, a wad of crime scene tape in his hand. I thanked him for contacting me and gave him a hug. Julian's hugs seemed to last a little longer than most people's, which was fine since he gave great hugs and always smelled awesome.

He and Nick gave each other chin lifts, but neither of them reached out to shake hands, which was unusual for both of them. But I didn't have time to dwell on whatever was going on there or the extra-macho man vibe that was rolling off them, making the air tight around us. I needed to keep my eyes open for clues about what happened here. My dad's future could depend on it.

The back door led directly into the kitchen. I'd visited my dad in restaurant kitchens in the U.S. and Colombia, but I hadn't come to the VIP Center in the month he'd been working here. I didn't want to make him look bad to his bosses by having relatives stop by. I had my dad back in the same city for the first time since just before my ninth birthday and I didn't want to screw it up.

The Center had an impressively large kitchen with absolutely everything a chef could need, all of it shiny and clean, until we got to the place on the floor where dried blood was spread over several tiles. Luckily, the air conditioning was set very low. This made the kitchen uncomfortably cold, but the smell wasn't as bad as it could have been.

The extra-long counter next to the blood was the closest one to the dining area, normally used to set platters full of food once they were ready. I knew from the crime scene photos that this was the place where the quiches and plates had been set out, and there were a few eggy crumbs still visible, apparently deemed too unimportant to warrant an evidence bag.

"The cops may not know Kim has a thing for bugs," Nick said. "I'm going to look around and see if I can find any of those tiny cameras or recording devices."

That was a good idea I hadn't thought of, which was why I'd wanted Nick here in the first place. Well, not the only reason, of course, but it was cool how our minds came up with different ideas but were still in sync when it most mattered. If the place was bugged, there was probably a computer somewhere that had video or audio of the murder.

While Nick walked around, opening vents and other fixtures

that might make good hiding places, I pulled up the crime scene photos on my phone and stood at the various angles the pictures were taken from. I swiped through images of the body, the quiches, the necklace, the knife...

I was disappointed that standing in the spot where everything happened didn't give me any new insight. My father had to have been here that night. Why else would he have been spirited away by the Microtologists?

So, who would be worth protecting?

Valerie, jealous over Alberto's trysts with other women? Jemima, the fresh face of Microtology, same reason? Loraine, Jason Kim's wife?

Julian was supposed to try to get some work and contact information for us today. We needed to figure out how to interview her without running into her husband.

I swiped my phone screen until the photos of quiches appeared. What did they have to do with the murder? Could they have been a peace offering? A romantic dinner?

But why two? One quiche was plenty for two people. Unless this wasn't a romantic dinner and my father and Al were here late, trying out new quiche recipes when...

What? What happened? How did a man end up dead?

I swiped through the pictures again. But this time, my finger stopped abruptly on the image of the quiches.

My father always topped his quiches with elongated herbs or spices like thyme, rosemary or even cinnamon sticks, depending on the type of quiche. He did this so he could make an artistic "M" on top for "Martín."

Personally, I thought this was just a wee bit egotistical, although I'd never say as much to him. But when my Aunt Madi mentioned it, my father replied with "Artists sign their creations, *hermanita,* just as God signed you with those eyes." This made me, my aunts and my grandmother feel fuzzy and melty because: a) We all had the same eyes. And b) my mother had these eyes and we knew how much he loved her.

Yes, my father was a charmer of all women, but, as far as I knew, he hadn't had a long-term relationship with anyone since my mother died and sometimes that made me sad.

"My dad didn't make either of these quiches," I told Nick. "They're missing his signature herbal signature."

Nick was on a step ladder checking a vent. "Signature herbal signature?" He climbed down and came over to see what I was talking about.

I did a quick search of *Diego Martín quiche.* Dozens of pictures popped up, some publicity shots for the restaurant, others Instagram-style meal photos. "Do you see what he does with the garnish?"

"Yeah."

I pulled up the crime scene photos. "Look at these. One is topped in tomato slices, the other has basil leaves around it. No 'M'."

"But if he was only experimenting with new recipes..." Nick began.

How did I say this without making my dad sound like an egomaniac? "He always signs his work. If he makes one at home in his own kitchen, he signs it. It's his art." I tapped over to the phone app. "I should tell the detectives."

Nick looked like he didn't want to say what he was about to say. "Rika, that's not going to mean a thing to cops. They won't relate to this artsy stuff."

Damn it! I felt like I couldn't catch a break in this case, even when I found new evidence. But the signature thing would only count as evidence to me and my family.

"But doesn't it seem strange that your dad was here, but he wasn't doing any of the cooking? Especially with quiche on the menu."

I shrugged and shook my head. So far, getting into the crime scene was raising more questions than it was answering.

Frustrated, I walked away from the counter and started opening things randomly—the oven, the storage room, the drawers. One of the drawers I opened contained a set of chef's knives organized into wooden slots. I lifted one out, recognizing it as my father's favorite brand—Drechsler, the only brand he used.

I slid the knife carefully back into its slot. "They're all here," I murmured, mostly to myself.

Nick came over and looked in the drawer, then back at me questioningly.

"The whole set is here," I said. I glanced around, realizing there were two other prep stations. I strode to the next one with Nick right behind me and opened the drawer. The knives were all in their places. The third station yielded the same results.

I turned to Nick, "Alberto was killed with a high-quality kitchen knife, but there are no knives missing."

"How do you know it wasn't an extra lying around somewhere?"

I tugged my phone out of my pocket and scrolled to the picture of the murder weapon. Before, I'd mostly noticed the blood on it. This time, I used my fingers to enlarge the image, focusing on the handle, which did not have the Drechsler copper heel.

"This isn't the brand my dad uses," I explained. "He only uses Drechsler."

"But there could be—" Nick began.

"No. He's really obsessive about his cuts," I interrupted. "He banishes all other knives as soon as he takes over a kitchen. He requires everyone working in his kitchen to use Drechsler."

Nick blew out a loud breath, his brows pushing down over his eyes. "You think someone brought a chef's knife with them to kill Alberto, knowing there was a kitchen full of knives here that couldn't be traced to them?"

I thought about the stupidity of the killer who would do such a thing. "I'm sure someone brought in a knife," I said. "I don't know what they intended to do with it. I only know what they ended up doing with it. If Alberto was entertaining a woman, he might have brought his own kit with him. Every chef has his or her preferences, and I don't think my dad would have objected to Alberto bringing his knives if it was for his own personal use."

"In that case," Nick said, "there's a kit out there missing a knife."

I sighed. "If Alberto brought his kit and one of his women came in, found him with another date and stabbed him with it..." I shook my head. Something wasn't right. "Jason Kim had time to remove whatever evidence he wanted and bury it in the desert. He could have taken Alberto's kit and anything else he wanted to hide."

Nick frowned. "But why not take the murder weapon, too?"

That was a good question. I considered it for a moment. "Maybe he wanted the murder scene to tell a story. He probably didn't know the knife wasn't from this kitchen. A man is found dead with a chef's knife in his body and the other chef is missing. He would have known running away would make my dad a prime suspect, even when there were a dozen women with more motive."

"And they had less to lose if your father was a suspect than if a Microtology member was the murderer, even more so if it was Valerie or Suzee, or Jemima, three high-profile members."

"So..." I tried to decide on our next move. "I guess, first, we need to visit Diana at home and find out what brand of knives Alberto preferred...and maybe see if his kit is at home."

I tapped my phone again, scrolling until I found Diana Viera's work number. "Hello?" a feminine young voice answered. "Oh, I mean, Viera and Associates."

I was pretty sure "associates" was stretching the truth a bit, unless they'd been hiding behind stacks of paper in her office.

"Hi, this is Detective Martin," I said. "My partner and I spoke to Ms. Viera about her husband's murder. We need to speak with her again. Is she in the office today?"

"No, sorry," the girl said. "She's in court today. Probably won't be done until after five. She won't be back in the office today."

"Then we'll swing by the house tonight. I don't have that address with me. Do you have it around there somewhere?"

"Oh, yeah!" she cried brightly. "She had me order some stuff to be delivered there." I smiled triumphantly at Nick as I put the phone on speaker and punched the address into my GPS app.

When I ended the call, I looked at Nick. "She's not supposed to be home until after six. I'm not sure what to do until then."

Nick considered what I said. "So, what we have here is a crime of passion, but with the weapon brought to the crime scene like in a premeditated murder."

Yeah, that wasn't going to help the cops either.

"Let's say Alberto brought in his own knife to make dinner for a woman without getting your dad's permission to entertain there after hours," Nick suggested. "Maybe he and your father got in a fight about it and—"

I resisted the urge to pull out the biggest Drechsler and use it on Nick.

"My father did not kill Alberto Viera!" I yelled.

"Okay..." Nick replied in a tone that said he was trying to calm me more than agree with me. "It was after hours. Maybe your dad let Al do his own thing with his own knives after hours and he was experimenting with quiches...or cooking for one of his many dates."

"Yeah, maybe," I agreed. My father was very particular about the food that was served under his name, but he wasn't a tyrant. If Al wanted to try out a new recipe or cook for a woman, he'd be fine with him doing it his own way. "But where are the rest of Al's knives?" I said. "He'd bring a chef's kit if he were going to cook."

"Maybe he brought the only knife he needed."

"Just like that? In his hand?" I felt like we were just talking around in circles and not getting anywhere.

I tapped my phone to get to messaging and sent one to Julian. *Do you know if another set of chef's knives were found at the scene?*

Didn't see any, he replied. *But didn't get all the way through murder book. Detectives were coming back.*

I showed the messages to Nick. "You texted someone who's standing right outside the door?"

I gave him a *what's the problem* look and he got back to business.

"So, we're back to anyone could have killed Al, possibly with his own knife," he said.

I leaned over, placing my elbows on the counter, my head bowed into my fingertips. "We're getting nowhere," I said. "The police are going to arrest my dad for murder."

"Maybe he'll be able to point them to the murderer when he gets his memory back."

"*If* he gets his memory back," I replied. "It may not matter, anyway. They don't seem to have any real evidence, and if it's his word against someone like Valerie or Jemima, who are the cops going to believe?"

Nick didn't reply because we both knew how fallible the police could be and how eager to close a case, especially a high-profile case with influential Hollywood types involved.

My phone vibrated and I checked my texts. *Shots were fired a couple blocks away,* Julian texted. *Heading there now. Could be a few hours. Back door locks automatically.*

No longer in the mood to speak, I handed the phone to Nick. He read the message and handed it back.

"Let's finish looking around," he said. "You never know."

We spent the next half hour trying to come up with places the cops might not have checked. Nick even removed the traps under the sinks. Finally, we decided to check the walk-in freezer, although what I hoped to find in there I didn't know.

Nick flipped the light on and we walked into the frigid room —huge, as walk-ins went.

Shelves lined the walls and two sets ran down the middle, splitting the room in half until near the back.

I glanced around at the meticulously stacked and labelled goods. My father used only fresh ingredients for his dishes, but I figured some of this stuff might be stored here for Microtology events or for use at the compound. I was working my way down one side of the middle shelves while Nick searched the other side. We met up between the end of the shelves and the back wall.

"I'm not finding anything here," Nick said. "Not even a camera."

I nodded slowly, trying to think what to do next. Too bad Julian was busy. I wanted to talk to Loraine, but didn't know how to reach her. The more I thought about it, the more viable she or Jason seemed as suspects. He sure seemed to be putting a lot of effort into cover up, even if he didn't have the best help doing it.

"I'm going to take my own pictures of the crime scene," I replied. "Then we can go."

We turned and started walking to the door...

And the lights went out.

CHAPTER TWENTY-FIVE

Nick

I looked to the ceiling as if the florescent tubes were going to tell me what was happening. A clunk echoed around us and my eyes snapped to the front of the walk-in where the door was. If it was still open like we left it, I'd see light coming from the kitchen.

There was no light.

We were in a freezer. How long could we survive in here? And we had no idea when workers would return to the kitchen. They had no head chef and were down a sous chef, plus, who would want to come eat in a restaurant where a murder had taken place a few days ago?

"Fuck!" I said as I sprinted to the door. There was no handle on the inside, so I pushed against it, hard, with both hands.

It didn't budge.

An awful, cold feeling swept through me, colder even than the air around me. How could I have been so stupid? The Microtologists had it in for us and we'd strolled right into a trap where they could shut us up for good and make it look like an accident.

As my eyes adjusted, I realized we weren't in complete darkness. A rectangular blue light glowed over the door. Hoping someone had happened by and closed the door by accident, I pounded on it for a minute or two, but nobody came.

I had to get Rika out of here. I'd seen her rubbing goose bumps from her arms when we were in the chilly kitchen before we even came into the freezer. She was so slender. Hardly any insulation on her at all.

Damn it, I wasn't going to let her die like this!

I took a few steps back, then ran at the door, smashing my shoulder into it.

It hurt like fuck, but the door wasn't affected at all.

"Nick!" Rika cried as she hurried over to stand next to me. "What are you doing?"

"Fuck!" I said again. It was the only word I could get to come out of my mouth. The others going through my head were too unthinkable to say aloud.

Rika is going to freeze to death in here.

A woman who felt just as important to me as my mom and my sister had called me here to help her, but I fucked up in the worst possible way.

My brain rewound to her last words. What was I doing? Wasn't it pretty obvious what I was doing? I was trying to save her from freezing to death, but she didn't even seem to realize we were in trouble.

I remembered my phone and pulled it from my pocket.

No bars. "Do you have any reception?" I asked Rika.

"Nick...?" she said in an odd voice. It was pretty dark, but she seemed freakishly calm. Somewhere in the back of my head it registered that she was talking to me like I'd lost my mind. But I didn't have time to figure out what she was thinking. I didn't know how much time we had before the freezing temperatures would render us unconscious.

Reaching around her, I slid her phone from her back pocket and checked it.

No bars.

Fuck!

I turned on my phone's flashlight and strode quickly along the perimeter, skimming the shelves for something to use to jimmy the door. Why had I come onto Jason Kim's turf without so much as a crow bar?

I'd gotten overconfident and it was about to get Rika killed.

Finding no useful tools, I shined the light on Rika's face to see how she was doing.

Still calm. But her head was tilted and she was watching me like I was putting on a stage show and she wanted to see how it ended. Maybe this was because of what happened to her mom. Maybe she'd expected to die young. I shook my head, trying to make sense of her reaction—or lack of one—because the Rika I'd known up until now was a survivor.

Whatever was going through her head, she had to survive this. I braced myself on the door frame and kicked the door with the sole of my boot, over and over and over. The only damage was a small dent right center of the door. I adjusted and did the same thing again, only closer to where the door met the frame.

When I saw that I hadn't made any progress, I tried banging —hard—again with my fists. I don't know if I did it for a minute or ten.

Her lips turned up at the corners. Was she smiling?

Maybe she was resigning herself to her fate.

Then I remembered Boy Band. "What was it Julian say in the text?" I asked. "Is he coming back?" Realizing I still had her phone, I pulled it from my pocket and looked for messages from Julian.

As much as I'd hated having him around, I'd gladly let him be Rika's hero if it saved her life.

"Not anytime soon, I don't think," she said. She was rubbing her arms, clearly cold. Would I have to watch her die?

I closed the space between us and gathered her to me, wrapping my body around hers. She felt like a Popsicle. I didn't know how much time we had, but, I needed her to know how I felt about her before it was all over.

Still holding her body against mine, I pulled my head back enough to look into her eyes. Now that I'd adjusted to the low light, I could see into them pretty well.

God, she was brave. She wasn't even crying.

I caressed her cheeks with my thumbs, memorizing her face, hoping we'd find each other in another life, although I'd never believed in reincarnation before.

"Rika..." Shutting my eyes, I sucked in a slow breath. "I'm sorry. I should have paid more attention..." I glanced at the door.

"It's okay, Nick," she began, but I brushed a thumb over her bottom lip and she stopped talking.

I leaned in, pressing my forehead to hers. "Before we—" I stopped myself from finishing the ominous phrase. "I need to tell you how I feel."

Her eyes widened and my heart tripped over itself. She was so bright and so beautiful. I tightened my hold on her.

"Rika, when you were in Bolo..." I paused and shook my head, trying to get my thoughts straight. "Since you left, I haven't been able to stop—"

She covered my lips with the fingers of her left hand. "No, Nick. You have someone..."

I had no idea what she was talking about and I didn't have time to figure it out. I was getting colder by the second and trying to share my last moments of body heat with her while I told her I loved her.

I peeled her hand from my mouth and kept talking. "I liked you the first night I saw you," I said. "Remember, when you were giving Danny a hard time?"

She nodded.

"And, well, we made a great team. There's no disputing that, but—" How did I explain to her how I felt about her? How she was different than every other woman in the world. How I couldn't stop thinking about her even when she was thousands of miles away.

"I was your attorney last summer and if I hadn't been, I don't think I would have been able to..." That wasn't what I wanted to say exactly. I needed to tell her I loved her. Her lips parted like she was about to speak. Her tongue came out and wet them.

I couldn't resist, I threaded my fingers through her hair and pressed my lips to hers. They were cold at first, but I heated them for her, my tongue tangling with hers as I went deeper with each thrust.

The more I touched her and kissed her, the more pressure I felt in my chest. How could I have let her leave my house? If I hadn't, she might be there now, safe in my bed.

I pulled my lips from hers, needing to say the words. "Paprika..." Her name came out in a gravelly whisper. "I want you to know that I—"

She jerked away suddenly. Her arm flung out, her palm hitting something on the wall near the door.

The door popped open.

"What the...?" I looked back and forth between her and the open door. My hands dropped away from her.

The door was freaking open and she'd opened it.

Multiple emotions raced through me at once—embarrassment that I'd been so ridiculous, anger that she hadn't told me she knew how to get out of here, but, worst of all, was the fact that I was about to confess my love to her and she didn't want to hear it.

I thought we had something. Something more than the attraction I'd felt for the women I'd dated and married. I thought she'd called me because she wanted me by her side during one of the hardest times of her life.

Damn it, I thought she loved me, too.

"How did you know?" I said, after I'd found my voice.

She shrugged. "Once, I was watching a movie where people

got stuck in a freezer like this. I thought with the liability involved and the litigious society we live in, it was weird that the companies who made these things wouldn't have made them safer than that, so I—"

"Googled it."

"Yeah, and I found out they come with these release buttons so employees can't get locked in."

My anger rose up, squashing all other emotions. "Why the hell didn't you tell me sooner?"

She wobbled her head from side to side, "Well...I was kind of fascinated."

"Fascinated."

"You're usually so calm and reasonable," she replied. "I was trying to figure out if you had claustrophobia or maybe some other type of phobia..."

"Yeah, I have a phobia about seeing you freeze to death," I said angrily before I walked out of the freezer and slammed the door behind me.

CHAPTER TWENTY-SIX

Rika

When we left the VIP Center, we sat in the Yukon for a half an hour, both of us using our phones to search for information on Jason Kim's wife. We both struck out with the name Loraine Kim. We found some Loraine Kims, but none of them were the right age and occupation. Marriage records searches didn't yield anything helpful either.

It was entirely possible the Kims were married in another state or even another country. Not to mention the possibility that she didn't take Jason's last name and she could be Loraine anybody. Julian was tied up with an arrest he'd made and wouldn't be free until later to snoop around for her work address.

Finally, we decided to go back to Chef Ben's house, since he must have worked with Loraine and might be able to fill in some of the details about her.

On the way over, neither of us spoke. An awkward silence hung between us and I felt guilty even though I had no reason to. I'd done the right thing. Nick was the one who was inappropriate. He had a woman and she wasn't me.

The whole freezer fiasco had seemed surreal.

I was intrigued, seeing Nick freak out like that. I'd seen him concerned, annoyed, and angry, but I'd never seen him this freaked out. Not when we found the devil worshippers, or when we were being shot at, or even when we were almost blown sky high. And considering all the embarrassment I'd suffered in front of him, not letting him know about the release button for a few minutes seemed like a fun practical joke at first.

And, maybe this makes me a bad person, but the geeky, chubby girl inside me was kind of hoping Mr. Quarterback, Mr. Eight-Pack, Mr. Freaking Perfect suffered from claustrophobia. I cringed inwardly at how mean I'd been, letting him get so upset on what turned out to be my behalf.

Stop feeling guilty! He's the horn dog who thinks he should get a crack at every woman on the continent!

Besides, it wasn't fair that he'd gotten to live his entire life as a hot guy, and, as hard as I'd fallen for him, at times, I still resented him for it.

Then he grabbed me and looked into my eyes, and I realized he thought we were going to freeze to death and was about to make a dying declaration. And by the way he was holding my face, I was pretty sure he was going to confess the feelings I'd wanted him to confess to me six months ago.

So why did the thought of him doing it scare the crap out of me?

Because he wasn't free to be with me. He had a hot blonde trophy girlfriend or fiancé or whatever, sharing a room with him at the Omni.

Because I knew anything he told me about his feelings for me would be null and void once we were out of the freezer. Then it would be permanently awkward between us and I wouldn't even be able to keep Nick Owen in my life as a friend.

My heart split open at the thought of losing him again. Now that I knew Nick existed in the world, I needed him in my life any way I could get him. Since I'd left Bolo, I felt like I'd left a part of me behind.

In that moment, the fear of losing him altogether became stronger than the need to hear him profess some profound feelings for me. And I'd regretted not letting him finish every second since, even though I was sure I did the right thing.

I swallowed the lump that had formed in my throat and tried to get my head back in the game. On one hand, since I knew my dad was alive and being taken care of, I didn't hear that doomsday clock ticking away in my brain. But seeing him jailed for the rest of his life for a crime he didn't commit was nearly as unthinkable as the alternative.

"How do you people live like this?" Nick asked as he cruised slowly by Ben's apartment building looking for a place to park. He still sounded angry which made me angry. What right did he have to bring Marla to town, then treat me like he cared about me?

"It helps if you don't have to find a spot large enough for a tank," I replied.

Nick cut his narrowed eyes at me, then went back to searching for a slice of curb. After circling the block once, we were back in front of the building and I couldn't wait another second to follow up on my lead.

"Look, Nick," I began, knowing he wouldn't like what I was about to say. "I can ask Ben the questions and be back before you find a spot." I released my seat belt and grabbed for the door handle.

"Damn it, Rika!" Nick yelled as he jammed on the brake.

I jumped out of the truck and jogged toward the building, waving without looking back at his sure-to-be-pissed-off face. I only had a question or two for Chef Ben, and the time apart would give Nick a chance to cool off.

I thought of the freezer and chuckled. *You'd think he would have cooled off in there.*

Guilt swept through me again. *Damn it, Lita! And Father Vargas who gave me all those Hail Mary's for calling people names inside my own head!*

Whatever. I shook it off and put my *Ben's bestie* face on.

When I got to his door, I rang the bell and he answered a minute later. He held a kitchen towel in one hand, but that barely registered because I couldn't take my eyes off his outfit.

I was no fashionista, but Ben's taste was bizarre to say the least. Today, he was wearing a suspender-shorts one-piece that resembled German lederhosen, except neon orange. On his feet, were black shoes with square buckles that looked like they'd been made by actual Pilgrims, but I guess they went as well with lederhosen as anything else. Perched on his nose were a pair of glass-less glasses that belonged on an owl dressed as a professor.

"Rika!" Chef Ben squealed as if we'd known each other for years. Although we'd only met once before, I'd really poured on the charm and made him like me. I was proud of myself. Maybe someday I could get my way with a wink and a compliment like Nick did.

Yeah, right.

Ben reached out to me and I went in for a hug, but then realized he was doing the cheek-kissing thing, which I was used to from the Latin immigrants in our neighborhood, but not so much with anyone else. I managed to change tactics mid-embrace and make a light kissing sound next to his ear.

He acted as if he didn't notice the awkwardness. "What brings you here today?" he asked as he stepped back to let me in.

I walked in and he shut the door behind us. "I was wondering if you could shed some light on a couple of things about the VIP Center restaurant," I replied.

"Sure," he said. "If you don't mind hanging out in my kitchen. I'm in the middle of making lunch." He led me into the next room.

Even if I hadn't known Ben lived here, I would have been sure the owner of this kitchen was a foodie by the high-end small appliances, six-burner gas stove and double ovens.

"I guess you had this place redone when you bought it?" I leaned my forearms on his beautiful granite island.

"I sure did!" He went over to his huge sink where a colander full of vegetables was waiting and turned on the water. Lined up on the counter next to the stove were spices and other ingredients.

When I made lunch, it typically consisted of a sandwich unless there were leftovers in the fridge. Then I made lunch by putting them on a plate and letting them spin around a few times in the microwave. I wouldn't tell Ben or my father this, but I'd always felt it was a waste of time to spend more time making meals than I did eating them.

"Are you having people over?" I asked.

"For lunch?" Ben turned on the water and started scrubbing the vegetables. "No, I think it's terrible that people will cook when others are around, but not cook for themselves. You should always treat yourself as a guest. I have a whole chapter of recipes under that heading in my book."

"How's work going on that?" I asked as if I cared about a cookbook.

"I'm almost finished." He took a bowl out of the refrigerator and set it in front of me. "Help yourself," he said. The strawberries in the bowl were huge and dark red. They looked delicious. Still, I was tempted to ask if he could dip them in chocolate for me.

"You seem to be feeling better than last time I saw you." I popped a strawberry in my mouth.

"That's because I've been treating myself as a guest," he replied half-jokingly. Then his voice dropped to a conspiratorial whisper. "And Rolf and I are back together."

"Ohhhh..." I added a semi-lecherous eyebrow wiggle. "No wonder you look so great!"

Sure, I was buttering him up, but the compliment was genuine. He did look a lot better than the last time I saw him, despite the lederhosen and Jimmy Neutron hair. I guess happiness does that for a person.

Chef Ben was beaming at me, so I figured I'd offered enough validation and it was time to get down to business.

"Can I show you a picture related to the murder?" I asked. He grimaced and clutched at his chest, so I added quickly, "It's from the crime scene, but it's nothing gory."

He took a deep breath. "Poor Alberto's crime scene," he murmured. "Okay, sure." He dried his hands on a dish towel and came to stand next to me.

I pulled out my phone, quickly dismissed the notifications on the screen without reading them, and pulled up the quiche photo. "Can you tell anything about who made these?"

He peered at the screen. "Well, that one with the cilantro garnish looks like Alberto's work. The other one..." He enlarged the picture. "Wouldn't it be likely that Diego Martín made it, since he was there that night?"

Chef Ben was being so helpful, I wanted to come clean and tell him Diego was my dad and I knew for a fact that wasn't one of his quiches, but he was still chummy with Steve and Valerie so I decided against confessing.

"I've been told by recent diners at the restaurant that these don't look anything like Diego Martín's work," I said.

Ben took another look at the photo. "Sorry. I don't recognize it."

I propped my back casually against the counter behind me. "What about Loraine, the sous chef, Jason Kim's wife?"

He seemed surprised to hear the name. "Loraine Frazier?" he said. "She left for another job a few months ago."

I watched him scrub a potato with a vegetable brush for a moment before asking, "Was she one of Alberto's conquests?"

He stopped what he was doing and turned completely

around, his eyes twinkling mischievously. "I wish I knew!" he said. "Al was flirtatious with her, like he was with all women and she teased him back, but I was never sure there was anything going on between them." He paused and tilted his head. "Plus, her husband was head of security in the same building, so it would have been pretty risky."

"If they'd been sneaking around and he found out, what do you think he would do?"

"Jason?" Ben winced. "He might murder both of them. He's pretty intense—you know, tightly wound. I never liked it when he came around my kitchen. The food can take on the mood of the cook, you know, and nobody wants a freaked-out frittata." He burst out laughing at his colorful alliteration, so I laughed along with him.

He was turning back to his veggies, but I asked, "Do you mind looking at another photo again?" I hadn't told Nick, but something had niggled at the back of my brain since the last time I'd shown Ben this photo. I wanted to gauge his reaction more carefully this time.

"Sure." He turned and gave me his full attention.

I found what I was looking for and held my phone out. He took it and peered into the screen.

"Remember this heart necklace that was found at the scene?" I asked.

Ben was squinting like he needed some actual lenses in his glasses, so I reached over and used my thumb and index finger to enlarge the photo. His chest jumped as he took in a shocked breath.

There it was! The same reaction I'd notice last time, but I passed off as my imagination getting the better of me. After all, I was desperate to find my dad. But this time I felt sure of what I'd seen.

"Do you recognize it?" I asked excitedly. "Did it belong to one of the women who worked at the VIP Center?"

He kept staring into the phone screen, stalling for time, I was sure of it. He clearly knew who the necklace belonged to, which meant if he would tell me, I'd probably know who the murderer was.

"One of the regular customers?" I prodded. "Or a hostess? Maybe one of the women Alberto was sleeping with?"

Ben took a deep breath, then set the phone on the counter. "Nope," he said. "For a second I thought I recognized it, but then I took a closer look..." He shrugged. "Those faux-birthstone necklaces are everywhere. I don't know who it belongs to."

He was lying. I knew because he'd made eye-contact with me each time he'd answered a question until I showed him this photo.

What woman would be important enough to Ben that he'd lie for her? About a murder, no less?

My mind flipped quickly through the possibilities—Jemima? Suzee? Valerie? One of the hostesses Alberto had his way with?

Then, my mind's brakes squealed as it stopped and backed up to Valerie. Ben had a deal with the Kaporskys. His books would be beneficial for all of them. A murder charge could throw a monkey wrench into all the projects they had their fingers in, including his.

"Are you sure?" I pushed. "Because it looked like maybe you recognized it."

Ben set a carrot on a cutting board and began chopping, but now it felt like an excuse not to look me in the eye.

"Sorry I can't help you," he said. "But I haven't seen that on any of the women from the center. His voice sounded certain, but his body had gone rigid when he looked at the picture and it was still tense now.

I needed to get him to tell me more. But if it wasn't in his best interest, I didn't think he'd talk unless he believed the truth was going to come out anyway.

I had an idea. "Could I use your bathroom?" I asked.

Ben's relaxed. "Sure. It's right down the hall." He pointed to a doorway off the living room.

I picked up my phone from the counter and stuck it in my pocket. "Thanks," I said cheerily as I headed in the direction he sent me.

The second I reached the bathroom, I locked myself inside and yanked my phone from my pocket.

Birthstone.

Ben had said it was a birthstone necklace. I didn't know much about them, so I bingged "birthstones," then tapped the "images" icon. I scrolled around a page full of stones until I found one a similar color to the one in the photo.

The stone was called a "peridot" for people born in the month of August.

I immediately pulled up a new search field.

Valerie Kaporsky Wikipedia, I typed in. When her page came up, I zeroed in on her birth date—April twenty-first.

Damn it!

I followed up with Jemima Harte and Suzee Driver. Neither of them had August birthdays either.

I blew out a frustrated breath and looked up at the eggshell-colored ceiling. What was I missing?

I placed my hands on the edges of the sink and peered into the mirror over it. "Think, Paprika," I whispered.

Then, something in the mirror caught my eye. I stared into the mirror, then turned to look behind me at a small framed picture hanging on the wall that I'd seen reflecting in it. The photo was a black and white of Chef Ben hand-in-hand with another man—a body-builder type. I recognized the shop behind them as one I'd seen the last time I was at Venice Beach.

Then the front of my brain caught up to the thing that had pinged at the back of it when I was looking in the mirror.

Necklaces.

Both men were wearing what appeared to be the same one,

but I was willing to bet the pendants would look different from each other if this were a color photo.

Well, they'd be different assuming the two men weren't born in the same month.

Holy mother of Zeus! How could I have been so dense?

I'd lived in L.A. all my life, where all kinds of people wore all kinds of things. A place where just because a piece of jewelry looked feminine did not mean it wouldn't be worn by men, especially when you factored in rock stars and gay guys!

I double checked the bathroom door to make sure it was locked then turned my attention back to my phone. My hands shook as I binged "Chef Ben Appétit Wikipedia."

A picture of him looking a bit slimmer than he was now popped onto the screen. Underneath it, were his vital statistics, including the fact that he was born August fifteenth.

The necklace belonged to Chef Ben!

CHAPTER TWENTY-SEVEN

My hands shook as I turned off the screen and shoved the phone back into my pocket. My heart thudded hard, did a flip and plunged into my stomach.

Okay maybe that's impossible, but that's certainly what it felt like. A moment later I couldn't feel it beating at all. Could a person in her mid-twenties die of terminal freak out?

Fuck, fuck, fuck...

I wrapped the fingers of my right hand around my left wrist and checked for a pulse as I paced the small bathroom, trying to decide how to proceed. Seconds later, I forgot about taking my pulse and clasped my hands together in front of my chest as I continued pacing the bathroom, which was so small, I had to turn around every four steps. Dizziness from all the turning overtook me and I sat on the toilet lid, deep-breathing.

I could probably just go, but where would that leave my dad? If he didn't regain his memory, he could end up in prison.

I needed to talk to Nick. Maybe the two of us could work out a trap like we set with JimBob McGwire in Bolo. Or maybe once Nick came in, we could confront Ben together. If he got violent, I had no doubt Nick could take him. We could make a citizen's arrest and shove the murderer right in Detective Hertz and Winchell's smug faces.

Ha! Call my dad a murderer, you idiots!

The shock of the Chef Ben revelation was wearing off and the idea of proving to L.A. Homicide how wrong they'd been sent a jolt of excitement through to my nerve endings.

I had to tell Nick!

As I was tugging my phone from my pocket, it made a beeping sound. I tried to remember what type of notification made a generic beep like that. I thought I'd personalized every sound my cell made.

When I looked at the screen, all I saw was black.

That couldn't be right.

I touched the screen, pushed the buttons on the sides...

Still black.

I pressed the On button and held it for fifteen seconds.

Nothing.

It was then my brain flashed back to this morning when I picked up my phone from the nightstand and noticed I hadn't plugged it in last night. My phone was my life. I almost never forgot to charge it, but I'd had an awful lot going on and was dead tired by the time I got into bed.

In my groggy stupor this morning, I simply told myself I'd plug it into the rapid charger I kept in my car, forgetting that Nick would insist we take his rental.

Stupid Nick!

Although, I guess it was just as much my fault because, in his presence, I seemed capable of forgetting absolutely anything, even the fact that my most important tool was running out of battery! Then it hit me that one of those notifications I dismissed when I was eager to show photos to Ben was probably a low battery warning.

Now I had no choice but to leave and explain things to Nick.

Since he was a trial lawyer, he would know whether we had enough evidence to go to the police.

I reached for the door handle.

Wait, a little voice in the back of my brain cried out.

I was alone in the home of a possible murderer. I needed to take some precautions, even though Ben didn't know I knew that he knew who the necklace belonged to.

But why would an up and coming chef, with so much to look forward to, kill his former sous chef? It made no sense. What motive could he possibly have? And the murder had the earmarks of a crime of passion. Was Alberto bi-sexual?

Maybe I was wrong.

Better safe than sorry...

I looked around for anything that could be used as a weapon in a pinch. I found some tweezers in the medicine cabinet, but I doubted they could do anything other than piss him off. Next to the tweezers were an eyelash curler and an electric razor.

The razor had a cord, but I wasn't tall enough to strangle him with it unless he was kind enough to lie down on the couch and hold still for me.

In a square yellow basket on top of the toilet were about a dozen hair products of different sizes. I picked up a travel-sized spray can of "hair freeze"—probably what he used to make his hair stick in that impossible style.

I read the ingredients. It contained a bunch of chemicals, but one of the first ingredients listed was alcohol. Surely that would burn if it got into someone's eyes.

I grabbed it and stuck it in the pouch in the front of my hoodie, feeling a little silly. It wasn't much of a weapon. But Ben had no idea I was on to him, anyway, and he wouldn't dare try to kill me in his fourth story apartment. How would he get rid of my body?

I unlocked and opened the door, then stuck my hands in the pockets of my hoodie and walked out...

Into a much darker hallway than I remembered from a few minutes ago. As I lifted my gaze, I realized it was darker because Ben was standing in the entrance to the hall, blocking the light from the living room.

It was a weird place to stand. In fact, try as I might, I couldn't come up with one benign reason he'd be hanging around that spot.

I smiled at him as if everything was completely normal, which it probably was. I was just freaking out because I thought Ben was the killer now. Anything he did would seem suspect.

"I just realized what time it was," I said. "I'd better get going."

Chef Ben didn't smile back at me. He stared at me with eyes that looked completely different than before.

Completely scary, that is.

In fact, if my grandmother saw the look on Ben's face, she'd say he had given me the evil eye and drag me to Mrs. Ruíz to have it taken away. This process would involve Mrs. Ruíz making little crisscrosses all over my body with an egg while praying in Latin. Then she'd break the raw egg into a glass of water and put it under my bed for the night.

Up until now, I thought the ritual was a ridiculous waste of time, but, as Chef Ben stared at me with his, now creepy, blue eyes, I kinda wished I had a little of Mrs. Ruíz's mojo.

"So, um...I'll just be going then," I said, hoping he'd move out of the way.

"Seems kind of sudden," he replied. "Why are you in such a hurry?"

Until this moment, I didn't realize just how big he was. He'd seemed so laughable when I first met him in his funny clothes and Jimmy Neutron hair, my mind didn't record the fact that he was a large man in width, height and weight. I checked his hands. He wasn't holding a weapon, but his hands were big. They could probably snap my neck like a twig.

"Lunch!" I blurted. Yes, that was the perfect excuse! "I just saw the time. I have a lunch date."

I took a step forward, but stopped when he didn't move out of the way.

"Not today," he said. "Well..." He half-shrugged. "...not any day, really."

Shit, shit, shit, shit, shit! The only way I could think of that he could keep me from any future lunch dates was to kill me.

I met his gaze again. One eye looked murderous and determined. The other eye looked freaked out about killing another person, but still determined.

I decided it was now or never. My hand slid over the tiny spray bottle in my pocket. My index finger positioned itself on the nozzle.

"You know what, Chef Ben?" I said, hoping he had a curious enough nature to want to know what I was going to say before attacking me. At the same time, I moved forward, gesturing with my left hand, aiming to distract him. I yanked the can out of my pocket and sprayed his face at point blank range.

He screamed like a Mandrake as his hands flew up to cover his eyes. I wasted no time, squeezing past him, running for the front door. I made it and turned the knob but the door wouldn't open. As I yanked desperately on it, I realized the keyed deadbolt was locked.

Ben had locked the door when he decided he was going to kill me.

I heard his footsteps coming up behind me. Instead of turning to face him, I waited the couple of seconds it took for him to get to me and swung my elbow back as hard as I could.

"Oomph!" he grunted as my elbow connected with his ribs. I whirled around to find him half-doubled over, so I kneed him in the forehead.

"Fuck!" he screamed.

He was kind of a wimp. I mean, sure, he was a chef, not some martial arts *sensei*, but my dad was a chef too and he was way more badass than this guy.

Maybe I could do this. Maybe I could get away.

I spotted a key on the coffee table and made a dash for it, hoping it was the door key. But just as I reached out to take it, an arm came around my middle, dragging me back.

Ben stepped to the side but kept his arm in motion.

I flew through the air and landed hard on the floor.

Luckily, the part of my body that took most of the impact was my ass, which was where most of my remaining fat accumulated and, for the first time, I was thankful for it.

Unluckily, Chef Ben was looming over me, looking huge and maybe not so wimpy after all.

"Hold on!" I yelled as he leaned down to do Zeus knows what to me. "Wait just a minute!"

He paused.

I couldn't believe that worked. I'd only been stalling to give myself a moment to make a new plan.

"What?" Chef Ben panted in a way that made me think he was glad for the break.

"If you're going to kill me, it's only fair that you tell me the truth first."

He tilted his head, eyes on the ceiling as he considered my request. "Yeah, I guess that is fair," he replied.

Uh...score! If I kept him talking long enough, Nick would knock on the door and I could scream for help. Maybe I could even incapacitate Ben for long enough to get the key and open the door for Nick.

"Okay," Ben said as he sat in the nearest chair, still huffing and puffing like he was going to blow a little pig's house down—me being the little pig in this scenario. My mind flashed back to the mean kids snorting at me as I walked by them in the halls of my junior high school. I don't know why something so irrelevant would try to clutter my mind at a time like this, unless it was the start of my life flashing before my eyes.

"So, what do you want to know?" Ben asked once he'd caught his breath.

I pushed myself up into a seated position as my mind searched for a question. "Why?" I asked. "Why did you kill Alberto?"

Ben wiped the sweat off his forehead with the back of his hand. "You have to understand," he began, "my cookbook deal was in the works for two years. Steve had introduced me to an editor at a big New York publishing house. She was really into my book, and my quiche recipes were going to figure prominently into it."

He looked at me expectantly, so I nodded encouragingly, assuming that when he stopped talking, he'd probably start murdering.

"Al was my sous chef, and I was excited, so I told him about the book. At the next Microtology event, he got Valerie to introduce him to another editor at the same publishing company. He pitched him an idea about his own quiche cookbook. That editor got excited about Al's story, you know, growing up on the streets of El Salvador or Nicaragua or wherever."

Maybe it was ridiculous at this point, but I couldn't help feeling a little insulted on Alberto's behalf. I mean, Ben had worked with him for at least a year, from what I could tell, and hadn't even bothered to get his home country straight before killing him.

But it probably wasn't a good idea to point that out to Ben right now, so I tried to look shocked at what Alberto had done.

"The publisher said they couldn't possibly publish quiche cookbooks from two separate authors. Our editors each fought for us, but in the end, Al's book won out. Not because his recipes were better. They weren't."

Ben shook his head, so I shook mine in agreement.

"They decided stories from his life that related to the recipes were going to be worked in with each recipe. The publisher said my Microtology angle would only be of interest to a niche group of people on the West Coast." Ben's eyes drifted off toward the window and my gaze followed automatically. "Said Al's 'tugged at the heartstrings,' which could make it a bestseller. I should have killed him, too."

The blinds were closed on the window he was looking at. By the expression on his face, I concluded he must be imagining himself beating the publisher to death with Al's cookbook.

"So, when you found out, you rushed over to the center and killed him?" I asked.

"No!" Ben yelled.

I was so unnerved already, my body jerked as if he'd kicked me, but I managed to keep my mouth shut. I raised my eyebrows and waited for the rest of the story because each time Ben seemed distracted by it, I'd begun scanning the room for possible weapons.

"Anyway, I challenged Al to a taste test. We would both make our signature quiches and whoever lost the taste test would bow out gracefully. I knew he couldn't resist the challenge. His ego was always too big for his cooking skills.

We asked Diego to judge the blind taste test, since he is considered one of the preeminent makers of quiche, and probably would have been offered the deal himself if he'd been in the country sooner and had any interest in writing a book. He'd never tasted either of our quiches because I left the restaurant before he took over, and Al had never been anything more than a sous chef there."

Ben's body stiffened as his face, which had been pink from exertion earlier, turned beet red. His clenched fist slid up to cover the left side of his chest and, for a moment I thought he might be having a heart attack.

Well, I hoped he was having a heart attack, which would have been a mean thing to hope under normal circumstances, but he was planning to kill me any minute so I figured my karma was in the clear.

"Then, Diego..." He spat out my father's name in a way that made me want to slap him across the face. "He chose Al's quiche. Maybe I should have known Al would cheat and tell him what to look for in advance. I mean they're both Mexican or whatever."

My lips parted, and the words *My father is Colombian!* nearly flew out of my mouth, but I jammed them together.

Ben continued, "I didn't think of that at the time. I just stood there with my mouth open in shock while Diego explained why he'd chosen the quiche he had—something about the texture and perfect balance of seasonings..."

His fist dropped down into his lap. "Things get a little blurry after that. All I could think about was how Al was going to steal my book deal...my life! I started to gather up my kit and saw the knife and put my hand on it. I think I put my hand on it and took it off more than once.

Then I heard Al laughing behind me. He and Diego had spoken to each other in Spanish, so I didn't know what they'd said. But at that moment I was sure Al was standing there laughing at me while he stole my life. Then Diego got a call and walked to the back of the kitchen."

Chef Ben's eyes held a faraway look. As I scanned the room again, I still didn't see anything I could use as a weapon.

"I don't even remember picking up the knife," he went on. "The next thing I knew, the knife was stuck in Al and my hand was on the handle. Al was grabbing at me and my necklace broke. Then Diego was yelling at me in Spanish.

He pushed me away and knelt over Al on the floor. I think he might have yelled at me to call 9-1-1 without realizing he was still speaking Spanish. He looked so shocked. I saw all the blood coming from Al and I just started backing up.

I don't remember coming home. In fact, the next thing I

remember is Jason Kim standing in my living room, telling me to keep my mouth shut and let him take care of things."

The thought went through my mind that this would make a good episode of *Snapped* on that channel with all the true crime shows.

His gaze drifted to the floor. "It's not like I planned to kill him or anything, but he was taking everything from me." His eyes met mine again. "You see, I'm just as much a victim as he is."

I felt my eyes grow wide at his last statement, even though I'd been telling myself to be cool and go along with him. But all I could see in that moment was the crime scene photo of Alberto, dead in a pool of blood, with a knife sticking out of his chest.

And I'd just learned he died over a quiche! Or a book deal, depending on how you looked at it.

I imagined my father's shock, thinking he was judging a harmless cooking contest then seeing his friend stabbed to death on the floor.

I forced myself to speak. "It's understandable. You're very passionate about what you do and he was trying to—"

"Don't patronize me!" Ben stood suddenly. The side chair he'd been sitting in reared up onto two legs with the force of it before settling down on all four again. He turned and looked at the striped area rug that visually anchored the couch and occasional chairs together.

"How tall are you?" he asked. "About five-two?"

"Five-four-and-a-half," I said automatically before realizing why he was asking.

Now, both of us were examining the rug.

Yep. It looked big enough to role my body up in. Too bad I'd lost all that weight or Ben would have known he couldn't possibly carry me out of here.

My Jilly Crane counselor was always telling me that thin people lived longer than fat ones.

Ha! I'd never had anyone try to kill me when I was heavy!

Now my life really was flashing before my eyes. Well, not my life, exactly, but all the foods I'd turned down in the past few years in order to be thin.

A pork rind is a terrible thing to waste.

I really, really didn't want to leave here rolled up in that rug. "Why the two glasses," I blurted. "Next to the quiches?"

"Oh, that was part of the agreement. Diego would take a sip of water before tasting the first quiche and another before tasting the second. We wanted two separate glasses to ensure he wasn't getting residual taste from the first quiche while trying to cleanse his palette for the second."

I rolled my eyes. *Foodies. Jeez.* I made a mental note to be more careful in the future about assumptions I made based on my own point of view. Nick and I had assumed a woman had to be on the scene and that the two glasses meant two people eating together like they would do on a date.

Oh, well, live and learn.

Except, I wasn't going to live if Ben had anything to say about it.

"Stay right there," he commanded as he walked to the kitchen.

As if!

Did he think I was an idiot? If there's one thing I'd learned from watching true crime docudramas, it was that you do *not* obey your potential murderer's instructions.

I pulled myself up and glanced around as I heard the knife drawer open. Actually, I heard a drawer open and assumed it was the knife drawer. I didn't think I had enough time to grab the key, get to the door and open it. My eyes caught on a large decorative platter on a side table. It was a long shot, but...

I grabbed it and stuffed it up under my shirt, hoping the thickness of the fabric and the front pouch would camouflage my armor. I also hoped that Ben didn't change his modus operandi and decide to slit my throat rather than stab me in the torso like he had Alberto.

I laced my fingers together and held them over my lower abdomen to keep the plate from sliding out.

Then, Ben was back, a determined gleam in his eyes, a large chef's knife in his hand. One that looked like the same brand as the murder weapon.

Damn it! If I'd only noticed while he was cutting the carrot, I probably could have gotten out of here.

"It'll be quieter this way," he murmured as if to himself. Did that mean he also had a gun at his disposal? Or maybe he meant stabbing me with a sharp knife would be quieter than beating me to death with a rolling pin.

But he was wrong. It would *not* be quieter, not if I could help it.

"Nooooo!" I screamed at the top of my lungs. I followed up with "Call 9-1-1!" in case the neighbors were home.

Ben lunged at me. But, instead of falling back like a fearful victim, I took a hard step forward, jamming my armored stomach directly into the tip of the knife as he was thrusting it forward.

Then, everything went into slow motion as the knife hit the platter and was jarred out of Chef Ben's hand. It flipped up, then end over end, as he tried to catch it. The attempt was almost comical. I realized that when Chef Ben was in school, he was probably every bit as P.E. challenged as I was.

After batting the knife around in the air several times, he finally caught it...

By the blade.

"Fuck!" he boomed. The knife clattered to the floor as blood streamed out of deep slices in at least three of his fingers.

As I crept backward toward the key, his eyes went crazy-wild. "I'm gonna fucking kill you!" He rushed me, his hands closing around my neck.

I stuck a hand under my hoodie to get the only weapon I had

—the platter—hoping to crack it on his head. But as I pulled it out, I slipped on some blood and we fell. He landed on top of me with such force it knocked the wind out of me.

I knew it was either worry about breathing now or worry about breathing for the rest of my life so I lifted the plate and used all my strength to smash it into the side of his face.

It exploded and a shard of ceramic sliced his cheek.

He let out a strangled sound. "You bitch!" He tried to grasp my throat with his slippery hands. The blood caused them to slide around on my skin, but I couldn't get away because of his substantial weight on top of me.

My lungs kicked back in and I gasped in as much oxygen as was possible with a chunky chef on my chest.

I placed both of my hands under me, palms down, and tried to scoot out from under him.

When that didn't work, I bucked and squirmed and bucked and squirmed until my neck was just out of his reach.

Thinking fast, I said, "Oh, my God! Your finger's gone!"

Sure, the fake distraction technique wasn't the most creative ploy, but there's a reason it's a classic.

It worked. Chef Ben stopped trying to strangle me and lifted his hand to examine his fingers. His right hand was so bloody, it took him a moment to assess his injuries. I took advantage of that moment—and the fact that some of his weight had transferred to his knees—and scrambled out from under him.

The doorbell rang.

Nick! my mind cried. *It has to be Nick!*

"Nick!" I yelled as I lunged for the door. In a panic, I twisted the knob back and forth, even though my brain kept trying to tell me it was useless. My head was swimming with words like "help," and "Chef Ben is the murderer and he's try to kill me!" But all that came out when I opened my mouth again was another long, loud "Niiiiiiiiiiiick!"

I heard a growl and turned to see Ben on his feet, his eyes glowing like a werewolf in a low-budget movie.

I stepped back and felt the door behind me. As Ben lunged at me again, I side-jerked out of his reach. At the same moment, I heard Nick say, "Get away from the door!"

I took several quick steps away as Ben turned to look at me and snarled, "I'll kill you and your fucking boyfri—"

His threat was cut short by a loud thud, then the door blew in, still in one piece, apparently torn from its hinges by the force.

Chef Ben had turned back at just the wrong moment so the door smashed him right in the face.

He, the door, and Nick landed on the floor, Nick on top.

Nick shook it off surprisingly fast, jumped up and looked around, searching for other assailants. "Is he it?" he asked.

"Yes," I replied defensively. "He's the murderer! And he's tougher than he looks!"

Nick gave me a look that said he thought my defensiveness was silly, and of course I couldn't take on a man twice my size. Then his expression changed, his eyes widening in alarm. "Rika..." he breathed.

He strode over to me and began examining my neck, running his fingers over my skin. "Where are you injured?" he asked.

"Injured?" I repeated, staring at him stupidly as I rewound the minutes before he broke the door down. I was sore and bruised, but I thought I'd come out of the situation pretty well.

Nick's eyes flicked from my neck to my chest to my stomach. As he lifted the bottom of my t-shirt gingerly, I slapped his hand, not wanting him to get up close and personal with the pounds I'd gained.

His eyes met mine. "Rika!" He said in a tone you'd use if you were trying to wake someone from a coma or bring a lunatic back to reality. He went back to examining my neck, sliding his thumbs from underneath my chin to my clavicle. "Where's the blood coming from?"

"Blood?" I tilted and peeked around him to check the decorative mirror on the wall. Blood was smeared on my cheeks and shirt. My neck was coated in it.

When I met his gaze again, his expression reminded me of the way he'd looked at me the night we'd been shot at in Bolo. And the night he'd rescued me from the church basement.

Maybe this makes me a sick person, but I liked that look.

"I think the blood is his." I gestured toward Chef Ben as he moaned underneath the door.

Nick exhaled a huge breath and his whole body relaxed. "Damn it, Rika," he said as if it was my fault Chef Ben had tried to carve me up like a Thanksgiving turkey.

Okay, maybe it was my fault. I'd lost patience and ditched Nick to come up to Ben's apartment alone, but it wasn't my fault he'd turned out to be psycho about his quiches. *Jeez.*

Suddenly, Nick's arms encircled me, pulling me into him, tight.

Then very tight.

Then awesomely, wonderfully, magnificently tight.

"Damn it, Paprika Anise Martín," he murmured in my ear. His voice held a combination of chastisement and affection. I noticed he'd pronounced my entire name correctly, even the last one. "You sure know how to put a scare in me."

I slid my arms around his waist, trying to hold him every bit as tightly as he was holding me.

I let myself stand there, wrapped up in him, surrounded by his heavenly scent, knowing at any moment, he'd let me go again. In fact, now that we knew who the murderer was, he'd be out of my life completely.

I squeezed my cheek against his pecs.

I never, ever, ever wanted him to go. In fact, I was willing to be attacked by a killer chef every day if this was what it got me.

Eyes closed, I focused on the feel of him, enjoying the closeness while I could, but dreading the loss of his comforting heat.

"You're trembling," he said. "It's okay. It's over. His leg's broken."

I looked down at Chef Ben, this time noting that his right leg was bent in an unnatural position.

"That's not why I'm trembling." Crap, had I said that aloud?

Nick pulled back and looked into my eyes.

Damn it! I *had* said that aloud. Me and my stupid blurting!

Embarrassed, I lowered my chin and pushed my face harder into his chest. Nick's hand slipped under the hem of my shirt, and he slid his hot palm up my spine.

What can I say? I was full of adrenaline and relief and now lust. I wasn't thinking straight. So, I didn't pull away. I shoved everything else out of my mind and let myself enjoy holding Nick, maybe for the last time.

But, then, the air in the room shifted and I opened my eyes. A shadow had replaced the sunlight that lit the room a moment before.

I glanced downward to make sure Chef Ben was still where Nick had left him.

Then my eyes moved to the doorway.

CHAPTER TWENTY-EIGHT

Rika

My spine went stiff. Nick must have felt the shift in my body because he stopped and looked down into my eyes questioningly. Then he loosened his grip on me and turned slowly, following my line of sight.

The man in the doorway was staring down at Chef Ben, wide-eyed in disbelief.

Unfortunately, his eyes weren't the only wide things on his body. He also had a thick neck, huge biceps and wide thighs. But, unlike Chef Ben, not one inch of his wideness could be attributed to sampling too many quiches.

This guy was buff and tough, his longish brown hair skimming his shoulders, which, like the rest of him, were too muscular to occur in nature.

He was freakishly tall, too, and dressed in a muscle shirt and body hugging bike shorts. The only people I'd ever seen who resembled this guy were professional wrestlers on ads for the WWE...

...and the man posing with Ben in the photo hanging in the master bath.

Holy mother of Zeus! This was Rolf!

"Benny!" he bellowed as he knelt and pulled the door off his boyfriend, tossing it aside like it was made of Styrofoam instead of wood.

Nick and I stood side by side watching him as I tried to come up with a way to explain to Ben's boyfriend why the love of his life was lying on the floor with a broken leg while we were practically making out next to his limp body.

As Rolf knelt over him, Ben's eyes shifted to me and Nick. They held a dangerous combination of hope and vengeance.

He lifted a shaky arm and pointed at us. "They're trying to kill me!" he cried. "They said they want me dead!"

I felt Nick tense beside me. "Fuck," he muttered in a tone that was way too quiet for the situation we were in at this moment.

My brain was screaming, *Fuck, fuck, fuck, fuck, fuuuuuuuck!!!* Which I thought was much more in line with our current circumstances.

"Look, buddy," Nick began. His voice was calm and amicable. The same voice he used when delivering an argument in front of a jury.

Rolf had been stroking Ben's drooping hair away from his forehead. I crossed my fingers that Nick's lawyer skills would work on the gentle giant.

But when he lifted his face to look up at us, my heart dropped to my stomach. There was only one word I could think of to describe that expression.

Rage.

"You need to know the whole story..." Nick continued calmly as Rolf stood to his full seven feet. I was pretty sure he could legally qualify as a giant, assuming there was such a legal designation. It was like facing down the Incredible Hulk.

Rolf's hands fisted as he closed the distance between him and Nick. He cocked his right arm and pulled back.

"Wait!" I cried as he took a wild swing at Nick. Nick jerked his head back, dodging the blow easily.

"We don't need to do this," Nick began again, still freakishly calm in the face of the monster.

While Rolf hadn't turned green like the Hulk, his veins were bulging out of all his muscles, not to mention the one in his forehead that looked like it could explode out of his face at any moment.

He threw another punch and, again, Nick dodged it easily.

"This guy's a murderer," Nick said as he pointed down at Chef Ben.

I winced. I was pretty sure calling Ben a murderer was not the best way to handle this. I mean, who would you believe? A couple of strangers? Or the man you loved?

Unfortunately, Nick was unaware that this muscle-bound menace was Ben's love interest.

Rolf went back to trying to hit Nick. The scene would have been hilarious on YouTube. His huge fists swung clumsily—not so much slicing through the air as batting it around. All Nick had to do to avoid them was jerk his head or take a step back. But the anger, followed by frustration, was turning Rolf's face bright red.

After several more misses, he finally caught on and followed up his right hook with a left jab. As they'd moved gradually around the room, I'd ended up behind Rolf and couldn't see what happened, but I heard a crack that caused nausea to sweep through my stomach.

I hoped he hadn't broken Nick's jaw because then Nick wouldn't be able to kiss me like he did last night.

I know it was weird to still be thinking about kissing at a time like this, but my mind and body had roller-coastered through quite a few emotions in the past twenty-four hours and all those pheromones and endorphins mixed with adrenaline had my emotions all over the place.

Pull it together, Paprika!

I checked the half of the living room I was stuck in, looking for something else to use as a weapon. Nick managed to recover and land some blows to Rolf's mid-section. Each time Rolf was hit—which was a lot of times—he took a step back, recovered almost instantly, and went back to the job of trying to smash Nick into oblivion.

I remembered the knife and looked around for it, then recalled there were more like it in the kitchen. Maybe I could squeeze by the men and grab one.

But anywhere I stabbed Rolf that would stop him from fighting could potentially kill him. As far as I knew, he had nothing to do with Alberto's death and was just protecting the man he loved.

After another sweep of the room, I raced over to an expensive-looking floor lamp and yanked the cord from the wall. When I picked it up from the middle, it was heavier than I expected, but I half-dragged it across the floor to where Rolf was panting like a wild animal as he pulled back to take another swing.

When I caught a glimpse of Nick's face, which now had a cut slanting across one eyebrow, *I* was the one filled with rage. Chef Ben's boyfriend would not destroy my boyfriend's—I mean, Nick's— beautiful face! Not while I had anything to say about it!

As the men traded more blows, I mustered up all my strength and lifted the floor lamp at an angle over my head. Since I wasn't used to holding floor lamps over my head, I miscalculated and swung it back too far. I teetered, nearly pulled backward by the weight of it.

But I regained control and swung as hard as I could, hitting Rolf across his back.

His only reaction was to glance over his shoulder at me as if I were an annoying insect buzzing around his head. He immediately discounted me as no threat at all and turned back to Nick just as Nick threw an uppercut. His fist caught Rolf squarely under the chin. Rolf took three involuntary steps backward, then stood, swaying, a dazed expression on his face.

The thought passed through my mind that someone should yell "Timberrrrr!" because he was surely about to go down.

But I watched in surprise as he shook his head hard, like something out of a cartoon, steadied himself and charged at Nick with renewed determination.

Holy freaking mother of Zeus!

I'd often yelled out loud at old movies when a female character stood by screaming while the man she loved was in a battle to the death. I liked kick-ass heroines who could beat the shit out of five men while flying through the air, doing cartwheels and making cool swooshing noises with their black robes.

Unfortunately, I hadn't gotten around to taking those martial arts classes I always planned to enroll in when I got thin. This was partly because of the P.E.-phobia that was left over from being the fattest girl in high school, and partly because I never truly felt like I'd lost all the weight I needed to.

Plus, most of those martial arts uniforms were white and white was not a slimming color.

So as the two men tumbled to the floor, Rolf on top, there was only one thing I could think to do.

CHAPTER TWENTY-NINE

Nick

This guy won't go down.

The sentence went through my head every time I landed a punch, and I landed a lot more punches than he did. He was slow and his boxing form was ridiculous, but he was huge and had a jaw of steel.

And after he finally landed a left that felt like I'd been hit in the head with a brick, it occurred to me that I hadn't been in a fight with someone this much bigger than I was since the time I stood up for LeeAnne against the junior high boys who were taunting her. In fact, once I finished growing, I didn't encounter a lot of guys much bigger, and I didn't enjoy fighting—hitting or getting hit—so I'd mostly won my battles with words.

In high school, as a freshman, all it took was one punch to the first senior who tried to fuck with me and nobody ever tried it again. Probably because he ended up with a broken nose and blood running down his face. Nobody wanted to have their face bloodied by a freshman.

Now, here I was, fighting with someone I'd never even met,

which I seemed to be doing a lot the past few days. But they were small potatoes compared to this guy.

When I landed that uppercut under his chin, I thought I had him for sure. It was the hardest punch I'd ever delivered and his eyes rolled up in his head as he stumbled backward.

That went on for about five seconds, long enough that I could have followed up with more blows to finish him off if I'd had any idea he'd come back from it. But I didn't believe in kicking someone when they were down and he was going down.

Then he didn't.

He shook it off and came at me like a cyborg who just needed a few seconds to repair itself before continuing its killing spree.

And this guy really wanted to kill me. I could see it in his eyes. It didn't help that Chef Ben was egging him on from the floor. He kept yelling, "Kill him! Kill him, baby, or he'll kill me!"

The "baby" part struck me as a strange way for one hefty man to address a much bigger man. Then it dawned on me that this might be Ben's boyfriend and he was protecting Gentle Ben, mild-mannered chef, from evil intruders. A person was always stronger when they were protecting someone they loved.

But I had someone to protect too. Who knew what would happen to Rika if I went down? I didn't mind taking chances with my wellbeing, but I couldn't stand the idea of anything happening to her.

"Run, Rika!" I called before the next fist came at me. The cyborg and I traded blows again, but, this time, he managed to wrap his arm around my neck and pull me off balance.

We crashed to the floor and I ended up underneath about three hundred pounds of steroid-enhanced muscle.

He went for my throat but I jerked my forearms apart, hitting him in just the right spots so the inside of his elbows collapsed and he lost his grip. But, seconds later, he managed to get his knee on my chest and shift his weight to it.

I couldn't catch my breath. At any moment, his weight was going to crush my ribcage.

As I tried twisting my body to dislodge him, he smashed his hammer fist into my head again and I saw stars.

Rika! someone yelled in my head. *You have to stay conscious for Rika!*

Then, suddenly, her face was in my sight line. I thought I was hallucinating because it seemed to be connected to the cyborg's head, her cheek squeezed against his.

The stars cleared and I realized she was on his back, one of her arms hooked around his iron neck in what was supposed to be a choke hold. With her slender arms, it would be better described as a *piss the big guy off even more* hold.

When that didn't work, her other hand came around and she pressed her thumb into the cyborg's right eye like she was trying to gouge it out.

That's when he seemed to forget about me completely. He screamed out in pain while grabbing at Rika's wrist and thumb.

This was my chance—maybe my only chance. Telling myself it was just like bench pressing in my home gym, I pushed upward against his bulk and managed to slide out from under him.

Somehow, Rika was still on his back. He started twisting and bucking like a wild bronc, trying to dislodge her, but she had a look of crazed determination on her face as she clung to his writhing back like a tiny rodeo bull rider.

He managed to get up on one knee as I made it to my feet.

"No!" I cried out, but, before I got a hold on either of them, he stood and twisted hard, flinging Rika off his back.

She hit the wall with a sickening crash and crumpled to the floor.

A feeling of rage boiled up inside me like I'd never known before. I hadn't wanted to hurt this guy, especially once I understood who he was.

That was when he was an innocent person. Now, he'd hurt

Rika and all bets were off. I turned and grabbed the wood coffee table and swung hard, smashing it into one side of his head.

He fell to the floor, unconscious.

I turned to Rika. She was breathing, but her eyes were closed. Yanking my phone out of my back pocket, I called 9-1-1. I told the operator to send ambulances and police to Chef Ben's address, then hung up as she was telling me to stay on the line.

I sat on the floor next to Rika, brushing her hair gently away from her face. Her chest was rising and falling and her color was good. But the awful sound her body made when she hit the wall...

I slid my hand around to the back of her head. No blood, but there was a good-sized lump.

"Rika," I whispered as I heard the first set of sirens approach. I cleared my throat. "Paprika Anise Martin!" I said as if the simple act of pronouncing her name wrong would bring her to consciousness.

Her eyes fluttered open. "Mar-*teen*," she said before they fell closed again.

CHAPTER THIRTY

Rika

The next night, Nick sat in one of my grandmother's upholstered chairs, while I sat on the sofa. We'd been rehashing the events of the past two days in the way people do when they need to get past the shock of an unfathomable situation.

The cops were at the hospital with Chef Ben when he was taken in for his leg. He was screaming, irate and in pain, and basically confessed to the crime during his rants.

The Kaporskys, Jason Kim, and his henchmen were all arrested for obstruction of justice, kidnapping and a few other charges. They weren't involved in the murder, but had tried to cover it up, more interested in how it would reflect on Micrology than whether justice was served.

Apparently, they'd thought they could brainwash my father into their cult and have him go right back to cooking for them at the center.

Detectives Hertz and Winchell wouldn't tell me much, but word from Julian was that Steve and Valerie insisted they were just trying to help my father get over the trauma he'd suffered, watching his friend get murdered.

They threw Jason Kim under the bus, saying if our claims about being followed and threatened were true, it must have been him who ordered the actions.

Kim was keeping his mouth shut on the advice of his attorney.

Today, we'd taken my father to a neurologist to get checked out, even though he kept insisting he was fine. The doctor agreed with Mrs. Ruíz that he'd make a full recovery except for some memory lapses that might be permanent.

For the rest of the day, I'd felt like a hippopotamus had been lifted from my shoulders. My *papi* was alive and well!

The whole family, Nick and LeeAnne were at the hospital, plus Mrs. Ruíz and Mr. Garza.

Once my father got a clean bill of health we all stopped at a restaurant and ate, then we came back home and everyone got back to whatever they were supposed to be doing.

My father was resting in my room at my grandmother's insistence. She was napping upstairs. I hadn't realized how little she'd been sleeping until I looked into her face at the hospital. I'd been too wrapped up in my investigation to notice the toll the abduction of my dad had taken on anyone else, not that they blamed me for it.

There was a lull in our conversation. It seemed like Nick and I had said all we had to say about the case, several times over. In fact, it felt like that moment, just before a person decides they've overstayed their welcome and starts excusing themselves from your presence.

God, I didn't want Nick to go.

My throat tightened at the thought of not seeing him every day.

"Paprika..." he said gently.

No, no, no, no, no! I didn't want to hear this.

Think of something! my mind cried, but I couldn't come up with anything that would make a damn bit of difference.

I raised my eyebrows and steeled myself for his next words. I'd lived through my mother's death. I'd lived through the separation from my father. I'd lived through leaving Nick in Bolo the last time. I would live through this, even if it didn't seem possible while he was looking into my eyes, murmuring my name.

"I, uh..." He pressed his lips together as if rethinking what he was going to say. "After you left, I missed having you around."

My heart squeezed so hard my hand jerked up to rub my chest. That wasn't what I was expecting him to say. And why was he torturing me with this when he already had another woman? In fact, why did he have another woman if he missed me so much?

Unless he missed me in a completely different way than I missed him. I mean, we worked well together. We were often on the same wave-length. He seemed to like the geeky things I said.

Maybe he just wanted a new bestie. But surely, he'd know we couldn't randomly visit each other as friends. How awkward would that be with Marla around?

Plus, if he thought we should just be friends, why had he kissed me?

He was being a jerk to me and Marla both

"You missed me?" I said sarcastically. "If you missed me, it seems like I would have heard from you in the past six months."

He cocked his head. "So that means you didn't miss me, I guess. Since you didn't call or text."

Damn him and his lawyer logic! Okay, maybe it was just regular logic, but I thought my feelings for him were pretty clear when I left Bolo, considering I was freaking *crying!*

Was he hoping I'd contact him all this time? Then why did he let me leave in the first place? An anger I couldn't quite explain erupted inside me. "This conversation is irrelevant," I said. "I doubt your new whatever she is—Marla—would approve of a friendship between us."

Nick's brows pushed together. "Marla?" He said her name almost as if he didn't remember who she was.

"Yeah," I replied. "Blonde? Legs up to her forehead?"

Nick stared at me for several seconds. Then his lips parted as something seemed to dawn on him. "You think Marla and I are...?" He threw his head back and laughed.

"What's so fucking funny?" I glanced around to make sure my grandmother was still out of earshot.

"All this time, you thought Marla and I were an item?"

Now I was confused. "Why wouldn't I? You showed up with a woman who looks just like your last two wives and didn't explain her presence. For all I knew, you'd met and married her since I saw you last."

"Married her?" Nick's face looked like he'd just smelled spoiled milk. And was that a shudder? "I would never marry Marla," he said with absolute certainty.

"So, she's your girlfriend." I shrugged. "Same difference. She wouldn't want us to be friends."

Nick shook his head. "Rika, I found her crying on the side of the road. She had car trouble, which she claimed caused a whole series of other bad stuff to happen. I let her stay at my house for a few days, I thought. Then she didn't leave and I wasn't sure what to do with her. Now, I'm pretty sure she was a con artist."

"But...but..." I stammered. Nick and Marla weren't together? *At all?* "You brought her with you. You shared a hotel room!"

He was looking at me like I was ridiculous. "You may not know this, since you've probably never had to stay there, but that particular hotel has more than one room for rent."

My mouth came open, but I was confused as to whether I wanted to celebrate Nick's single status or yell at him for letting me think he was with another woman, then standing here mansplaining to me like I'd made a ridiculous assumption.

Nick waved the subject away with a sweep of his hand. "Anyway, you solved that problem for me. A couple of days ago, she texted that she was going to stay at some producer's house in Brentwood. Told me thanks for everything."

"She broke up with you and you didn't even mention it?" I said.

"There was no breaking up because we weren't together," Nick reminded me. "I never even touched her, except for patting her on the back when I found her to try to stop her crying."

My mind kept rewinding the moments since I picked him up at the airport, looking for confirmation one way or the other. But now that I thought of it, Nick hadn't touched Marla at any time when I picked them up and took them to the hotel. And when she came by the house with Gucci, he didn't kiss her goodbye. He never said he needed to check on her or that he'd better get back to her.

Apparently, she was on my mind a lot more than she was ever on his.

"Anyway, she's somebody else's problem now," he said. He shook his head again. "I can't believe you thought I was with Marla."

I would have kept arguing that he didn't explain Marla, and how was I supposed to know he wasn't with her, etcetera, but I was glad I didn't have to imagine the two of them in his big bed in Bolo anymore.

But what was I supposed to do now? Confess my undying love and beg him to stay?

No. I cried in Bolo and he let me leave. I wasn't opening myself up to that humiliation again.

Then, something clicked in my head. I mean, I actually heard a click.

"Nick, I just had a thought..." *He'll never go for this*, that annoying voice in my head insisted. I pushed her down and sat on her. "I've been planning to open my own investigation firm. I have some ideas about how to get clients, make a splash out of the gate. You'd make a great partner."

Nick blinked at me like he thought he didn't hear me right. "I'm not a P.I." he said. "I'm an attorney. Totally different things."

"I know they're different. But, last I heard, you didn't really want to be a lawyer anymore."

As he stared at me, I could tell he was sorting through a bunch of thoughts that were rushing through his brain at the same time. Unfortunately, I couldn't read his mind, but he hadn't rejected the idea outright, so I thought maybe this was my chance to persuade him.

I decided to take a page from Judge Martínez's book when we were back in Bolo. "So, you're still moving away from Bolo?" I asked with mock enthusiasm. "Where are you going? What firm have you joined there?"

He narrowed his eyes, realizing what I was up to. "I haven't joined one," he admitted. "Not yet."

"And do you have a new address yet?"

His eyes narrowed even more. "No new address."

"Then what's stopping you from trying a different career?"

He looked down at the carpet for a moment. Then his gaze moved to the window. The blinds were open and a cat was crossing the street, but I knew he wasn't that interested in cats.

Holy mother of Zeus! He was taking time to consider my off-the-wall proposition!

I held my breath.

When his gaze met mine, his expression was unreadable. The suspense was killing me because if he agreed, I'd be able to see him every day. I couldn't take another breath until I heard his answer.

He extended his right hand. "Okay," he said. "Let's try it, partner."

As I placed my hand in his, the air I'd been holding in my lungs burst out of me all at once.

Nick looked at me as if he thought I might need medical attention. "You okay?"

"I'm awesome!" It took all my effort not to bounce off the couch and jump for joy. I wanted to throw my arms around his neck, but that wasn't the type of partnership we'd just agreed to.

I tried to focus on the fact that, for once, I was getting what I truly wanted. A private investigation firm. And Nick in my life.

"Paprika," my father said.

I turned and saw him coming in from the hall. I jumped up. "Papi, your head...be careful."

He laughed, his voice deep and resonant. I hadn't heard that sound nearly enough in my life. "I'm fine, *mi hija.* I've been in much worse battles than that one and I'm still alive." The chain was back around his neck, my mother's ring resting on the white t-shirt he was wearing.

"Nick is staying in town for a while," I blurted out, even though it had nothing to do with the subject at hand.

My father's gaze shifted to Nick. "He is, is he?"

"Yes, we're opening a business together." Crap. In my excitement, I was blurting too much, too soon. My father wouldn't like the idea of me being a P.I. He'd think it was too dangerous.

But he didn't ask about the business. Instead, he smiled again, but this time, the smile didn't reach his eyes. "Nick Owen," he said. "Come outside with me."

I swallowed hard and watched as Nick stood and followed my father out the door.

Nick

I wasn't sure why Rika's father wanted to talk to me outside, but, when he said my name, I felt like a kid who'd been called to the principal's office.

"Do we need to sit down?" I asked as we stepped off the porch. "You were just in the hospital..." I gestured to the steps.

"No," he replied. His voice was deep, the Spanish accent

somehow making it weightier. "I feel very, very healthy." The statement was innocent enough, but his tone seemed kind of threatening.

"Well...great," I said. "Glad to hear it."

He was a few inches shorter than I was, but when he put his arm around my shoulders and pressed down, my tension level rose. This was Rika's father. If he didn't want Rika and me to be partners, he might be able to stop it. I couldn't blame her for wanting to please a dad she'd basically lost as a kid, not to mention his very recent abduction.

"I saw how you looked at my Paprika," he said. "When we were at the hospital and she was talking to me."

I used to think I was in control of my reactions and expressions, but I knew Rika had proven me wrong. Sometimes I couldn't stop myself from gazing at her profile...and her ass.

Damn, I hoped he hadn't seen me checking out her ass!

"You know I lost Paprika's mother years ago. She was the only woman I ever loved with *todo mi corazón*—all my heart—and Paprika is all I have left of her. She's the only light in my life." His voice was full of emotion, but his eyes stared at me with steely determination.

I'd seen that same determination in Rika's gaze when she told me she would solve the murder she was suspected of. Hell, I think it was one of the things that impressed me so much when we were together in Texas.

Her father released me from his hold and folded his arms in front of him.

"You know I'm Colombian, yes?"

"Yes." I swallowed hard, unsure what was coming next.

"When you're from Colombia. You know people. Very good people..." he paused for effect like I'd done many times in the courtroom, "and very bad people. Over there...and right here in this city."

I nodded, even though I still wasn't sure where he was going with this.

"I know you're older than my daughter. So, if there is a relationship between you, you'll be the one responsible. I will *hold* you responsible."

Uh-oh. I was pretty sure I'd rather have a gun held on me again, than have this conversation with Rika's dad. Rika and I hadn't even talked about this stuff.

"What I'm trying to say, is that if you hurt the light of my life, I will make sure you forfeit your own."

Was he threatening to have me taken out?

I opened my mouth, but found I was speechless. Me. Nick Owen, attorney at law.

I mean, what do you say when the woman you...um...*like* an awful lot has a dad who threatens you with violence?

Diego threw his head back and laughed. "You should see the look on your face." He laughed some more. "I'm just fucking with you."

Relieved, I chuckled along with him. He got me, all right. But, hey, I was a good sport and that was pretty funny.

"But not really," he said, his face suddenly dead serious.

I quit laughing as his words sunk in. "Pardon?"

"I mean if you hurt her, you *will* pay." He stared at me, his dark eyes expectant.

What was I supposed to say? "I would never—" I began.

He started laughing again. "Why are you so serious? I told you I was just fucking with you."

I tried to laugh but it came out sounding awkward—halfway between my normal laugh and Sheldon Cooper's from *The Big Bang Theory*. I cleared my throat, hoping to sound normal again.

"I do know people though," he mused as if to himself.

I didn't laugh this time. I had no idea whether he was serious or not.

"Come on, let's go watch some *fútbol*," he said jovially.

Perfect! I wanted out of this bizarre conversation, and I knew everything about football. If I was going to have to spend some time with Rika's father, best to do it watching a football game.

"Oh." He chuckled. "I always forget, you Americans call it 'soccer'." He walked up the stairs and into the house.

Fuck. I didn't know much about soccer. Soccer didn't really exist in the tiny town I grew up in.

I looked at the screen door and asked myself if I really wanted to go in there. Not just because of the soccer. I guess I was asking myself whether I was ready for everything it would take to become a part of Rika's life. Starting a new career. Living in freaking Los Angeles. Ingratiating myself with her family *and* all the neighbors and friends who cared about her...

But as I stood there, in a city I never wanted to live in, on the verge of making changes I never would have imagined, I knew I didn't have a choice.

I'd experienced what it was like to spend time with Rika, then have her completely out of my life and, whatever did or didn't happen between us in the future, I couldn't face that again. Not now, anyway.

I pulled out my phone and bingged "Colombian soccer players." Then I took a deep breath and went back inside.

~

This book is over, but the story continues in ***Dead Men Don't Flip***. Sign up for my (Nina Cordoba's) reader group to be notified of new releases, get book extras (like answers to reader questions and hints about what's coming up), participate in Beta Reader or Early Reader-Reviewer programs (aka free books).

And, once in a blue moon, I even have a contest.

Sign up at NinaCordoba.com.

OTHER BOOKS BY NINA CORDOBA

Not Dreaming of You

Always Dreaming of You

Don't Make Me Make You Brownies

Mia Like Crazy

No More Mr. Nice Girl

Dead Men Don't Chew Gum